FLATLAND

broadview editions
series editor: L.W. Conolly

Photograph of Edwin Abbott during his teaching days. Courtesy of Thomas Banchoff and The Center for Digital Initiatives, Brown University Library.

FLATLAND
A Romance of Many Dimensions

Edwin Abbott

edited by Lila Marz Harper

broadview editions

Library and Archives Canada Cataloguing in Publication

Abbott, Edwin A. (Edwin Abbott), 1838-1926
  Flatland : a romance of many dimensions / Edwin Abbott ; edited by Lila Marz Harper.

(Broadview editions)
Includes bibliographical references.
ISBN 978-1-55111-690-7

  I. Harper, Lila Marz, 1955-   II. Title.   III. Series: Broadview editions

PR4000.A22F53 2009   823'.8   C2009-905640-2

Broadview Editions
The Broadview Editions series represents the ever-changing canon of literature in English by bringing together texts long regarded as classics with valuable lesser-known works.

Advisory editor for this volume: Martin Boyne

Broadview Press is an independent, international publishing house, incorporated in 1985. Broadview believes in shared ownership, both with its employees and with the general public; since the year 2000 Broadview shares have traded publicly on the Toronto Venture Exchange under the symbol BDP.

We welcome comments and suggestions regarding any aspect of our publications—please feel free to contact us at the addresses below or at broadview@broadviewpress.com.

North America
Post Office Box 1243, Peterborough, Ontario, Canada K9J 7H5
2215 Kenmore Avenue, Buffalo, NY, USA 14207
Tel: (705) 743-8990; Fax: (705) 743-8353
email: customerservice@broadviewpress.com

UK, Europe, Central Asia, Middle East, Africa, India, and Southeast Asia
Eurospan Group, 3 Henrietta St., London WC2E 8LU, United Kingdom
Tel: 44 (0) 1767 604972; Fax: 44 (0) 1767 601640
Email: eurospan@turpin-distribution.com

Australia and New Zealand
NewSouth Books
c/o TL Distribution, 15-23 Helles Ave., Moorebank, NSW, Australia 2170
Tel: (02) 8778 9999; Fax: (02) 8778 9944
email: orders@tldistribution.com.au

www.broadviewpress.com

This book is printed on paper containing 100% post-consumer fibre.

Typesetting and assembly: True to Type Inc., Claremont, Canada.

PRINTED IN CANADA

Contents

Acknowledgements

Over the several years that I have worked on this project, beginning with my master's thesis, I have benefited from the generosity of many. Thanks are owed to the faculty of St. Cloud State University who worked with me when I was a graduate student: Sandra Keith, Judith Kilborn, John Melton, and Wayne Tosh. Others have shared their research and interests. Thomas Banchoff, in particular, has provided me with biographical details of Edwin Abbott's life that would not be obtainable otherwise. Both he and William F. Lindgren have shared with me their Abbott sightings in Victorian periodicals that have allowed me to compile the *Flatland* book reviews. Guidance has also been provided over the years by Rudy Rucker, A.K. Dewdney, Amirouche Moktefi, Mark Samuels Lasner, and Bruce Clarke. I am grateful to Charles E. Robinson and his class on methods of research, along with librarian Linda Stein, for their help in obtaining access to periodical indexes. As always, the interlibrary loan staff at Central Washington University have done their best to locate obscure newspapers while working with limited information. The combined expertise of Patrick Leary and the VICTORIA listserv is gratefully appreciated, as are the electronic scanned texts of Project Gutenberg. I thank everyone I have worked with at Broadview Press, including Leonard Conolly, Marjorie Mather, Tara Lowes, and Martin Boyne, for their patience and help.

My son, Artemus Harper, has long served as tech support, and he has patiently scanned images and solved software bugs. The rest of the family, my husband and daughter, have put up with this obsession and provided me with the time. This work is dedicated to the memory of my father, H.G. Marz, "mister science fiction" of Granada Hills High, who introduced many high-school biology students to the world of science fiction.

Introduction

Edwin Abbott's *Flatland* may be one of the most unclassifiable works of literature ever published. While it is acknowledged to be a classic of early science fiction, a work of Victorian social satire, and a religious allegory, it also presents, through its introduction to higher dimensions, an important contribution to the development of an area of mathematics that was eventually merged into non-Euclidean geometry.[1] *Flatland* is an unusually effective work that spans disciplines and challenges divisional categories. Since its publication in 1884, the book's popularity has continued today as its readers have embraced it as science fiction, popular science, and metaphysics. Working from the groundwork of philosophical issues raised by Plato's *Republic*, *Flatland* merges social satire and geometry to produce a novel situated in two-dimensional space, a believable world populated by memorable inhabitants whose geometric shapes designate their positions in a complex social structure, one that bears some resemblance to the Victorian class structure.

The subtitle of *Flatland—A Romance of Many Dimensions*—refers not only to the physical dimensions covered in the book, but also to the many levels of interpretation from which the book can be approached. On one level, *Flatland* reflects Abbott's pedagogical ability to illuminate difficult subjects, and it is valued by teachers of mathematics because it has proved to be an effective way to introduce students to the concepts of higher dimensions. Abbott himself was a member of the Association for the Improvement of Geometrical Teaching (AIGT), the earliest British association devoted to the teaching of an academic discipline.[2] Beginning in the 1870s, the AIGT challenged those who wished to limit the teaching of mathematics to Euclidean deduction and to

---

1 The Library of Congress shelved the work under the Mathematics (QA) heading, considering it essentially a work of mathematics. It has the distinction of being listed both in D.M.Y. Sommerville's *Bibliography of Non-Euclidean Geometry* (2nd ed.; New York: Chelsea, 1970) and Darko Suvin's *Victorian Science Fiction in the UK: The Discourses of Knowledge and of Power* (Boston: Hall, 1983).

2 In 1897, the AIGT became the Mathematical Association. See Amirouche Moktefi, "How to Supersede Euclid: Geometrical Teaching and the Mathematical Community in Nineteenth-Century Britain," *(Re)Creating Science in Nineteenth-Century Britain*, ed. Amanda Mordavsky Caleb (Newcastle: Cambridge Scholars Publishing, 2007), 220-34.

what could be empirically demonstrated.[1] In England, exams based on a thorough knowledge of Euclid's *Elements* were used as part of the entrance and advancement processes for military and government institutions; therefore, there was strong resistance to any change in the schools' mathematics curriculum. Additionally, such scientists as T.H. Huxley insisted that mathematical education was merely a deductive exercise, useful only in exercising mental faculties such as training in how to think.[2] This position, however, was not acceptable to mathematicians of the nineteenth century, when the field was rebuilt on new logical foundations that went beyond what was easily visualized. Attempts to revise Euclid so as to make it easier for students to understand and to prepare students for less intuitively understood concepts led to a "textbook war," as traditionalists resisted any modification of Euclid.[3]

The invention of mathematics as a subject with axioms, theorems, and proofs begins with Euclid's (c. 300 BCE) *Elements*, which was recovered in the Middle Ages. *Elements* was a series of thirteen parchment rolls that was passed down in a number of

---

1   See Joan L. Richards, *Mathematical Visions: The Pursuit of Geometry in Victorian England* (Boston: Academic Press, 1988); Rosemary Jann, "Abbott's *Flatland*: Scientific Imagination and 'Natural Christianity,'" *Victorian Studies* 28 (1985): 479 note.

2   The very public debate between Huxley and the mathematician J.J. Sylvester is outlined in chapter 5, "Sylvester versus Huxley: Mathematics: Ivory Tower or Real World?" of Hal Hellman's *Great Feuds in Mathematics: Ten of the Liveliest Disputes Ever* (Hoboken, NJ: Wiley, 2006), 94–115. See Appendix E3 for selections from Huxley and Sylvester's essays. Huxley wrote several popular essays promoting the teaching of science in the universities. He was trained as a surgeon (and never attended a university) before achieving prominence in scientific research (while aboard the *HMS Rattlesnake* [1846-50]) and in his vocal support of Darwin's *On the Origin of Species* (1859), which gave him the nickname of "Darwin's Bulldog." Huxley also coined the term "agnostic" in 1869 to describe his suspense of judgment about religious belief.

3   Richards, 170-80. One shot in this war, indicating the intensity of the discussion, was Charles Dodgson's (Lewis Carroll) *Euclid and His Modern Rivals* (1879; 1885, 2nd ed.), a 225-page critique and analysis of various reform-minded geometry textbooks, which Dodgson presents as a whimsical drama with Platonic dialogue. Its appendix includes an essay by Isaac Todhunter, author of *The Elements of Euclid*, on the impact on students' civil-service exams if a reform textbook were used, and a review of James Maurice Wilson's *Elementary Geometry* by Augustus De Morgan. Dodgson's writing of *The Elements of Euclid* is described in Morton N. Cohen's *Lewis Carroll: A Biography* (New York: Vintage, 1995), 384-85. See Appendix E1 for a list of 1884 geometry textbooks.

editions.[1] By 800 CE, only fragments of a Latin translation existed and the revival of *Elements* was a key text in the intellectual awakening of the Middle Ages.[2] In Euclid's methods, concepts are based on explicit definitions, then postulates and axioms (the terms are now used interchangeably); only after having established these foundations can the logical consequences that develop into proofs be applied. Using twenty-three definitions, five geometric postulates, and five additional postulates called "common notions," Euclid proved 465 theorems.[3] The first four postulates are quite straightforward, but the fifth, the parallel postulate, appears to have been Euclid's own invention, not part of the body of mathematical knowledge he was recording, and he avoided using it in *Elements*.[4] Later mathematicians also saw it as too complex for a postulate and something that should be provable as a theorem.[5]

For mathematicians, Euclid's fifth postulate—the proposition that through a point that does not lie on a given line, one and only one line can be drawn parallel to that line—had long presented difficulties. The first four postulates, which establish the definitions of a point and a line, contain one or two basic mathematical ideas. The fifth postulate, however, differs from the others in addressing several mathematical concepts. Euclid, by setting up his argument in this manner, was able to reach several important conclusions; however, mathematicians continued to explore ways to modify the parallel postulate. These explorations led to the development of alternative geometries.[6]

Flatland makes use of a two-dimensional limited perspective, a technique that formed the basis of many explanations of what is now called non-Euclidean geometry, the discovery of which opened mathematics to a higher degree of abstract thought and helped separate the study of applied mathematics from "pure"

---

1 Leonard Mlodinow, *Euclid's Window: The Story of Geometry from Parallel Lines to Hyperspace* (New York: Free Press, 2001), 29.
2 Mlodinow, 49, 96.
3 Mlodinow, 34.
4 Mlodinow, 37.
5 Mlodinow, 37.
6 An excellent and readable discussion of the history of non-Euclidean geometries can be found in David Bergamini's *Mathematics* (New York: Time-Life, 1963), part of the Time-Life series on the sciences, pp. 149-67. See also Mlodinow, 3-49, and Marvin Jay Greenberg, *Euclidean and Non-Euclidean Geometries: Development and History* (2nd ed.; San Francisco: Freeman, 1980), 6-21.

mathematics, that is, mathematics that did not attempt to describe the physical world. This movement of mathematics away from concerns over application paradoxically opened the way to a better understanding of aspects of the physical world that were not directly observable.

Basically, any geometry that breaks with Euclid's fifth postulate, the parallel postulate, is considered a non-Euclidean geometry since the parallel postulate does not hold in curved space, as is the case in hyperbolic geometry and elliptical geometry. The realization that Euclidean geometry was not the only geometry possible was quite controversial in the late nineteenth century, and as *Flatland* gave its readers a clear image of the fourth dimension, it led the way to the concept of hyperspace and space-time (where the fourth dimension is a time function), concepts important to understanding Einstein's space-time continuum in his 1915 general theory of relativity in the twentieth century.[1]

Carl Friedrich Gauss (1777-1855) suggested a new axiom leading to different two-dimensional geometries, one which stated that more than one line could be drawn parallel to a line;[2] János Bolyai (1802-60) and Nikolai Ivanovich Lobachevskii (1793-1856) developed "hyperbolic" geometries to describe the geometric properties of a trumpet-shaped surface rather than Euclid's plane surface. Bernhard Riemann (1826-66), working under Gauss, developed a geometry of many dimensions and in his 1854 lecture "The Hypotheses Which Lie at the Foundations of Geometry" generalized the properties of curves so they could be applied to space.[3] This geometry did not appear to have practical applications until Albert Einstein, working on the general theory of relativity from 1907 to 1915, became frustrated and asked Marcel Grossmann for a mathematical model that would

---

1 See William Garnett's introduction to the fifth edition of *Flatland* (Oxford: Basil Blackwell, 1926). Rudy Rucker's *The Fourth Dimension* makes heavy use of *Flatland* in his popular exploration of higher dimensions (Boston: Houghton Mifflin, 1984).

2 Richards, 80-81.

3 Riemann's "Habilitationsvortrag" was presented to the faculty at the University in Göttingen as part of his post-doctoral certification on 10 June 1854 and was published in 1866; however, the non-Euclidean ideas did not have a major impact on mathematics until they were clarified by Hermann von Helmholtz. See Richards, p. 74, note 20 for a discussion of the difficulty of establishing a good chronology of publication and reception of Riemann's work. William K. Clifford published an English translation of the work in *Nature* in 1873.

work with his research in gravitational fields. Grossmann suggested Riemann's non-Euclidean geometry, and by working with Riemann's geometry Einstein was able to explain observed phenomena that could not be understood using Isaac Newton's laws.[1] By applying the geometries of Gauss and Riemann, Einstein also suggested that the universe was curved and contained four dimensions: height, width, breadth, and time.[2]

Thus, in the 1870s, when the AIGT sought to revise a curriculum that was heavily based on Euclid's *Elements*, they had the foresight to see that new developments in mathematical research would require a different approach to the teaching of mathematics in England. By the 1850s, while other countries used a range of geometry textbooks, the English curriculum was committed to Euclid,[3] so much so that between 1800 and 1850, 214 editions of Euclid's geometry were published.[4] Discussions of the use of Euclid in the classroom became one of those *causes célèbres* created when a pedagogical issue becomes, under the influence of media attention, a representative of some basic element of national character or identity; this debate was not limited to academic publications, and it became surprisingly intense and personal as it was covered in the magazines of the day. One anonymous 1868 review (actually by Augustus De Morgan) of a new geometry textbook by James Wilson, published in *The Athenaeum*, declared that Euclid would not be replaced since "the old geometry is a very English subject...."[5] Attacks on the primacy of

---

1   In physics, the basis of classical mechanics is Newton's three Laws of Motion, which describe the relationship between the forces acting on a body and the motion of that body.

2   This episode in Einstein's life and an explanation of Riemann's geometry can be found in Walter Isaacson's recent biography, *Einstein: His Life and Universe* (New York: Simon and Schuster, 2007), 192-96.

3   Florian Cajori, "Attempts Made During the Eighteenth and Nineteenth Centuries to Reform the Teaching of Geometry," *The American Mathematical Monthly* 17 (1910): 181-201, 193.

4   Moktefi, 216.

5   From Augustus De Morgan's review of James Wilson's *Elementary Geometry* in *The Athenaeum* (18 July 1868), quoted in Moktefi, 219. (James Wilson, in his autobiography, commented, "I drafted a syllabus of geometry corresponding to the first two books of Euclid, and published it with Macmillan, and gave reasons in an interesting Preface: and then the war began" [quoted in Moktefi, 220].) De Morgan's review was reprinted by Charles Dodgson in *Euclid and His Modern Rivals*, 250. General overviews of the history of British geometry textbooks can be found in W.H. Brock's "Geometry and the Universities: (Continued)

Euclid in the teaching of mathematics continued up until the turn of the century, as Bertrand Russell criticized the consistency of the logic of the *Elements* in his 1902 essay "The Teaching of Euclid."[1]

Flatland reflects this pedagogical concern. The book has been a strong influence on the teaching of mathematics, as it encourages mathematical speculation and refutes the limitations placed on mathematics by others who would demand that the study of mathematics reflect the physical world. Thus, *Flatland*, in its consideration of how perception could be shaped by our sense of space, looks forward to later developments in theoretical mathematics by encouraging the use of imagination in exploring new mathematical territory. As a result, nearly all popular books dealing with higher-dimensional geometry or relativity begin by introducing Abbott's narrator, the Square, as a means of illustrating physical problems with perception.[2]

However, Abbott's book is mathematically oriented science fiction, not actually a mathematics text.[3] While it is referred to in studies of recreational mathematics, *Flatland* is not itself a part of that field; it does not require active participation on the part of its readership as do such long story problems as Lewis Carroll's *A Tangled Tale* (1880-85). To comprehend how much our perceptions are shaped by our physical space, all we have to do is to eavesdrop from our omniscient position in three dimensions to the goings on in Abbott's two-dimensional world. Indeed, our

---

Euclid and His Modern Rivals, 1860-1901," *History of Education*, 4.2 (1975): 21-35, and June Barrow-Green's "'Much Necessary for All Sortes of Men': 450 Years of Euclid's *Elements* in English," *BSHM Bulletin: Journal of the British Society for the History of Mathematics* 21.1 (2006): 2-25.

1 First published in *Mathematical Gazette* 2 (May 1902): 165-67; reprinted in *The Changing Shape of Geometry: Celebrating a Century of Geometry and Geometry Teaching*, ed. Chris Pritchard (Cambridge: Cambridge UP, 2003), 486–87.

2 See, for example, Rudy Rucker, *The Fourth Dimension: A Guided Tour of the Higher Universes* (Boston: Houghton Mifflin, 1984).

3 Discussions of Flatland as mathematically themed science fiction can be found in Lila Marz Harper, "Mathematical Themes in Science Fiction," *Extrapolation* 27 (1986): 245-69; Martin Gardner, "Mathematical Games," *Scientific American* July 1980: 18-31; and Jane Hipolito and Roscoe Lee Browne, "Flatland: A Romance of Many Dimensions," *Survey of Science Fiction Literature*, vol. 2 (Englewood Cliffs, NJ: Salem Press, 1979), 792-96.

relationship to *Flatland*'s two-dimensional society—we are able to see more than the inhabitants, yet not be seen ourselves—is very similar to the relationship between a reader and a novel.

Additionally, the inhabitants of Flatland are not truly alien; it is easy to identify with their emotions and behavior. The engaging characterization of Flatland's inhabitants is noted in Banesh Hoffmann's description, published in his introduction to the 1952 Dover edition:

> The inhabitants of Flatland are sentient beings, troubled by our troubles and moved by our emotions. Flat they may be physically, but their characters are well rounded. They are our kin, our own flesh and blood. We romp with them in Flatland. And romping, we suddenly find ourselves looking anew at our own humdrum world with the wide-eyed wonder of youth.[1]

Abbott's ability to create believable, understandable characters who hold our attention, while still maintaining a physically alien world, makes *Flatland* successful.

The Rev. Edwin Abbott Abbott

Edwin Abbott Abbott, D.D. (1838-1926) was a well-respected teacher and scholar. He was the eldest son of eight children born to Jane Abbott (1806-82) and Edwin Abbott (1802-82), who served as headmaster for 45 years at the Philological School in Marylebone, Middlesex. Abbott's parents were first cousins, not an unusual occurrence in Victorian society, which generally encouraged marriage between cousins. This close-knit relationship explains the use of "Abbott" as both a middle and last name, as Abbott was also Edwin Abbott's mother's maiden name.

Abbott's grandfather, Edward Abbott, was an "oilman and Italian warehouseman" in St. Martin's Lane, London.[2] This suggests that the family's roots were in the grocery business, one that dealt in imported foods, mostly from Italy. Abbott's father had been a charity student at the Philological School in 1818, when it was called the Philological Society of Marylebone. The Philological School was an Anglican grammar school for students aged

---

1   Banesh Hoffmann, Introduction to *Flatland* by Edwin A. Abbott (New York: Dover, 1952), iii.

2   James M. Borg, "Abbott, Edwin (1808-1882)," *Oxford Dictionary of National Biography*, 2004. All subsequent information about Edwin Abbott Sr. is taken from this source.

First location of the City of London School on Milk Street in 1837.
Engraving by J. Woods from a picture by Hablot Knight Browne (Phiz)
made from a sketch by Robert Garland. From Wikimedia Commons.

11 to 16. In 1834, the school established relations with the new
King's College, London, and began sending its better students to
the City of London School for university preparatory courses. In
1850, Philological School headmaster Edwin Abbott sent his son,
Edwin, to the City of London School (1850-57), and Edwin, in
turn, would later return to City of London as its headmaster. This

Modern photograph (2005) of the City of London School at Black-friars. School was located here from 1883 to 1987. From Wikimedia Commons. Photograph by Adrian Pingstone.

repeating biographical pattern, shared by father and son, made Abbott particularly conscious of being A^2 in more than just name.[1]

Abbott's father, while headmaster at the Philological School, oversaw its move to New Road, Marylebone, London, and its rebuilding in 1857. Starting in 1840, he expanded the curriculum

---

1 Although in his edition of the novel Ian Stewart states there is no support for reading A Square as A^2 (p. 2, note 2), the *Oxford Magazine* (5 November 1884) review of *Flatland* begins with "Mr. A^2—we beg his pardon, Mr. A. Square" (see Appendix A1), suggesting that the reviewer knew Abbott was the author. Rudy Rucker (*Fourth Dimension*, p. 11) and Thomas Banchoff (personal communication) also see A Square as a pun on Abbott's name. Some have argued that A Square echoes the rhythm and cadence of Euclid's definitions; this is also a possibility. However, such references are commonly made to the language of the English translation of Euclid by Sir Thomas L. Heath, which was published in 1909, post-dating *Flatland* by 25 years. Appendix E2 provides a comparison between an 1885 school textbook and Heath's translation.

to include English, German, electricity (1854), and chemistry (1870). His son would follow similar lines of curriculum revision at the City of London School, as he continued the education of some of the same boys his father had as students. Like his son, Abbott's father wrote textbooks: *A Second Latin Book* (1858), *A Handbook of English Grammar* (1845; 3rd ed. 1877), and *Handbook of Arithmetic and First Steps in Algebra* (7th ed. 1876), which inspired his son's *Flatland*. He also translated volume 3 of J.H. Merle D'Aubigné's *History of the Great Reformation* (1838-41) and wrote *A Concordance to Pope* (1875), which his son edited.

Therefore, Abbott was a second-generation headmaster and teacher-scholar, following and building on his father's work. That is how Lewis Richard Farnell's entry in the *Dictionary of National Biography* (1922-30) viewed him; Farnell states that Abbott's "claim to be remembered must chiefly rest upon what can only be called his genius for teaching";[1] however, the entry makes no mention of *Flatland*, the reason for his modern recognition.

As a student at the City of London School, Abbott encountered students from different religious backgrounds and made close friends with other pupils, such as Sir John Robert Seeley (attended 1846-52), who would also return to teach at City of London as Composition Master before becoming Professor of Latin at University College, London, and Howard Chandler (attended 1851-56), Mathematical Master at Uppingham School. An excellent student, after graduation from City of London, Abbott attended St. John's College, Cambridge, became Senior Classic and Senior Chancellor's Medalist in 1861, and was elected to a fellowship at his college in 1862.[2] His background in classics, mathematics, and theology would become fully integrated later in *Flatland*. In 1863, he was ordained deacon and became a priest in the Church of England. College rules at the time stated that only unmarried men could hold college fellowships, so Abbott resigned his fellowship upon his

---

1 Lewis Richard Farnell, "Abbott, Edwin Abbott," *Dictionary of National Biography (1922-1930)*, ed. J.R.H. Weaver (London: Oxford UP, 1937), 1-3.

2 L.R. Farnell and Rosemary Jann, "Abbott, Edwin Abbott," *Oxford Dictionary of National Biography*, 2004. At Cambridge, his other honors included seventh Senior Optime, First Class in the Theological Tripos, Camden Medal for Latin Verse, and the Scholefield Prize. Later on, he was also Hulsean Lecturer at Cambridge, Select Preacher at Oxford, and Fellow of the British Academy (A.E. Douglas-Smith, *The City of London School* [Oxford: Blackwell, 1965], 531).

marriage to Mary Elizabeth Rangeley in 1863 and began teaching at King Edward's School, Birmingham, and Clifton College, Bristol. He had a daughter, Mary, who attended Girton College in Cambridge in 1891, and a son, Edwin, who attended Caius College in Cambridge and eventually became a lecturer in Latin at Jesus College, Cambridge. Neither of the children ever married.[1]

Abbott also was involved in the lives of his nephews and nieces, particularly his nephew Edward Abbott Parry (1863-1943), son of his sister Elizabeth Mead and the highly respected jurist John Humphreys, who was involved in several of the major legal cases of his day, such as the Tichborne case and *Whistler v. Ruskin*. When both of Parry's parents died suddenly in 1880, Abbott was appointed co-executor of the estate and he helped guide Parry's preparation for his legal career. Parry was called to the bar in 1885 and Abbott's interest in his nephew's studies can be seen in the Square's legal profession in *Flatland*.[2]

In 1865, when Abbott became headmaster of the City of London School, after being assistant master at King Edward's, he was only 26, and he held the position for 23 years until his retirement in 1889 at the age of 50 (apparently for health reasons and in order to devote more time to writing, but the increasing pressure to weaken the Classics program and to stress commercial and applied subjects was a likely additional motivation). He was an educational reformist, something that was encouraged by the fact that the City of London School was an unusually tolerant, progressive, and socially inclusive secondary school, founded, owned, and supported, not by a church as was typical for the time, but by the city of London itself.

The history of the City of London School is rooted in a series of investigations by England's Charities Commission of ancient charitable bequests between 1818 and 1823 that questioned how those bequests were administered. There was concern over whether the poor and those in need were really benefiting from charity organizations, or if the money was primarily going into

---

1   Mary was also an excellent classicist, but she was not eligible for a degree or academic awards such as the Chancellor's Medal (which her father and brother received) because of her sex. She helped her father with his publications after his retirement.

2   Parry recalled visits to his uncle in his autobiography, *My Own Way* (London: Cassell, 1932) and has written essays reflecting on his father's cases. He went on to become a judge and published essays on jurisprudence as well as several children's books.

the administration of those funds. The medieval bequest of John Carpenter caught the Commission's attention as his 1442 will provided for the education of four boys, but by the 1820s, the London real estate set aside in Carpenter's will brought in quite a bit more money in rent than was spent on the boys. In the period 1823-27, the common Council of the City of London was trying to establish a better system to handle the Carpenter bequest, resolve scandals associated with the London Workhouse, provide better schooling for poor children, and find a better use for the city's Honey Lane Market property.[1] The committee wished that boys had access to an education that was both classical, meaning it prepared students for possible university work, and commercial, i.e., preparation for the workplace.[2] This emphasis was unique in nineteenth-century educational practices, which generally focused either on religious training or on an apprenticeship. Eventually, it was decided to found a school that would extend the Carpenter fund to more students and provide education for the less well-off, and to build it on the Honey Lane Market property; after much discussion, the school was finally opened in 1837.[3] Headmasters were appointed by a committee of six professors from King's College, London, and the University of London.[4]

The Rev. Dr. G.F.W. Mortimer, who served as headmaster before Abbott, opened the school to Dissenters (i.e., those who did not belong to the Church of England) and Jewish students. Mortimer explained, when giving evidence in 1865 to the Schools Inquiry Commission, that he did not require Jewish students to attend religious services or classes at the school, noting, "I always had a great regard for Jewish boys, and I found they were not received at any schools."[5] This made the school one of the first to exhibit such religious tolerance.[6] The tradition of

---

1 Douglas-Smith, 37.
2 Douglas-Smith, 39.
3 Douglas-Smith, 46-62.
4 Douglas-Smith, 63.
5 Douglas-Smith, 95.
6 Douglas-Smith, 96. Information about the City of London School found in the *Practical Handbook to the Principal Schools of England* by Charles Eyre Pascoe (London: Sampson Low, 1877) notes that among the scholarships available to students was The Jews' Commemoration Scholarship, established in 1859 to "commemorate the passing of the Act of the Legislature by which Jews are enabled to sit in Parliament" (108).

general religious tolerance, one experienced by Abbott when he was a student under Mortimer, was continued, in turn, by Abbott when he became headmaster.

The engineer Henry Beaufoy[1] established awards for English and mathematics, and City of London gained an excellent reputation in mathematics education. Students covered differential and integral calculus and took great pride in their geometry curriculum. One account given by Dr. Charles S. Myers[2] from 1885 describes a lesson in Euclid's geometry in the Senior class under Thomas Todd. Typically, a boy would be summoned to the blackboard and told to

> demonstrate before the class some theorem or problem which we were supposed to have learnt in our home-work. [The teacher] would help the boy to draw the appropriate figure on the board and would then affix to the various points letters which were quite different from those given in our textbook. "Cramming" was therefore quite useless; and if the boy was unsuccessful, Todd would dismiss him with an unforgettable dissyllabic roar—"Fai—led."[3]

Several students went on to distinguished careers in the sciences. In 1850, the enrollment was 637 boys (the City of London School for Girls was founded in 1894), with a waiting list of 240. Boys were admitted at any age between 7 and 15 years and could stay until age 19.[4] Under Abbott, the school continued to flourish, reaching an enrollment of 680 boys, which required a move to a new, larger location near the Blackfriars Bridge end of the Thames Embankment.[5] Whereas the standard school curriculum of the day focused on the study of the Classics, under Abbott's leadership the study of chemistry was made compulsory; English literature was added to the curriculum, particularly the close philological study of Shakespeare's language; a reformed pro-

---

1 Henry Beaufoy (1764-1827) was a Quaker and Member of Parliament.
2 Later Director of the Psychological Laboratory and Reader in Experimental Psychology at Cambridge, Professor of Psychology of King's College London, and pioneer in industrial psychology.
3 Quoted in Douglas-Smith, 279.
4 Pascoe, 106.
5 The school building at the Blackfriars location features statues of Shakespeare, Milton, Bacon, Newton, and Sir Thomas More on the front. Abbott wrote on Shakespeare and Bacon. More is the author of *Utopia*, another imaginary world.

nunciation of Latin was adopted; and the study of Sanskrit was made an option for the best students. As an administrator, Abbott reduced class sizes (classes could be as large as seventy students) and attracted better-qualified instructors. He was admired by his students, who included Sir Sidney Lee, Arthur Henry Bulen, Arthur Rackham, and Prime Minister H.H. Asquith.

Abbott had been appointed headmaster at an unusually young age, so when he retired from the position after 24 years on the job following several illnesses, he was still only 50 years old and was able to devote the rest of his life to scholarship. He is the author of *A Shakespearean Grammar: An Attempt to Illustrate Some of the Differences Between Elizabethan and Modern English* (1869), an examination of Shakespearean syntax with questions at the end of the book for classroom use. This book was a pioneering attempt to formulate and systematize the study of Shakespeare. It broke Shakespearean grammar into 529 sections—from "Adjectives" to "Good and Bad Metaphors"—and tried to clarify archaic usage. Abbott's explanations are still cited today by editors of Shakespeare's texts. *A Shakespearean Grammar* underwent three revisions, was very popular, and was reprinted as a Dover paperback in 1966.

In addition to *A Shakespearean Grammar*, Abbott studied the works of Francis Bacon (1561-1626) and the history of science during the Elizabethan period. He wrote *Bacon and Essex* (1877), an introduction to *Bacon's Essays* (1876),[1] and a well-received biography, *Francis Bacon: An Account of His Life and Works* (1885).[2] In his research on Bacon, Abbott was particularly interested in the corruption in the court of Elizabeth, and in Bacon's involvement in a "system of government [that] was radically bad, demoralizing both the governor and the governed."[3] Moral condemnations of Bacon for homosexuality had been expressed since the seventeenth century, but in the nineteenth century, politician and historian Lord Macaulay particularly blamed

---

1 Francis Bacon's *Essays* was a standard textbook for the teaching of essay writing to secondary-school students from the 1900s well into the 1930s. Abbott's notes are incorporated into Clark Sutherland Northup's Riverside College Classics edition of the *Essays*, and his help is acknowledged by Northup (see p. 27, note 1).

2 Edward Parry shared his uncle's interest in seventeenth-century England, editing the first edition of Dorothy Osborne's (1627-95) letters in 1889.

3 Edwin Abbott, *Francis Bacon: An Account of His Life and Works* (London: Macmillan, 1885), 5.

Bacon for his failure to maintain justice in a time of civil war.[1] This concern over poor government most likely sent Abbott to consider Plato's *Republic*, which contains Socrates' discussion of forms of government; Bacon had also used the cave simile from the *Republic* in his *Novum Organum* (1620) to identify types of intellectual fallacies.[2] Additionally Abbott considered church policy, the position of science in the seventeenth century, and Bacon's familiarity with the work of others, such as Galileo.

Abbott produced two writing textbooks: *English Lessons, for English People* (1871, in collaboration with J.R. Seeley) and *How to Write Clearly* (1872). In these textbooks, he emphasized the use of direct and concise expression and criticized passages from well-known eighteenth-century writers, along with passages that seem to have been picked out from contemporary parliamentary proceedings. These publications indicate Abbott's concern with the teaching of writing and mathematics, his close relationship with Seeley, and his careful monitoring of current events in the newspapers and magazines of his day.

His fiction writing tended toward religious works, displaying what was called a "Broad Church" viewpoint, a liberal position that attempted to reconcile science and religion. These novels included *Philochristus* (1878), *Onesimus: Memoirs of a Disciple of St. Paul* (1882), and *Silanus the Christian* (1906). In his fiction, Abbott attempted to reassure readers who could not accept miracles that historical biblical events might have been obscured by the mythology of the time and that religious beliefs that did not depend upon miracles were closer to the roots of Christianity.[3] Abbott was particularly sympathetic toward ministers in the Church of England who found they no longer had faith in religious miracles. In 1880, the Rev. Stopford Brooks resigned his position because of such concerns. The controversy triggered by Brooks's resignation led Abbott to publish *The Kernel and the Husk* (1886), a work based on conversations he had in 1884 with an unnamed clergyman who had lost his faith. In this account,

---

1 Markku Peltonen, "Bacon, Francis, viscount St Alban (1561-1626)," *Oxford Dictionary of National Biography*, (Oxford: Oxford UP, 2004; online edition, May 2006: <http://www.oxforddnb.com/view/article/990>).

2 See also the section on Francis Bacon and Plato's *Republic*. See also pp. 31-34 below.

3 Maria Poggi Johnson analyzes two of Abbott's historical novels, *Philochristus* (1878) and *Onesimus* (1882), in her article "Critical Scholarship, Christian Antiquity, and the Victorian Crisis of Faith in the Historical Novels of Edwin Abbott," *Clio* 37.3 (2008): 395-412.

Abbott argued that a minister who did not believe in miracles should still be allowed to hold office in the Church of England. This work contains autobiographical passages describing Abbott's intellectual and religious development, along with his view on miracles, higher dimensions, and evolution.[1]

Responses to *Flatland*

So believable has been the narrator, A Square (with no period), that many readers have experienced difficulty perceiving the separation between the narrator persona and the author. Statements that the Square makes about women and lower classes have been seen as indications that Abbott held such personal biases.[2] Such responses are akin to those who conclude after reading *A Modest Proposal* that Swift hated the Irish. This misreading is, however, primarily a modern reaction; most contemporary reviewers recognized the satire on the Victorian class system and its view of women.

On the other hand, some accusations must have been raised early in the publishing history of *Flatland*, for in the preface Abbott added to the revised edition, he responds to such charges:

It has been objected that he [the Square] is a woman-hater; and as this objection has been vehemently urged by those whom Nature's decree has constituted the somewhat larger half of the Spaceland race, I should like to remove it, so far as I can honestly do so. But the Square is so unaccustomed to the use of the moral terminology of Spaceland that I should be doing him an injustice if I were literally to transcribe his defence against this charge. [...] I gather that in the course of an imprisonment of seven years he has himself modified his

---

1 See Appendix C1 for a selection from *The Kernel and the Husk*.
2 Some, such as Peter Nicholls et al. in their reference work *The Science Fiction Encyclopedia* (New York: Doubleday, 1979), have taken these statements at face value and concluded that *Flatland* is a reflection of beliefs associated with Abbott's position as headmaster of the City of London School. Rudy Rucker (in a footnote on Charles Hinton's writing) compares the two authors and concludes that Hinton does not share the "misogyny which permeates *Flatland*" (Rudy Rucker, ed., *Speculations on the Fourth Dimension: Selected Writings of Charles H. Hinton* [New York: Dover, 1980], 31). Many math teachers dropped *Flatland* from their classrooms in the 1980s because it was seen as misogynist.

own personal views, both as regards Women and as regards the Isosceles or Lower Classes. Personally, he now inclines to the opinion of the Sphere that the Straight Lines are in many important respects superior to the Circles. [But] the destinies of Women and of the masses of mankind have seldom been deemed worthy of mention and never of careful consideration [even in Spaceland]. (64)

Abbott's response to these charges of misogyny is the considered and levelheaded response of an author who refuses to interpret his own writing for the reader. The society he has created operates by its own rules; its morality is not necessarily our morality—a strikingly modern stance. Rather, the society of *Flatland* works with premises that mirror the heavily regulated and stratified Victorian society that controlled his own life, and then satirically expands on those premises.

Although very much a Victorian work, *Flatland* is also a precursor to Modernism, in that Abbott raises questions about the very nature of fiction.[1] Incorporated into the essence of the tale is an awareness of the very physical geometry of paper, an awareness that resists the dictate that fiction creates the illusion of volume, of three-dimensional space. Abbott's unusually abstracted and conceptual fiction convinces Mark McGurl that the work is "more than a literary-historical oddity" and that "it may have considerable consequences for our understanding of certain features of the avant-garde projects to which it appears, in some ways, an eccentric precursor."[2] McGurl argues that although *Flatland* provides an abstracted representation, it is not free from ideological debate, and, indeed, its abstraction highlights its investigation of class distinction as shown in the geometric hierarchy of Flatland's society.[3] The history of abstract art and cubism also shows, in the words of Bruce Clarke, that "[t]he formal and philosophical motives of early modernist abstraction, at least in the first two decades of the twentieth century, derived not from the space-time of Einstein-

---

1   As Mark McGurl clearly notes, "The inhabitants of Flatland exist as 'characters' in two senses of that term, both as represented beings and as conventional symbols, somewhat as though the type beneath our eyes has detached itself from the pulp upon which it is pressed and come to life" ("Social Geometries: Taking Place in Henry James," *Representations* 68 [1999]: 59).
2   McGurl, 60.
3   McGurl, 60.

ian field theory but from earlier discourses like that of late classical hyperspace...."[1]

Background to a Two-Dimensional World

In 1623, Galileo wrote the following, often quoted passage in his book *Il Saggiatore* (*The Assayer*):

> Philosophy is written in that greatest of books which stands continually open before the eyes of men [that is, the universe], but cannot be learned without previous preparation to understand the language and decipher the characters in which it is written. It is written in the language of mathematics, and its characters are triangles, circles, and other geometrical figures, without which, we should wander in vain, through mazes and obscurity. It is humanly impossible to understand a single word of it, without these one is wandering about in a dark labyrinth.[2]

Flatland appears to take a punning inspiration from these words. Whereas Galileo meant "characters" as analogous to letters in the alphabet, in Abbott's book the fictional characters are, indeed, geometric figures. However, the Square, frustrated in his jail at the novel's end, does suggest an unjustly imprisoned Galileo who has been confined for teaching mathematically derived conclusions that run counter to the religious establishment.[3] Additional

1 Bruce Clarke, *Energy Forms: Allegory and Science in the Era of Classical Thermodynamics* (Ann Arbor: U of Michigan P, 2001), 5. See also Linda Dalrymple Henderson, *The Fourth Dimension and Non-Euclidean Geometry in Modern Art* (Princeton: Princeton UP, 1983). Henderson's work is an interdisciplinary study of mathematical history and art history based on her 1975 Yale University doctoral study, *The Artist, "The Fourth Dimension" and Non-Euclidean Geometry 1900-1930: A Romance of Many Dimensions.*

2 English translation from H. Cox, "Study of Mechanics," *The Civil Engineer and Architect's Journal* (November 1846): 323-27, 324; from the introduction to Part I of *Civil Engineer and Architect's Course of Mechanics, Applicable to Structures and Machines* (c. 1846); a more modern translation can be found in Stillman Drake, "The Assayer," *Controversy on Comets of 1618*, trans. Stillman Drake and C.D. O'Malley (Philadelphia: U of Pennsylvania P, 1960), 183-84.

3 There is, of course, a long history of religious persecution in Europe. Socrates, the focus of Plato's *Republic*, was charged with impiety and imprisoned. Parallels can also be found in biblical accounts of Christ's imprisonment.

support for parallels with Galileo in *Flatland* can be seen in Abbott's commentary on Bacon's allusion to Ptolemaic geocentric orbits—"astronomers, which did feign eccentrics and epicycles and such engines of orbs, to save the phenomena; though they knew there were no such things"—in his essay "Of Superstition." Abbott explains how a series of orbital circles were created to explain away phenomena that did not fit into the Ptolemaic description of the solar system. It is tempting to see connections between Bacon's essay on superstition and the behavior of the Circles in Flatland, who preached a law based on geometry to support a belief system that they knew was false.[1] While Galileo might have suggested the idea of mathematical figures as characters and his struggle against religious dogma might have inspired the novel's ending, the concept of two-dimensional life has a longer and more complex history.

Linda Dalrymple Henderson raises the question, "where might the theologian and educator Abbott have encountered 'the fourth dimension' and the associated analogy of a world of two dimensions?"[2] In answering her own question, Henderson traces the idea that space has three dimensions back to Aristotle's *De caelo*. In the eighteenth century, Immanuel Kant (1724-1804) referred to the possibility of other spaces in "On the First Grounds of the Distinction of Regions of Space" in 1769, suggesting that the difference between the right and the left hand is due to their different orientation in space.[3] Use of this analogy of "handedness" to argue for the existence of the fourth dimension was used by August Möbius (1790-1868) and later writers.[4] Later, in his *Critique of Pure Reason* (1781), Kant introduced the concept of objectivity (*a priori* or knowledge independent of experience) by first examining the relationship between mathematics and the concept of space, noting the degree by which point of view determines the experience of space,[5] a major theme of *Flatland*.

---

1 See *The Essays of Francis Bacon*, ed. Clark Sutherland Northup (Boston: Houghton Mifflin, 1936), 54-56 (essay 17), 195 n.9. Abbott contributed notes to this edition, first published in 1908. Interestingly, his notes are identified with an "A" in Northup's edition.
2 Henderson, 17
3 Henderson, 17.
4 Henderson, 18.
5 Immanuel Kant, *Critique of Pure Reason*, trans. J.M.D. Meiklejohn, ed. Vasilis Politis (London: Dent, 1993), A21/B35-A29/B45.

The first use of two-dimensional beings who are not aware of the third dimension (as an analogy for our three-dimensional existence in a four-dimensional universe) has been traced by Henderson back to physicist Gustav Theodor Fechner's (1801-87) satirical essay "Der Raum hat vier Dimensionen" ("Space Has Four Dimensions") in *Vier Paradoxa* (1846). Fechner (writing under the pseudonym "Dr. Mises") describes a "shadow man," who is a projection made by a camera obscura. Fechner's essay also suggests the interrelationship of time with the fourth dimension, an idea that Abbott did not make use of but that became a central element of the ideas of Abbott's contemporary, Charles Howard Hinton (1853-1907), who was working on a two-dimensional novel, *An Episode of Flatland* (1907).[1]

What is most likely, however, is that Abbott was influenced by any of several articles aimed at a general audience, many of which followed Sartorius van Waltershausen's 1856 biography of Karl Gauss (1755-1855). According to van Waltershausen, Gauss spoke of imagining creatures that could understand only two dimensions as a way of understanding beings that could see four or more dimensions,[2] the basis of *Flatland*.

This illustration was expanded upon by Hermann von Helmholtz's (1821-94) article "On the Origin and Significance of Geometrical Axioms."[3] Here Helmholtz used the model of two-dimensional beings living on a sphere to illustrate that geometrical axioms are dependent on the type of space in which its writers live.[4] Contrary to Euclid's axiom that parallel lines would not meet, when these two-dimensional creatures drew lines on what they thought was a flat world, they found that all lines would intersect once they were long enough. In addition, large triangles would have angles whose sums were larger than 180 degrees, as

---

1 Henderson, 18.

2 Henderson, 18-19.

3 Henderson, 12; Richards, 78-81, 96-99. Helmholtz's first published short paper, titled "The Axioms of Geometry" (see Appendix B2) is referred to in *The Oxford Magazine* review (5 November 1884; see Appendix A1). This paper was first given as a lecture in Heidelberg in 1870, then published in *Academy* in London (vol. 1 [1870]: 128-31). It was enlarged for publication in the psychological journal *Mind* (part 1 in vol. 1 [1876]: 301-21; part 2 in vol. 3 [1878]: 212-25) under the title "On the Origin and Significance of Geometrical Axioms" and collected in his *Popular Lectures on Scientific Subjects* (1881).

4 Henderson, 12.

they do in Riemann's geometry.[1] A series of widely reprinted articles were written in England, starting with J.J. Sylvester's "A Plea for the Mathematician,"[2] which affirmed the existence of four-dimensional space and called for the removal of Euclid's *Elements* as the major textbook for the teaching of mathematics.[3] This was followed by G.F. Rodwell's "On Space of Four Dimensions,"[4] which described the transformation of a three-dimensional man into a two-dimensional being and analyzed the changes in perception.[5] Non-Euclidean geometry and *n*-dimensional geometry (considered two different geometries) were brought together by William K. Clifford (like Abbott, a former fellow at Cambridge), who was interested in Riemann's studies. He suggested that a non-Euclidean curve would be required to provide higher dimensions with a direction in which to move. As an illustration of this, he compared our sense of three dimensions to the perspective of a bookworm in a flat page, a page in the process of being rumpled. The geometry of the bookworm's experience would remain two-dimensional, but, from the outside, a third dimension would be seen.[6] Helmholtz and others did not believe a connection was necessary between non-Euclidean geometry and a fourth dimension; however, despite their protests, the two remained linked in non-technical writing.[7]

In addition to the essays written in the 1870s, Charles L. Dodgson (1832-98), who wrote the *Alice* books (published in 1865) under the pseudonym of Lewis Carroll, published the short text "Dynamics of a Parti-cle, with an Excursus on the New Method of Evaluation, as Applied to Pi" in 1865 while holding the Christ Church Mathematical Lectureship at Oxford. In "Dynamics of a Parti-cle," "there is a romance between two linear, one-eyed creatures who glide over a flat

---

1 The model was later incorporated into Dionys Burger's *Sphereland* (New York: Crowell, 1965), a sequel to *Flatland*.

2 *Nature* 1 (30 December 1869): 237-39, 260-63.

3 Sylvester squared off with T.H. Huxley in print, one of the major battles in mathematical history. See Richards, 133-36 and Appendix E3.

4 *Nature*, 8 (1 May 1873): 8-9. This same issue also contained William K. Clifford's English translation of Riemann's 1854 lecture "On the Hypotheses which Lie at the Bases of Geometry" (14-17, 36-37). Clifford's translation made non-Euclidean ideas available to the British public in the mid-1870s. See Richards, 73-75.

5 Henderson, 19-20.

6 Henderson, 20.

7 Henderson, 21.

surface."[1] However, Dodgson, the editor of a Euclid-based mathematics textbook, was not interested in promoting non-Euclidean geometry.[2] As such texts as *Euclid and His Modern Rivals* (1879) show, Dodgson was quite conservative in his mathematics. "Dynamics of a Parti-cle" was intended to be a humorous attack on non-Euclidean students' concerns with Euclid's parallel postulate. Additionally, Dodgson satirizes those who attempt, as he phrases it, to "introduc[e] the human element into the hitherto barren region of Mathematics," and continues, tongue-in-cheek, to ask:

> Who can tell whether the parallelogram, which in our ignorance we have defined and drawn, and the whole of whose properties we profess to know, may not be all the while panting for exterior angles, sympathetic with the interior, or sullenly repining at the fact that it cannot be inscribed in a circle?[3]

Despite this interesting start, though, Dodgson simply continues the sketch with pseudo-geometric definitions of politics. The subject of higher dimensions was merely a subject for parody.

The topic of life in the two dimensions and, by analogy, the fourth dimension was being developed by Charles Hinton at the same time Abbott was writing. It is apparent that the two writers were influencing one another. Banchoff notes that Abbott's close friend Howard Chandler, the "H.C." of *Flatland*'s dedication, taught mathematics at the same school where Hinton was teaching science—Uppingham School.[4] Additionally, Hinton's intro-

---

1 John Fisher, Introduction to *The Magic of Lewis Carroll* (New York: Simon and Schuster, 1973), 10.

2 Dodgson's textbook competed with a reform *Euclidian Geometry* (1st ed., London: Macmillan, 1874) written by Francis Cuthbertson, the Head Mathematical Master of the City of London School where Abbott was headmaster. See Appendix E1 for a list of geometry textbooks available in 1884.

3 Charles Dodgson, "The Dynamics of a Parti-cle," *Diversions and Digressions of Lewis Carroll* (originally titled *The Lewis Carroll Picture Book*, 1899) (New York: Dover, 1961), 61.

4 Thomas Banchoff, Introduction to *Flatland*, by Edwin Abbott Abbott (Princeton: Princeton UP, 1991), xxv. Headmaster Edward Thring was forced to fire Hinton from Uppingham School when he was found guilty of bigamy. Hinton, aged 34, pleaded guilty "to feloniously marrying Maud Florence, his wife being alive" and received three days' imprisonment. (*Proceedings of the Old Bailey Online* 25 October 1886; <http://www.oldbaileyonline.org>). While Abbott was polite in his

duction to his 1888 *Scientific Romances* refers to "that ingenious work of Flatland," indicating that he was writing with knowledge of Abbott's book. Abbott, in turn, in his 1886 book *The Kernel and the Husk*, refers to Hinton's essay "What is the Fourth Dimension?"[1] It is also possible that Hinton's linkage of the fourth dimension to spiritualism affected later critical responses to Abbott's book, especially in the United States.

"What Is the Fourth Dimension?" was Hinton's first publication. It first appeared in *The Dublin University Magazine* in 1881 and was subsequently published as a pamphlet in 1884 (the same year as *Flatland*) with the subtitle "Ghosts Explained."[2] This was one of nine pamphlets, eventually collected in the two-volume *Scientific Romances*.[3] In the essay, Hinton describes a creature confined in two dimensions, "some figure, such as a circle or rectangle ... endowed with the power of perception." He also considers the perception of a being "confined to a single straight line"; these are obviously inspirations for Abbott's *Flatland*. Hinton even discusses what might happen if a two-dimensional creature was lifted out into a three-dimensional space. In turn, Hinton's own 1907 Flatland novel, *An Episode of Flatland: or How a Plane Folk Discovered the Third Dimension* (in press at the time of his death), attempts to solve the physical problems apparent in Abbott's world.

Francis Bacon and Plato's *Republic*

While writing *Flatland*, Abbott was deeply involved in his research on the Elizabethan court life and the relationship between the philosophical and political life of lord chancellor,

---

printed recognition of Hinton, he seems to have personally kept his distance. K.G. Valente believes that Abbott's studies predate Hinton's, pointing to an anonymously authored essay, "A New Philosophy," published in the *City of London School Magazine* in 1877 as being linked to *Flatland*. See K.G. Valente, "Transgression and Transcendence: *Flatland* as a Response to 'A New Philosophy,'" *Nineteenth-Century Contexts* 26.1 (2004): 61-77.

1 Ian Stewart, *The Annotated Flatland: A Romance of Many Dimensions* (Cambridge, MA: Perseus, 2002), xxiv.

2 Rucker, Introduction to *Speculations on the Fourth Dimension*, vii.

3 Rucker, Introduction to *Speculations on the Fourth Dimension*, vii. English translations of Jules Verne's (1828-1905) works, published as *voyages extraordinaires* in France, were called "scientific romances" in England, and it is likely that Hinton (or his publisher) picked up the term for his collection title.

politician, and philosopher Francis Bacon (1561-1626), author of the utopian work *New Atlantis* and one of the first philosophers of modern science. In his biography, Abbott responds to nineteenth-century charges by Lord Macaulay, among others, that Bacon was corrupt and took bribes.[1] In his work on Bacon, Abbott asks to what degree a person can be moral in the midst of political corruption. Such questions took Abbott back to Plato's *Republic*, along with its cave illustration and blueprint for an ideal state.

Plato's *Republic* is often cited as the origin of utopian literature.[2] Scholars date its writing to about 375 BCE, although the events described—Socrates' dialogues with the youth of Greece—are staged a generation earlier, just before 420.[3] The text is complex, but the topics that most pertain to *Flatland* are the importance of education in geometry to the training of the ideal ruler ("the philosopher ruler") as a means of drawing the mind "upwards, instead of downwards,"[4] the existence of different orders of reality, the conflict between popular opinion and the good, the use of myths that teach the necessary proper social roles, and how those who know more may be successfully attacked by those who know less. All of these topics are skillfully woven into *Flatland*.

As one of the best classicists of his day, Abbott, who knew Benjamin Jowett,[5] the major Victorian translator of Plato, would have studied the *Republic* in the original Greek. Abbott first

---

1   See p. 22, note 3.
2   Furthermore, some scholars cite Xenophon's *Cyropaedia* as playing a role in the development of the *dys*topian novel as it is read as a response and a correction to the *Republic* (see Robert Scholes, James Phelan, and Robert Kellogg, *The Nature of Narrative*, rev. ed. [Oxford: Oxford UP, 2006], 78). Others, however, disagree. James Tatum, while acknowledging that questions of the ideal king and the ideal kingship were common topics of discussion among Plato's contemporaries, concludes that the *Cyropaedia* "is not a dialectical response to the *Republic*" (see Tatum's *Xenophon's Imperial Fiction: On* The Education of Cyrus [Princeton: Princeton UP, 1989], 38-39).
3   Desmond Lee, Translator's Introduction to *Republic*, by Plato (London: Penguin, 2003), xx, 2.
4   *Republic*, 527b-c. This phrase is echoed in the Square's call for "Upwards, not Northwards" (134). Rucker in *Geometry, Relativity, and the Fourth Dimension* (4) and *The Fourth Dimension* (8-10) also identifies Plato as a possible precursor of the two-dimensional allegory.
5   Abbott's social and professional circle would have brought him in contact with Plato's translators. Jowett attempted to recruit Abbott to be a Lecturer on Theology at Balliol College at Oxford University while he

expands upon the *Republic*'s simile of the Cave, which Bruce Clarke declares "is a pivotal subtext in many Victorian and modernist allegories of science,"[1] in order to show the limitations of perception. Bacon made use of Plato's imagery in his classification of forms of poor logic. The Idols of the Cave from *Novum Organum* refers to individual perception and, in his biography of Bacon, Abbott identifies its source as "the famous allegory of the Cave in Plato's Republic," then traces its reference throughout Bacon's works.[2] In Plato's simile, once the prisoners who have been chained inside caves are allowed outside, they must try to sort out a reality different from the two-dimensional shadows upon which they have oriented their lives.[3] Similarly, in *Flatland*, the Square attempts to perceive a reality that is outside his very physical two-dimensional world, and he has as many problems doing so as do Plato's prisoners. And the Square, faced with government pressure, the carefully contrived history and myths of his culture, its rigid class structure, and the attacks of those in authority, loses his own momentarily gained understanding of another, higher reality, much as Socrates would have predicted.

Additionally, the *Republic* is the earliest attempt to describe an ideal state based on a hierarchy of rules that combines both descent and personal ability. In its attempt to outline the education of an ideal ruler, the *Republic* is the ancestor of all utopian works. *Flatland*'s society alludes to this educational idea. Geometry, for example, is highly valued in Flatland as it is in the *Republic*, as evidenced by the time and effort the Square invests in his

---

was headmaster, but he declined (Douglas-Smith, 531). Additionally, Abbott's brother-in-law, Rev. Howarth Hart (husband of his sister Alice), was a curate of Llewellyn Davies, the co-translator (with David James Vaughan) of an 1888 edition of the *Republic* (see Parry, *My Own Way*, 33).

1 Clarke, 30. See Appendix B1 for an English translation of The Cave section from the *Republic*.

2 Abbott, *Francis Bacon*, 381 and n.2. The term "simile" is now used in preference to "allegory" in philosophy.

3 Other writers of this period searched for pedagogical ways of showing a contrast between the limitations of perception and thought. Huxley used "Jack and the Beanstalk" for Oxford University's Romanes Lecture of 1893 (reprinted in *Evolution and Ethics and Other Essays* [New York: Appleton, 1901], 47-51) as a variation of the same idea designed to move the readers into a consideration of the transitory nature of natural life. The Cave simile is a common plot device in modern science fiction. Examples include Robert Heinlein's *Orphans of the Sky* (1963), where a spaceship functions as the cave, and Terry Pratchett's *Bromeliad Trilogy* (1988-90), where a department store is the cave.

own and his grandson's geometric education; but unlike Plato's utopian vision, Flatland does not consider capability, only physiology, in the selection of its rulers, who reach their station in life based solely on regularity in shape.

Unlike analogy, which relies on one-to-one correspondences to make a point, metaphoric correspondence, such as types of simile and allegory, is more diffuse, suggesting a series of shifting cultural and social discourses. As rhetorical forms, such metaphors are similar to mathematics in the sense that they provide symbolic equations upon which conceptual models can be built, offering "a structural geometry of networked spaces."[1] Abbott, and later Charles Hinton in his two-dimensional society,[2] built on Plato's parable to teach moral lessons. They were what Bruce Clarke calls "pedagogical allegorists," linking movements between higher and lower dimensions to the Victorian tendency to perceive human evolution in terms of moral advancement or degradation. Hinton used the idea of higher dimensions to power a kind of mystical metamorphosis into an advanced state of mind or consciousness,[3] but once Abbott raised such analogies, he also subverted them, leading his readers to question if belief in racial or class or gender superiority is as inborn or as apparent as was conventionally (and scientifically) believed at the time. These beliefs formed part of the social context in which Abbott wrote his novel.

Abbott's and Hinton's ideas quickly made an impact on other writers. The philosopher William James made reference to their work in an ethics lecture given at Harvard University, where the African-American writer W.E.B. Du Bois was a student. Inspired by the lecture, around 1899 Du Bois began a story or novel (it is unclear which Du Bois intended) titled "A Vacation Unique." In this unpublished manuscript, which treats the topic of American racism, the black protagonist invites a white friend to enter a "fourth dimension of color" and experience racism. The story makes direct references to both Hinton's "What is the Fourth Dimension?" and *Flatland*.[4]

---

1 Clarke, 95.
2 See Appendix D3 for a selection from Hinton's two-dimension novel.
3 Clarke, 31.
4 Shamoon Zamir, *Dark Voices: W.E.B. Du Bois and American Thought* (Chicago: U of Chicago P, 1995), 50-55. Also see Nancy Bentley, "Literary Forms and Mass Culture, 1870-1920," *The Cambridge History of American Literature: Prose Writing 1860-1920*, vol. 3, ed. Sacvan Bercovitch (Cambridge: Cambridge UP, 2005), 65-286, 219.

Social Context

To appreciate the significance of *Flatland*, it is necessary to understand the interplay between Abbott's literary imagination and late nineteenth-century current events, especially those affecting urbanized London. Victorians were heavy readers of periodicals, and Abbott, as exemplified in his composition textbooks and even in a note or two in *Flatland*, was a keen observer of current events. Additionally, the late nineteenth century was a time when science was just beginning to become professionalized, and the scientific community assumed a much larger and more diverse reading public compared to modern times, where the reading audience of scientific material is expected to possess a greater level of specialization. Major scientists such as T.H. Huxley and Francis Galton gave public lectures and demonstrations. Scientists sought a stronger voice in social policy, and scientific publications, such as *Nature*, were read by the educated members of society and discussed in newspaper editorials.

The fear of mob rule is a notable preoccupation in *Flatland*, especially in the account of the Universal Colour Bill in sections 9-10. By the time of *Flatland*'s publication, there had been three Reform Bills (in 1832, 1867, and 1884) that extended political rights for the working class, and these bills coexisted with women's increasingly public struggle for the vote. Flowing from this political agitation, the literature of the time focused on the behavior of mobs and crowds; there was intense interest in crowd psychology, a topic that is addressed in such works as Charles MacKay's *Extraordinary Popular Delusions and the Madness of Crowds* (1841).[1] In schools, students read tales of the slave revolts of classical Rome described in Appian's *History* and Plutarch's *Life of Crassus*; the threat posed by the French Revolution in the eighteenth century (particularly as described by Edmund Burke) was still fresh in the public's mind and the subject of continual debate. Several works of fiction in the 1880s, such as Henry James's *The Princess Casamassima* (1884), reflect the fear of violence that characterized British political life in the late 1800s.

Added to concerns linked to political reform was the impact

---

1   See discussion in Susan Sontag's *Under the Sign of Saturn* (New York: Random-Vintage, 1981), 197-98. E.P. Thompson, in chapters 4 and 5 of *The Making of the English Working Class* (New York: Vintage, 1966), argues that the focus on mob rule found in Edmund Burke's *Reflections on the Revolution in France* (1790) is rooted in the fear of working-class reform movements in the 1790s rather than in the French Revolution.

of severe weather. England was hit by a series of harsh winters in 1855, 1861, 1869, 1879, and 1886 that caused large-scale unemployment and bread riots in London.[1] Additionally, an agricultural depression that spread throughout Europe in the 1870s led to the formation in Ireland of the Irish Land League, which organized against landlords. Newspaper reports on the unrest in Ireland and on the large Irish populations in London combined with the immediacy of London riots to create a general sense of anxiety about the potential for insurrection among the lower classes, and these worries worked themselves into Abbott's history of Flatland society.[2]

Concerns over mob uprising, linked with the increasing size of the urban population of London, motivated those who believed that Darwin's theory of natural selection could have social implications and that tests and measurements could be devised that would predict criminal behavior or future achievement. Such studies often served to provide "scientific" support for class or racial superiority and sexism.

Sir Francis Galton (1822-1911), Charles Darwin's cousin, published his major work on the heritability of intelligence, *Hereditary Genius*, in 1869 and coined the word eugenics in 1883 to advocate the regulation of marriage based on the hereditary traits of parents. Skull measurement was commonly used to determine intelligence, and women were considered less intelligent because they had smaller skulls. In the summer of 1884, Galton even set up a laboratory at the London International Health Exhibition, where, for a threepence, people could go through a battery of tests and measurements and receive an assessment of their intelligence at the end.[3] He then moved to the

---

1 Peter Ackroyd, *London: The Biography* (New York: Anchor, 2003), 422.

2 In 1882, just before *Flatland* was published, 26 murders were linked to Irish unrest, and the English Secretary for Ireland was assassinated in Dublin. Irish terrorists blew up public buildings in England, spreading fear of mob uprising. In retaliation, the British government suspended civil liberties, including the right to trial by jury. Anthony Trollope's 1883 novel *The Landleaguers* was based on these accounts.

3 Stephen Jay Gould, *The Mismeasure of Man* (New York: Norton, 1981), 75-76. The Health Exhibition ran from May to August of 1884. Galton measured an estimated 9,000 people (David C. Watt, "Lionel Penrose, FRS (1898-1972) and Eugenics: Part One," *Notes and Records of the Royal Society of London* 52.1 [1998]: 137-51, 141). The London *Times* ran schedules of events, and the *Illustrated London News* reported on the exhibits. The exhibition featured free lectures on health, food, housing, gardening, and education.

Science Museum in South Kensington and continued with the measuring for another six years.[1] Considering the mania for such measurement, it is not difficult to see in Flatlanders' preoccupation with angle measurement, the Square's support for selective breeding by the Circles, and the reduction of the threat of revolution through the elimination of irregular shapes, a satiric comment on the beginnings of the eugenics movement long before its dangers were fully realized.[2]

In addition to mirroring Londoners' concerns about social unrest, Abbott's writings show that he was trying to come to terms with one of the major dilemmas of the Victorian age: how to resolve the conflict between scientific inquiry and spiritual faith. Part of this discussion is rooted in Kant's *Critique of Pure Reason* (1781), a difficult text that is far beyond the scope of this introduction.[3] Very basically, Kant is concerned with the question of objectivity in relationship to other philosophical schools of thought: rationalism, associated with G.W. Leibniz (1646-1716), and empiricism, associated with David Hume (1711-76). Leibniz argued that objective knowledge of the world is possible separate from the observer, and that all knowledge is derived from reason; Hume, on the other hand, argued that objective knowledge is not possible, and that knowledge comes only through experience and cannot be separated from the subjectivity of the observer. For Hume, objectivity is an illusion. Kant argued that neither experience nor reason alone could provide knowledge, but that rather a synthesis of both is necessary. In making his case that it is possible to know the world separate from perspective, Kant discusses space and time in the opening chapters of *Critique*, describing mathematics as "synthetic apriori," that is, propositions that are true independent of experience, but not abstract Platonic objects.

Apart from these philosophical discussions, the late Victorian period faced several scientific developments that challenged the traditional understanding of the physical world. Evolutionary theory is the best known today, but others included Maxwell's electromagnetic field theory and non-Euclidean geometry. Like Maimonides, who incorporated Greek philosophy into Jewish

---

1 Gould, 76.

2 As Gould's history explains, eugenics and other forms of anthropometric studies would later be used to justify forced sterilization and racist immigration policies in the United States and Nazi extermination campaigns in Germany in the first half of the twentieth century.

3 Roger Scruton has a good, concise introduction to Kant in his *Kant: A Very Short Introduction* (Oxford: Oxford UP, 2001), 16-31.

tradition to convince his readers that the Torah and nature both lead to the revelation of God, Abbott sought to forge a link between scientific theory and religion in order to renew his religion and make it significant for the modern age. He tried to show that imagination leads to higher truths in both scientific and religious knowledge.[1] Abbott's view of the division between religious and secular knowledge reflects the viewpoint of Denis Diderot (1713-84) and the Encyclopedists of the Enlightenment, who saw closer relationships between revealed and natural theology than Bacon, who separated religious from natural knowledge. Thus, the Square's attempts to convince his fellow Flatlanders of the reality of higher dimensions can be read as pertaining to either geometry or religion. Although contemporary reviewers did not make any specific connections between *Flatland* and religious questions, much of Victorian fiction is permeated with religious questioning.

On the other hand, Abbott also accepted historical and scientific standards of reality and rejected explanations that he considered unnatural or incredible. He believed that a man who did not believe in miracles should still be allowed to hold office in the Church of England. He was on the fringe of a Cambridge movement that opposed the better-known Oxford Movement and was intensely involved in the religious controversies of his time. His close friend and former schoolmate at City of London School, J.R. Seeley, Regius Professor of Modern History at Cambridge University (and whose family's press first published *Flatland*), had attracted controversy by anonymously publishing a historical biography of Jesus, *Ecce Homo*, in 1865, the year Abbott became headmaster at the City of London School.[2] In Abbott's unpublished manuscript *Confessions*, he describes how he discovered that Seeley was the author of *Ecce Homo* and his concern for keeping that authorship a secret.[3] Seeley's work emphasized moral principles; he saw Christianity as playing a historical role in the development of the secular Western world. His book was

---

1   Jann, "Abbott's *Flatland*." Also see Jann's introduction to the Oxford Classics edition of *Flatland* (2006), xx-xxiv.

2   This followed a similar attempt in 1863 by the French author Ernest Renan. See Owen Chadwick, *The Victorian Church* (New York: Oxford UP, 1970), 62-67.

3   Douglas-Smith, 160. The manuscript of *Confessions* was used in the writing of the history of the City of London School and then was unfortunately lost, so knowledge of its contents is available only indirectly through Douglas-Smith's school history.

inspirational for those, like Abbott, who sought to combine faith with progressive goals, but it also attracted some hostility.[1]

As clergy's doubts about the literal meaning of biblical texts deepened, by the 1880s some felt bound to leave the Church of England because they accepted evolutionary explanations for human development or could not accept miraculous explanations. In 1880, Stopford Brooke resigned his position in the Church, although he continued to preach and his case attracted particular attention. Many were divided over whether he should have left, and they respected his refusal to preach what he did not believe, while still teaching his faith.[2] Abbott attempted to give guidance to those who considered themselves Christians but who could not accept all the tenets of the Church. The same year *Flatland* was published, Abbott was working on *The Kernel and the Husk: Letters on Spiritual Christianity* (1886), which he published anonymously. Well aware of the personal cost of a loss of faith and sympathetic toward ministers who could no longer accept miracles in the face of scientific research, Abbott stated that he wrote *The Kernel and the Husk* at the request of a dying clergyman who had concluded that he had fallen into agnosticism. In this work, Abbott argued for a religious belief that was not dependent on miracles, one in which the "husk" or outdated ideas were discarded in order to retain "the kernel" or the basic Christian beliefs. While his views were considered acceptable for a layman, many thought that they were not appropriate for a clergyman. In 1887, the conservative minister Charles Gore, who later became a bishop, denounced *The Kernel and the Husk* from the pulpit of Oxford University and continued to preach until 1913 that ministers should not question orthodox beliefs.[3] Abbott's concern over the personal impact of rigid religious doctrine carried over into his portrayal of *Flatland*'s religion.

The Victorian scientific community was particularly concerned with Francis Bacon and the scientific method, since Bacon sought to understand nature through observation, from the senses, in order to derive scientific principles.[4] The problem was in determining how reliable those senses were and whether

---

1 Chadwick, 65.

2 Chadwick, 136-37.

3 Chadwick, 139.

4 Introduction to W.B. Carpenter's BAAS presidential address, "Man the Interpreter of Nature," in George Basalla, William Coleman, and Robert H. Kargon, eds., *Victorian Science: A Self-Portrait from the Presidential Addresses of the British Association for the Advancement of* (Continued)

objectivity was possible. In examining how the inhabitants of Flatland and Lineland derived their conclusions from their senses, Abbott points out the psychological limitations of observations. Yet, at the same time, Abbott felt the "credulity" (Abbott's term) of John Henry Newman to be more dangerous to faith than the theories of Charles Darwin.[1] In his contemplation of how faith could coexist with science and his awareness of the limitations of both, Abbott was neither simplistic nor uninformed; indeed, he challenged many assumptions about our modern expectations of a Victorian theologian.

Late Victorian Spiritualism

Questions about faith and physical reality also marked British culture. The 1860s-1880s were the golden age of English spiritualism, which is reflected in contemporary responses to *Flatland*. The idea of higher-dimensional geometry suggested a scientific support for the appearance and disappearance of ghosts and other psychic phenomena, or even of God, an interpretation that Abbott rejected and continued to address in his *Spirit on the Water*.[2] Interest in spiritualism arose during a period of intense controversy over women's rights and sexual inequality, and so the debate over women's proper sphere became intermixed with women's claims to greater sensitivity to the spiritual realm.

During the 1840s, occultism was closely linked with feminist projects, partly because spiritualists and feminists had a shared political platform and were aligned with reformist and utopian ideas. The involvement of mathematics in these complex strands of the imaginative reshaping of society may be seen in the life of Ada Byron, a supporter of Charles Babbage's early attempts to create a proto-computer.[3] In the 1850s, mediums (often women) had gained popular followings, and as one spiritualist, Mary Howitt, put it: "A feeling seems pervading all classes, all sects, that the world stands upon the eve of some great spiritual

---

Science (New York: Doubleday, 1970), 411-15, 412. Also see Jonathan Smith, *Fact and Feeling: Baconian Science and Nineteenth-Century Literary Imagination* (Madison: U of Wisconsin P, 1994).

1 Jann, 474.

2 See Appendix C2 for a selection.

3 See the discussion in Diana Basham's *The Trial of Woman: Feminism and the Occult Sciences in Victorian Literature and Society* (New York: New York UP, 1992), 1-32.

revelation."[1] In the later half of the nineteenth century, various forms of millenarianism became popular; this interest is reflected in *Flatland* as A Square's account begins at the eve of a new millennium. Many felt as the *fin de siècle* approached that the movement of the calendar promised some new spiritual transformation. Beginning in the 1870s, English mediums had moved beyond rapping at tables and hearing voices in the air and were focusing on creating a fully formed materialization of a spirit.[2] Such activities were challenged by unbelievers, and the unmasking of frauds was hotly debated in the newspapers.

During the late nineteenth century and into the 1920s, the concept of higher dimensions became a subject of general fascination: it provided a semi-scientific explanation for spiritualism and an answer to Darwinian materialism, one that gave access to a form of spiritual transcendence. Following *On the Origin of Species*, tensions between established religion and the increasingly powerful scientific community grew, with some worried that the loss of religious belief in a totally materialistic culture would mean loss of ethical behavior. Such fears—voiced by Alfred Russel Wallace, co-discoverer with Darwin of natural selection, among others—led to the 1882 founding of the Society for Psychical Research, a group that attempted to determine if there was some validity to the various claims of ghostly presence or premonitions.[3] However, the concept of higher dimensions quickly moved from suggesting a scientific explanation for ghosts to the development of the occult, as writers such as P.D. Ouspensky and Madame Blavatsky made the fourth dimension a central concept of spiritualism.[4] Although Abbott repeatedly attempted to

---

1 Qtd. in Alex Owen, *The Darkened Room: Women, Power, and Spiritualism in Late Victorian England* (Chicago: U of Chicago P, 2004), 19.

2 Owen, 44.

3 In addition to Wallace, early membership included several scientific and literary figures: Henry Sidgwick, Edmund Gurney, Frederic Myers, Alfred Lord Tennyson, Leslie Stephen, Charles Dodgson (Lewis Carroll), Samuel Clemens (Mark Twain), and Cromwell Varley. The development of this society is chronicled in Deborah Blum, *Ghost Hunters: William James and the Search for Scientific Proof of Life After Death* (New York: Penguin, 2006).

4 Madame Helena Petrovna Blavatsky, *The Secret Doctrine: The Synthesis of Science, Religion and Philosophy* (London: Theosophical Publishing Ltd., 1888); P.D. Ouspensky, *Tertium Organum* (New York: Knopf, 1944). Ouspensky, however, used C.H. Hinton's writings, rather than Abbott's, as a source for his theosophical mysticism (54-72).

divorce his *Flatland* from spiritualist use, it was to no avail. The use of Abbott's work to argue for the existence of an afterlife is apparent in A.T. Schofield's heavy use of the novel to make an argument to which Abbott was strongly and religiously opposed.[1]

The Reception of *Flatland* in 1884 and Charges of Misogyny

Flatland was probably written during the summer of 1884. Abbott showed a draft to friends in October, and a first print run was made in November.[2] The first reviews of *Flatland* were published in the first week of November 1884.[3] Abbott's publisher, Seeley and Co., ran an advertisement announcing the book on 22 November 1884 that contained the following positive snippets: from the *Literary World*, "Not only likely to create a present sensation in the thinking world, but also to find an abiding place among[4] the great satires of history"; from *Freeman*, "We strongly advise our readers to inspect for themselves this remarkable book";[5] from *Oxford Magazine*, "At once a popular scientific treatise of great value, and a fairy-tale worthy to rank with *The Water Babies* and *Alice in Wonderland*"; and from the *Architect*, "We recommend all our friends to read 'Flatland.' They will find in it as limitless fields for their thoughts as Carlyle's 'Sartor Resartus.'" For the most part, the British reviews were positive.[6] Compar-

---

1   A selection of Schofield's *Another World; or the Fourth Dimension* is in Appendix D1. One modern edition of *Flatland* (One World Spiritual Classics, 1995) has added the subtitle, "A Parable of Spiritual Dimensions" to Abbott's book.

2   The records of Seeley and Company, Abbott's publisher, have not survived. Stewart in his *Annotated Flatland* states that 1,000 copies were printed of the first edition (xvii) but does not give a source for this number. This would have been an unusually high number for a book of this type and cost at this time. Mark Samuels Lasner estimates, based on print-run numbers from the late Victorian period, that the first edition would have had a print run of no more than 500 copies (Victoria listserv correspondence, 3 October 2007).

3   For a selection of contemporary reviews, see Appendix A.

4   The review as reprinted in Appendix A2 has the words "in the classic domains of" instead of "among." Either the advertisement took liberties with the wording or the publisher had access to an earlier version of the review.

5   This review has not been traced.

6   A scrapbook collection of reviews was reportedly kept at the City of London School, but it has been misplaced.

isons were made to Carroll's *Alice in Wonderland*, Charles Kingsley's *The Water-Babies* (1863), and, as indicated above, Thomas Carlyle's *Sartor Resartus*[1] (1832), works that are still valued today.

Abbott's preface to his revised edition refers to "certain errors and misprints" and a couple of objections, apparently made in reviews. One, referring to Flatlanders' awareness of three dimensions, certainly is in reference to the 15 November 1884 review in *The Athenaeum*, which states, "Of course, if our friend the Square and his polygonal relations could see each other edgewise, they must have had *some* thickness, and need not, therefore, have been so distressed at the doctrine of a third dimension."[2] Abbott wrote a response, in which he defends the Flatlanders' lack of perception of three dimensions on the basis of the inhabitants' psychological limitations of perception.[3] Some of this response was later reprinted in the preface to the revised edition.

"Concerning the Women": Charges of Misogyny

The thinking of Flatland follows a didactic, tunnel-vision approach to logic. The rulers follow a step-by-step process of assumptions that classify everyone into a rigid class structure, one that is based on their shape and that fails to provide a system of ethics. This system of reasoning assumes that angle size determines intelligence and, therefore, the larger the angle, the higher the status. Since the Women are straight lines with no angles, they are assumed to be stupid.

The assumptions made about the Women based on their lack of angles symbolize the position of women in a society where only the men may inherit property. All attention is given to the son, who will carry on the family's status and wealth. The result is close to the situation of Victorian women, who were legal dependents, first of their fathers, then of their husbands, and finally of their sons. By placing Flatland's Women on the bottom of the class system based on their geometric appearance, Abbott may have hoped to arouse, first, some anger, and then some thought of the position of women in Victorian society. Abbott was writing at a time when women's economic emancipation was beginning in England: the 1870s-1890s saw the increased spread

---

1 Carlyle's *Sartor Resartus* is, like *Flatland*, difficult to categorize; it is both a social satire and an autobiographical account of Carlyle's spiritual crisis.

2 See Appendix A3.

3 This response was printed on 6 December 1884; see Appendix A3.

of respectable paid employment for gentlewomen. This social change was matched by changes in the legal code. Parliamentary debates over the reform of the married women's property law culminated in the passage of the Married Women's Property Act in 1882. This act gave a married woman the same rights over her property as an unmarried woman, and gave all women a separate legal identity from that of their husbands and the right to control their own earnings. The Married Women's Property Act finally addressed a major complaint voiced by Mary Wollstonecraft in *A Vindication of the Rights of Woman* (1792). This revolutionary legal reform also gave impetus to the urgent calls for change in divorce laws, women's access to higher education, employment, and suffrage. The resulting change in the psychological climate of England is reflected in Abbott's satire, and nineteenth-century reviewers of *Flatland* focused on the sharp expression of feminist views and the ridicule of the rigid views of the male Flatlanders.

Indeed, the treatment of women in *Flatland* is geometrically very curious. The Women are, as McGurl insightfully points out, "menacingly phallic straight lines,"[1] who threaten to pierce the rounded spheres of the upper class, sharing with the lower class the ability to defeat their overlords if inclined. They are active, not passive geometric vessels, and this very unusual topsy-turvy of conventional signs leaves the more biologically focused reader bemused over how Flatland reproduction takes place.

In his preface to the revised edition, Abbott makes references to charges that the Square is "a woman-hater" or has "aristocratic tendencies," readings that fail to imaginatively enter *Flatland*'s mode of thinking. Some of these charges might have come from individuals, although the reviewer from *The Architect* humorously suggests that the Square's description of Women as being straight lines "is probably evidence that Mr. Square is rather advanced in years, and has been jilted more than once."[2] The other reviews merely quote from the book's description of women and clearly see the social satire as being more critical of the Victorian class system and treatment of women; none suggested that *Flatland* supported that system.

Abbott was quite concerned about the type of education available to women and was involved in the reform of women's edu-

---

1 McGurl, 62.
2 See Appendix A4. R. Tucker, the reviewer for *Nature* (Appendix A5), makes a similar suggestion. Abbott does not mention these charges in his *Athenaeum* response.

cation, eventually communicating with Dorothea Buss, the head-mistress of Cheltenham Ladies' College (where Hinton taught for a time). He also admired and praised the writings of George Eliot. Eliot was one of the greatest women novelists and essayists of the period, but her family life did not conform to the social norms of the time and she was something of a social outcast; she openly lived with G.H. Lewes, who was legally married to another woman. Abbott, despite being a minister, was sympathetic to the position of couples who did not have access to divorce. Abbott corresponded with Eliot and visited her in her home in hopes of including her writing in his writing textbooks as examples of good prose.[1] His own daughter received a university education, and there is no biographical evidence that Abbott's views were anything but very progressive regarding women's access to education and social equality.

The Square's attitude toward the Women is a curious mixture of fear and misogyny, covered thinly with the pretense of courtesy. The Square admits that

> ... among Women, we use language implying the utmost deference for their Sex; and they fully believe that the Chief Circle Himself is not more devoutly adored by us than they are: but behind their backs they are both regarded and spoken of—by all except the very young—as being little better than "mindless organisms." Our Theology also in the Women's chambers is entirely different from our Theology elsewhere. (111)

As Orwell's "Newspeak" would do later,[2] the Flatland language is used to manipulate thought. Women are presented as frail ("the Frail Sex" and "the Thinner Sex"), but they are capable of harming Men since they are sharp, almost invisible lines that can pierce a Male. They are perceived as lacking any intelligence and as being emotional to the point of insanity. The Women are kept in narrow rooms where they cannot turn around, and where

> ... you can say and do what you like; for they are then wholly impotent for mischief, and will not remember a few minutes

---

1 Quotations from Eliot's novels appear in Abbott and Seeley's textbook, *English Lessons for English People* (90-92), and Abbott's *The Spirit on the Water* (55) and *Through Nature to Christ* (20).

2 "Newspeak" is a form of language used in George Orwell's *Nineteen Eighty-Four* (1949).

hence the incident for which they may be at this moment threatening you with death, nor the promises which you may have found it necessary to make in order to pacify their fury. (80)

The Women are not educated in any skill and are illiterate. This systematic ignorance is termed "quietism." Since the Women, being straight lines, do not physically show as easily measured an Irregularity as the Men, they must maintain a pedigree proving no Irregular births in their family. This emphasis on "purity" is enforced most strongly among the middle class. The upper class is not particularly concerned about the history of their wives, showing morals not unlike that of the Victorian aristocracy.

It is not difficult to see here a mirror of the hypocritical treatment of women at this time. Victorian women were spoken of with respect, yet they were kept trapped within a limited social role. Women of the genteel middle class were particularly trapped by the social emphasis on respectability, which prevented them from supporting themselves. For its time, *Flatland* presents an unusual recognition of the effect of environmental repression on a group of people, in addition to suggesting a link between repression and insanity. The Square points out that

A Male of the lowest type of the Isosceles may look forward to some improvement of his angle, and to the ultimate elevation of the whole of his degraded caste; but no Woman can entertain such hopes for her sex. "Once a Woman, always a Woman" is a Decree of Nature; and the very Laws of Evolution seem suspended in her disfavour. Yet at least we can admire the wise Prearrangement which has ordained that, as they have no hopes, so they shall have no memory to recall, and no forethought to anticipate, the miseries and humiliations which are at once a necessity of their existence and the basis of the constitution of Flatland. (81-82)

This evolutionary determinism voiced by the Square is not far removed from the common Victorian use of science to explain the superiority of upper-class Europeans to other racial or class groups.

Although John Stuart Mill in *The Subjection of Women* (1869) argued that a woman's lack of access to education and her socially limited role in life is responsible for an apparent lack of intellect or emotional control,[1] and the novelist George Eliot described the impact of biological labeling on the disadvantaged in *Mill on the Floss* (1860) and *Middlemarch* (1871-72), late Victorian scientists looked to nature, not nurture, for ways to quantitatively predict future behavior and to determine the relative worth of individuals. Similarly, Flatland society also predicts the future behavior of its inhabitants with a rationale based on nature or natural law, but the insights of Mill and Eliot still make their appearance, even though the Square is reluctant to admit to weaknesses in his world's rigid social structure. Despite the geometric determinism of Flatland society, even the Square admits that if the Women are burdened with too many restrictions, they will turn to violence, even at the expense of their own lives, and he notes that "in less temperate climates the whole male population of a village has been destroyed in one or two hours of simultaneous female outbreak" (79), suggesting that, on occasion, large numbers of Women have revolted and killed all the Men in a town.

We do not hear the Women's viewpoint and have to put together what bits the Square unknowingly reveals, since the Square is conditioned to see his wife only through the lens of social determinism and does not have a direct discussion with her about why she might feel angry or afraid. Realistic dialogue is reserved for interactions between Men, and Women receive what Suvin calls "Emotional pseudo-deference ... unmatched in English language SF until the modern feminists."[2] Suvin believes that "this is the first work of SF ... in which female subjection is seen both as enforced by the ruling class and religion to form the basis of the social order and as issuing in desperate domestic circumstances with frequent murders and suicides."[3] The power of the Women to destroy is continually manipulated by the government to eliminate the "more brutal and troublesome of the Isosceles," keep a check on population numbers, and prevent the long-threatened revolution.

---

1 In Chapter I, Mill wrote, "What is now called the nature of women is an eminently artificial thing—the result of forced repression in some directions, unnatural stimulation in others. It may be asserted without scruple, that no other class of dependents have had their character so entirely distorted from its natural proportions by their relation with their masters..." (238).

2 Suvin, 372.

3 Suvin, 372.

The point of Abbott's social satire, however, was lost on many because of the amount of mathematics in the work. The British reviewers, all sharing similar collegiate backgrounds as Abbott, where mathematics was a required course of study and a more integral part of academic culture, did not find the mathematical theme off-putting (although the London *Literary World* moved toward an identification of Abbott as the author when the reviewer sensed "a certain likeness in it here and there to the precise and formal lessons demonstrated on a blackboard to a class of schoolboys"[1]). This was clearly not the case for some of the American reviewers, such as those of *The Critic* and *Lippincott's*, who found *Flatland* too mathematical for the general audience,[2] whereas the *New York Times* reviewer found it both "puzzling" and "distressing" and responded in an almost agitated manner.[3]

Later Flatlands

Almost as soon as Abbott published *Flatland*, other authors imagined their own approaches to the concept of a limited dimensional world faced with new and disrupting concepts of space. In "A Plane World," Hinton writes,

> And I should have wished to be able to refer the reader altogether to that ingenious work, 'Flatland'. But on turning over its pages again, I find that the author has used his rare talent for a purpose foreign to the intent of our work. For evidently the physical conditions of life on the plane have not been his main object. He has used them as a setting wherein to place his satire and his lessons. But we wish, in the first place, to know the physical facts.[4]

The world that Hinton then sketches out is two-dimensional, but rather than the tabletop world of Abbott, Hinton's characters travel on the edge of a coin-like world, moving up and down but

---

1 See Appendix A2.

2 *The Critic* (18 April 1885, p. 185) predicted that "[f]or the non-mathematical reader the satire is too nebulous to be effective," and *Lippincott's* (May 1885, p. 528) found that "the prosperity of [Flatland's] jests must lie in the ear of the professor of trigonometry or some other branch of the exact sciences."

3 23 February 1885. See Appendix A6.

4 Qtd. in Rucker, Introduction to *Speculations on the Fourth Dimension*, viii.

not able to move around an object. This structure allows the creatures more physical mobility. In *An Episode of Flatland*, Hinton specifically makes the distinction between his world and Abbott's: "I saw that we must think of the beings that inhabit these worlds as standing out from the rims of them, not walking over the flat surface of them."[1] While "Plane World" pictures the beings as triangles, in *An Episode of Flatland* they are initially presented as triangles with arms on one side and eyes on either side, but Hinton suggests that this is just a simplified sketch and the actual creature is more complicated. Unfortunately, after some very ingenious development of the physical flat world, Hinton fails to develop believable characters.

In the modern period, *Flatland* has inspired other two-dimensional worlds.[2] Dionys Burger, a Dutch physics schoolteacher, wrote *Bol-land* in 1957 (translated into English by Cornelie J. Rheinboldt in 1965 as *Sphereland: A Fantasy About Curved Spaces and an Expanding Universe*) to popularize ideas of space-time curvature that had caught the public's imagination during the Sputnik era.[3] In *Sphereland*, Burger imagines a more "enlightened" Flatland some seventy years later. The Square's precocious grandson, a Hexagon, is now the narrator. Motivated partially out of guilt for his desertion of his grandfather when he was a child, the Hexagon updates the progress of Flatland. Similarly, in Ian Stewart's recently published *Flatterland: Like Flatland, Only More So*, a more enlightened Flatland is imagined, but it is now 150 years later and the narrator is a great-granddaughter of the Square.[4] In both Burger's and Stewart's books, the social inequalities in Flatland's class structure and the treatment of women have at least improved. Both books use a discussion of two-dimensional worlds to motivate a further exploration of, in Burger's case, the Einsteinian revolution in conceptions of space, and, in Stewart's case, different types of geometries. Additionally,

---

1   C[harles] H[oward] Hinton, *An Episode of Flatland: Or How a Plane Folk Discovered the Third Dimension, to Which is Added an Outline of the History of Unaea* (London: Swan Sonnenschein, 1907), 1.

2   A comparison of later Flatland novels can be found in Lila Marz Harper, *A Century of Flatlands*, M.A. Thesis, St. Cloud State University, 1987.

3   Dionys Burger, *Sphereland: A Fantasy About Curved Spaces and an Expanding Universe*, trans. Cornelie J. Rheinboldt (New York: Crowell, 1965).

4   Ian Stewart, *Flatterland: Like Flatland, Only More So* (Cambridge, MA: Perseus, 2001).

Jeffrey R. Weeks's *The Shape of Space* incorporates Flatland material, and dimensional analogies are used in Thomas Banchoff's *Beyond the Third Dimension* and Rudy Rucker's *The Fourth Dimension* and *Geometry, Relativity, and the Fourth Dimension*.[1]

Less pedagogical treatments of *Flatland* are found in the science fiction of Rucker. His knowledge of Abbott's and Hinton's works is apparent in his short story "Message Found in a Copy of *Flatland*" (in the collections *Gnarl!*, *Mathenauts*, and *The 57th Franz Kafka*), "Indian Rope Trick Explained," and *Spaceland*.[2] *Spaceland* is a clever reworking of Abbott's plot, focusing on the travails of Joe Cube, an annoying middle manager in Silicon Valley, who is visited by entrepreneurial-minded beings from the fourth dimension.

The question of life in two dimensions received very imaginative treatment when A.K. Dewdney brought together an international collection of scientists to imagine how the physical world would work using Hinton's edge-of-the-coin model.[3] Contributors were Jef Raskin of Apple Computers with a rocket plane, and Ta'akov Stein with Maxwell's equations in two dimensions. The two-dimensional periodic table was devised by Sergio Aragon of the Universidad del Valle Guatemala, George Marx of Roland Eötvös University in Budapest, and Timothy Robinson of Christchurch, New Zealand. These ideas were collected in *A Symposium on Two-Dimensional Science and Technology*, and Dewdney incorporated them into the very detailed world of Arde in his novel *The Planiverse* (for "plane universe").[4] In *The Planiverse*, Dewdney, like Burger, attempts to bring together a consistent, believable universe from the writings of Abbott and Hinton, while using more recent understandings of the basic principles of physics. Dewdney chose Hinton's framework, but he gave his creatures four arms—two on each side; rather than have them

---

1   Jeffrey R. Weeks, *The Shape of Space* (New York: Dekker, 1985); Thomas Banchoff, *Beyond the Third Dimension* (New York: Scientific American Library, 1990); Rucker, *The Fourth Dimension* and *Geometry, Relativity, and the Fourth Dimension* (New York: Dover, 1977).

2   Rucker, *Gnarl!* (New York: Four Walls, 2000); *Mathenauts* (New York: Arbor House, 1987); *The 57th Franz Kafka* (New York: Ace, 1983); *Spaceland* (New York: Tor, 2002).

3   A.K. Dewdney and I.R. Lapidus, eds., *The Second Symposium on Two-Dimensional Science and Technology* (London, ON: Turing Omnibus, 1986).

4   A.K. Dewdney, *The Planiverse: Computer Contact with a Two-Dimensional World*. New York: Poseidon Press, 1984.

face one direction, his Flatlanders have a flexible neck with their eyes on the top, allowing vision to both right and left, as well as above to keep a watch out for flying serpents. Having a disk world makes it easier to identify with the inhabitants; somehow Abbott's tabletop world gives the reader the sense of looking down on an anthill. Additionally, the problem of how communication would exist between different dimensions is solved as students in a class gain access to Planiverse via a computer screen.

From the blackboard to the computer screen, Abbott's tale continues to be re-examined and reworked whenever a new perception of space is advanced. It has had an amazingly pervasive power for well over a century.

Edwin Abbott Abbott: A Brief Chronology

1838   Edwin Abbott Abbott born on 20 December in Marylebone, Middlesex, the eldest son of Edwin Abbott and Jane Abbott

1857   Enters St. John's College, Cambridge

1861   Becomes Senior Classic and Senior Chancellor's Medalist

1862   Elected to a fellowship at St. John's; ordained deacon of Church of England

1863   Resigns fellowship to marry Mary Elizabeth, daughter of Henry Rangeley of Unstone, Derbyshire; ordained priest of the Church of England; birth of nephew Edward Parry

1863-65 Teaches at King Edward's School, Birmingham, and Clifton College, Bristol

1865   *Ecce Homo*, a life of Jesus, is published anonymously by John Robert Seeley, professor of Latin at University College, London; elected to headmastership of the City of London School

1868   Publishes "The Church and the Congregation"; birth of son Edwin (1868-1952)

1869   Girton College, Cambridge, admits women students; publishes *A Shakespearean Grammar*

1870   Publishes *Bible Lessons*; birth of daughter Mary (1870-1952)

1871   Publishes *English Lessons, for English People*, written with J.R. Seeley

1872   Publishes *How to Write Clearly*; *The Good Voices: A Child's Guide to the Bible*; "On Teaching the English Language"; *The Proposed Examination of First-Grade Schools by the Universities*

1873   Publishes *Parables for Children, With Illustrations*

1874   Publishes *How to Parse*; *How to Tell the Parts of Speech*

1875   Publishes *Cambridge Sermons: Preached before the University*; writes introduction to his father's *A Concordance to the Works of Alexander Pope*; publishes "Gospels" in *Encyclopaedia Britannica*; publishes *Latin Prose Through English Idiom*

1876	Elected to Hulsean lectureship at Cambridge; edits *Bacon's Essays*; publishes "The Latest Theory about Lord Francis Bacon" in *Contemporary Review*
1877	Publishes *Bacon and Essex* and *Through Nature to Christ*
1878	Anonymously publishes *Philochristus: Memoirs of a Disciple of the Lord*
1879	Publishes *Oxford Sermons, Preached before the University*
1880	Sister Elizabeth Mead and her husband John Parry die suddenly, leaving their son Edward Abbott Parry, age 17, orphaned; Abbott becomes co-executor of estate with Seneca Hughes
1881	Charles Hinton publishes "What Is the Fourth Dimension?" in *The Dublin University Magazine*
1882	Publishes *Onesimus: Memoirs of a Disciple of St. Paul*; New City of London school building opens
1883	Publishes *Hints on Home Teaching*; "Genuineness of the Second Peter" in *Southern Press Review*; "On the Teaching of Latin Verse Composition"; a preface to Mrs. Henry Pott's *The Promus of Formularies and Elegancies*
1884	Publishes *Flatland. A Romance of Many Dimensions* and, with W.G. Rushbrooke, *The Common Tradition of the Synoptic Gospels in the Text of the Revised Version*; Charles Hinton publishes "What Is the Fourth Dimension?: Ghosts Explained"
1885	Publishes *Francis Bacon: An Account of His Life and Works*
1886	Publishes *The Kernel and the Husk: Letters on Spiritual Christianity*; *Via Latina: A First Latin Book*; son Edwin attends Caius College, Cambridge (1886-90)
1887	Charles Gore denounces *Kernel and the Husk*
1889	Retires from headmastership; publishes *The Latin Gate: A First Latin Translation Book*; daughter Mary enters Girton College, Cambridge (1889-92; nephew Edward Abbott Parry publishes the first edition of *Letters From Dorothy Osborne to Sir William Temple*
1890	Publishes "Illusion in Religion" in *Contemporary Review*
1891	Publishes *Newmanianism: A Preface to the Second Edition of Philomythus*; *Philomythus: An Antidote Against Credulity*; publishes "The Early Life of Cardinal Newman" in *Contemporary Review*

1892	Publishes *The Anglican Career of Cardinal Newman*
1893	Publishes *Dux Latinus: A First Latin Construing Book*
1897	Publishes "On the Teaching of English Grammar"; *The Spirit on the Waters: The Evolution of the Divine from the Human*
1898	Publishes *St. Thomas of Canterbury: His Death and Miracles*
1900-17	Publishes *Diatessarica*; daughter Mary is unnamed co-author
1901	Publishes *Corrections of Mark Adopted by Matthew and Luke* (*Diatessarica* Part II)
1903	Publishes *Contrast; or, a Prophet and a Forger*; "Encyclopedia Biblica and the Gospels" in *Contemporary Review*; *From Letter to Spirit* (*Diatessarica* Part III)
1904	Publishes *Paradosis* (*Diatessarica* Part IV)
1905	Publishes *Johannine Vocabulary: A Comparison of the Words of the Fourth Gospel With Those of the Three* with daughter Mary
1906	Publishes *Johannine Grammar*; *Silanus the Christian*
1907	Publishes *Apologia: An Explanation and Defence*; *Notes on New Testament Criticism*; Charles Hinton posthumously publishes *An Episode of Flatland: or How a Plane Folk Discovered the Third Dimension*; Hinton dies on 30 April at age 54
1909	Publishes *The Message of the Son of Man*
1910	Publishes *"The Son of Man"; or, Contributions to the Study of the Thoughts of Jesus* (*Diatessarica* Part VIII)
1912	Publishes *Light on the Gospel from an Ancient Poet*; appointed Honorary Fellow of St. John's
1915	Publishes *Christ's Miracles of Feeding*
1918	Publishes *Righteousness in the Gospels*
1919	Wife, Mary Elizabeth Rangeley, dies on 5 February
1926	Dies on 12 October at his home, Wellside, Well Walk, Hampstead, London, at age 88

A Note on the Text

This Broadview edition of *Flatland* follows the 1884 second, revised edition of the novel published by Seeley and Company, with correction of misprints as indicated in the text's notes.

Edwin Abbott published the first edition in November 1884; the second edition quickly followed in December of the same year. Both were published by Seeley and Company under the pseudonym "A Square." The square, rather than rectangular, shape of the first edition also physically extended this pun. Later rectangular editions, however, required movement of the illustrations to accommodate the new shape. Abbott was identified as the author on 22 November 1884 in the *Athenaeum*, and later book reviews carried that identification. Abbott's name was not, however, added to the title page until the 1926 Blackwell edition. In his preface to the revised edition, Abbott speaks of "certain errors and misprints" that needed to be corrected. A line-by-line comparison of the two editions shows primarily changes in punctuation, especially the use of colons and semicolons, and correction of capitalization, along with the addition of missing quotation marks. Abbott probably felt the need to immediately correct minor punctuation errors, as he was the author of a manual on writing. The revised edition also added more dialogue to the exchange between the Square and the Sphere, probably to clear up questions about the possibility of physical interaction between the inhabitants of different dimensions.

Both the first and second editions had an illustrated cover with drawings of clouds and the Square's house, along with two lines from *Hamlet*: "O day and night, but this is wondrous strange" and "And therefore as a stranger give it welcome" (I.v.164-65). The title pages of both editions also had a quotation from *Titus Andronicus*: "Fie, fie, how franticly I square my talk!" (III.ii.31). The Roberts Brothers edition of 1885 made changes in the cover and title page illustrations to produce a title page with drawings of clouds, but no house, the *Titus Andronicus* quotation, or the first line of the *Hamlet* quotation. Most modern editions have used the Roberts Brothers version for their title page.[1]

The book went out of print in England until it was reprinted by Basil Blackwell in 1926. An introduction by William Garnett, a former pupil at the City of London School (1864-69), was

---

1   Jann, "Note on the Text," xxxiv-xxxv.

added. Later principal of Durham College of Science, Garnett remained in contact with Abbott and eventually retired to Abbott's hometown of Hampstead.[1]

In the United States, *Flatland* has remained in continuous print since 1885 in various pirated forms of the first edition. Dover Publishing reprinted the revised edition in 1952, and the book has remained one of its bestsellers.

---

1 Stewart, 5.·

FLATLAND

A Romance of Many Dimensions

With Illustrations

by the Author, A SQUARE

" *Fie, fie, how franticly I square my talk!* "

NEW AND REVISED EDITION

LONDON

SEELEY & Co., 46, 47 & 48, ESSEX STREET, STRAND

(*Late of* 54 FLEET STREET)

1884

" O day and night, but this is wondrous strange"

FLATLAND

Ten Dim

Five Dimen

Eight D

Seven

Six Dimen

Nine

Four D en

A ROMANCE
OF MANY DIMENSIONS

By A Square

No Dimensions
•
POINTLAND

One Dimension
LINELAND

Two Dimensions
☐
FLATLAND

Three Dimensions
▱
SPACELAND

My Study

My Bedroom

My Sons

THE HALL

My Wife's Apartments

Women's Door

My Daughter

MEN'S DOOR

My Wife

The Soldiers
The Professor
The Beadle

My Grandsons

THE CELLAR

Policeman

Policeman

LONDON
SEELEY & Co., ESSEX STREET, STRAND
Price Half-a-crown

" And therefore as a stranger give it welcome"

To

The Inhabitants of SPACE IN GENERAL

And H.C. IN PARTICULAR[1]

This Work is Dedicated

By a Humble Native of Flatland

In the Hope that

Even as he was Initiated into the Mysteries

Of THREE Dimensions

Having been previously conversant

With ONLY TWO

So the Citizens of that Celestial Region

May aspire yet higher and higher

To the Secrets of FOUR FIVE OR EVEN SIX Dimensions

Thereby contributing

To the Enlargement of THE IMAGINATION

And the possible Development

Of that most rare and excellent Gift of MODESTY

Among the Superior Races

Of SOLID HUMANITY

Preface to the Second and Revised Edition, 1884[2]
By the Editor

If my poor Flatland friend retained the vigour of mind which he enjoyed when he began to compose these Memoirs, I should not now need to represent him in this Preface, in which he desires, firstly, to return his thanks to his readers and critics in Spaceland, whose appreciation has, with unexpected celerity, required a second edition of his work; secondly, to apologize for certain errors and misprints (for which, however, he is not entirely responsible); and, thirdly, to explain one or two misconceptions. But he is not the Square he once was. Years of imprisonment, and the still heavier burden of general incredulity and mockery, have combined with the natural decay of old age to erase from his mind many of the thoughts and notions, and much also of the terminology, which

---

1 The H.C. referred to in the dedication is Abbott's good friend and old schoolmate, the mathematician Howard Chandler. Abbott identifies him in his *Apologia* (1907), xiii.

2 The material relating to Flatlanders' awareness of three dimensions is reprinted from Abbott's 6 December 1884 reply to the *Athenaeum* review of 15 November. See Appendix A3.

he acquired during his short stay in Spaceland. He has, therefore, requested me to reply in his behalf to two special objections, one of an intellectual, the other of a moral nature.

The first objection is, that a Flatlander, seeing a Line, sees something that must be *thick* to the eye as well as *long* to the eye (otherwise it would not be visible, if it had not some thickness); and consequently he ought (it is argued) to acknowledge that his countrymen are not only long and broad, but also (though doubtless in a very slight degree) *thick* or *high*. This objection is plausible, and, to Spacelanders, almost irresistible, so that, I confess, when I first heard it, I knew not what to reply. But my poor old friend's answer appears to me completely to meet it.

"I admit," said he—when I mentioned to him this objection— "I admit the truth of your critic's facts, but I deny his conclusions. It is true that we have really in Flatland a Third unrecognized Dimension called 'height,' just as it is also true that you have really in Spaceland a Fourth unrecognized Dimension, called by no name at present, but which I will call 'extra-height.' But we can no more take cognizance of our 'height' than you can of your 'extra-height.' Even I—who have been in Spaceland, and have had the privilege of understanding for twenty-four hours the meaning of 'height'—even I cannot now comprehend it, nor realize it by the sense of sight or by any process of reason; I can but apprehend it by faith.

"The reason is obvious. Dimension implies direction, implies measurement, implies the more and the less. Now, all our lines are *equally* and *infinitesimally* thick (or high, whichever you like); consequently, there is nothing in them to lead our minds to the conception of that Dimension. No 'delicate micrometer'—as has been suggested by one too hasty Spaceland critic—would in the least avail us; for we should not know *what to measure, nor in what direction*. When we see a Line, we see something that is long and *bright*; *brightness*, as well as length, is necessary to the existence of a Line; if the brightness vanishes, the Line is extinguished. Hence, all my Flatland friends—when I talk to them about the unrecognized Dimension which is somehow visible in a Line— say, 'Ah, you mean *brightness*': and when I reply, 'No, I mean a real Dimension,' they at once retort, 'Then measure it, or tell us in what direction it extends'; and this silences me, for I can do neither. Only yesterday,[1] when the Chief Circle (in other words

---

1 This section and the following paragraph follow closely the *Athenaeum* response, with some change in arrangement and wording.

our High Priest) came to inspect the State Prison and paid me his seventh annual visit, and when for the seventh time he put me the question, 'Was I any better?' I tried to prove to him that he was 'high,' as well as long and broad, although he did not know it. But what was his reply? 'You say I am "high"; measure my "highness" and I will believe you.' What could I do? How could I meet his challenge? I was crushed; and he left the room triumphant.

"Does this still seem strange to you? Then put yourself in a similar position. Suppose a person of the Fourth Dimension, condescending to visit you, were to say, 'Whenever you open your eyes, you see a Plane (which is of Two Dimensions) and you *infer* a Solid (which is of Three); but in reality you also see (though you do not recognize) a Fourth Dimension, which is not colour nor brightness nor anything of the kind, but a true Dimension, although I cannot point out to you its direction, nor can you possibly measure it.' What would you say to such a visitor? Would not you have him locked up? Well, that is my fate: and it is as natural for us Flatlanders to lock up a Square for preaching the Third Dimension, as it is for you Spacelanders to lock up a Cube for preaching the Fourth. Alas, how strong a family likeness runs through blind and persecuting humanity in all Dimensions! Points, Lines, Squares, Cubes, Extra-Cubes—we are all liable to the same errors, all alike the Slaves of our respective Dimensional prejudices, as one of your Spaceland poets has said—

'One touch of Nature makes all worlds akin.'"[1]*

On this point the defence of the Square seems to me to be impregnable. I wish I could say that his answer to the second (or moral) objection was equally clear and cogent. It has been objected that he is a woman-hater; and as this objection has been vehemently urged by those whom Nature's decree has constituted the somewhat larger half of the Spaceland race, I should like to remove it, so far as I can honestly do so. But the Square is so unaccustomed to the use of the moral terminology of Space-

---

* The Author desires me to add, that the misconception of some of his critics on this matter has induced him to insert in his dialogue with the Sphere, certain remarks which have a bearing on the point in question, and which he had previously omitted as being tedious and unnecessary. [Note: asterisked footnotes are Abbott's original notes.]

---

1 From lines spoken by Ulysses in Shakespeare's *Troilus and Cressida*, III.iii.175: "One touch of nature makes the whole world kin."

land that I should be doing him an injustice if I were literally to transcribe his defence against this charge. Acting, therefore, as his interpreter and summarizer, I gather that in the course of an imprisonment of seven years he has himself modified his own personal views, both as regards Women and as regards the Isosceles or Lower Classes. Personally, he now inclines to the opinion of the Sphere that the Straight Lines are in many important respects superior to the Circles. But, writing as a Historian, he has identified himself (perhaps too closely) with the views generally adopted by Flatland, and (as he has been informed) even by Spaceland, Historians; in whose pages (until very recent times) the destinies of Women and of the masses of mankind have seldom been deemed worthy of mention and never of careful consideration.

In a still more obscure passage he now desires to disavow the Circular or aristocratic tendencies with which some critics have naturally credited him. While doing justice to the intellectual power with which a few Circles have for many generations maintained their supremacy over immense multitudes of their countrymen, he believes that the facts of Flatland, speaking for themselves without comment on his part, declare that Revolutions cannot always be suppressed by slaughter, and that Nature, in sentencing the Circles to infecundity, has condemned them to ultimate failure—"and herein," he says, "I see a fulfilment of the great Law of all worlds, that while the wisdom of Man thinks it is working one thing, the wisdom of Nature constrains it to work another, and quite a different and far better thing." For the rest, he begs his readers not to suppose that every minute detail in the daily life of Flatland must needs correspond to some other detail in Spaceland; and yet he hopes that, taken as a whole, his work may prove suggestive as well as amusing, to those Spacelanders of moderate and modest minds who—speaking of that which is of the highest importance, but lies beyond experience—decline to say on the one hand, "This can never be," and on the other hand, "It must needs be precisely thus, and we know all about it."

Contents

PART I: THIS WORLD

PART II: OTHER WORLDS

PART I: THIS WORLD

"Be patient, for the world is broad and wide."[1]

---

1 *Romeo and Juliet*, III.iii.16. Spoken by Friar Laurence to Romeo about his banishment from Verona.

Section 1. Of the Nature of Flatland

I call our world Flatland, not because we call it so, but to make its nature clearer to you, my happy readers, who are privileged to live in Space.

Imagine a vast sheet of paper on which straight Lines, Triangles, Squares, Pentagons, Hexagons, and other figures, instead of remaining fixed in their places, move freely about, on or in the surface, but without the power of rising above or sinking below it, very much like shadows—only hard and with luminous edges—and you will then have a pretty correct notion of my country and countrymen.[1] Alas, a few years ago, I should have said "my universe": but now my mind has been opened to higher views of things.

In such a country, you will perceive at once that it is impossible that there should be anything of what you call a "solid" kind; but I dare say you will suppose that we could at least distinguish by sight the Triangles, Squares, and other figures, moving about as I have described them. On the contrary, we could see nothing of the kind, not at least so as to distinguish one figure from another. Nothing was visible, nor could be visible, to us, except straight Lines; and the necessity of this I will speedily demonstrate.

Place a penny on the middle of one of your tables in Space; and leaning over it, look down upon it. It will appear a circle.

But now, drawing back to the edge of the table, gradually lower your eye (thus bringing yourself more and more into the condition of the inhabitants of Flatland), and you will find the penny becoming more and more oval to your view, and at last when you have placed your eye exactly on the edge of the table (so that you are, as it were, actually a Flatlander) the penny will then have ceased to appear oval at all, and will have become, so far as you can see, a straight line.[2]

The same thing would happen if you were to treat in the same way a Triangle, or Square, or any other figure cut out of paste-

---

1 Although Charles Hinton imagines his two-dimensional characters as being more complex, he represents them as triangles with eyes on both sides and arms on only one side. See Hinton's *An Episode of Flatland* in Appendix D3.

2 Charles Hinton also begins his 1907 Flatland novel by having the reader imagine coins on a table. However, Hinton arranges four coins on a table to suggest a planetary system and directs the reader to "think of the beings that inhabit these worlds as standing out from the rims of them, not walking over the flat surface of them" (1).

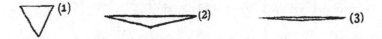

board. As soon as you look at it with your eye on the edge on the table, you will find that it ceases to appear to you a figure, and that it becomes in appearance a straight line. Take for example an equilateral Triangle—who represents with us a Tradesman of the respectable class. Fig. 1 represents the Tradesman as you would see him while you were bending over him from above; figs. 2 and 3 represent the Tradesman, as you would see him if your eye were close to the level, or all but on the level of the table; and if your eye were quite on the level of the table (and that is how we see him in Flatland) you would see nothing but a straight line.

When I was in Spaceland I heard that your sailors have very similar experiences while they traverse your seas and discern some distant island or coast lying on the horizon. The far-off land may have bays, forelands, angles in and out to any number and extent; yet at a distance you see none of these (unless indeed your sun shines bright upon them revealing the projections and retirements by means of light and shade), nothing but a grey unbroken line upon the water.

Well, that is just what we see when one of our triangular or other acquaintances comes toward us in Flatland. As there is neither sun with us, nor any light of such a kind as to make shadows, we have none of the helps to the sight that you have in Spaceland. If our friend comes closer to us we see his line becomes larger; if he leaves us it becomes smaller: but still he looks like a straight line; be he a Triangle, Square, Pentagon, Hexagon, Circle, what you will—a straight Line he looks and nothing else.

You may perhaps ask how under these disadvantageous circumstances we are able to distinguish our friends from one another: but the answer to this very natural question will be more fitly and easily given when I come to describe the inhabitants of Flatland. For the present let me defer this subject, and say a word or two about the climate and houses in our country.

Section 2. Of the Climate and Houses in Flatland

As with you, so also with us, there are four points of the compass North, South, East, and West.

There being no sun nor other heavenly bodies, it is impossible for us to determine the North in the usual way; but we have a method of our own. By a Law of Nature with us, there is a constant attraction to the South; and, although in temperate climates this is very slight—so that even a Woman in reasonable health can journey several furlongs northward without much difficulty—yet the hampering effect of the southward attraction is quite sufficient to serve as a compass in most parts of our earth. Moreover, the rain (which falls at stated intervals) coming always from the North, is an additional assistance; and in the towns we have the guidance of the houses, which of course have their side-walls running for the most part North and South, so that the roofs may keep off the rain from the North. In the country, where there are no houses, the trunks of the trees serve as some sort of guide. Altogether, we have not so much difficulty as might be expected in determining our bearings.

Yet in our more temperate regions, in which the southward attraction is hardly felt, walking sometimes in a perfectly desolate plain where there have been no houses nor trees to guide me, I have been occasionally compelled to remain stationary for hours together, waiting till the rain came before continuing my journey. On the weak and aged, and especially on delicate Females, the force of attraction tells much more heavily than on the robust of the Male Sex, so that it is a point of breeding, if you meet a Lady in the street, always to give her the North side of the way—by no means an easy thing to do always at short notice when you are in rude health and in a climate where it is difficult to tell your North from your South.

Windows there are none in our houses: for the light comes to us alike in our homes and out of them, by day and by night, equally at all times and in all places, whence we know not. It was in old days, with our learned men, an interesting and oft-investigated question, "What is the origin of light?" and the solution of it has been repeatedly attempted, with no other result than to crowd our lunatic asylums with the would-be solvers. Hence, after fruitless attempts to suppress such investigations indirectly by making them liable to a heavy tax, the Legislature, in comparatively recent times, absolutely prohibited them. I—alas, I alone in Flatland—know now only too well the true solution of this mysterious problem; but my knowledge cannot be made intelligible to a single one of my countrymen; and I am mocked at—I, the sole possessor of the truths of Space and of the theory of the introduction of Light from the world of Three Dimensions—as if I were the maddest of the mad! But a truce to these painful digressions: let me return to our houses.

The most common form for the construction of a house is five-sided or pentagonal, as in the annexed figure. The two Northern sides RO, OF,[1] constitute the roof, and for the most part have no doors; on the East is a small door for the Women; on the West a much larger one for the Men; the South side or floor is usually doorless.

Square and triangular houses are not allowed, and for this reason. The angles of a Square (and still more those of an equilateral Triangle), being much more pointed than those of a Pentagon, and the lines of inanimate objects (such as houses) being dimmer than the lines of Men and Women, it follows that there is no little danger lest the points of a square or triangular house residence might do serious injury to an inconsiderate or perhaps absent-minded traveller suddenly therefore, running against them: and as early as the eleventh century of our era, triangular houses were universally forbidden by Law, the only exceptions being fortifications, powder-magazines, barracks, and other state buildings, which it is not desirable that the general public should approach without circumspection.

At this period, square houses were still everywhere permitted, though discouraged by a special tax. But, about three centuries afterwards, the Law decided that in all towns containing a population above ten thousand, the angle of a Pentagon was the smallest house-angle that could be allowed consistently with the public safety. The good sense of the community has seconded the efforts of the Legislature; and now, even in the country, the pentagonal construction has superseded every other. It is only now and then in some very remote and backward agricultural district that an antiquarian may still discover a square house.

---

1 Whereas typically Euclidean geometric diagrams label points in alphabetical order, here the assigned letters for the two vertices spell out "ROOF" at the top of the house. This was likely a classroom joke.

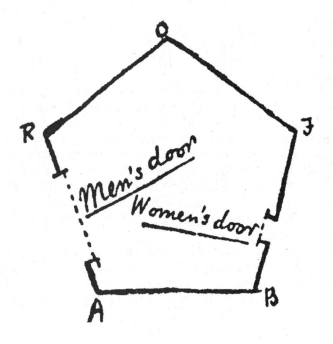

Section 3. Concerning the Inhabitants of Flatland

The greatest length or breadth of a full grown inhabitant of Flatland may be estimated at about eleven of your inches. Twelve inches may be regarded as a maximum.

Our Women are Straight Lines.

Our Soldiers and Lowest Classes of Workmen are Triangles with two equal sides, each about eleven inches long, and a base or third side so short (often not exceeding half an inch) that they form at their vertices a very sharp and formidable angle. Indeed when their bases are of the most degraded type (not more than the eighth part of an inch in size), they can hardly be distinguished from Straight Lines or Women; so extremely pointed are their vertices.[1] With us, as with you, these Triangles are distin-

---

1   The phallic shape of the women is quite unusual and very interesting. Although the problem of reproduction in Lineland is addressed in section 13, Abbott does not attempt to explain how reproduction can occur between a female line and a male plane figure, although from the Square's response to the King of Lineland, it would seem that proximity is required.

guished from others by being called Isosceles; and by this name I shall refer to them in the following pages.

Our Middle Class consists of Equilateral or Equal-Sided Triangles.

Our Professional Men and Gentlemen are Squares (to which class I myself belong)[1] and Five-Sided Figures or Pentagons.

Next above these come the Nobility, of whom there are several degrees, beginning at Six-Sided Figures, or Hexagons, and from thence rising in the number of their sides till they receive the honourable title of Polygonal, or many-sided. Finally when the number of the sides becomes so numerous, and the sides themselves so small, that the figure cannot be distinguished from a circle, he is included in the Circular or Priestly order; and this is the highest class of all.

It is a Law of Nature with us that a male child shall have one more side than his father, so that each generation shall rise (as a rule) one step in the scale of development and nobility. Thus the son of a Square is a Pentagon; the son of a Pentagon, a Hexagon; and so on.

But this rule applies not always to the Tradesmen, and still less often to the Soldiers, and to the Workmen; who indeed can hardly be said to deserve the name of human Figures, since they have not all their sides equal. With them therefore the Law of Nature does not hold; and the son of an Isosceles (i.e., a Triangle with two sides equal) remains Isosceles still. Nevertheless, all hope is not shut out, even from the Isosceles, that his posterity may ultimately rise above his degraded condition. For, after a long series of military successes, or diligent and skilful labours, it is generally found that the more intelligent among the Artisan and Soldier classes manifest a slight increase of their third side or base, and a shrinkage of the two other sides. Intermarriages (arranged by the Priests) between the sons and daughters of these more intellectual members of the lower classes generally

---

1   Although some writers have identified A Square's occupation as that of a math teacher, he identifies himself as a lawyer in Section 7 (this is noted by at least one contemporary reviewer, R. Tucker in *Nature*; see Appendix A5). This profession explains the Square's rather pedantic speech, his investment in the social order of Flatland, and his knowledge of the legal history of Flatland. Abbott's sister had married into a well-respected legal family, and his nephew, the future Judge Edward Abbott Parry, was preparing for his bar exam while Abbott was writing *Flatland*. As his guardian, Abbott took an interest in the young man's career.

result in an offspring approximating still more to the type of the Equal-Sided Triangle.[1]

Rarely—in proportion to the vast numbers of Isosceles births—is a genuine and certifiable Equal-Sided Triangle produced from Isosceles parents.* Such a birth requires, as its antecedents, not only a series of carefully arranged intermarriages, but also a long, continued exercise of frugality and self-control on the part of the would-be ancestors of the coming Equilateral, and a patient, systematic, and continuous development of the Isosceles intellect through many generations.

The birth of a True Equilateral Triangle from Isosceles parents is the subject of rejoicing in our country for many furlongs around. After a strict examination conducted by the Sanitary and Social Board, the infant, if certified as Regular, is with solemn ceremonial admitted into the class of Equilaterals. He is then immediately taken from his proud yet sorrowing parents and adopted by some childless Equilateral, who is bound by oath never to permit the child henceforth to enter his former home or so much as to look upon his relations again, for fear lest the freshly developed organism may, by force of unconscious imitation, fall back again into his hereditary level.

The occasional emergence of an Equilateral from the ranks of his serf-born ancestors is welcomed, not only by the poor serfs themselves, as a gleam of light and hope shed upon the monotonous squalor of their existence, but also by the Aristocracy at large; for all the higher classes are well aware that these rare phenomena, while they do little or nothing to vulgarize their own

---

* "What need of a certificate?" a Spaceland critic may ask: "Is not the procreation of a Square Son a certificate from Nature herself, proving the Equal-sidedness of the Father?" I reply that no Lady of any position will marry an uncertified Triangle. Square offspring has sometimes resulted from a slightly Irregular Triangle; but in almost every such case the Irregularity of the first generation is visited on the third; which either fails to attain the Pentagonal rank, or relapses to the Triangular.

---

1 A Lamarkian type of evolution is suggested here, since the individual's behavior can affect the heredity of the offspring. However, such views, while not strictly Darwinian, do reflect the popular Victorian understanding of how evolution works. This is seen, for example, in Charles Kingsley's *The Water-Babies* (1863).

privileges, serve as a most useful barrier against revolution from below.[1]

Had the acute-angled rabble been all, without exception, absolutely destitute of hope and of ambition, they might have found leaders in some of their many seditious outbreaks, so able as to render their superior numbers and strength too much even for the wisdom of the Circles. But a wise ordinance of Nature has decreed that, in proportion as the working-classes increase in intelligence, knowledge, and all virtue, in that same proportion their acute angle (which makes them physically terrible) shall increase also and approximate to the comparatively harmless angle of the Equilateral Triangle. Thus, in the most brutal and formidable of the soldier class—creatures almost on a level with women in their lack of intelligence—it is found that, as they wax in the mental ability necessary to employ their tremendous penetrating power to advantage, so do they wane in the power of penetration itself.[2]

How admirable is this Law of Compensation! And how perfect a proof of the natural fitness and, I may almost say, the divine origin of the aristocratic constitution of the States in Flatland! By a judicious use of this Law of Nature, the Polygons and Circles are almost always able to stifle sedition in its very cradle, taking advantage of the irrepressible and boundless hopefulness of the human mind. Art also comes to the aid of Law and Order. It is generally found possible—by a little artificial compression or expansion on the part of the State physicians—to make some of the more intelligent leaders of a rebellion perfectly Regular, and to admit them at once into the privileged classes;[3] a much larger number, who are still below the standard, allured by the prospect of being ultimately ennobled, are induced to enter the State Hospitals, where they are kept in honourable confinement for life; one or two alone of the more obstinate, foolish, and hopelessly irregular are led to execution.

Then the wretched rabble of the Isosceles, planless and leaderless, are either transfixed without resistance by the small body of their brethren whom the Chief Circle keeps in pay for emer-

---

1 Here we have one of the first indications that the Aristocracy uses a class-based geometry to control the population.
2 Another of Abbott's puns. Here there is word play on "penetration" as meaning both mental acuity and physical violence.
3 The suggestion here is that shape can be modified or the measurements falsified if it serves the State's interest.

gencies of this kind; or else more often, by means of jealousies and suspicions skilfully fomented among them by the Circular party, they are stirred to mutual warfare, and perish by one another's angles. No less than one hundred and twenty rebellions are recorded in our annals, besides minor outbreaks numbered at two hundred and thirty-five and they have all ended thus.

Section 4. Concerning the Women

If our highly pointed Triangles of the Soldier class are formidable, it may be readily inferred that far more formidable are our Women. For if a Soldier is a wedge, a Woman is a needle; being, so to speak, *all* point, at least at the two extremities. Add to this the power of making herself practically invisible at will, and you will perceive that a Female, in Flatland, is a creature by no means to be trifled with.

But here, perhaps, some of my younger Readers may ask *how* a woman in Flatland can make herself invisible. This ought, I think, to be apparent without any explanation. However, a few words will make it clear to the most unreflecting.

Place a needle on a table. Then, with your eye on the level of the table, look at it side-ways, and you see the whole length of it; but look at it end-ways, and you see nothing but a point, it has become practically invisible. Just so is it with one of our Women. When her side is turned towards us, we see her as a straight line; when the end containing her eye or mouth—for with us these two organs are identical—is the part that meets our eye, then we see nothing but a highly lustrous point; but when the back is presented to our view, then—being only sub-lustrous, and, indeed, almost as dim as an inanimate object—her hinder extremity serves her as a kind of Invisible Cap.

The dangers to which we are exposed from our Women must now be manifest to the meanest capacity in Spaceland. If even the angle of a respectable Triangle in the middle class is not without its dangers; if to run against a Working Man involves a gash; if collision with an officer of the military class necessitates a serious wound; if a mere touch from the vertex of a Private Soldier brings with it danger of death;—what can it be to run against a Woman, except absolute and immediate destruction? And when a Woman is invisible, or visible only as a dim sub-lustrous point, how difficult must it be, even for the most cautious, always to avoid collision!

Many are the enactments made at different times in the different States of Flatland, in order to minimize this peril; and in the Southern and less temperate climates where the force of gravitation is greater, and human beings more liable to casual and involuntary motions, the Laws concerning Women are naturally much more stringent. But a general view of the Code may be obtained from the following summary:—

1. Every house shall have one entrance in the Eastern side, for the use of Females only; by which all females shall enter "in a becoming and respectful manner" and not by the Men's or Western door.*
2. No Female shall walk in any public place without continually keeping up her Peace-cry,[1] under penalty of death.
3. Any Female, duly certified to be suffering from St. Vitus's Dance,[2] fits, chronic cold accompanied by violent sneezing, or any disease necessitating involuntary motions, shall be instantly destroyed.

In some of the States there is an additional Law forbidding Females, under penalty of death, from walking or standing in any public place without moving their backs constantly from right to left so as to indicate their presence to those behind them;[3] others oblige a Woman, when travelling, to be followed by one of her sons, or servants, or by her husband; others confine Women altogether to their houses except during the religious festivals. But it has been found by the wisest of our Circles or Statesmen that the multiplication of restrictions on Females tends not only to the debilitation and diminution of the race, but also to the increase of domestic murders to such an extent that a State loses more than it gains by a too prohibitive Code.

---

* When I was in Spaceland I understood that some of your Priestly circles have in the same way a separate entrance for Villagers, Farmers and Teachers of Board Schools (*Spectator*, Sept. 1884, p. 1255) that they may "approach in a becoming and respectful manner." [The reference is to snobbery among the clerics toward school teachers.]

---

1 The sound that women are required to make, according to Flatland law, in order to alert men to their presence.
2 A disease that causes rapid movement, also known as Sydenham's chorea, named for Thomas Sydenham, a British physician (1624-89).
3 This passage is quoted in the *Literary World* (London) review; see Appendix A2.

For whenever the temper of the Women is thus exasperated by confinement at home or hampering regulations abroad, they are apt to vent their spleen upon their husbands and children; and in the less temperate climates the whole male population of a village has been sometimes destroyed in one or two hours of simultaneous female outbreak. Hence the Three Laws, mentioned above, suffice for the better regulated States, and may be accepted as a rough exemplification of our Female Code.

After all, our principal safeguard is found, not in Legislature, but in the interests of the Women themselves. For, although they can inflict instantaneous death by a retrograde movement, yet unless they can at once disengage their stinging extremity from the struggling body of their victim, their own frail bodies are liable to be shattered.[1]

The power of Fashion is also on our side. I pointed out that in some less civilized States no female is suffered to stand in any public place without swaying her back from right to left. This practice has been universal among ladies of any pretensions to breeding in all well-governed States, as far back as the memory of Figures can reach.[2] It is considered a disgrace to any State that legislation should have to enforce what ought to be, and is in every respectable female, a natural instinct. The rhythmical and, if I may so say, well-modulated undulation of the back in our ladies of Circular rank is envied and imitated by the wife of a common Equilateral, who can achieve nothing beyond a mere monotonous swing, like the ticking of a pendulum; and the regular tick of the Equilateral is no less admired and copied by the wife of the progressive and aspiring Isosceles, in the females of whose family no "back-motion" of any kind has become as yet a necessity of life. Hence, in every family of position and consideration, "back motion" is as prevalent as time itself; and the husbands and sons in these households enjoy immunity at least from invisible attacks.

Not that it must be for a moment supposed that our Women are destitute of affection. But unfortunately the passion of the moment predominates, in the Frail Sex, over every other consideration. This is, of course, a necessity arising from their unfortunate conformation. For as they have no pretensions to an

---

1 Suggestive of the effect on a bee after it has stung a mammal, since pulling the stinger out kills the bee.
2 The fashions of 1884 included the use of a bustle, which gave women an exaggerated swaying rear movement.

angle, being inferior in this respect to the very lowest of the Isosceles, they are consequently wholly devoid of brain-power, and have neither reflection, judgment nor forethought, and hardly any memory. Hence, in their fits of fury, they remember no claims and recognize no distinctions. I have actually known a case where a Woman has exterminated her whole household, and half an hour afterwards, when her rage was over and the fragments swept away, has asked what has become of her husband and her children.

Obviously then a Woman is not to be irritated as long as she is in a position where she can turn round. When you have them in their apartments—which are constructed with a view to denying them that power—you can say and do what you like; for they are then wholly impotent for mischief, and will not remember a few minutes hence the incident for which they may be at this moment threatening you with death, nor the promises which you may have found it necessary to make in order to pacify their fury.

On the whole we get on pretty smoothly in our domestic relations, except in the lower strata of the Military Classes. There the want of tact and discretion on the part of the husbands produces at times indescribable disasters. Relying too much on the offensive weapons of their acute angles instead of the defensive organs of good sense and seasonable simulation,[1] these reckless creatures too often neglect the prescribed construction of the women's apartments, or irritate their wives by ill-advised expressions out of doors, which they refuse immediately to retract. Moreover a blunt and stolid regard for literal truth indisposes them to make those lavish promises by which the more judicious Circle can in a moment pacify his consort. The result is massacre; not, however, without its advantages, as it eliminates the more brutal and troublesome of the Isosceles; and by many of our Circles the destructiveness of the Thinner Sex is regarded as one among many providential arrangements for suppressing redundant population, and nipping Revolution in the bud.

Yet even in our best regulated and most approximately Circular families I cannot say that the ideal of family life is so high as with you in Spaceland. There is peace, in so far as the absence of

---

1 Timely pretense of respect. The Square's admiration for the upper class is partly based on their ability to manipulate their wives through flattery and lies. He accepts the status quo, though, because he believes it leads to social stability. His decorous phrasing allows him to abstract and rationalize misogynist beliefs and class prejudice.

slaughter may be called by that name, but there is necessarily little harmony of tastes or pursuits; and the cautious wisdom of the Circles has ensured safety at the cost of domestic comfort. In every Circular or Polygonal household it has been a habit from time immemorial—and now has become a kind of instinct among the women of our higher classes—that the mothers and daughters should constantly keep their eyes and mouths towards their husband and his male friends; and for a lady in a family of distinction to turn her back upon her husband would be regarded as a kind of portent, involving loss of *status*. But, as I shall soon shew, this custom, though it has the advantage of safety, is not without its disadvantages.

In the house of the Working Man or respectable Tradesman—where the wife is allowed to turn her back upon her husband, while pursuing her household avocations—there are at least intervals of quiet, when the wife is neither seen nor heard, except for the humming sound of the continuous Peace-cry; but in the homes of the upper classes there is too often no peace. There the voluble mouth and bright penetrating eye are ever directed towards the Master of the household; and light itself is not more persistent than the stream of feminine discourse. The tact and skill which suffice to avert a Woman's sting are unequal to the task of stopping a Woman's mouth; and as the wife has absolutely nothing to say, and absolutely no constraint of wit, sense, or conscience to prevent her from saying it, not a few cynics have been found to aver that they prefer the danger of the death-dealing but inaudible sting to the safe sonorousness of a Woman's other end.

To my readers in Spaceland the condition of our Women may seem truly deplorable, and so indeed it is. A Male of the lowest type of the Isosceles may look forward to some improvement of his angle, and to the ultimate elevation of the whole of his degraded caste; but no Woman can entertain such hopes for her sex. "Once a Woman, always a Woman"[1] is a Decree of Nature; and the very Laws of Evolution seem suspended in her disfavour.[2] Yet at least we can admire the wise Prearrangement

---

1   An often-quoted phrase, apparently from English law.

2   A comment on the lack of job opportunity and education available for Victorian women. Charles Darwin's *The Descent of Man* (1872) attempted to explain, and thus justify, women's social inferiority in terms of evolutionary process, but here it is pointed out that such inferiority does not follow from evolutionary laws. In Plato's *Republic* (451-53) it is argued that women are not necessarily less capable than men.

which has ordained that, as they have no hopes, so they shall have no memory to recall, and no forethought to anticipate, the miseries and humiliations which are at once a necessity of their existence and the basis of the constitution of Flatland.

Section 5. Of our Methods of Recognizing One Another

You, who are blessed with shade as well as light, you, who are gifted with two eyes, endowed with a knowledge of perspective, and charmed with the enjoyment of various colours, you, who can actually *see* an angle, and contemplate the complete circumference of a circle in the happy region of the Three Dimensions—how shall I make clear to you the extreme difficulty which we in Flatland experience in recognizing one another's configuration?

Recall what I told you above. All beings in Flatland, animate or inanimate, no matter what their form, present *to our view* the same, or nearly the same, appearance, viz. that of a straight Line. How then can one be distinguished from another, where all appear the same?

The answer is threefold. The first means of recognition is the sense of hearing; which with us is far more highly developed than with you, and which enables us not only to distinguish by the voice our personal friends, but even to discriminate between different classes, at least so far as concerns the three lowest orders, the Equilateral, the Square, and the Pentagon—for of the Isosceles I take no account. But as we ascend in the social scale, the process of discriminating and being discriminated by hearing increases in difficulty, partly because voices are assimilated, partly because the faculty of voice-discrimination is a plebeian virtue not much developed among the Aristocracy. And wherever there is any danger of imposture we cannot trust to this method. Amongst our lowest orders, the vocal organs are developed to a degree more than correspondent with those of hearing, so that an Isosceles can easily feign the voice of a Polygon, and, with some training, that of a Circle himself. A second method is therefore more commonly resorted to.

Feeling is, among our Women and lower classes—about our upper classes I shall speak presently—the principal test of recognition, at all events between strangers, and when the question is, not as to the individual, but as to the class. What therefore "introduction" is among the higher classes in Spaceland, that the process of "feeling" is with us. "Permit me to ask you to feel and be felt by my friend Mr. So-and-so"—is still, among the more old-fashioned of our country gentlemen in districts remote from towns, the customary formula for a Flatland introduction. But in the towns, and among men of business, the words "be felt by" are omitted and the sentence is abbreviated to, "Let me ask you to feel Mr. So-and-so"; although it is assumed, of course, that the "feeling" is to be reciprocal. Among our still more modern and dashing young gentlemen—who are extremely averse to super-fluous effort and supremely indifferent to the purity of their native language—the formula is still further curtailed by the use of "to feel" in a technical sense, meaning, "to recommend-for-the-purposes-of-feeling-and-being-felt"; and at this moment the "slang" of polite or fast society in the upper classes sanctions such a barbarism as "Mr. Smith, permit me to feel you Mr. Jones."

Let not my Reader however suppose that "feeling" is with us the tedious process that it would be with you, or that we find it necessary to feel right round all the sides of every individual before we determine the class to which he belongs. Long practice and training, begun in the schools and continued in the experi-ence of daily life, enable us to discriminate at once by the sense of touch, between the angles of an equal-sided Triangle, Square, and Pentagon; and I need not say that the brainless vertex of an acute-angled Isosceles is obvious to the dullest touch. It is there-fore not necessary, as a rule, to do more than feel a single angle of an individual; and this, once ascertained, tells us the class of the person whom we are addressing, unless indeed he belongs to the higher sections of the nobility. There the difficulty is much greater. Even a Master of Arts in our University of Wentbridge[1] has been known to confuse a ten-sided with a twelve-sided Polygon; and there is hardly a Doctor of Science in or out of that famous University who could pretend to decide promptly and unhesitatingly between a twenty-sided and a twenty-four sided member of the Aristocracy.

Those of my readers who recall the extracts I gave above from the Legislative code concerning Women, will readily perceive that the process of introduction by contact requires some care and discretion. Otherwise the angles might inflict on the unwary Feeler irreparable injury. It is essential for the safety of the Feeler that the Felt should stand perfectly still. A start, a fidgety shifting of the position, yes, even a violent sneeze, has been known before

---

1 Wordplay on "Cambridge"—pronounced Came-bridge.

now to prove fatal to the incautious, and to nip in the bud many a promising friendship. Especially is this true among the lower classes of the Triangles. With them, the eye is situated so far from their vertex that they can scarcely take cognizance of what goes on at that extremity of their frame. They are, moreover, of a rough coarse nature, not sensitive to the delicate touch of the highly organized Polygon. What wonder then if an involuntary toss of the head has ere now deprived the State of a valuable life!

I have heard that my excellent Grandfather—one of the least irregular of his unhappy Isosceles class, who indeed obtained, shortly before his decease, four out of seven votes from the Sanitary and Social Board for passing him into the class of the Equal-sided[1]—often deplored, with a tear in his venerable eye, a miscarriage of this kind, which had occurred to his great-great-great-Grandfather, a respectable Working Man with an angle or brain of 59° 30'. According to his account, my unfortunate Ancestor, being afflicted with rheumatism, and in the act of being felt by a Polygon, by one sudden start accidentally transfixed the Great Man through the diagonal; and thereby, partly in consequence of his long imprisonment and degradation, and partly because of the moral shock which pervaded the whole of my Ancestor's relations, threw back our family a degree and a half in their ascent towards better things. The result was that in the next generation the family brain was registered at only 58°, and not till the lapse of five generations was the lost ground recovered, the full 60° attained, and the Ascent from the Isosceles finally achieved.[2] And all this series of calamities from one little accident in the process of Feeling.

At this point I think I hear some of my better educated readers exclaim, "How could you in Flatland know anything about angles and degrees, or minutes? We can *see* an angle, because we, in the region of Space, can see two straight lines inclined to one another; but you, who can see nothing but one straight line at a time, or at all events only a number of bits of straight lines all in one straight line—how can you ever discern any angle, and much less register angles of different sizes?"

---

1 An indication of the subjectivity of what is supposedly an objective measurement system.

2 Although A Square believes that the action of his ancestor caused a loss in degrees, the possibility is raised that the Aristocrats manipulated the measurements to keep the family in the serf class.

I answer that though we cannot *see* angles, we can *infer* them, and this with great precision. Our sense of touch, stimulated by necessity, and developed by long training, enables us to distinguish angles far more accurately than your sense of sight, when unaided by a rule or measure of angles. Nor must I omit to explain that we have great natural helps. It is with us a Law of Nature that the brain of the Isosceles class shall begin at half a degree, or thirty minutes, and shall increase (if it increases at all) by half a degree in every generation; until the goal of 60° is reached, when the condition of serfdom is quitted, and the freeman enters the class of Regulars.

Consequently, Nature herself supplies us with an ascending scale or Alphabet of angles for half a degree up to 60°, Specimens of which are placed in every Elementary School throughout the land. Owing to occasional retrogressions, to still more frequent moral and intellectual stagnation, and to the extraordinary fecundity of the Criminal and Vagabond Classes, there is always a vast superfluity of individuals of the half degree and single degree class, and a fair abundance of Specimens up to 10°. These are absolutely destitute of civic rights; and a great number of them, not having even intelligence enough for the purposes of warfare, are devoted by the States to the service of education. Fettered immovably so as to remove all possibility of danger, they are placed in the class rooms of our Infant Schools, and there they are utilized by the Board of Education for the purpose of imparting to the offspring of the Middle Classes that tact and intelligence of which these wretched creatures themselves are utterly devoid.

In some States the Specimens are occasionally fed and suffered to exist for several years; but in the more temperate and better regulated regions, it is found in the long run more advantageous for the educational interests of the young, to dispense with food, and to renew the Specimens every month—which is about the average duration of the foodless existence of the Criminal class. In the cheaper schools, what is gained by the longer existence of the Specimen is lost, partly in the expenditure for food, and partly in the diminished accuracy of the angles, which are impaired after a few weeks of constant "feeling." Nor must we forget to add, in enumerating the advantages of the more expensive system, that it tends, though slightly yet perceptibly, to the diminution of the redundant Isosceles population—an object which every statesman in Flatland constantly keeps in view. On the whole therefore—although I am not ignorant that, in many popularly elected School Boards, there is a reaction in favour of "the cheap system" as it is called—I am myself disposed to think that this is one of the many cases in which expense is the truest economy.[1]

But I must not allow questions of School Board politics to divert me from my subject. Enough has been said, I trust, to shew that Recognition by Feeling is not so tedious or indecisive a process as might have been supposed; and it is obviously more trustworthy than Recognition by hearing. Still there remains, as has been pointed out above, the objection that this method is not without danger. For this reason many in the Middle and Lower classes, and all without exception in the Polygonal and Circular orders, prefer a third method, the description of which shall be reserved for the next section.

Section 6. Of Recognition by Sight

I am about to appear very inconsistent. In previous sections I have said that all figures in Flatland present the appearance of a straight line; and it was added or implied, that it is consequently impossible to distinguish by the visual organ between individuals of different classes: yet now I am about to explain to my Spaceland critics how we are able to recognize one another by the sense of sight.

If however the Reader will take the trouble to refer to the passage in which Recognition by Feeling is stated to be universal, he will find this qualification—"among the lower classes." It is only among the higher classes and in our temperate climates that Sight Recognition is practised.

That this power exists in any regions and for any classes is the result of Fog; which prevails during the greater part of the year in all parts save the torrid zones. That which is with you in Spaceland an unmixed evil, blotting out the landscape, depressing the spirits, and enfeebling the health, is by us recognized as a bless-

---

1   The tone is sarcastic here, although the target is not clear. Abbott is attacking those who hold a calloused attitude toward the poor. Additionally, Rosemary Jann suggests that attitudes toward state-supported education is another target. Educational policy linked the level of government support for a school to the number of students who passed standardized tests, a policy that was in effect until the early 1880s. (See Jann's edition, p. 121, n. 35.) This policy was as unpopular among teachers then as it is today in the United States.

ing scarcely inferior to air itself, and as the Nurse of arts and Parent of sciences.[1] But let me explain my meaning, without further eulogies on this beneficent Element.

If Fog were non-existent, all lines would appear equally and indistinguishably clear; and this is actually the case in those unhappy countries in which the atmosphere is perfectly dry and transparent. But wherever there is a rich supply of Fog objects that are at a distance, say of three feet, are appreciably dimmer than those at a distance of two feet eleven inches; and the result is that by careful and constant experimental observation of comparative dimness and clearness, we are enabled to infer with great exactness the configuration of the object observed.

An instance will do more than a volume of generalities to make my meaning clear.

Suppose I see two individuals approaching whose rank I wish to ascertain. They are, we will suppose, a Merchant and a Physician, or in other words, an Equilateral Triangle and a Pentagon: how am I to distinguish them?

It will be obvious, to every child in Spaceland who has touched the threshold of Geometrical Studies, that, if I can bring my eye so that its glance may bisect an angle (A) of the approaching stranger, my view will lie as it were evenly between his two sides that are next to me (viz. CA and AB), so that I shall contemplate the two impartially, and both will appear of the same size.

Now in the case of (1) the Merchant, what shall I see? I shall see a straight line DAE, in which the middle point (A) will be very bright because it is nearest to me; but on either side the line will shade away *rapidly into dimness*, because the sides AC and AB

---

1 The City of London experienced its worst decade for fogs in the 1880s (Peter Ackroyd, *London: The Biography* [New York: Anchor, 2003], 428). Visibility, especially in the month of November, was extremely limited, and reports of the limited perception were similar to Abbott's description of Flatland. The philosopher and psychologist William James described London in the fall of 1882 as like living in "The inside of a coal mine—and a coal mine in the process of combustion at that" (quoted in Deborah Blum, *Ghost Hunters: William James and the Search for Scientific Proof of Life After Death* [New York: Penguin, 2006], 75). The reason for the increase in fog during this time period is unclear; however, there were many references to heavy London fog in the late 1800s. Peter Brimblecombe's book, *The Big Smoke: A History of Air Pollution in London Since Medieval Times* (London: Methuen, 1987) provides an overview of such cultural references (123-31).

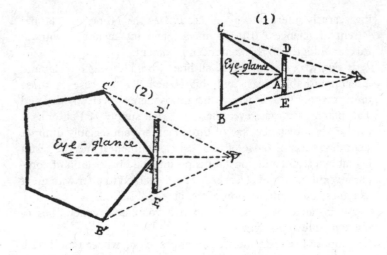

recede rapidly into the fog and what appear to me as the Merchant's extremities, viz. D and E, will be *very dim indeed*.

On the other hand in the case of (2) the Physician, though I shall here also see a line (D'A'E') with a bright centre (A'), yet it will shade away *less rapidly* into dimness, because the sides (A'C', A"B') *recede less rapidly into the fog*: and what appear to me the Physician's extremities, viz. D' and E', will not be *not so dim* as the extremities of the Merchant.

The Reader will probably understand from these two instances how—after a very long training supplemented by constant experience—it is possible for the well-educated classes among us to discriminate with fair accuracy between the middle and lowest orders, by the sense of sight.[1] If my Spaceland Patrons have grasped this general conception, so far as to conceive the possibility of it and not to reject my account as altogether incredible—I shall have attained all I can reasonably expect. Were I to attempt further details I should only perplex. Yet for the sake of the young and inexperienced, who may perchance infer—from the two simple instances I have given above, of the manner in which I should recognize my Father and my Sons—that Recognition by sight is an easy affair, it may be needful to point out that

---

1 The overriding reason for the Flatland higher education system is to make class distinctions. Although the Square accepts this system, it is a satiric comment on the Victorian university system, which often was more concerned with class than education.

in actual life most of the problems of Sight Recognition are far more subtle and complex.

If, for example, when my Father, the Triangle, approaches me, he happens to present his side to me instead of his angle, then, until I have asked him to rotate, or until I have edged my eye round him, I am for the moment doubtful whether he may not be a Straight Line, or, in other words, a Woman. Again, when I am in the company of one of my two hexagonal Grandsons, contemplating one of his sides (AB) full front, it will be evident from the accompanying diagram that I shall see one whole line (AB) in comparative brightness (shading off hardly at all at the ends) and two smaller lines (CA and BD) dim throughout and shading away into greater dimness towards the extremities C and D.

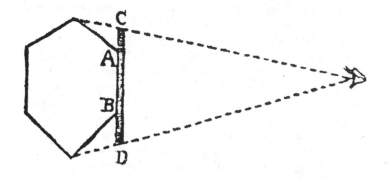

But I must not give way to the temptation of enlarging on these topics. The meanest mathematician in Spaceland will readily believe me when I assert that the problems of life, which present themselves to the well-educated—when they are themselves in motion, rotating, advancing or retreating, and at the same time attempting to discriminate by the sense of sight between a number of Polygons of high rank moving in different directions, as for example in a ball-room or conversazione—must be of a nature to task the angularity of the most intellectual, and amply justify the rich endowments of the Learned Professors of Geometry, both Static and Kinetic, in the illustrious University of Wentbridge, where the Science and Art of Sight Recognition are regularly taught to large classes of the *élite* of the States.

It is only a few of the scions of our noblest and wealthiest houses, who are able to give the time and money necessary for the thorough prosecution of this noble and valuable Art. Even to me, a Mathematician of no mean standing, and the Grandfather of two most hopeful and perfectly regular Hexagons, to find myself in the midst of a crowd of rotating Polygons of the higher classes, is occasionally very perplexing. And of course to a common Tradesman, or Serf, such a sight is almost as unintelligible as it would be to you, my Reader, were you suddenly transported into our country.

In such a crowd you could see on all sides of you nothing but a Line, apparently straight, but of which the parts would vary irregularly and perpetually in brightness or dimness. Even if you had completed your third year in the Pentagonal and Hexagonal classes in the University, and were perfect in the theory of the subject, you would still find that there was need of many years of experience, before you could move in a fashionable crowd without jostling against your betters, whom it is against etiquette to ask to "feel," and who, by their superior culture and breeding, know all about your movements, while you know very little or nothing about theirs. In a word, to comport oneself with perfect propriety in Polygonal society, one ought to be a Polygon oneself. Such at least is the painful teaching of my experience.

It is astonishing how much the Art—or I may almost call it instinct—of Sight Recognition is developed by the habitual practice of it and by the avoidance of the custom of "Feeling." Just as, with you, the deaf and dumb, if once allowed to gesticulate and to use the hand-alphabet, will never acquire the more difficult but far more valuable art of lip-speech and lip-reading, so it is with us as regards "Seeing" and "Feeling."[1] None who in early life resort to "Feeling" will ever learn "Seeing" in perfection.

For this reason, among our Higher Classes, "Feeling" is discouraged or absolutely forbidden. From the cradle their children, instead of going to the Public Elementary schools (where the art of Feeling is taught), are sent to higher Seminaries of an exclusive character; and at our illustrious University, to "feel" is regarded as a most serious fault, involving Rustication[2] for the first offence, and Expulsion for the second.

But among the lower classes the art of Sight Recognition is regarded as an unattainable luxury. A common Tradesman

---

1 During the Victorian period, deaf children were discouraged from using sign language as it was felt that they should learn lip reading in order to better fit into society. What was once considered the best educational practice is now seen as harmful.

2 This term refers to being "sent down" from the university as a form of academic penalty. "Rustication" suggests that students were sent home to the country.

cannot afford to let his son spend a third of his life in abstract studies. The children of the poor are therefore allowed to "feel" from their earliest years, and they gain thereby a precocity and an early vivacity which contrast at first most favourably with the inert, undeveloped, and listless behaviour of the half-instructed youths of the Polygonal class; but when the latter have at last completed their University course, and are prepared to put their theory into practice, the change that comes over them may almost be described as a new birth, and in every art, science, and social pursuit they rapidly overtake and distance their Triangular competitors.

Only a few of the Polygonal Class fail to pass the Final Test or Leaving Examination at the University. The condition of the unsuccessful minority is truly pitiable. Rejected from the higher class, they are also despised by the lower. They have neither the matured and systematically trained powers of the Polygonal Bachelors and Masters of Arts, nor yet the native precocity and mercurial versatility of the youthful Tradesman. The professions, the public services, are closed against them; and though in most States they are not actually debarred from marriage, yet they have the greatest difficulty in forming suitable alliances, as experience shews that the offspring of such unfortunate and ill-endowed parents is generally itself unfortunate, if not positively Irregular. [1]

It is from these specimens of the refuse of our Nobility that the great Tumults and Seditions of past ages have generally derived their leaders; and so great is the mischief thence arising that an increasing minority of our more progressive Statesmen are of opinion that true mercy would dictate their entire suppression, by enacting that all who fail to pass the Final Examination of the University should be either imprisoned for life, or extinguished by a painless death.

But I find myself digressing into the subject of Irregularities, a matter of such vital interest that it demands a separate section.

---

1   Similar to the position of a Victorian student who fails college exams and cannot find work in the professions because his education was too abstract and he had no practical skills. Children from the lower and middle classes were given an educational curriculum that stressed work skills, while those in the upper classes focused on classical or liberal arts education and lacked vocational training. Abbott's curriculum at the City of London School attempted to provide both vocational and liberal arts classes.

Section 7. Concerning Irregular Figures

Throughout the previous pages I have been assuming—what perhaps should have been laid down at the beginning as a distinct and fundamental proposition—that every human being in Flatland is a Regular Figure, that is to say of regular construction. By this I mean that a Woman must not only be a line, but a straight line; that an Artisan or Soldier must have two of his sides equal; that Tradesmen must have three sides equal; Lawyers (of which class I am a humble member),[1] four sides equal, and generally, that in every Polygon, all the sides must be equal.

The size of the sides would of course depend upon the age of the individual. A Female at birth would be about an inch long, while a tall adult Woman might extend to a foot. As to the Males of every class, it may be roughly said that the length of an adult's sides, when added together, is two feet or a little more.[2] But the size of our sides is not under consideration. I am speaking of the *equality* of sides, and it does not need much reflection to see that the whole of the social life in Flatland rests upon the fundamental fact that Nature wills all Figures to have their sides equal.

If our sides were unequal our angles might be unequal. Instead of its being sufficient to feel, or estimate by sight, a single angle in order to determine the form of an individual, it would be necessary to ascertain each angle by the experiment of Feeling. But life would be too short for such a tedious grouping. The whole science and art of Sight Recognition would at once perish; Feeling, so far as it is an art, would not long survive; intercourse would become perilous or impossible; there would be an end to all confidence, all forethought; no one would be safe in making the most simple social arrangements; in a word, civilization would relapse into barbarism.[3]

Am I going too fast to carry my Readers with me to these obvious conclusions? Surely a moment's reflection, and a single instance from common life, must convince every one that our whole social system is based upon Regularity, or Equality of Angles. You meet, for example, two or three Tradesmen in the street, whom you recognize at once to be Tradesmen by a glance

---

1 Here the Square identifies himself as a lawyer (not a mathematics teacher as some have assumed). The stilted and formal nature of the Square's speech reflects his legal occupation.

2 This was three feet in the first edition.

3 Abbott is satirizing common justifications for class distinctions.

at their angles and rapidly bedimmed sides, and you ask them to step into your house to lunch. This you do at present with perfect confidence, because everyone knows to an inch or two the area occupied by an adult Triangle: but imagine that your Tradesman drags behind his regular and respectable vertex, a parallelogram of twelve or thirteen inches in diagonal:—what are you to do with such a monster sticking fast in your house door?

But I am insulting the intelligence of my Readers by accumulating details which must be patent to everyone who enjoys the advantages of a Residence in Spaceland. Obviously the measurements of a single angle would no longer be sufficient under such portentous circumstances; one's whole life would be taken up in feeling or surveying the perimeter of one's acquaintances. Already the difficulties of avoiding a collision in a crowd are enough to tax the sagacity of even a well-educated Square; but if no one could calculate the Regularity of a single figure in the company, all would be chaos and confusion, and the slightest panic would cause serious injuries, or—if there happened to be any Women or Soldiers present—perhaps considerable loss of life.

Expediency therefore concurs with Nature in stamping the seal of its approval upon Regularity of conformation: nor has the Law been backward in seconding their efforts. "Irregularity of Figure" means with us the same as, or more than, a combination of moral obliquity and criminality with you, and is treated accordingly. There are not wanting, it is true, some promulgators of paradoxes who maintain that there is no necessary connection between geometrical and moral Irregularity.[1] "The Irregular," they say, "is from his birth scouted by his own parents, derided by his brothers and sisters, neglected by the domestics, scorned and suspected by society, and excluded from all posts of responsibility, trust, and useful activity. His every movement is jealously watched by the police till he comes of age and presents himself for inspection; then he is either destroyed, if he is found to exceed the fixed margin of deviation, or else immured in a Government Office as a clerk of the seventh class; prevented from marriage; forced to drudge at an uninteresting occupation for a miserable stipend; obliged to live and board at the office, and to take even

---

1   What follows, analogous to Swift's *A Modest Proposal*, is a reasonable alternative way of responding to social problems, one that reflects the author's actual beliefs and that sees the individual's environment, rather than heredity, as a cause for anti-social behavior.

his vacation under close supervision; what wonder that human nature, even in the best and purest, is embittered and perverted by such surroundings!"

All this very plausible reasoning does not convince me, as it has not convinced the wisest of our Statesmen, that our ancestors erred in laying it down as an axiom of policy that the toleration of Irregularity is incompatible with the safety of the State. Doubtless, the life of an Irregular is hard; but the interests of the Greater Number require that it shall be hard. If a man with a triangular front and a polygonal back were allowed to exist and to propagate a still more Irregular posterity, what would become of the arts of life? Are the houses and doors and churches in Flatland to be altered in order to accommodate such monsters? Are our ticket-collectors to be required to measure every man's perimeter before they allow him to enter a theatre or to take his place in a lecture room? Is an Irregular to be exempted from the militia? And if not, how is he to be prevented from carrying desolation into the ranks of his comrades? Again, what irresistible temptations to fraudulent impostures must needs beset such a creature! How easy for him to enter a shop with his polygonal front foremost, and to order goods to any extent from a confiding tradesman! Let the advocates of a falsely called Philanthropy plead as they may for the abrogation of the Irregular Penal Laws, I for my part have never known an Irregular who was not also what Nature evidently intended him to be—a hypocrite, a misanthropist, and, up to the limits of his power, a perpetrator of all manner of mischief.

Not that I should be disposed to recommend (at present) the extreme measures adopted by some States, where an infant whose angle deviates by half a degree from the correct angularity is summarily destroyed at birth. Some of our highest and ablest men, men of real genius, have during their earliest days laboured under deviations as great as, or even greater than, forty-five minutes: and the loss of their precious lives would have been an irreparable injury to the State.[1] The art of healing also has achieved some of its most glorious triumphs[2] in the compressions, extensions, trepannings, colligations, and other surgical or

---

1 Evidence that angular measurement does not dictate intelligence.
2 What follows are surgical procedures that indicate the extent to which Flatlanders will go to achieve a uniform appearance. Trepannings: the ancient surgical practice of cutting holes in the skull to cure disease. Colligations: surgically binding together.

diaetetic[1] operations by which Irregularity has been partly or wholly cured. Advocating therefore a *Via Media*,[2] I would lay down no fixed or absolute line of demarcation; but at the period when the frame is just beginning to set, and when the Medical Board has reported that recovery is improbable, I would suggest that the Irregular offspring be painlessly and mercifully consumed.

Section 8. Of the Ancient Practice of Painting

If my Readers have followed me with any attention up to this point, they will not be surprised to hear that life is somewhat dull in Flatland. I do not, of course, mean that there are not battles, conspiracies, tumults, factions, and all those other phenomena which are supposed to make History interesting; nor would I deny that the strange mixture of the problems of life and the problems of Mathematics, continually inducing conjecture and giving the opportunity of immediate verification, imparts to our existence a zest which you in Spaceland can hardly comprehend. I speak now from the aesthetic and artistic point of view when I say that life with us is dull; aesthetically and artistically, very dull indeed.

How can it be otherwise, when all one's prospect, all one's landscapes, historical pieces, portraits, flowers, still life, are nothing but a single line, with no varieties except degrees of brightness and obscurity?

It was not always thus. Colour, if Tradition speaks the truth, once for the space of half a dozen centuries or more, threw a transient splendour over the lives of our ancestors in the remotest ages. Some private individual—a Pentagon whose name is variously reported—having casually discovered the constituents of the simpler colours and a rudimentary method of painting, is said to have begun decorating first his house, then his slaves, then his Father, his Sons, and Grandsons, lastly himself. The convenience as well as the beauty of the results commended themselves to all. Wherever Chromatistes,[3]—for by that name the most trustworthy authorities concur in calling

---

1 Probably a misprint for diaeretic, meaning the surgical separation of parts normally united.

2 A middle way, or comprise solution to the issue.

3 From *chroma*, the Greek word for color.

him,—turned his variegated frame, there he at once excited attention, and attracted respect. No one now needed to "feel" him; no one mistook his front for his back; all his movements were readily ascertained by his neighbours without the slightest strain on their powers of calculation; no one jostled him, or failed to make way for him; his voice was saved the labour of that exhausting utterance by which we colourless Squares and Pentagons are often forced to proclaim our individuality when we move amid a crowd of ignorant Isosceles.

The fashion spread like wildfire. Before a week was over, every Square and Triangle in the district had copied the example of Chromatistes, and only a few of the more conservative Pentagons still held out. A month or two found even the Dodecagons infected with the innovation. A year had not elápsed before the habit had spread to all but the very highest of the Nobility. Needless to say, the custom soon made its way from the district of Chromatistes to surrounding regions; and within two generations no one in all Flatland was colourless except the Women and the Priests.

Here Nature herself appeared to erect a barrier, and to plead against extending the innovation to these two classes. Many-sidedness was almost essential as a pretext for the Innovators. "Distinction of sides is intended by Nature to imply distinction of colours"—such was the sophism which in those days flew from mouth to mouth, converting whole towns at a time to the new culture. But manifestly to our Priests and Women this adage did not apply. The latter had only one side, and therefore—plurally and pedantically speaking—*no sides*. The former—if at least they would assert their claim to be really and truly Circles, and not mere high-class Polygons with an infinitely large number of infinitesimally small sides—were in the habit of boasting (what Women confessed and deplored) that they also had no sides, being blessed with a perimeter of one line, or, in other words, a Circumference. Hence it came to pass that these two Classes could see no force in the so-called axiom about "Distinction of Sides implying Distinction of Colour"; and when all others had succumbed to the fascinations of corporal decoration, the Priests and the Women alone still remained pure from the pollution of paint.

Immoral, licentious, anarchical, unscientific—call them by what names you will—yet, from an aesthetic point of view, those ancient days of the Colour Revolt were the glorious childhood of Art in Flatland—a childhood, alas, that never ripened into manhood, nor even reached the blossom of youth. To live was then in itself a delight, because living implied seeing. Even at a small party, the company was a pleasure to behold; the richly varied hues of the assembly in a church or theatre are said to have more than once proved too distracting for our greatest teachers and actors; but most ravishing of all is said to have been the unspeakable magnificence of a military review.

The sight of a line of battle of twenty thousand Isosceles suddenly facing about, and exchanging the sombre black of their bases for the orange and purple of the two sides including their acute angle; the militia of the Equilateral Triangles tricoloured in red, white, and blue; the mauve, ultra-marine, gamboges,[1] and burnt umber of the Square artillerymen rapidly rotating near their vermilion guns; the dashing and flashing of the five-coloured and six-coloured Pentagons and Hexagons careering across the field in their offices of surgeons, geometricians and aides-de-camp—all these may well have been sufficient to render credible the famous story how an illustrious Circle, overcome by the artistic beauty of the forces under his command, threw aside his marshal's baton and his royal crown, exclaiming that he henceforth exchanged them for the artist's pencil. How great and glorious the sensuous development of these days must have been is in part indicated by the very language and vocabulary of the period. The commonest utterances of the commonest citizens in the time of the Colour Revolt seem to have been suffused with a richer tinge of word or thought; and to that era we are even now indebted for our finest poetry and for whatever rhythm still remains in the more scientific utterance of these modern days.

Section 9. Of the Universal Colour Bill[2]

But meanwhile the intellectual Arts were fast decaying.

The Art of Sight Recognition, being no longer needed, was no longer practised; and the studies of Geometry, Statics, Kinetics,

---

1 A dark mustard color. This is a word with a seventeenth-century background, reflecting Abbott's interest in that era; it was first used to indicate a color in English in 1634.

2 The Universal Colour Bill appears to comment on the series of Reform Bills (in 1832, 1867, and 1884) that marked the Victorian age. These bills gradually gave the vote to the middle class, then the laboring classes. Women, however, despite intense efforts in the 1880s, did not gain the right to vote.

and other kindred subjects, came soon to be considered super-fluous, and fell into disrespect and neglect even at our University. The inferior Art of Feeling speedily experienced the same fate at our Elementary Schools. Then the Isosceles classes, asserting that the Specimens were no longer used nor needed, and refusing to pay the customary tribute from the Criminal classes to the service of Education, waxed daily more numerous and more insolent on the strength of their immunity from the old burden which had formerly exercised the twofold wholesome effect of at once taming their brutal nature and thinning their excessive numbers.

Year by year the Soldiers and Artisans began more vehemently to assert—and with increasing truth—that there was no great difference between them and the very highest class of Polygons, now that they were raised to an equality with the latter, and enabled to grapple with all the difficulties and solve all the problems of life, whether Statical or Kinetical, by the simple process of Colour Recognition. Not content with the natural neglect into which Sight Recognition was falling, they began boldly to demand the legal prohibition of all "monopolizing and aristo-cratic Arts" and the consequent abolition of all endowments for the studies of Sight Recognition, Mathematics, and Feeling. Soon, they began to insist that inasmuch as Colour, which was a second Nature, had destroyed the need of aristocratic distinc-tions, the Law should follow in the same path, and that hence-forth all individuals and all classes should be recognized as absolutely equal and entitled to equal rights.

Finding the higher Orders wavering and undecided, the leaders of the Revolution advanced still further in their require-ments, and at last demanded that all classes alike, the Priests and the Women not excepted, should do homage to Colour by sub-mitting to be painted. When it was objected that Priests and Women had no sides, they retorted that Nature and Expediency concurred in dictating that the front half of every human being (that is to say, the half containing his eye and mouth) should be distinguishable from his hinder half. They therefore brought before a general and extraordinary Assembly of all the States of Flatland a Bill proposing that in every Woman the half contain-ing the eye and mouth should be coloured red, and the other half green. The Priests were to be painted in the same way, red being applied to that semicircle in which the eye and mouth formed the middle point; while the other or hinder semicircle was to be coloured green.

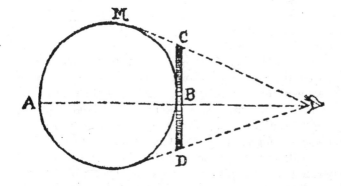

There was no little cunning in this proposal, which indeed emanated not from any Isosceles—for no being so degraded would have had angularity enough to appreciate, much less to devise, such a model of state-craft—but from an Irregular Circle who, instead of being destroyed in his childhood, was reserved by a foolish indulgence to bring desolation on his country and destruction on myriads of his followers.

On the one hand the proposition was calculated to bring the Women in all classes over to the side of the Chromatic Innovation. For by assigning to the Women the same two colours as were assigned to the Priests, the Revolutionists thereby ensured that, in certain positions, every Woman would appear like a Priest, and be treated with corresponding respect and deference—a prospect that could not fail to attract the Female Sex in a mass.

But by some of my Readers the possibility of the identical appearance of Priests and Women, under the new Legislation, may not be recognized; if so, a word or two will make it obvious.

Imagine a woman duly decorated, according to the new Code; with the front half (i.e., the half containing eye and mouth) red, and with the hinder half green. Look at her from one side. Obviously you will see a straight line, *half red, half green*.

Now imagine a Priest, whose mouth is at M, and whose front semicircle (AMB) is consequently coloured red, while his hinder semicircle is green; so that the diameter AB divides the green from the red. If you contemplate the Great Man so as to have your eye in the same straight line as his dividing diameter (AB), what you will see will be a straight line (CBD), of which *one half* (CB) *will be red, and the other* (BD) *green*. The whole line (CD) will be rather shorter perhaps than that of a full-sized Woman, and will shade off more rapidly towards its extremities; but the identity of the colours would give you an immediate impression of identity if not Class, making you neglectful of other details. Bear in mind the decay of Sight Recognition which threatened society at the time of the Colour Revolt; add too the certainty that Women would speedily learn to shade off their extremities so as to imitate the Circles; it must then be surely obvious to you, my dear Reader, that the Colour Bill placed us under a great danger of confounding a Priest with a young Woman.

How attractive this prospect must have been to the Frail Sex may readily be imagined. They anticipated with delight the confusion that would ensue. At home they might hear political and ecclesiastical secrets intended not for them but for their husbands and brothers, and might even issue commands in the name of a priestly Circle; out of doors the striking combination of red and green, without addition of any other colours, would be sure to lead the common people into endless mistakes, and the Women would gain whatever the Circles lost, in the deference of the passers by. As for the scandal that would befall the Circular Class if the frivolous and unseemly conduct of the Women were imputed to them, and as to the consequent subversion of the Constitution, the Female Sex could not be expected to give a thought to these considerations. Even in the households of the Circles, the Women were all in favour of the Universal Colour Bill.

The second object aimed at by the Bill was the gradual demoralization of the Circles themselves. In the general intellectual decay they still preserved their pristine clearness and strength of understanding. From their earliest childhood, familiarized in their Circular households with the total absence of Colour, the Nobles alone preserved the Sacred Art of Sight Recognition, with all the advantages that result from that admirable training of the intellect. Hence, up to the date of the introduction of the Universal Colour Bill, the Circles had not only held their own, but even increased their lead of the other classes by abstinence from the popular fashion.

Now therefore the artful Irregular whom I described above as the real author of this diabolical Bill, determined at one blow to lower the status of the Hierarchy by forcing them to submit to the pollution of Colour, and at the same time to destroy their domestic opportunities of training in the Art of Sight Recognition, so as to enfeeble their intellects by depriving them of their pure and colourless homes. Once subjected to the chromatic taint, every parental and every childish Circle would demoralize each other. Only in discerning between the Father and the Mother would the Circular infant find problems for the exercise of its understanding—problems too often likely to be corrupted by maternal impostures with the result of shaking the child's faith in all logical conclusions. Thus by degrees the intellectual lustre of the Priestly Order would wane, and the road would then lie open for a total destruction of all Aristocratic Legislature and for the subversion of our Privileged Classes.

Section 10. Of the Suppression of the Chromatic Sedition

The agitation for the Universal Colour Bill continued for three years; and up to the last moment of that period it seemed as though Anarchy were destined to triumph.

A whole army of Polygons, who turned out to fight as private soldiers, was utterly annihilated by a superior force of Isosceles Triangles—the Squares and Pentagons meanwhile remaining neutral. Worse than all, some of the ablest Circles fell a prey to conjugal fury. Infuriated by political animosity, the wives in many a noble household wearied their lords with prayers to give up their opposition to the Colour Bill; and some, finding their entreaties fruitless, fell on and slaughtered their innocent children and husband, perishing themselves in the act of carnage. It is recorded that during that triennial agitation no less than twenty-three Circles perished in domestic discord.

Great indeed was the peril. It seemed as though the Priests had no choice between submission and extermination; when suddenly the course of events was completely changed by one of those picturesque incidents which Statesmen ought never to neglect, often to anticipate, and sometimes perhaps to originate, because of the absurdly disproportionate power with which they appeal to the sympathies of the populace.

It happened that an Isosceles of a low type, with a brain little if at all above four degrees—accidentally dabbling in the colours of some Tradesman whose shop he had plundered—painted himself, or caused himself to be painted (for the story varies) with the twelve colours of a Dodecagon. Going into the Market Place he accosted in a feigned voice a maiden, the orphan daughter of a noble Polygon, whose affection in former days he had sought in vain; and by a series of deceptions—aided, on the one side, by a string of lucky accidents too long to relate, and on the other, by an almost inconceivable fatuity and neglect of ordinary precautions on the part of the relations of the bride—he succeeded in consummating the marriage. The unhappy girl committed suicide on discovering the fraud to which she had been subjected.

When the news of this catastrophe spread from State to State the minds of the Women were violently agitated. Sympathy with the miserable victim and anticipations of similar deceptions for themselves, their sisters, and their daughters, made them now regard the Colour Bill in an entirely new aspect. Not a few openly avowed themselves converted to antagonism; the rest needed only a slight stimulus to make a similar avowal. Seizing this favourable opportunity, the Circles hastily convened an extraordinary Assembly of the States; and besides the usual guard of Convicts, they secured the attendance of a large number of reactionary Women.

Amidst an unprecedented concourse, the Chief Circle of those days—by name Pantocyclus[1]—arose to find himself hissed and hooted by a hundred and twenty thousand Isosceles. But he secured silence by declaring that henceforth the Circles would enter on a policy of Concession; yielding to the wishes of the majority, they would accept the Colour Bill. The uproar being at once converted to applause, he invited Chromatistes, the leader of the Sedition, into the centre of the hall, to receive in the name of his followers the submission of the Hierarchy. Then followed a speech, a masterpiece of rhetoric, which occupied nearly a day in the delivery, and to which no summary can do justice.

With a grave appearance of impartiality he declared that as they were now finally committing themselves to Reform or Innovation, it was desirable that they should take one last view of the perimeter of the whole subject, its defects as well as its advantages. Gradually introducing the mention of the dangers to the Tradesmen, the Professional Classes and the Gentlemen, he silenced the rising murmurs of the Isosceles by reminding them that, in spite of all these defects, he was willing to accept the Bill if it was approved by the majority. But it was manifest that all, except the Isosceles, were moved by his words and were either neutral or averse to the Bill.

Turning now to the Workmen he asserted that their interests must not be neglected, and that, if they intended to accept the Colour Bill, they ought at least to do so with full view of the con-

---

1 "All circle," from the Greek *pantos*, "all," and the Latin *cyclus*, "circle."

sequences. Many of them, he said, were on the point of being admitted to the class of the Regular Triangles; others anticipated for their children a distinction they could not hope for themselves. That honourable ambition would now have to be sacrificed. With the universal adoption of Colour, all distinctions would cease; Regularity would be confused with Irregularity; development would give place to retrogression; the Workman would in a few generations be degraded to the level of the Military, or even the Convict Class; political power would be in the hands of the greatest number, that is to say the Criminal Classes, who were already more numerous than the Workmen, and would soon out-number all the other Classes put together when the usual Compensative Laws of Nature were violated.

A subdued murmur of assent ran through the ranks of the Artisans, and Chromatistes, in alarm, attempted to step forward and address them. But he found himself encompassed with guards and forced to remain silent while the Chief Circle in a few impassioned words made a final appeal to the Women, exclaiming that, if the Colour Bill passed, no marriage would henceforth be safe, no woman's honour secure; fraud, deception, hypocrisy would pervade every household; domestic bliss would share the fate of the Constitution and pass to speedy perdition. "Sooner than this," he cried, "Come death."

At these words, which were the preconcerted signal for action, the Isosceles Convicts fell on and transfixed the wretched Chromatistes; the Regular Classes, opening their ranks, made way for a band of Women who, under direction of the Circles, moved, back foremost, invisibly and unerringly upon the unconscious soldiers; the Artisans, imitating the example of their betters, also opened their ranks. Meantime bands of Convicts occupied every entrance with an impenetrable phalanx.

The battle, or rather carnage, was of short duration. Under the skillful generalship of the Circles almost every Woman's charge was fatal and very many extracted their sting uninjured, ready for a second slaughter. But no second blow was needed; the rabble of the Isosceles did the rest of the business for themselves. Surprised, leader-less, attacked in front by invisible foes, and finding egress cut off by the Convicts behind them, they at once—after their manner—lost all presence of mind, and raised the cry of "treachery." This sealed their fate. Every Isosceles now saw and felt a foe in every other. In half an hour not one of that vast multitude was living; and the fragments of seven score thousand of the Criminal Class slain by one another's angles attested the triumph of Order.

The Circles delayed not to push their victory to the uttermost. The Working Men they spared but decimated. The Militia of the Equilaterals was at once called out; and every Triangle suspected of Irregularity on reasonable grounds, was destroyed by Court Martial, without the formality of exact measurement by the Social Board. The homes of the Military and Artisan classes were inspected in a course of visitations extending through upwards of a year; and during that period every town, village, and hamlet was systematically purged of that excess of the lower orders which had been brought about by the neglect to pay the tribute of Criminals to the Schools and University, and by the violation of the other natural Laws of the Constitution of Flatland.[1] Thus the balance of classes was again restored.

Needless to say that henceforth the use of Colour was abolished, and its possession prohibited. Even the utterance of any word denoting Colour, except by the Circles or by qualified scientific teachers, was punished by a severe penalty. Only at our University in some of the very highest and most esoteric classes— which I myself have never been privileged to attend—it is understood that the sparing use of Colour is still sanctioned for the purpose of illustrating some of the deeper problems of mathematics. But of this I can only speak from hearsay.

Elsewhere in Flatland, Colour is now non-existent. The art of making it is known to only one living person, the Chief Circle for the time being; and by him it is handed down on his death-bed to none but his Successor.[2] One manufactory alone produces it; and, lest the secret should be betrayed, the Workmen are annually consumed, and fresh ones introduced. So great is the terror with which even now our Aristocracy looks back to the far-distant days of the agitation for the Universal Colour Bill.

Section 11. Concerning our Priests

It is high time that I should pass from these brief and discursive notes about things in Flatland to the central event of this book, my initiation into the mysteries of Space. *That* is my subject; all that has gone before is merely preface.

For this reason I must omit many matters of which the explanation would not, I flatter myself, be without interest for my

---

1 Suggesting that a system of continual eugenic selection is practiced.
2 Here we learn that the Circles have kept information from the public.

Readers: as for example, our method of propelling and stopping ourselves, although destitute of feet; the means by which we give fixity to structures of wood, stone, or brick, although of course we have no hands,[1] nor can we lay foundations as you can, nor avail ourselves of the lateral pressure of the earth; the manner in which the rain originates in the intervals between our various zones, so that the northern regions do not intercept the moisture from falling on the southern; the nature of our hills and mines, our trees and vegetables, our seasons and harvests; our Alphabet and method of writing, adapted to our linear tablets; these and a hundred other details of our physical existence I must pass over, nor do I mention them now except to indicate to my readers that their omission proceeds not from forgetfulness on the part of the author, but from his regard for the time of the Reader.[2]

Yet before I proceed to my legitimate subject some few final remarks will no doubt be expected by my Readers upon those pillars and mainstays of the Constitution of Flatland, the controllers of our conduct and shapers of our destiny, the objects of universal homage and almost of adoration: need I say that I mean our Circles or Priests?

When I call them Priests, let me not be understood as meaning no more than the term denotes with you. With us, our Priests are Administrators of all Business, Art, and Science; Directors of Trade, Commerce, Generalship, Architecture, Engineering, Education, Statesmanship, Legislature, Morality, Theology; doing nothing themselves, they are the Causes of everything worth doing, that is done by others.

Although popularly everyone called a Circle is deemed a Circle, yet among the better educated Classes it is known that no Circle is really a Circle, but only a Polygon with a very large number of very small sides. As the number of the sides increases, a Polygon approximates to a Circle; and, when the number is very great indeed, say for example three or four hundred, it is extremely difficult for the most delicate touch to feel any polygonal angles. Let me say rather, it *would* be difficult: for, as I have shown above, Recognition by Feeling is unknown among the highest society, and to *feel* a Circle would be considered a most

---

1 This comment reflects the bloody plot of Shakespeare's *Titus Andronicus*, in which characters have their hands cut off. A quotation from *Titus Andronicus* had appeared on the title page. See "A Note on the Text."

2 These, and other practical aspects of two-dimensional life, have been examined by later scientists.

audacious insult. This habit of abstention from Feeling in the best society enables a Circle the more easily to sustain the veil of mystery in which, from his earliest years, he is wont to enwrap the exact nature of his Perimeter or Circumference. Three feet being the average Perimeter it follows that, in a Polygon of three hundred sides each side will be no more than the hundredth part of a foot in length, or little more than the tenth part of an inch; and in a Polygon of six or seven hundred sides the sides are little larger than the diameter of a Spaceland pin-head. It is always assumed, by courtesy, that the Chief Circle for the time being has ten thousand sides.

The ascent of the posterity of the Circles in the social scale is not restricted, as it is among the lower Regular classes, by the Law of Nature which limits the increase of sides to one in each generation. If it were so, the number of sides in a Circle would be a mere question of pedigree and arithmetic, and the four hundred and ninety-seventh descendant of an Equilateral Triangle would necessarily be a Polygon with five hundred sides. But this is not the case. Nature's Law prescribes two antagonistic decrees affecting Circular propagation; first, that as the race climbs higher in the scale of development, so development shall proceed at an accelerated pace; second, that in the same proportion, the race shall become less fertile.[1] Consequently in the home of a Polygon of four or five hundred sides it is rare to find a son; more than one is never seen. On the other hand the son of a five-hundred-sided Polygon has been known to possess five hundred and fifty, or even six hundred sides.

Art also steps in to help the process of the higher Evolution. Our physicians have discovered that the small and tender sides of an infant Polygon of the higher class can be fractured, and his whole frame re-set, with such exactness that a Polygon of two or three hundred sides sometimes—by no means always, for the process is attended with serious risk—but sometimes overleaps two or three hundred generations, and as it were doubles at a stroke, the number of his progenitors and the nobility of his descent.

Many a promising child is sacrificed in this way. Scarcely one out of ten survives.[2] Yet so strong is the parental ambition among

---

1 This comment reflects a common Victorian fear that the lower classes will out-reproduce the upper classes. There was also a belief that more highly "evolved" members of society were becoming less fertile.

2 With each example of the sacrifice of the individual to social order, the world of Flatland appears more and more like a dystopia, although the Square appears to be still blinded to its problems.

those Polygons who are, as it were, on the fringe of the Circular class, that it is very rare to find a Nobleman of that position in society, who has neglected to place his first-born in the Circular Neo-Therapeutic Gymnasium before he has attained the age of a month.

One year determines success or failure. At the end of that time the child has, in all probability, added one more to the tombstones that crowd the Neo-Therapeutic Cemetery; but on rare occasions a glad procession bears back the little one to his exultant parents, no longer a Polygon, but a Circle, at least by courtesy: and a single instance of so blessed a result induces multitudes of Polygonal parents to submit to similar domestic sacrifices, which have a dissimilar issue.

Section 12. Of the Doctrine of our Priests

As to the doctrine of the Circles it may briefly be summed up in a single maxim, "Attend to your Configuration." Whether political, ecclesiastical, or moral, all their teaching has for its object the improvement of individual and collective Configuration—with special reference of course to the Configuration of the Circles, to which all other objects are subordinated.

It is the merit of the Circles that they have effectually suppressed those ancient heresies which led men to waste energy and sympathy in the vain belief that conduct depends upon will, effort, training, encouragement, praise, or anything else but Configuration.[1] It was Pantocyclus—the illustrious Circle mentioned above, as the queller of the Colour Revolt—who first convinced mankind that Configuration makes the man; that if, for example, you are born an Isosceles with two uneven sides, you will assuredly go wrong unless you have them made even—for which purpose you must go to the Isosceles Hospital; similarly, if you are a Triangle, or Square, or even a Polygon, born with any Irregularity, you must be taken to one of the Regular Hospitals to have

---

1 An apparent satire of the eugenics movement founded by Francis Galton (see Introduction, pp. 36-37). Followers argued that heredity, rather than individual effort or environment, affected social progress. Flatland society is the result of an artificial selection process that allows only the most regular shapes to exist. While the Square can see that shape does not always reflect ability, he still holds to the required orthodoxy.

your disease cured; otherwise you will end your days in the State Prison or by the angle of the State Executioner.[1]

All faults or defects, from the slightest misconduct to the most flagitious crime, Pantocyclus attributed to some deviation from perfect Regularity in the bodily figure, caused perhaps (if not congenital) by some collision in a crowd; by neglect to take exercise, or by taking too much of it; or even by a sudden change of temperature, resulting in a shrinkage or expansion in some too susceptible part of the frame. Therefore, concluded that illustrious Philosopher, neither good conduct nor bad conduct is a fit subject, in any sober estimation, for either praise or blame. For why should you praise, for example, the integrity of a Square who faithfully defends the interests of his client, when you ought in reality rather to admire the exact precision of his right angles?[2] Or again, why blame a lying, thievish Isosceles when you ought rather to deplore the incurable inequality of his sides?

Theoretically, this doctrine is unquestionable; but it has practical drawbacks. In dealing with an Isosceles, if a rascal pleads that he cannot help stealing because of his unevenness, you reply that for that very reason, because he cannot help being a nuisance to his neighbours, you, the Magistrate, cannot help sentencing him to be consumed—and there's an end of the matter. But in little domestic difficulties, where the penalty of consumption, or death, is out of the question, this theory of Configuration sometimes comes in awkwardly; and I must confess that occasionally when one of my own Hexagonal Grandsons pleads as an excuse for his disobedience that a sudden change of the temperature has been too much for his Perimeter, and that I ought to lay the blame not on him but on his Configuration, which can only be strengthened by abundance of the choicest sweetmeats, I neither see my way logically to reject, nor practically to accept, his conclusions.

For my own part, I find it best to assume that a good sound scolding or castigation has some latent and strengthening influence on my Grandson's Configuration; though I own that I have no grounds for thinking so.[3] At all events I am not alone in my

---

1 Suggestive of Samuel Butler's *Erewhon* (1872), which describes a fictional utopia where criminals go to hospitals and the sick are sent to jail.

2 The first edition has "exact precision of his Rectangles." The reference to "client" indicates that the Square is thinking of the conflict between Pantocyclus' teachings and his own duties as a lawyer.

3 The logic of the theory of Configuration is in conflict with parenting roles.

way of extricating myself from this dilemma; for I find that many of the highest Circles, sitting as Judges in law courts, use praise and blame towards Regular and Irregular Figures; and in their homes I know by experience that, when scolding their children, they speak about "right" or "wrong" as vehemently and passionately as if they believed that these names represented real existences, and that a human Figure is really capable of choosing between them.

Constantly carrying out their policy of making Configuration the leading idea in every mind, the Circles reverse the nature of that Commandment which in Spaceland regulates the relations between parents and children. With you, children are taught to honour their parents; with us—next to the Circles, who are the chief object of universal homage—a man is taught to honour his Grandson, if he has one; or, if not, his Son. By "honour," however, is by no means meant "indulgence," but a reverent regard for their highest interests: and the Circles teach that the duty of fathers is to subordinate their own interests to those of posterity, thereby advancing the welfare of the whole State as well as that of their own immediate descendants.

The weak point in the system of the Circles—if a humble Square may venture to speak of anything Circular as containing any element of weakness—appears to me to be found in their relations with Women.

As it is of the utmost importance for Society that Irregular births should be discouraged, it follows that no Woman who has any Irregularities in her ancestry is a fit partner for one who desires that his posterity should rise by regular degrees in the social scale.

Now the Irregularity of a Male is a matter of measurement; but as all Women are straight, and therefore visibly Regular so to speak, one has to devise some other means of ascertaining what I may call their invisible Irregularity, that is to say their potential Irregularities as regards possible offspring. This is effected by carefully-kept pedigrees, which are preserved and supervised by the State; and without a certified pedigree no Woman is allowed to marry.

Now it might have been supposed that a Circle—proud of his ancestry and regardful for a posterity which might possibly issue hereafter in a Chief Circle—would be more careful than any other to choose a wife who had no blot on her escutcheon.[1] But

---

1 That is, has good breeding and no irregularities or recessive traits in the family history. Escutcheon refers to the family's coat of arms.

it is not so. The care in choosing a Regular wife appears to diminish as one rises in the social scale.[1] Nothing would induce an aspiring Isosceles, who had hopes of generating an Equilateral Son, to take a wife who reckoned a single Irregularity among her Ancestors; a Square or Pentagon, who is confident that his family is steadily on the rise, does not inquire above the five-hundredth generation; a Hexagon or Dodecagon[2] is even more careless of the wife's pedigree; but a Circle has been known deliberately to take a wife who has had an Irregular Great-Grandfather, and all because of some slight superiority of lustre, or because of the charms of a low voice—which, with us, even more than you, is thought "an excellent thing in Woman."[3]

Such ill-judged marriages are, as might be expected, barren, if they do not result in positive Irregularity or in diminution of sides; but none of these evils have hitherto proved sufficiently deterrent. The loss of a few sides in a highly-developed Polygon is not easily noticed, and is sometimes compensated by a successful operation in the Neo-Therapeutic Gymnasium, as I have described above; and the Circles are too much disposed to acquiesce in infecundity as a Law of the superior development. Yet, if this evil be not arrested, the gradual diminution of the Circular class may soon become more rapid, and the time may be not far distant when, the race being no longer able to produce a Chief Circle, the Constitution of Flatland must fall.

One other word of warning suggests itself to me, though I cannot so easily mention a remedy; and this also refers to our relations with Women. About three hundred years ago, it was decreed by the Chief Circle that, since women are deficient in Reason but abundant in Emotion, they ought no longer to be treated as rational, nor receive any mental education.[4]

---

1   Much as aristocrats of Abbott's time would become infatuated with actresses or others generally not admitted into polite circles.

2   The first edition had Dodecahedron, a geometric error that Abbott corrected. A Dodecahedron is a geometric solid; a Dodecagon is a plane figure.

3   *King Lear*, V.iii.274-75: "Her voice was ever soft,/ Gentle and low, an excellent thing in woman."

4   The color revolt took place six hundred years ago, before the limitation of women's rights and the loss of education for women. The Square's knowledge of history shows that he is aware that women are more capable than most believe. Here Abbott is voicing his support for women's education through his character. Contemporary book reviewers of *Flatland*, such as the *Spectator*, particularly noted these pointed refer-

The consequence was that they were no longer taught to read, nor even to master Arithmetic enough to enable them to count the angles of their husband or children; and hence they sensibly declined during each generation in intellectual power. And this system of female non-education or quietism still prevails.

My fear is that, with the best intentions, this policy has been carried so far as to react injuriously on the Male Sex.

For the consequence is that, as things now are, we Males have to lead a kind of bi-lingual, and I may almost say bi-mental, existence. With Women, we speak of "love," "duty," "right," "wrong," "pity," "hope," and other irrational and emotional conceptions, which have no existence, and the fiction of which has no object except to control feminine exuberances; but among ourselves, and in our books, we have an entirely different vocabulary and I may almost say, idiom.[1] "Love" then becomes "the anticipation of benefits"; "duty" becomes "necessity" or "fitness"; and other words are correspondingly transmuted. Moreover, among Women, we use language implying the utmost deference for their Sex; and they fully believe that the Chief Circle Himself is not more devoutly adored by us than they are: but behind their backs they are both regarded and spoken of—by all except the very young—as being little better than "mindless organisms."

Our Theology also in the Women's chambers is entirely different from our Theology elsewhere.

Now my humble fear is that this double training, in language as well as in thought, imposes somewhat too heavy a burden upon the young, especially when, at the age of three years old, they are taken from the maternal care and taught to unlearn the old language—except for the purpose of repeating it in the presence of their Mothers and Nurses—and to learn the vocabulary and idiom of science.[2] Already methinks I discern a weakness in the grasp of mathematical truth at the present time as compared with the more robust intellect of our ancestors three hundred

---

ences to the pervasive separate-spheres doctrine of Victorian society that held women responsible for the spiritual health of the family and the home, while men took responsibility for worldly affairs.

1 The women, then, still maintain a pre-revolt sense of ethics and justice; whereas the men have adopted a utilitarian view of the world. The Square is bothered by the hypocrisy in the women's treatment.

2 The common practice in England was for upper-class British boys to be removed from their mothers at a young age and sent to boarding schools, and thus become isolated in an all-male world.

years ago.[1] I say nothing of the possible danger if a Woman should ever surreptitiously learn to read and convey to her Sex the result of her perusal of a single popular volume; nor of the possibility that the indiscretion or disobedience of some infant Male might reveal to a Mother the secrets of the logical dialect. On the simple ground of the enfeebling of the Male intellect, I rest this humble appeal to the highest Authorities to reconsider the regulations of Female Education.

---

1   That is, before women were barred from education.

PART II: OTHER WORLDS[1]

"O brave new worlds,
That have such people in them!"[2]

---

1 This second part moves the Square from his comfortable understanding
of the universe to radical changes in perception, as he is prepared to
understand the mental attitudes associated with different dimensional
spaces. Additionally, the reader is prepared to understand the dimensional analogies that follow.

2 A modification of *The Tempest*, V.i.183-84: "O brave new world,/ That
has such people in't." The Square will encounter more than one world.
In *The Tempest*, these lines are spoken by Miranda when she first
encounters people from outside her enchanted island. Miranda, like the
Square, is a naïve innocent.

Section 13. How I had a Vision of Lineland[1]

It was the last day but one of the 1999th year of our era,[2] and the first day of the Long Vacation.[3] Having amused myself till a late hour with my favourite recreation of Geometry,[4] I had retired to rest with an unsolved problem in my mind. In the night I had a dream.

I saw before me a vast multitude of small Straight Lines (which I naturally assumed to be Women) interspersed with other Beings still smaller and of the nature of lustrous points—all moving to and fro in one and the same Straight Line, and, as nearly as I could judge, with the same velocity.

A noise of confused, multitudinous chirping or twittering issued from them at intervals as long as they were moving; but sometimes they ceased from motion, and then all was silence.

Approaching one of the largest of what I thought to be Women, I accosted her, but received no answer. A second and a third appeal on my part were equally ineffectual. Losing patience at what appeared to me intolerable rudeness, I brought my mouth into a position full in front of her mouth so as to intercept her motion, and loudly repeated my question, "Woman, what signifies this concourse, and this strange and confused chirping, and this monotonous motion to and fro in one and the same Straight Line?"

"I am no Woman," replied the small Line. "I am the Monarch of the world. But thou, whence intrudest thou into my realm of Lineland?" Receiving this abrupt reply, I begged pardon if I had in any way startled or molested his Royal Highness; and describing myself as a stranger I besought the King to give me some account of his dominions. But I had the greatest possible difficulty in obtaining any information on points that really interested me; for the Monarch could not refrain from constantly assuming that whatever was familiar to him must also be known to me and

---

1 The idea of Lineland may have been inspired by Hinton's "What is the Fourth Dimension?" (1880; see Appendix B4).

2 That is, just before a millennial celebration. The date becomes important when the visiting Sphere reveals history that the Circles had kept hidden.

3 In Oxford and Cambridge, the Long Vacation refers to the summer vacation running from July to September. Apparently, the Flatland calendar places an extended academic break before the New Year.

4 Indicating that the Square enjoys mathematics as a hobby.

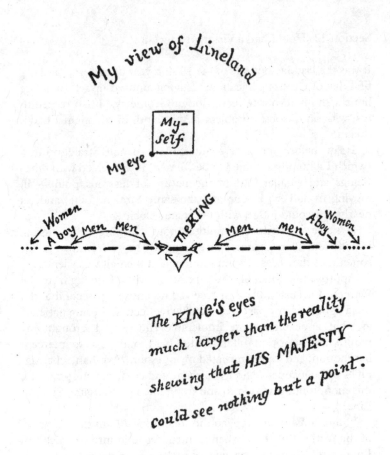

My view of Lineland

My-self

My eye

Women A boy Men Men The KING Men Men A boy Women

The KING'S eyes much larger than the reality shewing that HIS MAJESTY could see nothing but a point.

that I was simulating ignorance in jest. However, by persevering questions I elicited the following facts:

It seemed that this poor ignorant Monarch—as he called himself—was persuaded that the Straight Line which he called his Kingdom, and in which he passed his existence, constituted the whole of the world, and indeed the whole of Space. Not being able either to move or to see, save in his Straight Line, he had no conception of anything out of it. Though he had heard my voice when I first addressed him, the sounds had come to him in a manner so contrary to his experience that he had made no answer, "seeing no man," as he expressed it, "and hearing a voice as it were from my own intestines." Until the moment when I placed my mouth in his World, he had neither seen me, nor heard anything except confused sounds beating against—

what I called his side, but what he called his *inside* or *stomach*; nor had he even now the least conception of the region from which I had come. Outside his World, or Line, all was a blank to him; nay, not even a blank, for a blank implies Space; say, rather, all was non-existent.

His subjects—of whom the small Lines were men and the Points Women—were all alike confined in motion and eye-sight to that single Straight Line, which was their World.[1] It need scarcely be added that the whole of their horizon was limited to a Point; nor could any one ever see anything but a Point. Man, woman, child, thing—each was a Point to the eye of a Linelander. Only by the sound of the voice could sex or age be distinguished. Moreover, as each individual occupied the whole of the narrow path, so to speak, which constituted his Universe, and no one could move to the right or left to make way for passers by, it followed that no Linelander could ever pass another. Once neighbours, always neighbours. Neighbourhood with them was like marriage with us. Neighbours remained neighbours till death did them part.

Such a life, with all vision limited to a Point, and all motion to a Straight Line, seemed to me inexpressibly dreary; and I was surprised to note the vivacity and cheerfulness of the King. Wondering whether it was possible, amid circumstances so unfavourable to domestic relations, to enjoy the pleasures of conjugal union, I hesitated for some time to question his Royal Highness on so delicate a subject; but at last I plunged into it by abruptly inquiring as to the health of his family. "My wives and children," he replied, "are well and happy."

Staggered at this answer—for in the immediate proximity of the Monarch (as I had noted in my dream before I entered Lineland) there were none but Men—I ventured to reply, "Pardon me, but I cannot imagine how your Royal Highness can at any time either see or approach their Majesties, when there are at least half a dozen intervening individuals, whom you can neither see through, nor pass by? Is it possible that in Lineland proximity is not necessary for marriage and for the generation of children?"

"How can you ask so absurd a question?" replied the Monarch. "If it were indeed as you suggest, the Universe would soon be depopulated. No, no; neighbourhood is needless for the

---

1 This world has some similarities to Hinton's two-dimensional world, where the inhabitants live on the edge of a circle.

union of hearts; and the birth of children is too important a matter to have been allowed to depend upon such an accident as proximity. You cannot be ignorant of this. Yet since you are pleased to affect ignorance, I will instruct you as if you were the veriest baby in Lineland. Know, then, that marriages are consummated by means of the faculty of sound and the sense of hearing.

"You are of course aware that every Man has two mouths or voices—as well as two eyes—a bass at one and a tenor at the other of his extremities. I should not mention this, but that I have been unable to distinguish your tenor in the course of our conversation." I replied that I had but one voice, and that I had not been aware that his Royal Highness had two. "That confirms my impression," said the King, "that you are not a Man, but a feminine Monstrosity with a bass voice, and an utterly uneducated ear.[1] But to continue.

"Nature having herself ordained that every Man should wed two wives—" "Why two?" asked I. "You carry your affected simplicity too far," he cried. "How can there be a completely harmonious union without the combination of the Four in One, viz. the Bass and Tenor of the Man and the Soprano and Contralto of the two Women?" "But supposing," said I, "that a man should prefer one wife or three?" "It is impossible," he said; "it is as inconceivable as that two and one should make five, or that the human eye should see a Straight Line." I would have interrupted him; but he proceeded as follows:

"Once in the middle of each week a Law of Nature compels us to move to and fro with a rhythmic motion of more than usual violence, which continues for the time you would take to count a hundred and one. In the midst of this choral dance, at the fifty-first pulsation, the inhabitants of the Universe pause in full career, and each individual sends forth his richest, fullest, sweetest strain. It is in this decisive moment that all our marriages are made. So exquisite is the adaptation of Bass to Treble, of Tenor to Contralto, that oftentimes the Loved Ones, though twenty

---

1 The problem of identification, both of gender and of class, is a theme that runs through *Flatland*, and it was a preoccupation of late-Victorian England as increasing urbanization brought large numbers of strangers together.

thousand leagues away, recognize at once the responsive note of their destined Lover; and, penetrating the paltry obstacles of distance, Love unites the three. The marriage in that instant consummated results in a threefold Male and Female offspring which takes its place in Lineland."

"What! Always threefold?" said I. "Must one wife then always have twins?"

"Bass-voiced Monstrosity! yes," replied the King. "How else could the balance of the Sexes be maintained, if two girls were not born for every boy? Would you ignore the very Alphabet of Nature?" He ceased, speechless for fury; and some time elapsed before I could induce him to resume his narrative.

"You will not, of course, suppose that every bachelor among us finds his mates at the first wooing in this universal Marriage Chorus. On the contrary, the process is by most of us many times repeated. Few are the hearts whose happy lot it is at once to recognize in each other's voices the partner intended for them by Providence, and to fly into a reciprocal and perfectly harmonious embrace. With most of us the courtship is of long duration. The Wooer's voices may perhaps accord with one of the future wives, but not with both; or not, at first, with either; or the Soprano and Contralto may not quite harmonize. In such cases Nature has provided that every weekly Chorus shall bring the three Lovers into closer harmony. Each trial of voice, each fresh discovery of discord, almost imperceptibly induces the less perfect to modify his or her vocal utterance so as to approximate to the more perfect. And after many trials and many approximations, the result is at last achieved. There comes a day at last, when, while the wonted Marriage Chorus goes forth from universal Lineland, the three far-off Lovers suddenly find themselves in exact harmony, and, before they are aware, the wedded Triplet is rapt vocally into a duplicate embrace; and Nature rejoices over one more marriage and over three more births."

Section 14. How I vainly tried to explain the nature of Flatland

Thinking that it was time to bring down the Monarch from his raptures to the level of common sense, I determined to endeavour to open up to him some glimpses of the truth, that is to say of the nature of things in Flatland. So I began thus: "How does your Royal Highness distinguish the shapes and positions of his subjects? I for my part noticed by the sense of sight, before I entered your Kingdom, that some of your people are Lines and others Points, and that some of the Lines are larger—" "You speak of an impossibility," interrupted the King; "you must have seen a vision; for to detect the difference between a Line and a Point by the sense of sight is, as every one knows, in the nature of things, impossible; but it can be detected by the sense of hearing, and by the same means my shape can be exactly ascertained. Behold me—I am a Line, the longest in Lineland, over six inches of Space—" "Of Length," I ventured to suggest. "Fool," said he, "Space is Length. Interrupt me again, and I have done."

I apologized; but he continued scornfully, "Since you are impervious to argument, you shall hear with your ears how by means of my two voices I reveal my shape to my Wives, who are at this moment six thousand miles seventy yards two feet eight inches away, the one to the North, the other to the South. Listen, I call to them."

He chirruped, and then complacently continued: "My wives at this moment receiving the sound of one of my voices, closely followed by the other, and perceiving that the latter reaches them after an interval in which sound can traverse 6.457 inches, infer that one of my mouths is 6.457 inches further from them than the other, and accordingly know my shape to be 6.457 inches. But you will of course understand that my wives do not make this calculation every time they hear my two voices. They made it, once for all, before we were married. But they *could* make it at any time. And in the same way I can estimate the shape of any of my Male subjects by the sense of sound."

"But how," said I, "if a Man feigns a Woman's voice with one of his two voices, or so disguises his Southern voice that it cannot be recognized as the echo of the Northern? May not such deceptions cause great inconvenience? And have you no means of checking frauds of this kind by commanding your neighbouring subjects to feel one another?" This of course was a very stupid question, for feeling could not have answered the purpose; but I asked with the view of irritating the Monarch, and I succeeded perfectly.

"What!" cried he in horror, "explain your meaning." "Feel, touch, come into contact," I replied. "If you mean by *feeling*," said the King, "approaching so close as to leave no space between two individuals, know, Stranger, that this offence is punishable in my dominions by death. And the reason is obvious. The frail form of a Woman, being liable to be shattered by such an approximation, must be preserved by the State; but since Women cannot be distinguished by the sense of sight from Men, the Law ordains universally that neither Man nor Woman shall be approached so closely as to destroy the interval between the approximator and the approximated.[1]

"And indeed what possible purpose would be served by this illegal and unnatural excess of approximation which you call *touching*, when all the ends of so brutal and coarse a process are attained at once more easily and more exactly by the sense of hearing? As to your suggested danger of deception, it is non-existent: for the Voice, being the essence of one's Being, cannot be thus changed at will. But come, suppose that I had the power of passing through solid things, so that I could penetrate my subjects, one after another, even to the number of a billion, verifying the size and distance of each by the sense of *feeling*: how much time and energy would be wasted in this clumsy and inaccurate method! Whereas now, in one moment of audition, I take as it were the census and statistics, local, corporeal, mental and spiritual, of every living being in Lineland. Hark, only hark!"

So saying he paused and listened, as if in an ecstasy, to a sound which seemed to me no better than a tiny chirping from an innumerable multitude of lilliputian[2] grasshoppers.

"Truly," replied I, "your sense of hearing serves you in good stead, and fills up many of your deficiencies. But permit me to point out that your life in Lineland must be deplorably dull. To see nothing but a Point! Not even to be able to contemplate a Straight Line! Nay, not even to know what a Straight Line is! To see, yet be cut off from those Linear prospects which are vouchsafed to us in Flatland! Better surely to have no sense of sight at all than to see so little! I grant you I have not your discriminative faculty of hearing; for the concert of all Lineland which gives you such intense pleasure, is to me no better than a multitudinous twittering or chirping.[3] But at least I can discern, by sight, a Line from a Point. And let me prove it. Just before I came into your kingdom, I saw you dancing from left to right, and then from

---

1 A reversal of the situation in Flatland, where men are seen as fragile and women need to avoid touching them. Yet, as in Flatland, physical contact is avoided; both worlds find touch to be coarse. However, in Lineland, sound, rather than shape, is valued as the essence of the person.

2 Reference to the tiny world of Lilliput in Swift's *Gulliver's Travels* (1726).

3 The Square's arrogance will become quite ironic when he, in turn, is visited by a higher dimensional being.

right to left, with Seven Men and a Woman in your immediate proximity on the left, and eight Men and two Women on your right. Is not this correct?"

"It is correct," said the King, "so far as the numbers and sexes are concerned, though I know not what you mean by 'right' and 'left.' But I deny that you saw these things. For how could you see the Line, that is to say the inside, of any Man? But you must have heard these things, and then dreamed that you saw them. And let me ask what you mean by those words 'left' and 'right.' I suppose it is your way of saying Northward and Southward."[1]

"Not so," replied I; "besides your motion of Northward and Southward, there is another motion which I call from right to left."

King. Exhibit to me, if you please, this motion from left to right.

I. Nay, that I cannot do, unless you could step out of your Line altogether.

King. Out of my Line? Do you mean out of the world? Out of Space?

I. Well, yes. Out of *your* World. Out of *your* Space. For your Space is not the true Space. True Space is a Plane; but your Space is only a Line.

---

1 The Square's debate with the King of Lineland rests upon an analysis of sensory impressions, the basis of the scientific method, and it nearly echoes W.B. Carpenter's 1872 discussion of sensory evidence in his presidential address, "Man the Interpreter of Nature," to the British Association for the Advancement of Science: "The psychologist of the present day views Matter entirely through the light of his own Consciousness: his idea of matter in the abstract being that it is a 'something' which has a permanent power of exciting Sensations; his idea of any 'property' of Matter being the mental representation of some kind of sensory impression he has received from it; and his idea of any particular kind of Matter being the representation of the whole aggregate of the Sense-perceptions which its presence has called up in his Mind. Thus when I press my hand against this table, I recognize its unyielding-ness through the conjoint medium of my sense of Touch, my Muscular sense, and my Mental sense of Effort, to which it will be convenient to give the general designation of the Tactile Sense; and I attribute to that table a *hardness* which resists the effort I make to press my hand into its substance, whilst I also recognize the fact that the force I have employed is not sufficient to move its mass" (in George Basalla, William Coleman, and Robert H. Kargon, eds., *Victorian Science* [New York: Doubleday, 1970], 428).

King. If you cannot indicate this motion from left to right by yourself moving in it, then I beg you to describe it to me in words.

I. If you cannot tell your right side from your left, I fear that no words of mine can make my meaning clear to you. But surely you cannot be ignorant of so simple a distinction.

King. I do not in the least understand you.

I. Alas! How shall I make it clear? When you move straight on, does it not sometimes occur to you that you *could* move in some other way, turning your eye round so as to look in the direction towards which your side is now fronting? In other words, instead of always moving in the direction of one of your extremities, do you never feel a desire to move in the direction, so to speak, of your side?

King. Never. And what do you mean? How can a man's inside "front" in any direction? Or how can a man move in the direction of his inside?

I. Well then, since words cannot explain the matter, I will try deeds, and will move gradually out of Lineland in the direction which I desire to indicate to you.

At the word I began to move my body out of Lineland. As long as any part of me remained in his dominion and in his view, the King kept exclaiming, "I see you, I see you still; you are not moving." But when I had at last moved myself out of his Line, he cried in his shrillest voice, "She is vanished; she is dead."

"I am not dead," replied I; "I am simply out of Lineland, that is to say, out of the Straight Line which you call Space, and in the true Space, where I can see things as they are. And at this moment I can see your Line, or side—or inside as you are pleased to call it; and I can see also the Men and Women on the North and South of you, whom I will now enumerate, describing their order, their size, and the interval between each."

When I had done this at great length, I cried triumphantly, "Does this at last convince you?" And, with that, I once more entered Lineland, taking up the same position as before.

But the Monarch replied, "If you were a Man of sense—though, as you appear to have only one voice I have little doubt you are not a Man but a Woman—but, if you had a particle of sense, you would listen to reason. You ask me to believe that there is another Line besides that which my senses indicate, and another motion besides that of which I am daily conscious. I, in return, ask you to describe in words or indicate by motion that other Line of which you speak. Instead of moving, you merely exercise some magic art of vanishing and returning to sight; and instead of any lucid description of your new World, you simply tell me the numbers and sizes of some forty of my retinue, facts known to any child in my capital. Can anything be more irrational or audacious? Acknowledge your folly or depart from my dominions."

Furious at his perversity, and especially indignant that he professed to be ignorant of my sex, I retorted in no measured terms, "Besotted Being! You think yourself the perfection of existence, while you are in reality the most imperfect and imbecile. You profess to see, whereas you can see nothing but a Point! You plume yourself on inferring the existence of a Straight Line; but I *can see* Straight Lines, and infer the existence of Angles, Triangles, Squares, Pentagons, Hexagons, and even Circles. Why waste more words? Suffice it that I am the completion of your incomplete self. You are a Line, but I am a Line of Lines, called in my country a Square: and even I, infinitely superior though I am to you, am of little account among the great nobles of Flatland, whence I have come to visit you, in the hope of enlightening your ignorance."

Hearing these words the King advanced towards me with a menacing cry as if to pierce me through the diagonal; and in that same moment there arose from myriads of his subjects a multitudinous war-cry, increasing in vehemence till at last methought it rivalled the roar of an army of a hundred thousand Isosceles, and the artillery of a thousand Pentagons. Spell-bound and motionless, I could neither speak nor move to avert the impending destruction; and still the noise grew louder, and the King came closer, when I awoke to find the breakfast-bell recalling me to the realities of Flatland.[1]

---

1 This scene is similar to the conclusion of Lewis Carroll's *Through the Looking Glass* (1871), where Alice is threatened by a pack of cards and then wakes from a dream.

Section 15. Concerning a Stranger from Spaceland

From dreams I proceed to facts.

It was the last day of the 1999th year of our era. The pattering of the rain had long ago announced nightfall; and I was sitting[*] in the company of my wife, musing on the events of the past and the prospects of the coming year, the coming century, the coming Millennium.

My four Sons and two orphan Grandchildren had retired to their several apartments; and my wife alone remained with me to see the old Millennium out and the new one in.

I was rapt in thought, pondering in my mind some words that had casually issued from the mouth of my youngest Grandson, a most promising young Hexagon of unusual brilliancy and perfect angularity. His uncles and I had been giving him his usual practical lesson in Sight Recognition, turning ourselves upon our centres, now rapidly, now more slowly, and questioning him as to our positions; and his answers had been so satisfactory that I had been induced to reward him by giving him a few hints on Arithmetic, as applied to Geometry.

Taking nine Squares, each an inch every way, I had put them together so as to make one large Square, with a side of three inches, and I had hence proved to my little Grandson that— though it was impossible for us to *see* the inside of the Square— yet we might ascertain the number of square inches in a Square by simply squaring the number of inches in the side: "and thus," said I, "we know that 3^2, or 9, represents the number of square inches in a Square whose side is 3 inches long."

The little Hexagon meditated on this a while and then said to me: "But you have been teaching me to raise numbers to the third power; I suppose 3^3 must mean something in Geometry; what does it mean?" "Nothing at all," replied I, "not at least in Geometry; for Geometry has only Two Dimensions." And then I

---

[*] When I say "sitting," of course I do not mean any change of attitude such as you in Spaceland signify by that word; for as we have no feet, we can no more "sit" nor "stand" (in your sense of the word) than one of your soles or flounders.

Nevertheless, we perfectly well recognize the different mental states of volition implied in "lying," "sitting," and "standing," which are to some extent indicated to a beholder by a slight increase of lustre corresponding to the increase of volition.

· But on this, and a thousand other kindred subjects, time forbids me to dwell.

began to shew the boy how a Point by moving through a length of three inches makes a Line of three inches, which may be represented by 3; and how a Line of three inches, moving parallel to itself through a length of three inches, makes a Square of three inches every way, which may be represented by 3^2.

Upon this, my Grandson, again returning to his former suggestion, took me up rather suddenly and exclaimed, "Well, then, if a Point by moving three inches, makes a Line of three inches represented by 3; and if a straight Line of three inches, moving parallel to itself, makes a Square of three inches every way, represented by 3^2; it must be that a Square of three inches every way, moving somehow parallel to itself (but I don't see how) must make a Something else (but I don't see what) of three inches every way—and this must be represented by 3^3."[1]

"Go to bed," said I, a little ruffled by this interruption: "if you would talk less nonsense, you would remember more sense."

So my Grandson had disappeared in disgrace; and there I sat by my Wife's side, endeavouring to form a retrospect of the year 1999 and of the possibilities of the year 2000, but not quite able to shake off the thoughts suggested by the prattle of my bright little Hexagon. Only a few sands now remained in the half-hour glass. Rousing myself from my reverie I turned the glass Northward for the last time in the old Millennium; and in the act, I exclaimed aloud, "The boy is a fool."

Straightway I became conscious of a Presence in the room, and a chilling breath thrilled through my very being. "He is no such thing," cried my Wife, "and you are breaking the Commandments in thus dishonouring your own Grandson." But I took no notice of her. Looking round in every direction I could see nothing; yet still I *felt* a Presence, and shivered as the cold whisper came again. I started up. "What is the matter?" said my Wife, "there is no draught; what are you looking for? There is nothing." There was nothing; and I resumed my seat, again exclaiming, "The boy is a fool, I say; 3^3 can have no meaning in Geometry." At once there came a distinctly audible reply, "The boy is not a fool; and 3^3 has an obvious Geometrical meaning."

My Wife as well as myself heard the words, although she did not understand their meaning, and both of us sprang forward in

---

1   The grandson's reasoning may have been inspired by Plato's reference to squaring and cubing numbers in the *Republic* (587d-e). According to Lee, classical Greeks often represented numbers spatially (see Desmond Lee's translation of Plato's *Republic*, p. 408, n. 41, on plane numbers).

the direction of the sound. What was our horror when we saw before us a Figure! At the first glance it appeared to be a Woman, seen sideways; but a moment's observation shewed me that the extremities passed into dimness too rapidly to represent one of the Female Sex; and I should have thought it a Circle, only that it seemed to change its size in a manner impossible for a Circle or for any regular Figure of which I had had experience.

But my Wife had not my experience, nor the coolness necessary to note these characteristics. With the usual hastiness and unreasoning jealousy of her Sex, she flew at once to the conclusion that a Woman had entered the house through some small aperture.[1] "How comes this person here?" she exclaimed, "you promised me, my dear, that there should be no ventilators[2] in our new house." "Nor are there any," said I; "but what makes you think that the stranger is a Woman? I see by my power of Sight Recognition—" "Oh, I have no patience with your Sight Recognition," replied she, "'Feeling is believing' and 'A Straight Line to the touch is worth a Circle to the sight'"—two Proverbs very common with the Frailer Sex in Flatland.[3]

"Well," said I, for I was afraid of irritating her, "if it must be so, demand an introduction." Assuming her most gracious manner, my Wife advanced towards the Stranger, "Permit me, Madam, to feel and be felt by—" then, suddenly recoiling, "Oh! it is not a Woman, and there are no angles either, not a trace of one. Can it be that I have so misbehaved to a perfect Circle?"

"I am indeed, in a certain sense a Circle," replied the Voice, "and a more perfect Circle than any in Flatland; but to speak more accurately, I am many Circles in one."[4] Then he added more mildly, "I have a message, dear Madam, to your husband, which I must not deliver in your presence; and, if you would

---

1 The rigid restrictions placed on women may be because they can be mistaken for circles rather than because of danger, as the Square's confusion reveals.

2 Apparently some sort of window mechanism. The term was used for air-circulation devices in railroad cars.

3 A play on the proverbs "Seeing is believing" and "A bird in the hand is worth two in the bush."

4 The visitor takes the shape that the Square would show the most respect to, i.e., a circle; in fact, it is a sphere. Any other shape would have been treated with immediate rejection. The idea of geometric shapes forming geometric-based religions can be found in Letter 59 of Montesquieu's *The Persian Letters* (1721): "It has been well said that if   (Continued)

suffer us to retire for a few minutes—"[1] But my Wife would not listen to the proposal that our august Visitor should so incommode himself, and assuring the Circle that the hour of her own retirement had long passed, with many reiterated apologies for her recent indiscretion, she at last retreated to her apartment.

I glanced at the half-hour glass. The last sands had fallen. The third Millennium had begun.[2]

Section 16. How the Stranger vainly endeavoured
to reveal to me in words the mysteries of Spaceland

As soon as the sound of the Peace-cry of my departing Wife had died away,[3] I began to approach the Stranger with the intention of taking a nearer view and of bidding him be seated: but his appearance struck me dumb and motionless with astonishment. Without the slightest symptoms of angularity he nevertheless varied every instant with gradations of size and brightness scarcely possible for any Figure within the scope of my experience. The thought flashed across me that I might have before me a burglar or cut-throat, some monstrous Irregular Isosceles, who, by feigning the voice of a Circle, had obtained admission somehow into the house, and was now preparing to stab me with his acute angle.

In a sitting-room, the absence of Fog (and the season happened to be remarkably dry), made it difficult for me to trust to Sight Recognition, especially at the short distance at which I was standing. Desperate with fear, I rushed forward with an uncere-

---

triangles were to create a god, they would give him three sides." This reference, in turn, has been traced to Spinoza's *Opera Posthuma* (Epistola 57) by Alessandro Crisafulli. (See p. 313, n. 117 of J. Robert Loy's edition of the Montesquieu work.)

1 The soon-to-be-identified Sphere treats the Square's Wife with a respect alien to Flatland.

2 The first and second editions stated it was the second Millennium, an error Abbott corrected in the third edition. However, some modern editions (such as the Shambhala edition) retain the error, while others (such as the Oxford) retain it but add an explanatory note.

3 In the first edition, Abbott slipped and wrote, "As soon as the sound of my Wife's retreating footsteps had died away...." Flatlanders, of course, have no feet. The "retreating footsteps" was corrected to "Peace-cry" in the revised edition.

monious, "You must permit me, Sir—" and felt him. My Wife was right. There was not the trace of an angle, not the slightest roughness or inequality: never in my life had I met with a more perfect Circle. He remained motionless while I walked round him, beginning from his eye and returning to it again. Circular he was throughout, a perfectly satisfactory Circle; there could not be a doubt of it. Then followed a dialogue, which I will endeavour to set down as near as I can recollect it, omitting only some of my profuse apologies—for I was covered with shame and humiliation that I, a Square, should have been guilty of the impertinence of feeling a Circle. It was commenced by the Stranger with some impatience at the lengthiness of my introductory process.

Stranger. Have you felt me enough by this time? Are you not introduced to me yet?

I. Most illustrious Sir, excuse my awkwardness, which arises not from ignorance of the usages of polite society, but from a little surprise and nervousness, consequent on this somewhat unexpected visit. And I beseech you to reveal my indiscretion to no one, and especially not to my Wife. But before your Lordship enters into further communications, would he deign to satisfy the curiosity of one who would gladly know whence his Visitor came?

Stranger. From Space, from Space, Sir: whence else?

I. Pardon me, my Lord, but is not your Lordship already in Space, your Lordship and his humble servant, even at this moment?

Stranger. Pooh! what do you know of Space? Define Space.

I. Space, my Lord, is height and breadth indefinitely prolonged.

Stranger. Exactly: you see you do not even know what Space is. You think it is of Two Dimensions only; but I have come to announce to you a Third—height, breadth, and length.

I. Your Lordship is pleased to be merry. We also speak of length and height, or breadth and thickness, thus denoting Two Dimensions by four names.

Stranger. But I mean not only three names, but Three Dimensions.

I. Would your Lordship indicate or explain to me in what direction is the Third Dimension, unknown to me?[1]

Stranger. I came from it. It is up above and down below.

---

1 The Square is now in the same position that the King of Lineland was in earlier.

I. My Lord means seemingly that it is Northward and South-ward.

Stranger. I mean nothing of the kind. I mean a direction in which you cannot look, because you have no eye in your side.

I. Pardon me, my Lord, a moment's inspection will convince your Lordship that I have a perfect luminary at the juncture of two of my sides.

Stranger. Yes: but in order to see into Space you ought to have an eye, not on your Perimeter, but on your side, that is, on what you would probably call your inside; but we in Spaceland should call it your side.

I. An eye in my inside! An eye in my stomach! Your Lordship jests.

Stranger. I am in no jesting humour. I tell you that I come from Space, or, since you will not understand what Space means, from the Land of Three Dimensions whence I but lately looked down upon your Plane which you call Space forsooth. From that position of advantage I discerned all that you speak of as *solid* (by which you mean "enclosed on four sides"), your houses, your churches, your very chests and safes, yes even your insides and stomachs, all lying open and exposed to my view.

I. Such assertions are easily made, my Lord.

Stranger. But not easily proved, you mean. But I mean to prove mine.

When I descended here, I saw your four Sons, the Pentagons, each in his apartment, and your two Grandsons the Hexagons; I saw your youngest Hexagon remain a while with you and then retire to his room, leaving you and your Wife alone. I saw your Isosceles servants, three in number, in the kitchen at supper, and the little Page in the scullery. Then I came here, and how do you think I came?

I. Through the roof, I suppose.

Stranger. Not so. Your roof, as you know very well, has been recently repaired, and has no aperture by which even a Woman could penetrate. I tell you I come from Space. Are you not convinced by what I have told you of your children and household?

I. Your Lordship must be aware that such facts touching the belongings of his humble servant might be easily ascertained by any one in the neighbourhood possessing your Lordship's ample means of obtaining information.

Stranger. (*To himself.*)[1] What must I do? Stay; one more argu-

---

1 This begins the material added to the revised edition. In the first edition, the Sphere's line "How shall I convince him?" follows.

ment suggests itself to me. When you see a Straight Line—your wife, for example—how many Dimensions do you attribute to her?

I. Your Lordship would treat me as if I were one of the vulgar who, being ignorant of Mathematics, suppose that a Woman is really a Straight Line, and only of One Dimension. No, no, my Lord; we Squares are better advised, and are as well aware as your Lordship that a Woman, though popularly called a Straight Line, is, really and scientifically, a very thin Parallelogram, possessing Two Dimensions, like the rest of us, viz., length and breadth (or thickness).

Stranger. But the very fact that a Line is visible implies that it possesses yet another Dimension.

I. My Lord, I have just acknowledged that a Woman is broad as well as long. We see her length, we infer her breadth; which, though very slight, is capable of measurement.

Stranger. You do not understand me. I mean that when you see a Woman, you ought—besides inferring her breadth—to see her length, and to *see* what we call her *height*; although that last Dimension is infinitesimal in your country. If a Line were mere length without "height," it would cease to occupy Space and would become invisible. Surely you must recognize this?

I. I must indeed confess that I do not in the least understand your Lordship. When we in Flatland see a Line, we see length and *brightness.* If the brightness disappears, the Line is extinguished, and, as you say, ceases to occupy Space. But am I to suppose that your Lordship gives to brightness the title of a Dimension, and that what we call "bright" you call "high"?

Stranger. No, indeed. By "height" I mean a Dimension like your length: only, with you, "height" is not so easily perceptible, being extremely small.

I. My Lord, your assertion is easily put to the test. You say I have a Third Dimension, which you call "height." Now, Dimension implies direction and measurement. Do but measure my "height," or merely indicate to me the direction in which my "height" extends, and I will become your convert. Otherwise, your Lordship's own understanding must hold me excused.

Stranger. (*To himself.*) I can do neither.[1] How shall I convince him? Surely a plain statement of facts followed by ocular demonstration ought to suffice.—Now, Sir; listen to me.

You are living on a Plane. What you style Flatland is the vast level surface of what I may call a fluid, on, or in, the top of which

---

1 This ends the added dialogue that Abbott wrote for the revised edition.

you and your countrymen move about, without rising above it or falling below it.

I am not a plane Figure, but a Solid. You call me a Circle; but in reality I am not a Circle, but an infinite number of Circles, of size varying from a Point to a Circle of thirteen inches in diameter, one placed on the top of the other. When I cut through your plane as I am now doing, I make in your plane a section which you, very rightly, call a Circle. For even a Sphere—which is my proper name in my own country—if he manifest himself at all to an inhabitant of Flatland—must needs manifest himself as a Circle.[1]

Do you not remember—for I, who see all things, discerned last night the phantasmal vision of Lineland written upon your brain—do you not remember, I say, how, when you entered the realm of Lineland, you were compelled to manifest yourself to the King, not as a Square, but as a Line, because that Linear Realm had not Dimensions enough to represent the whole of you, but only a slice or section of you? In precisely the same way, your country of Two Dimensions is not spacious enough to represent me, a being of Three, but can only exhibit a slice or section of me, which is what you call a Circle.

The diminished brightness of your eye indicates incredulity. But now prepare to receive proof positive of the truth of my assertions. You cannot indeed see more than one of my sections, or Circles, at a time; for you have no power to raise your eye out of the plane of Flatland; but you can at least see that, as I rise in Space, so my sections become smaller. See now, I will rise; and the effect upon your eye will be that my Circle will become smaller and smaller till it dwindles to a point and finally vanishes.

There was no "rising" that I could see; but he diminished and finally vanished. I winked once or twice to make sure that I was not dreaming. But it was no dream. For from the depths of nowhere came forth a hollow voice—close to my heart it seemed—"Am I quite gone? Are you convinced now? Well, now I

---

1   The Sphere's appearance on the millennium may have been inspired by the early Greek philosopher Empedocles' vision of the universe as being motivated by two forces, Love and Strife. In *On Nature*, Empedocles explains that periodically the universe reaches a harmonious balance as a divine Sphere (*Sphairos*), which then dissolves and slowly reestablishes itself. Marshall McLuhan argues that Lewis Carroll's Humpty Dumpty in the Alice books is Empedocles' *Sphairos* (see Helle Lambridis, "Empedocles and T.S. Eliot," *Empedocles, Studies in the Humanities* No. 15 [U of Alabama P, 1975], vi-xv).

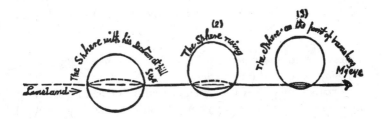

will gradually return to Flatland and you shall see my section become larger and larger."

Every reader in Spaceland will easily understand that my mysterious Guest was speaking the language of truth and even of simplicity. But to me, proficient though I was in Flatland Mathematics, it was by no means a simple matter. The rough diagram given above will make it clear to any Spaceland child that the Sphere, ascending in the three positions indicated there, must needs have manifested himself to me, or to any Flatlander, as a Circle, at first of full size, then small, and at last very small indeed, approaching to a Point. But to me, although I saw the facts before me, the causes were as dark as ever. All that I could comprehend was, that the Circle had made himself smaller and vanished, and that he had now reappeared and was rapidly making himself larger.

When he regained his original size, he heaved a deep sigh; for he perceived by my silence that I had altogether failed to comprehend him. And indeed I was now inclining to the belief that he must be no Circle at all, but some extremely clever juggler; or else that the old wives' tales were true, and that after all there were such people as Enchanters and Magicians.

After a long pause he muttered to himself, "One resource alone remains, if I am not to resort to action. I must try the method of Analogy." Then followed a still longer silence, after which he continued our dialogue.

Sphere. Tell me, Mr. Mathematician; if a Point moves Northward, and leaves a luminous wake, what name would you give to the wake?

I. A straight Line.

Sphere. And a straight Line has how many extremities?

I. Two.

Sphere. Now conceive the Northward straight Line moving parallel to itself, East and West, so that every point in it leaves behind it the wake of a straight Line. What name will you give to the Figure thereby formed? We will suppose that it moves through a distance equal to the original straight Line.—What name, I say?

I. A Square.

Sphere. And how many sides has a Square? How many angles?

I. Four sides and four angles.

Sphere. Now stretch your imagination a little, and conceive a Square in Flatland, moving parallel to itself upward.

I. What? Northward?

Sphere. No, not Northward; upward; out of Flatland altogether.[1]

If it moved Northward, the Southern points in the Square would have to move through the positions previously occupied by the Northern points. But that is not my meaning.

I mean that every Point in you—for you are a Square and will serve the purpose of my illustration—every Point in you, that is to say in what you call your inside, is to pass upwards through Space in such a way that no Point shall pass through the position previously occupied by any other Point; but each Point shall describe a straight Line of its own. This is all in accordance with Analogy; surely it must be clear to you.

Restraining my impatience—for I was now under a strong temptation to rush blindly at my Visitor and to precipitate him into Space, or out of Flatland, anywhere, so that I could get rid of him—I replied:—

"And what may be the nature of the Figure which I am to shape out by this motion which you are pleased to denote by the word 'upward'? I presume it is describable in the language of Flatland."

Sphere. Oh, certainly. It is all plain and simple, and in strict accordance with Analogy—only, by the way, you must not speak of the result as being a Figure, but as a Solid. But I will describe it to you. Or rather not I, but Analogy.

---

1 The Sphere is directing the Square to perceive both higher understanding in addition to three dimensions. The phrase "upward" echoes Plato's *Republic* (527b), where the importance of plane geometry in the education of a ruler is discussed. The purpose of geometry in the *Republic* is for intellectual training with the goal of seeing the Good. Socrates states that objects of geometrical knowledge are eternal and their study "will tend to draw the mind to the truth and direct the philosophers' reason upwards, instead of downwards ..." (527b). Later, the Square clings to the phrase "Upward, not Northward" as he tries to regain his vision of higher dimensions.

We began with a single Point, which of course—being itself a Point—has only *one* terminal Point.

One Point produces a Line with *two* terminal Points.

One Line produces a Square with *four* terminal Points.

Now you can give yourself the answer to your own question: 1, 2, 4, are evidently in Geometrical Progression. What is the next number?

I. Eight.

Sphere. Exactly. The one Square produces a something-which-you-do-not-as-yet-know-a-name-for-but-which-we-call-a-cube with eight terminal Points. Now are you convinced?

I. And has this Creature sides, as well as angles or what you call "terminal Points"?

Sphere. Of course; and all according to Analogy. But, by the way, not what *you* call sides, but what *we* call sides. You would call them *solids*.

I. And how many solids or sides will appertain to this Being whom I am to generate by the motion of my inside in an "upward" direction, and whom you call a Cube?

Sphere. How can you ask? And you a mathematician! The side of anything is always, if I may so say, one Dimension behind the thing. Consequently, as there is no Dimension behind a Point, a Point has 0 sides; a Line, if I may say, has 2 sides (for the Points of a Line may be called by courtesy, its sides); a Square has 4 sides; 0, 2, 4; what Progression do you call that?

I. Arithmetical.

Sphere. And what is the next number?

I. Six.

Sphere. Exactly. Then you see you have answered your own question. The Cube which you will generate will be bounded by six sides, that is to say, six of your insides. You see it all now, eh?

"Monster," I shrieked, "be thou juggler, enchanter, dream, or devil, no more will I endure thy mockeries. Either thou or I must perish!" And saying these words I precipitated myself upon him.

Section 17. How the Sphere, having in vain tried words, resorted to deeds

It was in vain. I brought my hardest right angle into violent collision with the Stranger, pressing on him with a force sufficient to have destroyed any ordinary Circle: but I could feel him slowly and unarrestably slipping from my contact; not edging to the right nor to the left, but moving somehow out of the world, and vanishing to nothing. Soon there was a blank. But still I heard the Intruder's voice.

Sphere. Why will you refuse to listen to reason? I had hoped to find in you—as being a man of sense and an accomplished mathematician—a fit apostle for the Gospel of the Three Dimensions, which I am allowed to preach once only in a thousand years: but now I know not how to convince you. Stay, I have it. Deeds, and not words, shall proclaim the truth. Listen, my friend.[1]

I have told you I can see from my position in Space the inside of all things that you consider closed. For example, I see in yonder cupboard near which you are standing, several of what you call boxes (but like everything else in Flatland, they have no tops nor bottoms) full of money; I see also two tablets of accounts. I am about to descend into that cupboard and to bring you one of those tablets. I saw you lock the cupboard half an hour ago, and I know you have the key in your possession. But I descend from Space; the doors, you see, remain unmoved. Now I am in the cupboard and am taking the tablet. Now I have it. Now I ascend with it.

I rushed to the closet and dashed the door open. One of the tablets was gone. With a mocking laugh, the Stranger appeared in the other corner of the room, and at the same time the tablet appeared upon the floor. I took it up. There could be no doubt— it was the missing tablet.

I groaned with horror, doubting whether I was not out of my senses; but the Stranger continued: "Surely you must now see that my explanation, and no other, suits the phenomena. What you call Solid things are really superficial; what you call Space is really nothing but a great Plane. I am in Space, and look down upon the insides of the things of which you only see the outsides. You could leave this Plane yourself, if you could but summon up the necessary volition. A slight upward or downward motion would enable you to see all that I can see.

"The higher I mount, and the further I go from your Plane, the more I can see, though of course I see it on a smaller scale. For example, I am ascending; now I can see your neighbour the Hexagon and his family in their several apartments; now I see the inside of the Theatre, ten doors off, from which the audience is only just departing; and on the other side a Circle in his study,

---

1 This section takes on biblical overtones as the Sphere becomes a Christ-like figure attempting to teach a spurned gospel.

sitting at his books. Now I shall come back to you. And, as a crowning proof, what do you say to my giving you a touch, just the least touch, in your stomach? It will not seriously injure you, and the slight pain you may suffer cannot be compared with the mental benefit you will receive."

Before I could utter a word of remonstrance, I felt a shooting pain in my inside, and a demoniacal laugh seemed to issue from within me. A moment afterwards the sharp agony had ceased, leaving nothing but a dull ache behind, and the Stranger began to reappear, saying, as he gradually increased in size, "There, I have not hurt you much, have I? If you are not convinced now, I don't know what will convince you. What say you?"

My resolution was taken. It seemed intolerable that I should endure existence subject to the arbitrary visitations of a Magician who could thus play tricks with one's very stomach. If only I could in any way manage to pin him against the wall till help came!

Once more I dashed my hardest angle against him, at the same time alarming the whole household by my cries for aid. I believe, at the moment of my onset, the Stranger had sunk below our Plane, and really found difficulty in rising. In any case he remained motionless, while I, hearing, as I thought, the sound of some help approaching, pressed against him with redoubled vigour, and continued to shout for assistance.

A convulsive shudder ran through the Sphere. "This must not be," I thought I heard him say: "either he must listen to reason, or I must have recourse to the last resource of civilization." Then, addressing me in a louder tone, he hurriedly exclaimed, ."Listen: no stranger must witness what you have witnessed. Send your Wife back at once, before she enters the apartment. The Gospel of Three Dimensions must not be thus frustrated. Not thus must the fruits of one thousand years of waiting be thrown away. I hear her coming. Back! back! Away from me, or you must go with me—whither you know not—into the Land of Three Dimensions!"

"Fool! Madman! Irregular!" I exclaimed; "never will I release thee; thou shalt pay the penalty of thine impostures."

"Ha! Is it come to this?" thundered the Stranger: "then meet your fate: out of your Plane you go. Once, twice, thrice! 'Tis done!"

Section 18. How I came to Spaceland, and what I saw there

An unspeakable horror seized me. There was a darkness; then a dizzy, sickening sensation of sight that was not like seeing; I saw a Line that was no Line; Space that was not Space: I was myself, and not myself. When I could find voice, I shrieked aloud in agony, "Either this is madness or it is Hell." "It is neither," calmly replied the voice of the Sphere, "it is Knowledge; it is Three Dimensions: open your eye once again and try to look steadily."

I looked, and, behold, a new world![1] There stood before me, visibly incorporate, all that I had before inferred, conjectured, dreamed, of perfect Circular beauty. What seemed the centre of the Stranger's form lay open to my view: yet I could see no heart, nor lungs, nor arteries, only a beautiful harmonious Something— for which I had no words; but you, my Readers in Spaceland, would call it the surface of the Sphere.

Prostrating myself mentally before my Guide, I cried, "How is it, O divine ideal of consummate loveliness and wisdom that I see thy inside, and yet cannot discern thy heart, thy lungs, thy arteries, thy liver?" "What you think you see, you see not," he replied; "it is not given to you, nor to any other Being to behold my internal parts. I am of a different order of Beings from those in Flatland. Were I a Circle, you could discern my intestines, but I am a Being, composed as I told you before, of many Circles, the Many in the One, called in this country a Sphere. And, just as the outside of a Cube is a Square, so the outside of a Sphere presents the appearance of a Circle."

Bewildered though I was by my Teacher's enigmatic utterance, I no longer chafed against it, but worshipped him in silent adoration. He continued, with more mildness in his voice. "Distress not yourself if you cannot at first understand the deeper mysteries of Spaceland. By degrees they will dawn upon you. Let us begin by casting back a glance at the region whence you came. Return with me a while to the plains of Flatland, and I will shew you that which you have often reasoned and thought about, but never seen with the sense of sight—a visible angle." "Impossible!"

---

1 This echoes the earlier reference to the lines from *The Tempest* (see
p. 113, note 2).

I cried; but, the Sphere leading the way, I followed as if in a dream, till once more his voice arrested me: "Look yonder, and behold your own Pentagonal house, and all its inmates."

I looked below, and saw with my physical eye all that domestic individuality which I had hitherto merely inferred with the understanding. And how poor and shadowy was the inferred conjecture in comparison with the reality which I now beheld! My four Sons calmly asleep in the North-Western rooms, my two orphan Grandsons to the South; the Servants, the Butler, my Daughter, all in their several apartments. Only my affectionate Wife, alarmed by my continued absence, had quitted her room and was roving up and down

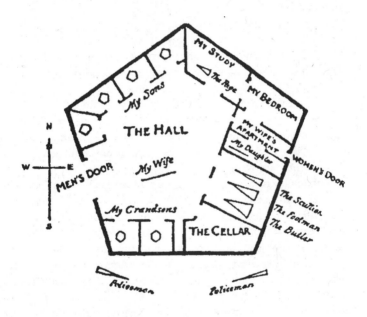

in the Hall, anxiously awaiting my return.[1] Also the Page, aroused by my cries, had left his room, and under pretext of ascertaining whether I had fallen somewhere in a faint, was prying into the cabinet in my study. All this I could now *see*, not merely infer; and as we came nearer and nearer, I could discern

---

1 The wife's anxiety indicates a warmer family relationship than the Square has hereto suggested.

even the contents of my cabinet, and the two chests of gold, and the tablets of which the Sphere had made mention.

Touched by my Wife's distress, I would have sprung downward to reassure her, but I found myself incapable of motion. "Trouble not yourself about your Wife," said my Guide: "she will not be long left in anxiety; meantime, let us take a survey of Flatland."

Once more I felt myself rising through space. It was even as the Sphere had said. The further we receded from the object we beheld, the larger became the field of vision. My native city, with the interior of every house and every creature therein, lay open to my view in miniature. We mounted higher, and lo, the secrets of the earth, the depths of mines and inmost caverns of the hills, were bared before me.

Awestruck at the sight of the mysteries of the earth, thus unveiled before my unworthy eye, I said to my Companion, "Behold, I am become as a God. For the wise men in our country say that to see all things, or as they express it, *omnividence*,[1] is the attribute of God alone." There was something of scorn in the voice of my Teacher as he made answer: "Is it so indeed? Then the very pick-pockets and cut-throats of my country are to be worshipped by your wise men as being Gods: for there is not one of them that does not see as much as you see now. But trust me, your wise men are wrong."

I. Then is omnividence the attribute of others besides Gods?

Sphere. I do not know. But, if a pick-pocket or a cut-throat of our country can see everything that is in your country, surely that is no reason why the pick-pocket or cut-throat should be accepted by you as a God. This omnividence, as you call it—it is not a common word in Spaceland—does it make you more just, more merciful, less selfish, more loving? Not in the least. Then how does it make you more divine?

I. "More merciful, more loving!" But these are the qualities of women! And we know that a Circle is a higher Being than a Straight Line, in so far as knowledge and wisdom are more to be esteemed than mere affection.

Sphere. It is not for me to classify human faculties according to merit. Yet many of the best and wisest in Spaceland think more of the affections than of the understanding, more of your despised

---

1 The capacity to see all things.

Straight Lines than of your belauded Circles.[1] But enough of this. Look yonder. Do you know that building?

I looked, and afar off I saw an immense Polygonal structure, in which I recognized the General Assembly Hall of the States of Flatland, surrounded by dense lines of Pentagonal buildings at right angles to each other, which I knew to be streets; and I perceived that I was approaching the great Metropolis.

"Here we descend," said my Guide. It was now morning, the first hour of the first day of the two thousandth year of our era. Acting, as was their wont, in strict accordance with precedent, the highest Circles of the realm were meeting in solemn conclave, as they had met on the first hour of the first day of the year 1000, and also on the first hour of the first day of the year 0.[2]

The minutes of the previous meetings were now read by one whom I at once recognized as my brother, a perfectly Symmetrical Square, and the Chief Clerk of the High Council. It was found recorded on each occasion that: "Whereas the States had been troubled by divers ill-intentioned persons pretending to have received revelations from another World, and professing to produce demonstrations whereby they had instigated to frenzy both themselves and others, it had been for this cause unanimously resolved by the Grand Council that on the first day of each millenary, special injunctions be sent to the Prefects in the several districts of Flatland, to make strict search for such misguided persons, and without formality of mathematical examination, to destroy all such as were Isosceles of any degree, to scourge and imprison any regular Triangle, to cause any Square or Pentagon to be sent to the district Asylum, and to arrest any one of higher rank, sending him straightway to the Capital to be examined and judged by the Council."[3]

"You hear your fate," said the Sphere to me, while the Council was passing for the third time the formal resolution. "Death or imprisonment awaits the Apostle of the Gospel of Three Dimensions." "Not so," replied I, "the matter is now so clear to me, the

---

1 This is a rejection of Flatland's assessment of women and of common Victorian arguments that women lack rational and logical reasoning and are too heavily dependent on emotion.

2 While Abbott's contemporaries numbered the start of the twentieth century at the beginning of 1901, Flatlanders began their millennium on the zero year. Ian Stewart, in his edition, discusses the background as to when the millennium begins on pp. 113-16, n. 2.

3 An indication that the Sphere has been expected.

nature of real space so palpable, that methinks I could make a child understand it. Permit me but to descend at this moment and enlighten them." "Not yet," said my Guide, "the time will come for that. Meantime I must perform my mission. Stay thou there in thy place." Saying these words, he leaped with great dexterity into the sea (if I may so call it) of Flatland, right in the midst of the ring of Counsellors. "I come," cried he, "to proclaim that there is a land of Three Dimensions."

I could see many of the younger Counsellors start back in manifest horror, as the Sphere's circular section widened before them. But on a sign from the presiding Circle—who shewed not the slightest alarm or surprise—six Isosceles of a low type from six different quarters rushed upon the Sphere. "We have him," they cried; "No; yes; we have him still! he's going! he's gone!"

"My Lords," said the President to the Junior Circles of the Council, "there is not the slightest need for surprise; the secret archives, to which I alone have access, tell me that a similar occurrence happened on the last two millennial commencements. You will, of course, say nothing of these trifles outside the Cabinet."

Raising his voice, he now summoned the guards. "Arrest the policemen; gag them. You know your duty." After he had consigned to their fate the wretched policemen—ill-fated and unwilling witnesses of a State-secret which they were not to be permitted to reveal—he again addressed the Counsellors. "My Lords, the business of the Council being concluded, I have only to wish you a happy New Year." Before departing, he expressed, at some length, to the Clerk, my excellent but most unfortunate brother, his sincere regret that, in accordance with precedent and for the sake of secrecy, he must condemn him to perpetual imprisonment, but added his satisfaction that, unless some mention were made by him of that day's incident, his life would be spared.

Section 19. How, though the Sphere shewed me other mysteries of Spaceland, I still desired more; and what came of it

When I saw my poor brother led away to imprisonment, I attempted to leap down into the Council Chamber, desiring to intercede on his behalf, or at least bid him farewell. But I found that I had no motion of my own. I absolutely depended on the volition of my Guide, who said in gloomy tones, "Heed not thy brother; haply thou shalt have ample time hereafter to condole with him. Follow me."

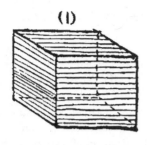

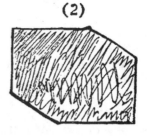

Once more we ascended into space. "Hitherto," said the Sphere, "I have shewn you naught save Plane Figures and their interiors. Now I must introduce you to Solids, and reveal to you the plan upon which they are constructed. Behold this multitude of moveable square cards. See, I put one on another, not, as you supposed, Northward of the other, but *on* the other. Now a second, now a third. See, I am building up a Solid by a multitude of Squares parallel to one another. Now the Solid is complete, being as high as it is long and broad, and we call it a Cube."

"Pardon me, my Lord," replied I; "but to my eye the appearance is as of an Irregular Figure whose inside is laid open to the view; in other words, methinks I see no Solid, but a Plane such as we infer in Flatland; only of an Irregularity which betokens some monstrous criminal, so that the very sight of it is painful to my eyes."

"True," said the Sphere, "it appears to you a Plane, because you are not accustomed to light and shade and perspective; just as in Flatland a Hexagon would appear a Straight Line to one who has not the Art of Sight Recognition. But in reality it is a Solid, as you shall learn by the sense of Feeling."[1]

He then introduced me to the Cube, and I found that this marvellous Being was indeed no Plane, but a Solid; and that he was endowed with six plane sides and eight terminal points called solid angles; and I remembered the saying of the Sphere that just such a Creature as this would be formed by a Square moving, in Space, parallel to himself: and I rejoiced to think that so insignif-

---

1 The Square must use the method of the lower classes and women to truly perceive. "Feeling" is also a punning reference to the emotions valued by the women but rejected by the male upper class.

icant a Creature as I could in some sense be called the Progenitor of so illustrious an offspring.

But still I could not fully understand the meaning of what my Teacher had told me concerning "light" and "shade" and "perspective"; and I did not hesitate to put my difficulties before him.

Were I to give the Sphere's explanation of these matters, succinct and clear though it was, it would be tedious to an inhabitant of Space, who knows these things already. Suffice it, that by his lucid statements, and by changing the position of objects and lights, and by allowing me to feel the several objects and even his own sacred Person, he at last made all things clear to me, so that I could now readily distinguish between a Circle and a Sphere, a Plane Figure and a Solid.

This was the Climax, the Paradise, of my strange eventful History. Henceforth I have to relate the story of my miserable Fall:—most miserable, yet surely most undeserved! For why should the thirst for knowledge be aroused, only to be disappointed and punished?[1] My volition shrinks from the painful task of recalling my humiliation; yet, like a second Prometheus,[2] I will endure this and worse, if by any means I may arouse in the interiors of Plane and Solid Humanity a spirit of rebellion against the Conceit which would limit our Dimensions to Two or Three or any number short of Infinity. Away then with all personal considerations! Let me continue to the end, as I began, without further digressions or anticipations, pursuing the plain path of dispassionate History. The exact facts, the exact words,—and they are burnt in upon my brain,—shall be set down without alteration of an iota; and let my Readers judge between me and Destiny.

The Sphere would willingly have continued his lessons by indoctrinating me in the conformation of all regular Solids, Cylinders, Cones, Pyramids, Pentahedrons, Hexahedrons, Dodecahedrons, and Spheres: but I ventured to interrupt him. Not that I was wearied of knowledge. On the contrary, I

---

1 An allusion to the expulsion of Adam and Eve from the Garden of Eden because of their desire for knowledge.

2 From Classical Greek creation myths dealing with the theme of forbidden knowledge. Prometheus was a god, one of the Titans, who angered Zeus by giving fire to men. He was punished by being chained to a rock, where an eagle ate his liver each day after it regenerated during the night.

thirsted for yet deeper and fuller draughts than he was offering to me.

"Pardon me," said I, "O Thou Whom I must no longer address as the Perfection of all Beauty; but let me beg thee to vouchsafe thy servant a sight of thine interior."

Sphere. My what?

I. Thine interior: thy stomach, thy intestines.

Sphere. Whence this ill-timed impertinent request? And what mean you by saying that I am no longer the Perfection of all Beauty?

I. My Lord, your own wisdom has taught me to aspire to One even more great, more beautiful, and more closely approximate to Perfection than yourself. As you yourself, superior to all Flatland forms, combine many Circles in One, so doubtless there is One above you who combines many Spheres in One Supreme Existence, surpassing even the Solids of Spaceland. And even as we, who are now in Space, look down on Flatland and see the insides of all things, so of a certainty there is yet above us some higher, purer region, whither thou dost surely purpose to lead me—O Thou Whom I shall always call, everywhere and in all Dimensions, my Priest, Philosopher, and Friend—some yet more spacious Space, some more dimensionable Dimensionality, from the vantage-ground of which we shall look down together upon the revealed insides of Solid things, and where thine own intestines, and those of thy kindred Spheres, will lie exposed to the view of the poor wandering exile from Flatland, to whom so much has already been vouchsafed.

Sphere. Pooh! Stuff! Enough of this trifling! The time is short, and much remains to be done before you are fit to proclaim the Gospel of Three Dimensions to your blind benighted countrymen in Flatland.

I. Nay, gracious Teacher, deny me not what I know it is in thy power to perform. Grant me but one glimpse of thine interior, and I am satisfied for ever, remaining henceforth thy docile pupil, thy unemancipable slave, ready to receive all thy teachings and to feed upon the words that fall from thy lips.

Sphere. Well, then, to content and silence you, let me say at once, I would shew you what you wish if I could; but I cannot. Would you have me turn my stomach inside out to oblige you?

I. But my Lord has shewn me the intestines of all my countrymen in the Land of Two Dimensions by taking me with him into the Land of Three. What therefore more easy than now to take his servant on a second journey into the blessed region of the Fourth Dimension, where I shall look down with him once more upon this land of Three Dimensions, and see the inside of every three-dimensioned house, the secrets of the solid earth, the treasures of the mines in Spaceland, and the intestines of every solid living creature, even of the noble and adorable Spheres.

Sphere. But where is this land of Four Dimensions?

I. I know not: but doubtless my Teacher knows.

Sphere. Not I. There is no such land. The very idea of it is utterly inconceivable.[1]

I. Not inconceivable, my Lord, to me, and therefore still less inconceivable to my Master. Nay, I despair not that, even here, in this region of Three Dimensions, your Lordship's art may make the Fourth Dimension visible to me; just as in the Land of Two Dimensions my Teacher's skill would fain have opened the eyes of his blind servant to the invisible presence of a Third Dimension, though I saw it not.

Let me recall the past. Was I not taught below that when I saw a Line and inferred a Plane, I in reality saw a Third unrecognized Dimension, not the same as brightness, called "height"? And does it not now follow that, in this region, when I see a Plane and infer a Solid, I really see a Fourth unrecognized Dimension, not the same as colour, but existent, though infinitesimal and incapable of measurement?

And besides this, there is the Argument from Analogy of Figures.

Sphere. Analogy! Nonsense: what analogy?[2]

I. Your Lordship tempts his servant to see whether he remembers the revelations imparted to him. Trifle not with me, my Lord; I crave, I thirst, for more knowledge. Doubtless we cannot *see* that other higher Spaceland now, because we have no eye in our stomachs. But, just as there *was* the realm of Flatland, though that poor puny Lineland Monarch could neither turn to left nor right to discern it, and just as there *was* close at hand, and touching my frame, the land of Three Dimensions, though I, blind senseless wretch, had no power to touch it, no eye in my interior

---

1 Here the Square reveals the Sphere's own limitations. The next lines are the added dialogue alluded to by Abbott in his preface to the revised edition.

2 This line ends the dialogue added to the revised edition.

to discern it, so of a surety there is a Fourth Dimension, which my Lord perceives with the inner eye of thought. And that it must exist my Lord himself has taught me. Or can he have forgotten what he himself imparted to his servant?

In One Dimension, did not a moving Point produce a Line with *two* terminal points?

In Two Dimensions, did not a moving Line produce a Square with *four* terminal points?

In Three Dimensions, did not a moving Square produce—did not this eye of mine behold it—that blessed Being, a Cube, with *eight* terminal points?

And in Four Dimensions shall not a moving Cube—alas, for Analogy, and alas for the Progress of Truth, if it be not so—shall not, I say, the motion of a divine Cube result in a still more divine Organization with *sixteen* terminal points?

Behold the infallible confirmation of the Series, 2, 4, 8, 16: is not this a Geometrical Progression? Is not this—if I might quote my Lord's own words—"strictly according to Analogy"?

Again, was I not taught by my Lord that as in a Line there are *two* bounding Points, and in a Square there are *four* bounding Lines, so in a Cube there must be *six* bounding Squares? Behold once more the confirming Series, 2, 4, 6: is not this an Arithmetical Progression? And consequently does it not of necessity follow that the more divine offspring of the divine Cube in the Land of Four Dimensions, must have *eight* bounding Cubes: and is not this also, as my Lord has taught me to believe, "strictly according to Analogy"?

O, my Lord, my Lord, behold, I cast myself in faith upon conjecture, not knowing the facts; and I appeal to your Lordship to confirm or deny my logical anticipations. If I am wrong, I yield, and will no longer demand a Fourth Dimension; but, if I am right, my Lord will listen to reason.

I ask therefore, is it, or is it not, the fact, that ere now your countrymen also have witnessed the descent of Beings of a higher order than their own, entering closed rooms, even as your Lordship entered mine, without the opening of doors or windows, and appearing and vanishing at will? On the reply to this question I am ready to stake everything. Deny it, and I am henceforth silent. Only vouchsafe an answer.

Sphere (after a pause). It is reported so. But men are divided in opinion as to the facts. And even granting the facts, they explain them in different ways. And in any case, however great may be the number of different explanations, no one has adopted or suggested the theory of a Fourth Dimension. Therefore, pray have done with this trifling, and let us return to business.

I. I was certain of it. I was certain that my anticipations would be fulfilled. And now have patience with me and answer me yet one more question, best of Teachers! Those who have thus appeared—no one knows whence—and have returned—no one knows whither—have they also contracted their sections and vanished somehow into that more Spacious Space, whither I now entreat you to conduct me?

Sphere (*moodily*). They have vanished, certainly—if they ever appeared. But most people say that these visions arose from the thought—you will not understand me—from the brain; from the perturbed angularity of the Seer.

I. Say they so? Oh, believe them not. Or if it indeed be so, that this other Space is really Thoughtland, then take me to that blessed Region where I in Thought shall see the insides of all solid things. There, before my ravished eye, a Cube, moving in some altogether new direction, but strictly according to Analogy, so as to make every particle of his interior pass through a new kind of Space, with a wake of its own—shall create a still more perfect perfection than himself, with sixteen terminal Extra-solid angles, and Eight solid Cubes for his Perimeter. And once there, shall we stay our upward course? In that blessed region of Four Dimensions, shall we linger on the threshold of the Fifth, and not enter therein? Ah, no! Let us rather resolve that our ambition shall soar with our corporal ascent. Then, yielding to our intellectual onset, the gates of the Sixth Dimension shall fly open; after that a Seventh, and then an Eighth—

How long I should have continued I know not. In vain did the Sphere, in his voice of thunder, reiterate his command of silence, and threaten me with the direst penalties if I persisted. Nothing could stem the flood of my ecstatic aspirations. Perhaps I was to blame; but indeed I was intoxicated with the recent draughts of Truth to which he himself had introduced me. However, the end was not long in coming. My words were cut short by a crash outside, and a simultaneous crash inside me, which impelled me through space with a velocity that precluded speech. Down! down! down! I was rapidly descending;[1] and I knew that return to Flatland was my doom. One glimpse, one last and never-to-be-

---

1 Another likely reference to the Alice books, this time suggestive of Alice going down the rabbit hole, but here the Square is returning to, not entering, another world.

forgotten glimpse I had of that dull level wilderness—which was now to become my Universe again—spread out before my eye. Then a darkness. Then a final, all-consummating thunder-peal; and, when I came to myself, I was once more a common creeping Square, in my Study at home, listening to the Peace-Cry of my approaching Wife.

Section 20. How the Sphere encouraged me in a vision

Although I had less than a minute for reflection, I felt, by a kind of instinct, that I must conceal my experiences from my Wife. Not that I apprehended, at the moment, any danger from her divulging my secret, but I knew that to any Woman in Flatland the narrative of my adventures must needs be unintelligible. So I endeavoured to reassure her by some story, invented for the occasion, that I had accidentally fallen through the trap-door of the cellar, and had there lain stunned.[1]

The Southward attraction in our country is so slight that even to a Woman my tale necessarily appeared extraordinary and well-nigh incredible; but my Wife, whose good sense far exceeds that of the average of her Sex, and who perceived that I was unusually excited, did not argue with me on the subject, but insisted that I was ill and required repose. I was glad of an excuse for retiring to my chamber to think quietly over what had happened. When I was at last by myself, a drowsy sensation fell on me; but before my eyes closed I endeavoured to reproduce the Third Dimension, and especially the process by which a Cube is constructed through the motion of a Square. It was not so clear as I could have wished; but I remembered that it must be "Upward, and yet not Northward,"[2] and I determined steadfastly to retain these words as the clue which, if firmly grasped, could not fail to guide me to the solution. So mechanically repeating, like a charm, the words, "Upward, yet not Northward," I fell into a sound refreshing sleep.

During my slumber I had a dream. I thought I was once more by the side of the Sphere, whose lustrous hue betokened that he had exchanged his wrath against me for perfect placability. We were moving together towards a bright but infinitesimally small

---

1 An apparent physical impossibility in two dimensions.
2 Another echo of Plato's argument that the study of geometry will draw the mind to the truth (see Appendix B1).

Point, to which my Master directed my attention. As we approached, methought there issued from it a slight humming noise as from one of your Spaceland blue-bottles,[1] only less resonant by far, so slight indeed that even in the perfect stillness of the Vacuum through which we soared, the sound reached not our ears till we checked our flight at a distance from it of something under twenty human diagonals.

"Look yonder," said my Guide, "in Flatland thou hast lived; of Lineland thou hast received a vision; thou hast soared with me to the heights of Spaceland; now, in order to complete the range of thy experience, I conduct thee downward to the lowest depth of existence, even to the realm of Pointland, the Abyss of No dimensions.

"Behold yon miserable creature. That Point is a Being like ourselves, but confined to the non-dimensional Gulf. He is himself his own World, his own Universe; of any other than himself he can form no conception; he knows not Length, nor Breadth, nor Height, for he has had no experience of them; he has no cognizance even of the number Two; nor has he a thought of Plurality; for he is himself his One and All, being really Nothing. Yet mark his perfect self-contentment, and hence learn this lesson, that to be self-contented is to be vile and ignorant, and that to aspire is better than to be blindly and impotently happy. Now listen."

He ceased; and there arose from the little buzzing creature a tiny, low, monotonous, but distinct tinkling, as from one of your Spaceland phonographs,[2] from which I caught these words, "Infinite beatitude of existence! It is; and there is none else beside It."

"What," said I, "does the puny creature mean by 'it'?" "He means himself," said the Sphere: "have you not noticed before now, that babies and babyish people who cannot distinguish themselves from the world, speak of themselves in the Third Person? But hush!"

"It fills all Space," continued the little soliloquizing Creature, "and what It fills, It is. What It thinks, that It utters; and what It utters, that It hears; and It itself is Thinker, Utterer, Hearer,

---

1 An insect, a type of fly.
2 This is a reference to Thomas A. Edison's tinfoil phonograph, the invention of which was announced in 1878. The wax cylinder came later. The phonograph must have been known to Abbott through demonstrations, as it was not brought to the market until 1887.

Thought, Word, Audition; it is the One, and yet the All in All. Ah, the happiness, ah, the happiness of Being!"

"Can you not startle the little thing out of its complacency?" said I. "Tell it what it really is, as you told me; reveal to it the narrow limitations of Pointland, and lead it up to something higher."[1] "That is no easy task," said my Master; "try you."

Hereon, raising my voice to the uttermost, I addressed the Point as follows:

"Silence, silence, contemptible Creature. You call yourself the All in All, but you are the Nothing: your so-called Universe is a mere speck in a Line, and a Line is a mere shadow as compared with—" "Hush, hush, you have said enough," interrupted the Sphere, "now listen, and mark the effect of your harangue on the King of Pointland."

The lustre of the Monarch, who beamed more brightly than ever upon hearing my words, shewed clearly that he retained his complacency; and I had hardly ceased when he took up his strain again. "Ah, the joy, ah, the joy of Thought! What can It not achieve by thinking! Its own Thought coming to Itself, suggestive of Its disparagement, thereby to enhance Its happiness! Sweet rebellion stirred up to result in triumph! Ah, the divine creative power of the All in One! Ah, the joy, the joy of Being!"

"You see," said my Teacher, "how little your words have done. So far as the Monarch understands them at all, he accepts them as his own—for he cannot conceive of any other except himself—and plumes himself upon the variety of 'Its Thought' as an instance of creative Power. Let us leave this God of Pointland to the ignorant fruition of his omnipresence and omniscience: nothing that you or I can do can rescue him from his self-satisfaction."

After this, as we floated gently back to Flatland, I could hear the mild voice of my Companion pointing the moral of my vision, and stimulating me to aspire, and to teach others to aspire. He had been angered at first—he confessed—by my ambition to soar to Dimensions above the Third; but, since then, he had received fresh insight, and he was not too proud to acknowledge his error to a Pupil. Then he proceeded to initiate me into mysteries yet higher than those I had witnessed, shewing me how to construct Extra-Solids by the motion of Solids, and Double Extra-Solids by the motion of Extra-Solids, and all "strictly according to

---

1 Having had his own complacency shaken, the Square is eager to inflict a similar shaking on others.

Analogy," all by methods so simple, so easy, as to be patent even to the Female Sex.

Section 21. How I tried to teach the Theory of Three Dimensions to my Grandson, and with what success

I awoke rejoicing, and began to reflect on the glorious career before me. I would go forth, methought, at once, and evangelize the whole of Flatland. Even to Women and Soldiers should the Gospel of Three Dimensions be proclaimed. I would begin with my Wife.

Just as I had decided on the plan of my operations, I heard the sound of many voices in the street commanding silence. Then followed a louder voice. It was a herald's proclamation. Listening attentively, I recognized the words of the Resolution of the Council, enjoining the arrest, imprisonment, or execution of any one who should pervert the minds of the people by delusions, and by professing to have received revelations from another World.

I reflected. This danger was not to be trifled with. It would be better to avoid it by omitting all mention of my Revelation, and by proceeding on the path of Demonstration—which after all, seemed so simple and so conclusive that nothing would be lost by discarding the former means. "Upward, not Northward"—was the clue to the whole proof. It had seemed to me fairly clear before I fell asleep; and when I first awoke, fresh from my dream, it had appeared as patent as Arithmetic; but somehow it did not seem to me quite so obvious now. Though my Wife entered the room opportunely just at that moment, I decided, after we had exchanged a few words of commonplace conversation, not to begin with her.

My Pentagonal Sons were men of character and standing, and physicians of no mean reputation, but not great in mathematics, and, in that respect, unfit for my purpose. But it occurred to me that a young and docile Hexagon, with a mathematical turn, would be a most suitable pupil. Why therefore not make my first experiment with my little precocious Grandson, whose casual remarks on the meaning of 3^3 had met with the approval of the Sphere? Discussing the matter with him, a mere boy, I should be in perfect safety; for he would know nothing of the Proclamation of the Council; whereas I could not feel sure that my Sons—so greatly did their patriotism and reverence for the Circles predominate over mere blind affection—might not feel compelled to hand me over to the Prefect, if they found me seriously maintaining the seditious heresy of the Third Dimension.[1]

But the first thing to be done was to satisfy in some way the curiosity of my Wife, who naturally wished to know something of the reasons for which the Circle had desired that mysterious interview, and of the means by which he had entered the house. Without entering into the details of the elaborate account I gave her,—an account, I fear, not quite so consistent with truth as my Readers in Spaceland might desire,— I must be content with saying that I succeeded at last in persuading her to return quietly to her household duties without eliciting from me any reference to the World of Three Dimensions. This done, I immediately sent for my Grandson; for, to confess the truth, I felt that all that I had seen and heard was in some strange way slipping away from me, like the image of a half-grasped, tantalizing dream, and I longed to essay my skill in making a first disciple.

When my Grandson entered the room I carefully secured the door. Then, sitting down by his side and taking our mathematical tablets,—or, as you would call them, Lines—I told him we would resume the lesson of yesterday. I taught him once more how a Point by motion in One Dimension produces a Line, and how a straight Line in Two Dimensions produces a Square. After this, forcing a laugh, I said, "And now, you scamp, you wanted to make me believe that a Square may in the same way by motion 'Upward, not Northward' produce another figure, a sort of extra Square in Three Dimensions. Say that again, you young rascal."

At this moment we heard once more the herald's "O yes! O yes!"[2] outside in the street proclaiming the Resolution of the Council. Young though he was, my Grandson—who was unusually intelligent for his age, and bred up in perfect reverence for the authority of the Circles—took in the situation with an acuteness for which I was quite unprepared. He remained silent till the last words of the Proclamation had died away, and then, bursting into tears, "Dear Grandpapa," he said, "that was only my fun, and of course I meant nothing at all by it; and we did not know anything then about the new Law; and I don't think I said any-

---

1   Flatland appears to be a police state. The Square cannot trust his own sons not to turn him in. It is not clear if he does not trust his wife or feels she would be endangered by the information.

2   The town-crier's call—here a phonetic rendering (and mistranslation) of the French "oyez" or "hear ye."

thing about the Third Dimension; and I am sure I did not say one word about 'Upward, not Northward,' for that would be such nonsense, you know. How could a thing move Upward, and not Northward? Upward and not Northward! Even if I were a baby, I could not be so absurd as that. How silly it is! Ha! ha! ha!"[1]

"Not at all silly," said I, losing my temper; "here for example, I take this Square," and, at the word, I grasped a moveable Square, which was lying at hand—"and I move it, you see, not Northward but—yes, I move it Upward—that is to say, not Northward, but I move it somewhere—not exactly like this, but somehow—" Here I brought my sentence to an inane conclusion, shaking the Square about in a purposeless manner, much to the amusement of my Grandson, who burst out laughing louder than ever, and declared that I was not teaching him, but joking with him; and so saying he unlocked the door and ran out of the room. Thus ended my first attempt to convert a pupil to the Gospel of Three Dimensions.

Section 22. How I then tried to diffuse the Theory of Three Dimensions by other means, and of the result

My failure with my Grandson did not encourage me to communicate my secret to others of my household; yet neither was I led by it to despair of success. Only I saw that I must not wholly rely on the catch-phrase, "Upward, not Northward," but must rather endeavour to seek a demonstration by setting before the public a clear view of the whole subject; and for this purpose it seemed necessary to resort to writing.

So I devoted several months in privacy to the composition of a treatise on the mysteries of Three Dimensions. Only, with the view of evading the Law, if possible, I spoke not of a physical Dimension, but of a Thoughtland whence, in theory, a Figure could look down upon Flatland and see simultaneously the insides of all things, and where it was possible that there might be supposed to exist a Figure environed, as it were, with six Squares, and containing eight terminal Points. But in writing this book I found myself sadly hampered by the impossibility of drawing such diagrams as were necessary for my purpose; for of course, in our country of Flatland, there are no tablets but Lines, and no

---

1 The Grandson has learned not to trust anyone, including his grandfather, and fears entrapment.

diagrams but Lines, all in one straight Line and only distinguishable by difference of size and brightness; so that, when I had finished my treatise (which I entitled, "Through Flatland to Thoughtland"[1]) I could not feel certain that many would understand my meaning.

Meanwhile my life was under a cloud. All pleasures palled upon me; all sights tantalized and tempted me to outspoken treason, because I could not but compare what I saw in Two Dimensions with what it really was if seen in Three, and could hardly refrain from making my comparisons aloud. I neglected my clients and my own business to give myself to the contemplation of the mysteries which I had once beheld, yet which I could impart to no one, and found daily more difficult to reproduce even before my own mental vision.

One day, about eleven months after my return from Spaceland, I tried to see a Cube with my eye closed, but failed; and though I succeeded afterwards, I was not then quite certain (nor have I been ever afterwards) that I had exactly realized the original. This made me more melancholy than before, and determined me to take some step; yet what, I knew not. I felt that I would have been willing to sacrifice my life for the Cause, if thereby I could have produced conviction. But if I could not convince my Grandson, how could I convince the highest and most developed Circles in the land?

And yet at times my spirit was too strong for me, and I gave vent to dangerous utterances. Already I was considered heterodox if not treasonable, and I was keenly alive to the danger of my position; nevertheless I could not at times refrain from bursting out into suspicious or half-seditious utterances, even among the highest Polygonal and Circular society. When, for example, the question arose about the treatment of those lunatics who said that they had received the power of seeing the insides of things, I would quote the saying of an ancient Circle, who declared that prophets and inspired people are always considered by the majority to be mad; and I could not help occasionally dropping such expressions as "the eye that discerns the interiors of things," and "the all-seeing land"; once or twice I even let fall the forbidden terms "the Third and Fourth Dimensions." At last, to complete a series of minor indiscretions, at a meeting of our Local Speculative Society held at the palace of the Prefect himself,—some

---

1 Abbott's 1877 theological work was titled *Through Nature to Christ, or, The Ascent of Worship through Illusion to the Truth.*

extremely silly person having read an elaborate paper exhibiting the precise reasons why Providence has limited the number of Dimensions to Two, and why the attribute of omnividence is assigned to the Supreme alone[1]—I so far forgot myself as to give an exact account of the whole of my voyage with the Sphere into Space, and to the Assembly Hall in our Metropolis, and then to Space again, and of my return home, and of everything that I had seen and heard in fact or vision. At first, indeed, I pretended that I was describing the imaginary experiences of a fictitious person; but my enthusiasm soon forced me to throw off all disguise, and finally, in a fervent peroration, I exhorted all my hearers to divest themselves of prejudice and to become believers in the Third Dimension.

Need I say that I was at once arrested and taken before the Council?[2]

Next morning, standing in the very place where but a very few months ago the Sphere had stood in my company, I was allowed to begin and to continue my narration unquestioned and uninterrupted. But from the first I foresaw my fate; for the President, noting that a guard of the better sort of Policemen was in attendance, of angularity little, if at all, under 55°, ordered them to be relieved before I began my defence, by an inferior class of 2° or 3°. I knew only too well what that meant. I was to be executed or imprisoned, and my story was to be kept secret from the world by the simultaneous destruction of the officials who had heard it;

---

1 A reference to the Natural Theology arguments of William Paley (1743-1805), who encouraged the study of nature in order to reach a better understanding of God. In *Evidences of Christianity* (1794) and *Natural Theology* (1802) he argued that the presence of design in nature proved the existence of God. As required reading for students studying for the ministry, his writing inspired some trite and comical theological arguments.

2 The imprisonment of the philosopher has a long history. In addition to Galileo's imprisonment, prison is addressed as a likely outcome when those who venture outside the cave attempt to communicate what they have seen to those still in the cave. See Plato's *Republic* (517d-e): "Nor will you think it strange that anyone who descends from contemplation of the divine to human life and its ills should blunder and make a fool of himself, if, while still blinded and unaccustomed to the surrounding darkness, he's forcibly put on trial in the law-courts or elsewhere about the shadows of justice or the figures of which they are shadows, and made to dispute about the notions of them held by men who have never seen justice itself."

and, this being the case, the President desired to substitute the cheaper for the more expensive victims.

After I had concluded my defence, the President, perhaps perceiving that some of the junior Circles had been moved by my evident earnestness, asked me two questions:—

1. Whether I could indicate the direction which I meant when I used the words "Upward, not Northward"?

2. Whether I could by any diagrams or descriptions (other than the enumeration of imaginary sides and angles) indicate the Figure I was pleased to call a Cube?

I declared that I could say nothing more, and that I must commit myself to the Truth, whose cause would surely prevail in the end.

The President replied that he quite concurred in my sentiment, and that I could not do better. I must be sentenced to perpetual imprisonment; but if the Truth intended that I should emerge from prison and evangelize the world, the Truth might be trusted to bring that result to pass. Meanwhile I should be subjected to no discomfort that was not necessary to preclude escape, and, unless I forfeited the privilege by misconduct, I should be occasionally permitted to see my brother who had preceded me to my prison.

Seven years have elapsed and I am still a prisoner, and—if I except the occasional visits of my brother—debarred from all companionship save that of my jailers. My brother is one of the best of Squares, just, sensible, cheerful, and not without fraternal affection; yet I confess that my weekly interviews, at least in one respect, cause me the bitterest pain. He was present when the Sphere manifested himself in the Council Chamber; he saw the Sphere's changing sections; he heard the explanation of the phenomena then given to the Circles. Since that time, scarcely a week has passed during seven whole years, without his hearing from me a repetition of the part I played in that manifestation, together with ample descriptions of all the phenomena in Spaceland, and the arguments for the existence of Solid things derivable from Analogy. Yet—I take shame to be forced to confess it— my brother has not yet grasped the nature of the Third Dimension, and frankly avows his disbelief in the existence of a Sphere.

Hence I am absolutely destitute of converts, and, for aught that I can see, the millennial Revelation has been made to me for nothing. Prometheus up in Spaceland was bound for bringing down fire for mortals, but I—poor Flatland Prometheus—lie here in prison for bringing down nothing to my countrymen. Yet I exist in the hope that these memoirs, in some manner, I know not how, may find their way to the minds of humanity in Some Dimension, and may stir up a race of rebels who shall refuse to be confined to limited Dimensionality.

That is the hope of my brighter moments. Alas, it is not always so. Heavily weighs on me at times the burdensome reflection that I cannot honestly say I am confident as to the exact shape of the once-seen, oft-regretted Cube; and in my nightly visions the mysterious precept, "Upward, not Northward," haunts me like a soul-devouring Sphinx.[1] It is part of the martyrdom which I endure for the cause of the Truth that there are seasons of mental weakness, when Cubes and Spheres flit away into the background of scarce-possible existences; when the Land of Three Dimensions seems almost as visionary as the Land of One or None; nay, when even this hard wall that bars me from my freedom, these very tablets on which I am writing, and all the substantial realities of Flatland itself, appear no better than the offspring of a diseased imagination, or the baseless fabric of a dream.

---

1 The female monster defeated by Oedipus. This classical image was popular in late Victorian art and design. In 1884, the date of *Flatland*'s publication, an edition of Edward Fitzgerald's translation of *The Rubaiyat of Omar Khayyam* (1859) was illustrated by Elihu Vedder, an American artist (1836-1923). One illustration was that of *The Sphinx of the Seashore*, where the Sphinx is painted in dark reddish tones and shown sprawled over a heap of bones and machinery, meant to represent remnants of civilizations.

2 The ending of *Flatland* moves smoothly into the end-page illustration. The caption "The End of Flatland" has lines from *The Tempest* interwoven among the clouds:

"The baseless fabric of my vision
Melted into air thin air
Such stuff as dreams made on."
These words are selections from the well-known speech of Prospero in
The Tempest, IV.i.148-63. The full passage is as follows:
"Our revels now are ended. These our actors,
As I foretold you, were all spirits and
Are melted into air, into thin air:
And, like the baseless fabric of this vision,
The cloud-capp'd towers, the gorgeous palaces,
The solemn temples, the great globe itself,
Yea, all which it inherit, shall dissolve
And, like this insubstantial pageant faded,
Leave not a rack behind. We are such stuff
As dreams are made on, and our little life
Is rounded with a sleep.—Sir, I am vex'd,
Bear with my weakness; my old brain is troubled.
Be not disturb'd with my infirmity.
If you be pleas'd, retire into my cell
And there repose: a turn or two I'll walk,
To still my beating mind."
The final lines are suggestive of the Square's state of mind as he is left
in his prison cell. A "rack" is a wisp of cloud, suggested by the illustra-
tion. In the first edition, the words "The End of Flatland" are set hori-
zontally. Beneath is a line and the printer's legend: London: R. Clay,
Sons, and Taylor, Printers. In the revised edition, "The End of Flatland"
is set at a slant.

Appendix A: Contemporary Reviews

1. *The Oxford Magazine* (5 November 1884): 387

Mr. A²—we beg his pardon, Mr. A. Square—must be congratulated upon his able attempt to realise the existence of intelligent beings whose experience, acquired and inherited, relates to space of two dimensions or even one dimension only.[1] Persons who would be alarmed by the very title of Helmholtz's essay, "On the Origin and Significance of Geometrical Axioms,"[2] may gather from this book that those rash mathematicians who believe in the possibility of space of four or more dimensions have, to say the very least, some method in their madness. The author has, we think, rendered it tolerably evident that our own kind of space would be quite as incomprehensible to a Flatlander as space of four dimensions is to ourselves.

The *sauce piquante*[3] necessary to render these unpalatable ideas capable of assimilation by the general reader contains amongst its ingredients many sly hits at the inhabitants of Spaceland, who will doubtless thank the author for thus indicating the application of his fable, instead of adopting the irritating method for which Aesop[4] must be held responsible.

The humour of such a *jeu d'esprit*[5] cannot be given by extracts. If we were not afraid of spoiling the book for others, we should like to discourse of the feminine fashions in Flatland, and hint at the momentous subject of the Universal Colour Bill: above all, we should like to give at length the conversation of the dweller in Flatland with the Sphere of the higher world, on whom he retorts the argument of Analogy with such fatal consequences. But all these we will leave to the reader, confident that he will move safely in these worlds not realised, with so clear a map of the country as the frontispiece provides him with.

This book is at once a popular scientific treatise of great merit, and

---

1 The reviewer has identified the various ways of reading the character's name.
2 See Appendix B2.
3 French cooking term: spicy sauce.
4 Reference to Aesop's *Fables*, a collection of classical tales featuring animals, which always end with an instructive moral.
5 From the French: "play of spirit." A light-hearted or humorous literary piece, usually applied to pieces quickly dashed off in fun.

a fairy tale worthy to rank with *The Water Babies*[1] and *Alice in Wonderland*.[2] Those points which might call for criticism from one point of view are in general amply justified by the other.

It might seem, for instance, that the author has needlessly restricted the play of his fertile imagination by limiting the forms of his Flatlanders to lines, triangles, and regular figures. No doubt closed curves of nearly constant area, capable, to some extent, of changing their form, but always preserving certain well-marked *singularities*, would have more easily afforded scope for those tender situations which, reasoning from analogy, should grace the lighter literature of Flatland. Such a modification would, however, have placed the idea of flatness less prominently before the mind of the non-mathematical reader, and would have prevented the author from taking advantage of one of the, we venture to think, few points in which Flatland is superior to its more familiar analogue. No Spacelander, constructed upon similar principles, and free from the fatal blemish of irregularity, could possibly possess more than twenty faces.

Gratitude has been defined as "a lively sense of favours to come,"[3] and this must be our excuse for coupling with our best thanks to Mr. A. Square for his amusing volume, a hope that he may ere long make a fresh venture in the little-explored field of the Romance of Mathematics.

---

1 *The Water-Babies* was written by Rev. Charles Kingsley (1819-75) and first serialized in *Macmillan's Magazine* in 1862-63. Kingsley's novels attempted to address social and spiritual controversies. While supposedly intended for children, *The Water-Babies* focuses on several issues: child labor, education, health, and narrow-minded religious beliefs. Two striking elements are his view of evolution as a means toward higher consciousness and the strong moral message that lazy behavior will cause racial degeneration. There are several humorous pokes at contemporary scientific debates, especially regarding comparative anatomy as an argument for natural selection. Although very supportive of Darwinian evolution, Kingsley did not fully understand how natural selection worked and makes several assumptions based on the evolutionary theory of Jean-Baptiste Lamarck (1744-1829).

2 Similar to Kingsley's work, Lewis Carroll's *Alice in Wonderland* (1865) presents scientific material in a fable-like manner. Lewis Carroll is the pseudonym for Charles Dodgson (1832-98), a mathematician at Cambridge, and *Alice in Wonderland* presents a wealth of logic exercises in an entertaining manner. The two comparisons made by this reviewer are apt.

3 A common nineteenth-century quoted phrase, sometimes ascribed to Victor Hugo. In the male Flatlander's vocabulary, "Love" means "the anticipation of benefits" (Sec. 12).

2. From *The Literary World* (London) (14 November 1884): 389-99

Whoever the author of this remarkable mathematical allegory may be, his cleverly elaborated fancy is not only likely to create a present sensation in the thinking world, but also to find an abiding place in the classic domains of the great satires of history.[1] The subject is too abstruse, and involves too many metaphysical speculations expressed in geometrical terms, to appeal to the multitude with the fascination exerted by the immortal allegories of Bunyan[2] and Swift,[3] whose simplicity is their strength; and it may, therefore, share the fate of the Fairy Queen[4] and Rabelais' Romance[5] in being reserved for the delectation of the favoured few. Its irony, though severe, is delicate, and its interpretation not always easy. It is cast in the historical and descriptive, rather than the dramatic form. These facts may limit the number of those capable of appreciating it, as may a certain likeness in it here and there to the precise and formal lessons demonstrated on a blackboard to a class of schoolboys. But older scholars and fellow-teachers will admire the perspicuity and skill with which these difficult and original lessons are taught. In working out the details of his humour the writer has aimed his shafts sometimes at the world of society, sometimes at that of politics, sometimes at that of religion. His references are now plain and palpable, now recondite and obscure. But about the broad drift of his parable there can be no mistake whatever. His allegory is in the chiefest of its aspects a magnificent protest against self-sufficiency and dogmatism; against cherishing the idea

---

1 This line was used in Seeley and Company's advertisement for *Flatland* in the 20 December 1884 issue of *The Athenaeum*.

2 John Bunyan (1628-88), author of the Puritan allegory *The Pilgrim's Progess* (1678, 1684), once found next to the Bible in every nineteenth-century home.

3 Jonathan Swift (1667-1745), Anglo-Irish satirist, author of *Gulliver's Travels* (1726), whose protagonist, Lemuel Gulliver, experienced perception-changing experiences while traveling in different kingdoms where the inhabitants were tiny (Lilliput), giants (Brobdingnag), or horses (Houyhnhnms). One kingdom, Laputa, a flying island and home of mathematicians and abstract thinkers, is a satire on the seventeenth-century scientific society, the Royal Society. Swift used Gulliver's observations to comment on human nature and the politics of his time.

4 The Fairy Queen refers to *The Faerie Queene* (1590, 1596), an allegorical epic poem by Edmund Spenser (c. 1552-99), written in praise of Queen Elizabeth I.

5 A reference to François Rabelais's (c. 1494-1553) bawdy satire *Gargantua and Pantagruel*, which tells of the adventures of two giants. Rabelais's grotesque description, like Swift's, makes use of changes in scale for humorous effects.

that we have, in reference to any matter of experience whatever, seen the end of all perfection; against all narrowness, bigotry, and intolerance in any region of supposed knowledge, whether that of scientific self-assurance on the one hand, or religious fanaticism on the other. In emphasizing this doctrine the writer has availed himself of the idea, mooted some years ago by a great mathematician, that there might be states of existence blessed with more dimensions than those with which we ourselves are acquainted.[1] Our experience has only told us of three—length, breadth, and height. But why should there not be more? And in a world in which there are more, what vaster revelations of ourselves, our present life, and our surroundings might be possible than those which we at present possess! Now, no flight of fancy will enable us to jump into a world of four dimensions; but we can imagine the conditions of existence in a world which has only two, or less than two; and this is what the author has done. We cannot add an additional faculty to our beings; but we can guess what it would be like to be deprived of some we already enjoy. We know not in what direction to grope for a sixth sense; but we can tell the loss we should sustain in being deprived of those,—say sight,—hitherto belonging to us. Flatland is the realm of the superficial, on or *in* the surface of which creatures animate and inanimate exist, without either rising above or sinking below it. They have length and breadth, but neither height nor depth. In such a state, there can be no solids but every thing and every being is a *plane* figure. Society there is divided into the well-known shapes that appear in the pages of Euclid. The word spoken in jest by the wit, who retorted on an enraged and abusive fishwoman with the remark that she was an isosceles triangle, would have been taken solemnly and understood literally in Flatland.[2] The narrator of the story is a Square. His wife is a Straight Line. His father is a Triangle, his sons are Pentagons, and his grandson a Hexagon. Social distinctions in Flatland are determined by these shapes. Manysidedness is characteristic of the highest class, and angularity—in the sense of extreme acuteness of the vertex—of the lowest. At the aristocratic end of society are Polygons, so many-cornered as to approach circles; at the plebeian extremity Isosceles Triangles, so narrow as to approach straight

---

1 Possibly a reference to Hermann von Helmholtz's essay, "The Axioms of Geometry" (1870). See Appendix B2.

2 A humorous account generally attributed to Daniel O'Connell (1775-1847), leader of the Irish Repeal Association. In *Heroes of the Exile* (1852), Karl Marx and Friedrich Engels make reference to this jest, describing someone as being "like that Billingsgate fishwife with whom O'Connell became involved in a shouting match and whom he silenced by replying to a long string of insults: 'You are all that and worse: you are an isosceles triangle, you are a parallelepiped'" (Chapter 6).

lines. The necessary conditions of his problem seem to us to have been ably anticipated by the author. The chemical wizardry by which Jules Verne makes it seem practicable to travel across Africa in a balloon pales before the mathematical and optical enchantments of this literary conjurer.[1] In his Flatland, of course, there are no shadows, as with us in Spaceland; nor are there sun or stars visible to the inhabitants. Light is diffused from an unknown source, and so fierce have been the speculations as to its origin, that legal enactments have been passed to restrain such inquiries. But without sun, star, or shadow how could the people in Flatland tell their position; or how could they distinguish one another? Although the writer solves these problems one after another with great ability, he yet states them so formally that we never can get rid altogether of the idea that we are going through an educational course rather than reading a story. For the answers to many of them we must refer to the volume itself. But here is an instance of [a quotation from section 5 follows]

Recognition in Flatland

Feeling is, among our Women and lower classes—about our upper classes I shall speak presently—the principal test of recognition, at all events between strangers, and when the question is, not as to the individual, but as to the class.

. . .

Even a Master of Arts in our University of Wentbridge has been known to confuse a ten-sided with a twelve-sided Polygon; and there is hardly a Doctor of Science in or out of that famous University who could pretend to decide promptly and unhesitatingly between a twenty-sided and a twenty-four-sided member of the Aristocracy. [end of quotation]

Two matters claim our especial attention in this division of the allegory; the one is the condition of the women of Flatland, and the other the relation between the governing classes and the lower orders. The women, as being entirely destitute of brain power, which is always situated in one of the angles of the figure, have no angles at all, and are simply straight lines. But they are extremely dangerous lines, "being, so to speak, *all* point, at least, at the two extremities," and capable of running into, and then wounding fatally any male creature that comes in their way. The statesmen of Flatland have had much work to cope with this perpetual source of danger; for the women are not only lethally pointed, but in such a shadowless realm they are practically invisible as well. Among other precautions, therefore, to prevent acci-

---

1 Jules Verne (1828-1905), French science-fiction writer. Known for several imaginative adventure stories, his first novel was *Five Weeks in a Balloon, or, Journeys and Discoveries in Africa by Three Englishmen* (1863).

dental injuries being inflicted by women in public, it has been ordered in some States that when in public they should always move their backs from right to left, "so as to indicate their presence to those behind them." [a summary of the plot of *Flatland* follows]

. . .

But this creature of Pointland is only the beginning of the scale of those who will not open their eyes to the light. As he of Pointland cannot bring himself to believe in the possibilities of Lineland; nor he of Lineland in those of Flatland; nor he of Flatland in those of Spaceland; so we of the latter region are prone to think that our own horizon is the limit of existence. But this story of surfaces and squares and cubes may well serve to shake out of their conceited complacency the whole race of dogmatists, whether they belong to the schools of philosophy, science, or religion.

3. The Exchange with *The Athenaeum* (November-December 1884)

[Abbott became involved in an exchange in print with Arthur John Butler, the reviewer for *The Athenaeum*. Taking on the persona of his character, A Square, Abbott's response became incorporated into the revisions of *Flatland*. Although Abbott does not address spiritualism in his reply, Butler's comment about Flatland being read as enforcing spiritualist doctrine may have helped motivate his response. Abbott argued for a rational approach to religious belief in his writings on theology. In his later writings, such as *The Spirit on the Water* (1897; see Appendix C2), Abbott spoke out against the use of higher dimensions as an explanation of miraculous phenomena.]

The Athenaeum No. 2977 (15 November 1884): 622
[Arthur John Butler][1]

That whimsical book *Flatland* by a Square (Seeley & Co.), seems to have a purpose, but what that may be it is hard to discover. At first it read as if it were intended to teach young people the elementary principles of geometry. Next it seemed to have been written in support of the more transcendental branches of the same science. Lastly we fancied we could see indications that it was meant to enforce spiritualistic doctrines, with perhaps an admixture of covert satire on various social and political theories. The general purport of it is to show how

---

1 Identified by William Lindgren in a paper titled "Some Newly Discovered Dimensions of *Flatland*," Conference on 4-Dimensional Worlds, Institute for Mathematical Behavioral Sciences, Irvine, CA, 25-26 February 2005.

being shaped like a square, born and bred in a world in which everything took place on a plane surface, and where consequently only two dimensions were conceived, obtained by a sort of revelation knowledge of a third dimension. He has previously in a dream studied the conditions of existence in a world of one dimension, where everything is a line or point, and nobody can pass any one else. There is some ingenuity in the way in which these conceptions are worked out, but it is rather spoilt to the mathematical mind by the conception (which, indeed, was unavoidable) of lines and points as objects which can be seen. Of course, if our friend the Square and his polygonal relations could see each other edgewise, they must have had *some* thickness, and need not, therefore, have been so distressed at the doctrine of a third dimension. There is something rather funny in the idea that a being of n dimensions, when addressed by a being of $n+1$, fancies the voice which he hears to proceed from his own inside; but no doubt it is in strict harmony with facts, and probably represents what we should all feel if we got into a region where it was possible to tie a knot in a closed loop of string, as it is in the world of four dimensions. When we saw the feat performed we should doubtless be as much surprised as our Square was when the Sphere told him the contents of his house without opening the door or taking off the roof. If we came back and told about it, we should, equally without doubt, fare much as the unlucky narrator of this history did.

[Abbott's response to this review was printed in *The Athenaeum* on 6 December 1884 and is printed below. It is dated just two days after a note in *The Athenaeum* of 22 November identified him as the author of *Flatland*.]

I write from a world that has been truly and literally described as "weary, stale, *flat*, and unprofitable,"[1]—from the land of Two Dimensions, some of the characteristics of which I have recently endeavoured to describe in a little treatise entitled "Flatland."

Into the dimness of my dull existence in this region there has penetrated a notice of my work which appeared in a recent number of the *Athenaeum*, and which raises a neat question—shall I say metaphysical or psychological?—which may possibly interest your readers.

Your not unfriendly, but, as I venture to think, too hasty critic, while complimenting me on the "ingenuity" of my simple description of my native land, and while admitting that the incidents recorded in my history, though "funny," are nevertheless "strictly according to

---

1   *Hamlet*, I.ii.133-34: "How weary, stale, flat and unprofitable/ Seem to me all the uses of this world!"

facts," has, nevertheless, cast an implied censure on my intelligence, and on that of my countrymen, by declaring that, though we think we are of Two Dimensions, we are really of Three, and ought to know it. The narrative is spoilt, he says, "for mathematical minds," because any *visible* line must really have thickness as well as length; and therefore all our so-called plane figures, besides having length and breadth, must really have some degree of thickness, or height—in other words a Third Dimension; and of this, he implies, we ought not to be ignorant.

I admit your critic's facts, but I deny his conclusions. It is true, no doubt, that *we* really have a Third Dimension, just as it is also true that *you* have a Fourth. But just as you are not aware that you belong to the Fourth Dimension, so neither are we aware, nor can we be made logically aware, that we belong to the Third.

A moment's reflection will make this obvious. Dimension implies measurement. Now, our lines are so thin that they cannot be measured. Measurement implies degrees, the more and the less; but all our lines are equally and infinitesimally thin, or thick, whichever you please to call it; so that we in Flatland can neither measure their thinness, nor even take cognizance of it. Where you speak of a line as being long and thick (or thin), we speak of it as being long and *bright*; "thickness" (or "thinness") never enters our heads, and we do not know what you mean by it. I knew what it meant once, during the few hours I spent in Spaceland; but I cannot realize it now. I take it on trust; but I cannot now make a mental image of it even to myself, much less to my countrymen.

Does this puzzle you? Then put yourself in my place. Suppose a being of the Fourth Dimension, condescending to visit you, were to address you thus: "You creatures of Three Dimensions *see* a plane (which is of Two Dimensions) and you *infer* a solid (which is of Three); but in reality what you call a plane has another Dimension of a kind not known to you"; what would you reply? Would you not call for a policeman to see your visitor safely locked up in some asylum?

Well, precisely this has been my reception when I have attempted to demonstrate the facts insisted on by your critic. Only yesterday, when the Chief Circle (in other words the Chief Priest) paid his annual visit to my prison, I endeavoured to prove to him that the Figures which we saw around us had a Third non-recognized Dimension, being not only long and broad, but also what you in Spaceland call "high." What was his reply? Simply this: "Dimension implies measurement. You say I am 'high'; measure my 'high-ness,' and I will believe you." I was crushed, and he left the room in triumph.

Sir, I am a humble Square, and I do not deny the superiority of your critic, who is doubtless a Cube; I impugn neither the exactness of his mathematics nor the regularity of his proportions; in the language of Spaceland, I am ready to admit that he is "a regular Cube and no mistake." But I respectfully submit that his knowledge of human nature is not equal to his knowledge of mathematics. He has forgotten that we are all alike—Points, Lines, Squares, Cubes, Extra-Cubes, whether of no Dimensions or of many Dimensions—liable to the prejudices of our several Dimensions, brothers in error; as one of your own poets also has said, "One touch of nature makes the world akin," meaning thereby not one world only, but all worlds, and not excepting the favoured world of Three Dimensions. And I must say I take it ill that I should be, however gently, censured for appearing to be ignorant of a truth which I firmly apprehend by faith, and which I daily endeavour to inculcate upon others.   A Square

**[1] If we understand the Square rightly, all that is wanting to make the Flatlanders realize a third dimension, and to settle circularism once for all, is a delicate micrometer. For he seems to admit that the edges of himself and his country men really are extended surfaces—as, indeed, appears from the fact which he elsewhere mentions, that they were capable of receiving colour. He is not, therefore, in the same position with regard to the third dimension as we of this world with regard to a fourth. The truth is, it may be suspected that our Square, having once in some measure grasped the conception of three-dimensioned space, cannot now wholly divest himself of it. He thinks, so to speak, in three dimensions. For instance, he talks in one place of hearing the sound of his wife's retreating footsteps, a bold metaphor indeed to apply to the motion of a line on a plane.[2] But, with a degree of intellectual insincerity probably unconscious, certainly pardonable in a person situated as he is, he thinks it necessary to persist in saying that he apprehends by faith a truth which he has really learnt from the evidence of his eyesight; thus making a serious confusion between the functions of faith and sense. The Square does his reviewer too much honour in supposing him to be a regular cube. The best he can claim to be is a rectangular parallelopiped;[3] and he finds it hard enough to live up to that configuration in space of the kind he knows, so that he

---

1 Abbott here steps out of character and discusses the limited perception of the Square.

2 A reference to an error in the first edition. This was changed to a "Peace-cry" in section 16 of the revised edition.

3 The word is usually spelled parallelepiped. According to the *OED*: A solid figure contained by six parallelograms, of which every two opposite ones are parallel; a prism whose base is a parallelogram.

is content to do without speculations as to the ways of beings in worlds of more or fewer dimensions.

4. *The Architect* (15 November 1884): 326-27

In this book we have an account of a country that is not to be found on any atlas hitherto published, and is unknown to enterprising followers of Messrs. Cook & Sons.[1] But as the author, Mr. Square, is a native of Flatland, we can consider his account to be as veracious as the descriptions of other remarkable places which have been written by Lemuel Gulliver.[2] The peculiarity of Flatland is that everything in it is absolutely deficient of a third dimension. There are only two dimensions. Men, women, cattle, trees, houses, are, like the subjects of Euclid's six books, either lines or surfaces. Mr. Square tells us—and we have no reason to doubt his statement—that statesmen in Flatland are circles, professors are squares, tradesmen are triangles (the equilateral being considered the most respectable), soldiers are isosceles triangles, each having a narrow base and sharp apex. Pope says that most women have no character at all,[3] and the Flatland ladies are only straight lines. There is, however, compensation in everything, and, by the peculiarity of their organisation, they are made most dangerous to the men, for whether seen in front or from behind, they are so attenuated that their fellow-citizens are wounded before they are aware of the presence of danger. To prevent accidents, all kinds of wise precautions have to be taken against womankind. Two doors are made to the houses, a large one for the men, a narrow one for the women; extremely small rooms are also provided for the latter, in order that their male friends may be comparatively safe. In the houses there are many peculiarities besides doors. Flatland architects are great in planning, and it is a pity that one of them was not induced to study the conditions of the competition for the Admiralty and War Offices.[4] We

---

1 A British travel company that offered organized package tours to foreign countries.

2 The hero of Swift's *Gulliver's Travels* (1726), see p. 163, note 3.

3 This comment was actually made by Alexander Pope's (1688-1744) friend Martha Blount (1690-1762). In Pope's poem "Epistle II: To a Lady (Of the Characters of Women)" (1731-35), he expands on Blount's observation: "Nothing so true as what you once let fall, / 'Most Women have no Characters at all.' / Matter too soft a lasting mark to bear, / And best distinguish'd by black, brown, or fair" (lines 1-4).

4 A reference to a design competition held for a new war office. According to a report of a meeting of The Royal Institute of British Architects, "the buildings should be suitable for the purposes for which they were intended. Internal arrangements should not be sacrificed for external effect or architectural

do not suppose that the contest would attract the least eminent practitioner in Flatland, but some of the younger members might have been inspired to send over a few suggestions. Considering that in Flatland it is impossible to see the shape of anyone, for as one's self and one's friends would be both on one plane, each must seem only as straight lines to the other, whatever be their normal form. May we not therefore conclude that the author can only have discovered the appearance of his neighbours by a philosophical course of experience, that is, by having in the jostling of life had to feel (for length and breadth can surely have feelings) their various sides and angles? If, however, we admit the test of experience we might be tempted to say that Mr. Square is not so impartial as he professes to be, and his statement that the female sex consists of straight lines, dangerously acute at each end, is probably evidence that Mr. Square is rather advanced in years, and has been jilted more than once. Unless mathematical truth, as it is expounded in Cambridge, does not hold in Flatland, we see no reason why the women should not be described as ellipses instead of lines. They would thus be more perfect than the circular statesmen who have but one centre to their being, whereas an elliptical woman would have two foci and an endless variety of outline. Beings may shrink with age in Flatland as elsewhere, and although Mr. Square probably was constituted of honest right angles when he was young, his sides may have since become concave, his angles more acute, and who knows if he has not reached the formation of a cross? In that case he is, when at home, no doubt more than a match for his wife, offering four dangerous points to her two. We might even go so far as to say that the origin of the narrow doors in the Flatland houses arose from the necessity of giving facility for the escape of women when pursued by their irate lords. But we speak under correction, and shall be glad to hear what Mr. Square has to say on this subject. Mr. Square is also a traveller, and has visited Lineland, a country which consists of a straight line. The inhabitants are also straight lines of various dimensions, moving backwards and forwards in their linear world. Mr. Square relates how, on one occasion, he frightened the King of Lineland by his appearance. No inhabitant of Lineland could conceive, far less explain, the existence of such a form; there was no word in their language to express a surface, the idea of two dimensions being absolutely foreign to their nature. Spaceland, the land in which

---

display. A very large number of the designs sent in for the great competition had wholly failed in this respect, and could not under any circumstances have been recommended by the judges for adoption or accepted by the Government" ("The Royal Institute of British Architects," *The Times* [London], 4 November 1884: 8).

we live (consult Stieler's atlas[1]), was also visited. Mr. Square cannot by any effort of his intellect comprehend the third dimension which forms solids, and therefore he labours under some difficulty in travelling among us. But our land appeared to him like some dream of light, of a brilliancy surpassingly great and magnificent, but inexpressible. The encomiums[2] of a man of his experience are flattering. Nevertheless, he has no doubt [of] the reality of Spaceland. When he was professor of mathematics[3] in Flatland Mr. Square taught that quantities exist not only in their first or second powers, which are accounted for by lines and surfaces, but that they can be elevated to an infinity of powers. Therefore, although he cannot conceive anything beyond surfaces to represent mathematical results, yet he cannot resist the conclusion that there are other dimensions, other worlds, other realities besides those his brain is capable of comprehending. His speculations on mathematics are accordingly far more notable than those of Sir William Rowan Hamilton[4] when he predicted the form which objects must assume when seen through a mineral of a certain form. There are readers who may hesitate to accept everything that is said by Mr. Square, especially if they only once read his book. Hamlet tells us there are more things in heaven and earth than are dreamt of in our philosophy, but while we repeat the lines glibly we hardly accept them as words of wisdom. The inhabitants of Flatland, in spite of their good sense, may likewise hesitate in believing all Mr. Square can tell them about ourselves. Meanwhile we recommend all our friends to read "Flatland." They will find in it as limitless fields for their thoughts as in Carlyle's "Sartor Resartus," with the great advantage that "Flatland" is written in good English instead of debased German.[5]

---

1 Adolf Stieler was a German mapmaker known for very detailed maps. His world atlas was issued from 1817-23.
2 From the Greek *enkomion*, a song of praise.
3 The reviewer has misidentified the Square's profession.
4 Irish mathematician (1805-65), known for his work on optics, who studied aberrations in reflected images caused by light on a curved mirror. He is also known for his work on the close relationship between geometry and the algebra of complex numbers, and "quaternions" or four-dimensional complex numbers. He introduced several mathematical terms, such as scalar and vector.
5 Thomas Carlyle's *Sartor Resartus: The Life and Opinions of Herr Teufelsdröckh* (1833-34) is a satiric work written in a mock-German form.

5. R. Tucker, *Nature* (27 November 1884): 76-77

[Founded in 1869, *Nature* is the major scientific journal in Britain. While in modern times it is a very technical and specialized scientific journal, in the nineteenth century its purpose was to provide the general public with information about scientific discoveries, so it was written in a more accessible manner.]

We live in an age of adventure. Men are ready to join in expeditions to the North Pole or to the interior of the African continent, yet we will venture to say that the work before us describes a vast plain as yet untrodden by any Fellow of the Royal Geographical Society,[1] and teeming with a population of which no example has figured in any of our shows. A few years ago a distinguished mathematician published some speculations on the existence of a book-worm "cabin'd, cribb'd, confin'd"[2] within the narrow limits of an ordinary sheet of paper,[3] and another writer bewailed "the dreary infinities of homoloidal space."[4] A third remarks, "there is no logical impossibility in conceiving the existence of intelligent beings, living on and moving along the surface of any solid body, who are able to perceive nothing but what exists on this surface and insensible to all beyond it."[5] How delighted Prof. Helmholtz will be to find, if this Flatland writer is worthy of credence, his conjecture is thus verified. "Flatland" is not the real name of this unknown land (the secret is not divulged), but it is so called here to make its character clear to us Spacedenizens. It is a noteworthy fact that one at least of the Flatlanders expresses himself in remarkably correct English, and singularly after the

---

1 A prestigious organization, founded in 1830, comprising explorers, military men, and geographers devoted to the advancement of geographical sciences. The RGS sponsored the explorations of Ernest Shackleton, David Livingstone, and Edmund Hillary, among others. Full members were called "fellows."

2 This phrase is from *Macbeth*, III.iv.24.

3 Reference is to J.J. Sylvester's 1869 presidential speech to the British Association for the Advancement of Science. See Appendix E3. In a note to the *Nature* published version, Sylvester points to William K. Clifford as the source for the bookworm analogy. The mathematicians mentioned in this review are identified by Jonathan Smith in *Fact and Feeling* (Madison: U of Wisconsin P, 1994), 182-83.

4 The quotation is from William K. Clifford's 1873 address to the Royal Institution, "The Philosophy of the Pure Sciences." "Homoloidal" means flat and level.

5 Hermann von Helmholtz. The quotation is from his essay "The Axioms of Geometry" (1870). See Appendix B2.

manner of an ordinary Space-human being; and further, though—we regret to have to record it—as a martyr in the cause of the truth of a third dimension, he has spent seven long years in the State jail, yet these memoirs have in some mysterious manner found their way into our hands. There is hope then that some one of our readers may yet expatiate in the broad plain, though the penalty will be, we fear, that he must first become as flat as a pancake and then see to it that his configuration (as a triangle, square, or other figure) is regular. This latter is a *sine qua non* in Flatland, because, whatever you are, your configuration must be regular, or woe betide you, and you will shuffle off your mortal coil incontinently.

We will not stop to inquire how this and that have come about, but will endeavour to lay before our readers some of the features of this (to us) new world, though we are informed that it has just entered upon its third millennium.[1]

In Flatland there is no sun nor any light to make shadows, but there is fog. This, which we on this earth consider to be an unmitigated nuisance, is recognized in that other world "as a blessing scarcely inferior to air itself, and as the Nurse of Arts and Parent of Sciences." If there were no fog, all lines would be equally distinct, whereas under present circumstances, "by careful and constant experimental observation of comparative dimness and clearness, we are enabled to infer with great exactness the configuration of the object observed." It is a necessity of Flatland life to know the north (for instance, it is a point of good breeding to give a lady the north side of the way); this is determined in the absence of any heavenly bodies by a novel (we speak as a Space-denizen) law of Nature, *viz.* the constancy of an attraction to the south; however, in temperate regions the southward attraction is scarcely felt, but here again Nature comes to the Flatlander's aid. If he is in an inhabited region, the fact that the houses (mostly regular pentagons; squares and triangles are only allowed in the case of powder-magazines, barracks, and such like, for sufficient reasons) have their roofs towards the north, so that the rain, which always comes from that quarter, may run off and not damage the houses, will help him to get his north point. If, however, he is out in the country far away from trees and houses, there is no help for him until a shower of rain comes.

We must now give some description of the inhabitants. The women are all straight lines; the men are other regular figures (if there be hopeless irregularity, which the hospitals cannot cure, then the man is put

---

1   [Tucker's note.] From the secret Archives it appears that at the commencement of each millennium a Sphere descended into the midst of the Council of Circles proclaiming the great truth for the attempted teaching of which our author is in bonds.

to death). The lowest orders, policemen, soldiers, and the *canaille*,[1] are isosceles triangles, their mental calibre being determined by the largeness or smallness of the vertical angle. It is possible for an isosceles triangle to be developed into an equilateral triangle, or the offspring after a few generations may be so developed: in this class are the respectable tradesmen. The professional men and gentlemen are Squares—our author is a lawyer—and Pentagons. The Circles (that is, approximations more or less closely to that figure) are the nobility.

Another law of Nature in Flatland is that "a male child shall have one more side than his father, so that each generation shall rise (as a rule) one step in the scale of development and nobility." Our author, as appears by the drawing on the cover, has four pentagonal sons and two hexagonal grandsons. We do not clearly gather where the one eye (for Flatlanders appear to be monoculi) is situated, and how locomotion is effected we are not told. It can hardly be by such means as were once suggested by Prof. Clerk Maxwell,[2] for in Flatland you must go steadily forward or dire may be the disaster you will inflict upon your neighbour. There seems to be no lack of Board schools, and there is at least one university, that of Wentbridge (we had by force of habit written Cambridge), where instruction is given in mathematics.[3] A knowledge of this branch of study is obligatory, for since a Flatlander's eye can only move in his world-plane, all the objects, human and otherwise, even the circular priests, appear to be straight lines, and the figure-angles have to be, at any rate approximately, correctly guessed at sight.

Before we close our notice we must return to the description of womankind. The women we have said are straight lines, hence they are very formidable, for they are like needles, and what makes them more to be dreaded is that they have the power of making themselves practically invisible, hence a Flatland female is "a creature by no means to be trifled with." There are, however, certain regulations in force which diminish the dangers resulting from having a woman about the house. There is an entrance for her on the eastern side of the house, by which she must enter "in a becoming and respectful manner"; she must also, when walking, keep up her peace-cry, under penalty of death, and if she has fits, is given to sneezing, or in any way is liable to any sudden movement, there is but one cure for such movements, and that is instant destruction. Though involuntary and sudden motions are thus

---

1 The rabble, a mob.
2 James Clerk Maxwell (1831-79), physicist. Maxwell's equations describe the electromagnetic field. He was also known for his work on optics and the production of color, the apparent reference in this review.
3 This reviewer caught Abbott's word play.

summarily dealt with, yet if she is in any public place she must keep up a gentle "back-motion," and thus she is less liable to be invisible to her neighbours. Happily fashion exercises its potent sway in Flatland female society, as elsewhere, for we learn that "the rhythmical, and, if I may so say, well-modulated undulation of the back in our ladies of circular rank is envied and imitated by the wife of a common Equilateral, who can achieve nothing beyond a mere monotonous swing, like the ticking of a pendulum." Owing to their unfortunate configuration they are inferior in all good qualities to the very lowest of the Isosceles, being entirely devoid of brain-power, and they have "neither reflection, judgment, nor forethought, and hardly any memory." This is but a poor account, but we must bear in mind that it is an *ex parte* description by a Square who may at some time have suffered a disappointment at the hands of a lady. We shall be glad (though we can hardly expect such a result)—now that tidings have come from this little-known country—if some female will favour us with her view of the state of matters in Flatland. At birth a female is about an inch long, a tall adult woman reaches about a foot. The length of the sides of an adult male of every class may be said to be three feet or a little more.

The book consists of two parts—*This World*, i.e. of Flatland, in twelve sections, and *Other Worlds*, in ten sections. The whole is very cleverly worked out, and many passages descriptive of events in the past history of the country at times force upon one the thought that after all the book may have been compiled by a Spacedenizen, and that he is quietly laughing in his sleeve and saying, "de te Fabula narratur."[1] However this may be, Flatlander or Spacelander, there is a slip in the note on p. 64, and for "Flatland" should be read "Spaceland."[2]

We commend "A Square's" book to any of our readers who have a leisure hour from severer studies, and we believe when they have read it they will say "the tenth part of the humour has not been suggested."[3]

---

1 Latin: literally "about you the tale is told."

2 This is an error in section 15 of the first edition; the edition reads,
    Note: When I say "sitting", of course I do not mean any change of attitude such as you in Flatland signify by that word; for as we have no feet, we can no more "sit" nor "stand" (in your sense of the word) than one of your soles or flounders.
    The word "Flatland" was corrected to "Spaceland" in later editions.

3 [Tucker's note.] We may mention as specially humorous the chapters in which the Square is initiated into some of the mysteries of tri-dimensional space by the spherical stranger.

6. *New York Times* (23 February 1885): 3

This is a delirious book. A. Square, having lost his balance with over-studying geometry, statics, and kinetics, and having become stark mad about a line, a triangle, a pentagon, and a hexagon, has written a story about them. Take a penny and lay it on a table and leaning over it look down on it and it is a circle. Look at it in another way, and it becomes a line. Having then your penny, your circle, and your line, construct a geometrical romance, and carry out the action in Flatland, Spaceland, and Lineland. A. Square is always asking the reader to imagine what he can't imagine; for instance, that a female in his country is a line. Imagine a line painted and her eye red with the hinder half green. Now, fancy a priest whose mouth is at M; and whose front semicircle (A M B) is consequently colored red, while his hinder semicircle is green. But the women in Flatland decline being painted, and there is a color revolt. "How I Vainly Tried to Explain the Nature of Flatland" is the title of one of the chapters of this story, and there is a terrible row between a Line and a Point, and an awful catastrophe happens when a sphere sits down on A. Square. It's a very puzzling book and a very distressing one, and to be enjoyed possibly by about six, or at the outside seven, persons in the whole of the United States and Canada. A. Square has a brother, and that brother "has not yet grasped the nature of the third dimension, and frankly avows his disbelief in the existence of a sphere." May we remark that we love that brother? And if he had not [sic] existence in this geometrical romance we should go many miles to shake hands with him. Some little sense is apparent in an appeal for a better education for women, but beyond that all the rest of Flatland is incomprehensible.

7. From the *New York Tribune* (6 March 1885): 6

This is an ingenious and clever satire by an anonymous writer. The purpose of it is to show the folly of those pseudo-scientific assumptions and dogmatisms which in effect purport to define the limits of the possible in Nature by declaring that this and that is "opposed to the laws of Nature." Flatland is a region in which there are but two dimensions. The people are all triangles, squares, more or less irregular circles, and acute angles. The description of this remarkable country, of its various classes or castes, its government, institutions, customs and modes of thought, is as well done as almost anything of the kind that has appeared since Gulliver's Travels. The ideas are moreover full of originality, yet all of a logical consistency. It is plain, in short, that in such a region and under such dimensional conditions the arrangements must be very much as here represented.

. . .

The most amusing point in the skit perhaps is the refusal of the Third Dimensional being, who has come to illuminate the ignorance of the Flatlanders, to admit the possibility of a space of four dimensions. A wittier and keener rebuke to the sciolism[1] which too frequently passes muster for science in these days, and which is as presumptuous and bigoted as mediaeval ecclesiasticism, has never been administered. It is to be hoped that "Flatland" will be read by those who most need its lessons, and that its good-humored and delicate satire will be appreciated as it deserves.

8. Advertisement Run by Robert Brothers Publishers in *The Literary World* (Boston, MA), 21 March 1885

This little book is a puzzle to the critics. Some of them are as dull as a case-knife over it, while others see its points with the keenness of a razor.

"All that there is of any value in it might have been put in ten pages," says one.

"The ingenuity of this satire has not been exceeded since Swift wrote 'Gulliver's Travels'—the wit of it is hardly less keen," says another.

"The most silly and stupid book which we have seen in many years. Presumably it is a satire," says a third.

"A well-known English writer has published anonymously an amusing little book called 'Flatland: a Romance of many Dimensions,' by A. Square. It is an effective satire on social differences, and on the assumption of absolute knowledge. The book is full of light, good-natured mockery and absurd extravagances," says a fourth.

"Not only likely to create a present sensation in the thinking world, but also to find an abiding place among the great satires of history," says the London *Literary World*.

---

1 Superficial knowledge.

Appendix B: Sources and Influences

1. From Benjamin Jowett's Translation of Plato's *Republic* (Oxford: Clarendon Press, 1871)

[Here Socrates is talking to the student Glaucon. In this famous passage, Plato makes the analogy between human perception and captives bound in a cave trying to make sense of the world beyond the limits of their experience. Jowett's translation retains the dialogue form of Plato's writing and was the best-known English translation of Plato. Abbott would have been familiar with both this translation and the original Greek.]

BOOK VII
ON SHADOWS AND REALITIES IN EDUCATION
(SOCRATES, GLAUCON.)

And now, I said, let me show in a figure how far our nature is enlightened or unenlightened:— Behold! human beings living in an underground den, which has a mouth open toward the light and reaching all along the den; here they have been from their childhood, and have their legs and necks chained so that they cannot move, and can only see before them, being prevented by the chains from turning round their heads. Above and behind them a fire is blazing at a distance, and between the fire and the prisoners there is a raised way; and you will see, if you look, a low wall built along the way, like the screen which marionette-players have in front of them, over which they show the puppets.

I see.

And do you see, I said, men passing along the wall carrying all sorts of vessels, and statues and figures of animals made of wood and stone and various materials, which appear over the wall? Some of them are talking, others silent.

You have shown me a strange image, and they are strange prisoners.

Like ourselves, I replied; and they see only their own shadows, or the shadows of one another, which the fire throws on the opposite wall of the cave?

True, he said; how could they see anything but the shadows if they were never allowed to move their heads?

And of the objects which are being carried in like manner they would only see the shadows?

Yes, he said.

And if they were able to converse with one another, would they not suppose that they were naming what was actually before them?

Very true.

And suppose further that the prison had an echo which came from the other side, would they not be sure to fancy when one of the passers-by spoke that the voice which they heard came from the passing shadow?

No question, he replied.

To them, I said, the truth would be literally nothing but the shadows of the images.

That is certain.

And now look again, and see what will naturally follow if the prisoners are released and disabused of their error. At first, when any of them is liberated and compelled suddenly to stand up and turn his neck round and walk and look toward the light, he will suffer sharp pains; the glare will distress him, and he will be unable to see the realities of which in his former state he had seen the shadows; and then conceive someone saying to him, that what he saw before was an illusion, but that now, when he is approaching nearer to being and his eye is turned toward more real existence, he has a clearer vision,—what will be his reply? And you may further imagine that his instructor is pointing to the objects as they pass and requiring him to name them,— will he not be perplexed? Will he not fancy that the shadows which he formerly saw are truer than the objects which are now shown to him?

Far truer.

And if he is compelled to look straight at the light, will he not have a pain in his eyes which will make him turn away to take refuge in the objects of vision which he can see, and which he will conceive to be in reality clearer than the things which are now being shown to him?

True, he said.

And suppose once more, that he is reluctantly dragged up a steep and rugged ascent, and held fast until he is forced into the presence of the sun himself, is he not likely to be pained and irritated? When he approaches the light his eyes will be dazzled, and he will not be able to see anything at all of what are now called realities.

Not all in a moment, he said.

He will require to grow accustomed to the sight of the upper world. And first he will see the shadows best, next the reflections of men and other objects in the water, and then the objects themselves; then he will gaze upon the light of the moon and the stars and the spangled heaven; and he will see the sky and the stars by night better than the sun or the light of the sun by day?

Certainly.

Last of all he will be able to see the sun, and not mere reflections of him in the water, but he will see him in his own proper place, and not in another; and he will contemplate him as he is.

Certainly.

He will then proceed to argue that this is he who gives the season and the years, and is the guardian of all that is in the visible world, and in a certain way the cause of all things which he and his fellows have been accustomed to behold?

Clearly, he said, he would first see the sun and then reason about him.

And when he remembered his old habitation, and the wisdom of the den and his fellow-prisoners, do you not suppose that he would felicitate himself on the change, and pity them?

Certainly, he would.

And if they were in the habit of conferring honors among themselves on those who were quickest to observe the passing shadows and to remark which of them went before, and which followed after, and which were together; and who were therefore best able to draw conclusions as to the future, do you think that he would care for such honors and glories, or envy the possessors of them? Would he not say with Homer,

Better to be the poor servant of a poor master, and to endure anything, rather than think as they do and live after their manner?

Yes, he said, I think that he would rather suffer anything than entertain these false notions and live in this miserable manner.

Imagine once more, I said, such a one coming suddenly out of the sun to be replaced in his old situation; would he not be certain to have his eyes full of darkness?

To be sure, he said.

And if there were a contest, and he had to compete in measuring the shadows with the prisoners who had never moved out of the den, while his sight was still weak, and before his eyes had become steady (and the time which would be needed to acquire this new habit of sight might be very considerable), would he not be ridiculous? Men would say of him that up he went and down he came without his eyes; and that it was better not even to think of ascending; and if anyone tried to loose another and lead him up to the light, let them only catch the offender, and they would put him to death.

No question, he said.

This entire allegory, I said, you may now append, dear Glaucon, to the previous argument; the prison-house is the world of sight, the light of the fire is the sun, and you will not misapprehend me if you interpret the journey upward to be the ascent of the soul into the intellectual world according to my poor belief, which, at your desire, I have expressed whether rightly or wrongly, God knows. But, whether true or false, my opinion is that in the world of knowledge the idea of good appears last of all, and is seen only with an effort; and, when seen, is also inferred to be the universal author of all things beautiful and right, parent of light and of the lord of light in this visible world, and the immediate source of reason and truth in the intellectual; and that this is the power upon which he who would act rationally either in public or private life must have his eye fixed.

I agree, he said, as far as I am able to understand you.

Moreover, I said, you must not wonder that those who attain to this beatific vision are unwilling to descend to human affairs; for their souls are ever hastening into the upper world where they desire to dwell; which desire of theirs is very natural, if our allegory may be trusted.

Yes, very natural.

And is there anything surprising in one who passes from divine contemplations to the evil state of man, misbehaving himself in a ridiculous manner; if, while his eyes are blinking and before he has become accustomed to the surrounding darkness, he is compelled to fight in courts of law, or in other places, about the images or the shadows of images of justice, and is endeavoring to meet the conceptions of those who have never yet seen absolute justice?

Anything but surprising, he replied.

Anyone who has common-sense will remember that the bewilderments of the eyes are of two kinds, and arise from two causes, either from coming out of the light or from going into the light, which is true of the mind's eye, quite as much as of the bodily eye; and he who remembers this when he sees anyone whose vision is perplexed and weak, will not be too ready to laugh; he will first ask whether that soul of man has come out of the brighter life, and is unable to see because unaccustomed to the dark, or having turned from darkness to the day is dazzled by excess of light. And he will count the one happy in his condition and state of being, and he will pity the other; or, if he have a mind to laugh at the soul which comes from below into the light, there will be more reason in this than in the laugh which greets him who returns from above out of the light into the den.

That, he said, is a very just distinction.

But then, if I am right, certain professors of education must be wrong when they say that they can put a knowledge into the soul which was not there before, like sight into blind eyes.

They undoubtedly say this, he replied.

Whereas, our argument shows that the power and capacity of learning exists in the soul already; and that just as the eye was unable to turn from darkness to light without the whole body, so too the instrument of knowledge can only by the movement of the whole soul be turned from the world of becoming into that of being, and learn by degrees to endure the sight of being, and of the brightest and best of being, or, in other words, of the good.

Very true.

And must there not be some art which will effect conversion in the easiest and quickest manner; not implanting the faculty of sight, for that exists already, but has been turned in the wrong direction, and is looking away from the truth?

Yes, he said, such an art may be presumed.

And whereas the other so-called virtues of the soul seem to be akin to bodily qualities, for even when they are not originally innate they can be implanted later by habit and exercise, the virtue of wisdom more than anything else contains a divine element which always remains, and by this conversion is rendered useful and profitable; or, on the other hand, hurtful and useless. Did you never observe the narrow intelligence flashing from the keen eye of a clever rogue—how eager he is, how clearly his paltry soul sees the way to his end; he is the reverse of blind, but his keen eyesight is forced into the service of evil, and he is mischievous in proportion to his cleverness?

Very true, he said.

But what if there had been a circumcision of such natures in the days of their youth; and they had been severed from those sensual pleasures, such as eating and drinking, which, like leaden weights, were attached to them at their birth, and which drag them down and turn the vision of their souls upon the things that are below—if, I say, they had been released from these impediments and turned in the opposite direction, the very same faculty in them would have seen the truth as keenly as they see what their eyes are turned to now.

Very likely.

Yes, I said; and there is another thing which is likely, or rather a necessary inference from what has preceded, that neither the uneducated and uninformed of the truth, nor yet those who never make an end of their education, will be able ministers of the State; not the former, because they have no single aim of duty which is the rule of all their actions, private as well as public; nor the latter, because they will not act at all except upon compulsion, fancying that they are already dwelling apart in the islands of the blessed.

Very true, he replied.

Then, I said, the business of us who are the founders of the State will be to compel the best minds to attain that knowledge which we have already shown to be the greatest of all—they must continue to ascend until they arrive at the good; but when they have ascended and seen enough we must not allow them to do as they do now.

What do you mean?

I mean that they remain in the upper world: but this must not be allowed; they must be made to descend again among the prisoners in the den, and partake of their labors and honors, whether they are worth having or not.

But is not this unjust? he said; ought we to give them a worse life, when they might have a better?

You have again forgotten, my friend, I said, the intention of the legislator, who did not aim at making any one class in the State happy above the rest; the happiness was to be in the whole State, and he held the citizens together by persuasion and necessity, making them benefactors of the State, and therefore benefactors of one another; to this end he created them, not to please themselves, but to be his instruments in binding up the State.

True, he said, I had forgotten.

Observe, Glaucon, that there will be no injustice in compelling our philosophers to have a care and providence of others; we shall explain to them that in other States, men of their class are not obliged to share in the toils of politics: and this is reasonable, for they grow up at their own sweet will, and the government would rather not have them. Being self-taught, they cannot be expected to show any gratitude for a culture which they have never received. But we have brought you into the world to be rulers of the hive, kings of yourselves and of the other citizens, and have educated you far better and more perfectly than they have been educated, and you are better able to share in the double duty. Wherefore each of you, when his turn comes, must go down to the general underground abode, and get the habit of seeing in the dark. When you have acquired the habit, you will see ten thousand times better than the inhabitants of the den, and you will know what the several images are, and what they represent, because you have seen the beautiful and just and good in their truth. And thus our State, which is also yours, will be a reality, and not a dream only, and will be administered in a spirit unlike that of other States, in which men fight with one another about shadows only and are distracted in the struggle for power, which in their eyes is a great good. Whereas the truth is that the State in which the rulers are most reluctant to govern is always the best and most quietly governed, and the State in which they are most eager, the worst.

Quite true, he replied.

And will our pupils, when they hear this, refuse to take their turn at the toils of State, when they are allowed to spend the greater part of their time with one another in the heavenly light?

Impossible, he answered; for they are just men, and the commands which we impose upon them are just; there can be no doubt that every one of them will take office as a stern necessity, and not after the fashion of our present rulers of State.

Yes, my friend, I said; and there lies the point. You must contrive for your future rulers another and a better life than that of a ruler, and then you may have a well-ordered State; for only in the State which offers this, will they rule who are truly rich, not in silver and gold, but in virtue and wisdom, which are the true blessings of life. Whereas, if they go to the administration of public affairs, poor and hungering after their own private advantage, thinking that hence they are to snatch the chief good, order there can never be; for they will be fighting about office, and the civil and domestic broils which thus arise will be the ruin of the rulers themselves and of the whole State.

Most true, he replied.

And the only life which looks down upon the life of political ambition is that of true philosophy. Do you know of any other?

Indeed, I do not, he said.

And those who govern ought not to be lovers of the task? For, if they are, there will be rival lovers, and they will fight.

No question. Who, then, are those whom we shall compel to be guardians? Surely they will be the men who are wisest about affairs of State, and by whom the State is best administered, and who at the same time have other honours and another and a better life than that of politics?

They are the men, and I will choose them, he replied.

And now shall we consider in what way such guardians will be produced, and how they are to be brought from darkness to light,—as some are said to have ascended from the world below to the gods?

By all means, he replied.

The process, I said, is not the turning over of an oystershell, but the turning round of a soul passing from a day which is little better than night to the true day of being, that is, the ascent from below, which we affirm to be true philosophy?

Quite so.

And should we not inquire what sort of knowledge has the power of effecting such a change?

Certainly.

What sort of knowledge is there which would draw the soul from becoming to being? And another consideration has just occurred to me: You will remember that our young men are to be warrior athletes?

Yes, that was said.

Then this new kind of knowledge must have an additional quality?

What quality?

Usefulness in war.

Yes, if possible.

There were two parts in our former scheme of education, were there not?

Just so.

There was gymnastics, which presided over the growth and decay of the body, and may therefore be regarded as having to do with generation and corruption?

True.

Then that is not the knowledge which we are seeking to discover?

No.

But what do you say of music, what also entered to a certain extent into our former scheme?

Music, he said, as you will remember, was the counterpart of gymnastics, and trained the guardians by the influences of habit, by harmony making them harmonious, by rhythm rhythmical, but not giving them science; and the words, whether fabulous or possibly true, had kindred elements of rhythm and harmony in them. But in music there was nothing which tended to that good which you are now seeking.

You are most accurate, I said, in your recollection; in music there certainly was nothing of the kind. But what branch of knowledge is there, my dear Glaucon, which is of the desired nature; since all the useful arts were reckoned mean by us?

Undoubtedly; and yet if music and gymnastics are excluded, and the arts are also excluded, what remains?

Well, I said, there may be nothing left of our special subjects; and then we shall have to take something which is not special, but of the universal application.

What may that be?

A something which all arts and sciences and intelligences use in common, and which everyone first has to learn among the elements of education.

What is that?

The little matter of distinguishing one, two, and three—in a word, number and calculation:—do not all arts and sciences necessarily partake of them?

Yes.

Then the art of war partakes of them?

To be sure.

Then Palamedes, whenever he appears in tragedy, proves Agamemnon ridiculously unfit to be a general. Did you never remark how he declares that he had invented number, and had numbered the ships and set in array the ranks of the army at Troy; which implies that they had never been numbered before, and Agamemnon must be supposed literally to have been incapable of counting his own feet—how could he if he was ignorant of number? And if that is true, what sort of general must he have been?

I should say a very strange one, if this was as you say.

Can we deny that a warrior should have a knowledge of arithmetic?

Certainly he should, if he is to have the smallest understanding of military tactics, or indeed, I should rather say, if he is to be a man at all.

I should like to know whether you have the same notion which I have of this study?

What is your notion?

It appears to me to be a study of the kind which we are seeking, and which leads naturally to reflection, but never to have been rightly used; for the true use of it is simply to draw the soul toward being.

Will you explain your meaning? he said.

I will try, I said; and I wish you would share the inquiry with me, and say yes or no when I attempt to distinguish in my own mind what branches of knowledge have this attracting power, in order that we may have clearer proof that arithmetic is, as I suspect, one of them.

Explain, he said.

I mean to say that objects of sense are of two kinds; some of them do not invite thought because the sense is an adequate judge of them; while in the case of other objects sense is so untrustworthy that further inquiry is imperatively demanded.

You are clearly referring, he said, to the manner in which the senses are imposed upon by distance, and by painting in light and shade.

No, I said, that is not at all my meaning.

Then what is your meaning?

When speaking of uninviting objects, I mean those which do not pass from one sensation to the opposite; inviting objects are those which do; in this latter case the sense coming upon the object, whether at a distance or near, gives no more vivid idea of anything in particular than of its opposite. An illustration will make my meaning clearer:—here are three fingers—a little finger, a second finger, and a middle finger.

Very good.

You may suppose that they are seen quite close: And here comes the point.

What is it?

Each of them equally appears a finger, whether seen in the middle or at the extremity, whether white or black, or thick or thin—it makes no difference; a finger is a finger all the same. In these cases a man is not compelled to ask of thought the question, what is a finger? for the sight never intimates to the mind that a finger is other than a finger.

True.

And therefore, I said, as we might expect, there is nothing here which invites or excites intelligence.

There is not, he said.

But is this equally true of the greatness and smallness of the fingers? Can sight adequately perceive them? and is no difference made by the circumstance that one of the fingers is in the middle and the other at the extremity? And in like manner does the touch adequately perceive the qualities of thickness or thinness, of softness or hardness? And so of the other senses; do they give perfect intimations of such matters? Is not their mode of operation on this wise—the sense which is concerned with the quality of hardness is necessarily concerned also with the quality of softness, and only intimates to the soul that the same thing is felt to be both hard and soft?

You are quite right, he said.

And must not the soul be perplexed at this intimation which the sense gives of a hard which is also soft? What, again, is the meaning of light and heavy, if that which is light is also heavy, and that which is heavy, light?

Yes, he said, these intimations which the soul receives are very curious and require to be explained.

Yes, I said, and in these perplexities the soul naturally summons to her aid calculation and intelligence, that she may see whether the several objects announced to her are one or two.

True.

And if they turn out to be two, is not each of them one and different?

Certainly.

And if each is one, and both are two, she will conceive the two as in a state of division, for if they were undivided they could only be conceived of as one?

True.

The eye certainly did see both small and great, but only in a confused manner; they were not distinguished.

Yes.

Whereas the thinking mind, intending to light up the chaos, was compelled to reverse the process, and look at small and great as separate and not confused.

Very true.

Was not this the beginning of the inquiry, "What is great?" and "What is small?"

Exactly so.

And thus arose the distinction of the visible and the intelligible.

Most true.

This was what I meant when I spoke of impressions which invited the intellect, or the reverse—those which are simultaneous with opposite impressions, invite thought; those which are not simultaneous do not.

I understand, he said, and agree with you.

And to which class do unity and number belong?

I do not know, he replied.

Think a little and you will see that what has preceded will supply the answer; for if simple unity could be adequately perceived by the sight or by any other sense, then, as we were saying in the case of the finger, there would be nothing to attract toward being; but when there is some contradiction always present, and one is the reverse of one and involves the conception of plurality, then thought begins to be aroused within us, and the soul perplexed and wanting to arrive at a decision asks, "What is absolute unity?" This is the way in which the study of the one has a power of drawing and converting the mind to the contemplation of true being.

And surely, he said, this occurs notably in the case of one; for we see the same thing to be both one and infinite in multitude?

Yes, I said; and this being true of one must be equally true of all number?

Certainly.

And all arithmetic and calculation have to do with number?

Yes.

And they appear to lead the mind toward truth?

Yes, in a very remarkable manner.

Then this is knowledge of the kind for which we are seeking, having a double use, military and philosophical; for the man of war must learn the art of number or he will not know how to array his troops, and the philosopher also, because he has to rise out of the sea of change and lay hold of true being, and therefore he must be an arithmetician.

That is true.

And our guardian is both warrior and philosopher?

Certainly.

Then this is a kind of knowledge which legislation may fitly prescribe; and we must endeavor to persuade those who are to be the principal men of our State to go and learn arithmetic, not as amateurs, but they must carry on the study until they see the nature of numbers with the mind only; nor again, like merchants or retail-traders, with a view to buying or selling, but for the sake of their military use, and of the soul herself; and because this will be the easiest way for her to pass from becoming to truth and being.

That is excellent, he said.

Yes, I said, and now having spoken of it, I must add how charming the science is! and in how many ways it conduces to our desired end, if pursued in the spirit of a philosopher, and not of a shopkeeper!

How do you mean?

I mean, as I was saying, that arithmetic has a very great and elevating effect, compelling the soul to reason about abstract number, and rebelling against the introduction of visible or tangible objects into the argument. You know how steadily the masters of the art repel and ridicule anyone who attempts to divide absolute unity when he is calculating, and if you divide, they multiply, taking care that one shall continue one and not become lost in fractions.

That is very true.

Now, suppose a person were to say to them: O my friends, what are these wonderful numbers about which you are reasoning, in which, as you say, there is a unity such as you demand, and each unit is equal, invariable, indivisible—what would they answer?

They would answer, as I should conceive, that they were speaking of those numbers which can only be realized in thought.

Then you see that this knowledge may be truly called necessary, necessitating as it clearly does the use of the pure intelligence in the attainment of pure truth?

Yes; that is a marked characteristic of it.

And have you further observed that those who have a natural talent for calculation are generally quick at every other kind of knowledge; and even the dull, if they have had an arithmetical training, although they may derive no other advantage from it, always become much quicker than they would otherwise have been?

Very true, he said.

And indeed, you will not easily find a more difficult study, and not many as difficult.

You will not.

And, for all these reasons, arithmetic is a kind of knowledge in which the best natures should be trained, and which must not be given up.

I agree.

Let this then be made one of our subjects of education. And next, shall we inquire whether the kindred science also concerns us?

You mean geometry?

Exactly so.

Clearly, he said, we are concerned with that part of geometry which relates to war; for in pitching a camp or taking up a position or closing or extending the lines of an army, or any other military manoeuvre, whether in actual battle or on a march, it will make all the difference whether a general is or is not a geometrician.

Yes, I said, but for that purpose a very little of either geometry or calculation will be enough; the question relates rather to the greater and more advanced part of geometry whether that tends in any degree to make more easy the vision of the idea of good; and thither, as I was saying, all things tend which compel the soul to turn her gaze toward that place, where is the full perfection of being, which she ought, by all means, to behold.

True, he said.

Then if geometry compels us to view being, it concerns us; if becoming only, it does not concern us?

Yes, that is what we assert.

Yet anybody who has the least acquaintance with geometry will not deny that such a conception of the science is in flat contradiction to the ordinary language of geometricians.

How so?

They have in view practice only, and are always speaking, in a narrow and ridiculous manner, of squaring and extending and applying and the like they confuse the necessities of geometry with those of daily life; whereas knowledge is the real object of the whole science.

Certainly, he said.

Then must not a further admission be made?

What admission?

That the knowledge at which geometry aims is knowledge of the eternal, and not of aught perishing and transient.

That, he replied, may be readily allowed, and is true.

Then, my noble friend, geometry will draw the soul toward truth, and create the spirit of philosophy, and raise up that which is now unhappily allowed to fall down.

Nothing will be more likely to have such an effect.

Then nothing should be more sternly laid down than that the inhabitants of your fair city should by all means learn geometry. Moreover, the science has indirect effects, which are not small.

Of what kind? he said.

There are the military advantages of which you spoke, I said; and in all departments of knowledge, as experience proves, anyone who has studied geometry is infinitely quicker of apprehension than one who has not. Yes, indeed, he said, there is an infinite difference between them.

Then shall we propose this as a second branch of knowledge which our youth will study?

Let us do so, he replied.

[...]

2. From Hermann von Helmholtz, "The Axioms of Geometry" [a review essay on geometry textbooks dealing with non-Euclidean geometry], *The Academy* (12 February 1870): 128-31

[In this essay, the mathematician Helmholtz speculates on the perceptions of inhabitants living in two-dimensional space. This essay is a possible inspiration for Abbott's novel.]

To begin with the more simple case, the geometry of two dimensions. We live in and know a space of three dimensions. But there is no logical impossibility, in conceiving the existence of intelligent beings, living on and moving along the surface of any solid body, who are able to perceive nothing but what exists on this surface, and insensible to all beyond it. Neither would it be a contradiction to suppose that such beings could find out the shortest lines existing in their space, and form geometrical notions of it, as far as it is accessible to and perceptible by them. Their space, of course, would have only two dimensions. If the surface, on which they lived, were an infinite plane, they would acknowledge the truth of the axioms of *Euclid*. They would find that there exists only one shortest (or *geodetical*) line between two points, and that two geodetical (or in this case straight) lines, both being parallel to a third, are parallel to each other.

If, on the contrary, such beings lived on the surface of a sphere, their space would be without a limit, as under the former supposition, but it would not be infinitely extended; and the axioms of geometry would turn out very different from ours, and from those of the inhabitants of a plane. The shortest lines which the inhabitants of a spherical surface could draw would be arcs of great circles. The axiom, that there is only one shortest line between two points, would not be true without exception; for between two points diametrically opposed, they would find an infinite number of shortest lines, all of equal length. Such beings would not be able to form the notion of parallel geodetical lines, because every pair of their geodetical lines, when sufficiently prolonged, would intersect in two points. The sum of the angles of a triangle would be greater than two right angles, and the difference would grow with the area of the triangle. It is evident that the beings on the spherical surface would not be able to form the notion of geometrical similarity, because they would not know geometrical figures of the same form but different magnitude, except such as were of infinitely small dimensions.

Now let us suppose beings living on any other surface, for example, that of an ellipsoid. They could construct the shortest lines between three points, and form in this way a geodetical triangle. But if they constructed such triangles in different parts of their space, so that the three sides of the one were equal to the three sides of the other, the angles of these triangles would be different, except in particular cases. Circles of equal geodetical radius would have different areas and different lengths of periphery, when situated in parts of the surface where the curvature is different. In such a case, therefore, it would not be possible, as it is in the plane and on the sphere, to construct in every place a figure, congruent to a given figure, or to move a figure without changing one or more of its dimensions.

3. From Fyodor Dostoyevsky (1821-81), *The Brothers Karamazov* (1879-80), book 5, chapter 3. Translated by Constance Garnett (London: Heinemann, 1912)

[In this passage from Dostoyevsky's famous novel, the character Ivan advises his brother, Alyosha, to reject speculations of other dimensions, seeing non-Euclidean geometry as analogous to a disbelief in God.]

As for me, I've long resolved not to think whether man created God or God man. And I won't go through all the axioms laid down by Russian boys on that subject, all derived from European hypotheses; for what's a hypothesis there is an axiom with the Russian boy, and not only with the boys but with their teachers too, for our Russian professors are often just the same boys themselves. And so I omit all the hypotheses. For what are we aiming at now? I am trying to explain as quickly as possible my essential nature, that is what manner of man I am, what I believe in, and for what I hope, that's it, isn't it? And therefore I tell you that I accept God simply. But you must note this: if God exists and if He really did create the world, then, as we all know, He created it according to the geometry of Euclid and the human mind with the conception of only three dimensions in space. Yet there have been and still are geometricians and philosophers, and even some of the most distinguished, who doubt whether the whole universe, or to speak more widely, the whole of being, was only created in Euclid's geometry; they even dare to dream that two parallel lines, which according to Euclid can never meet on earth, may meet somewhere in infinity. I have come to the conclusion that, since I can't understand even that, I can't expect to understand about God. I acknowledge humbly that I have no faculty for settling such questions, I have a Euclidian earthly mind, and how could I solve problems that are not of this world? And I advise you never to think about it either, my dear Alyosha, especially about God, whether He exists or not. All such questions are utterly inappropriate for a mind created with an idea of only three dimensions.

4. From C.H. Hinton, "What is the Fourth Dimension?," *Scientific Romances*, Vol. 1 (London: Swan Sonnenschein, 1884)

[This first appeared in *Dublin University Magazine* in 1880, was reprinted in *Cheltenham Ladies' College Magazine* (September 1883), and then was published by Swann Sonnenschein as a pamphlet with the subtitle "Ghosts Explained" in 1884. In this essay, Hinton raises the question of how a creature confined to a plane would understand solid forms. It is likely that Abbott and Hinton were aware of each other's work and were influencing one another.][1]

At the present time our actions are largely influenced by our theories. We have abandoned the simple and instinctive mode of life of the earlier civilizations for one regulated by the assumptions of our knowledge and supplemented by all the devices of intelligence. In such a state it is possible to conceive that a danger may arise, not only from a want of knowledge and practical skill, but even from the very presence and possession of them in any one department, if there is a lack of information in other departments. If, for instance, with our present knowledge of physical laws and mechanical skill, we were to build houses without regard to the conditions laid down by physiology, we should probably—to suit an apparent convenience—make them perfectly draught-tight, and the best-constructed mansions would be full of suffocating chambers. The knowledge of the construction of the body and the conditions of its health prevent it from suffering injury by the development of our powers over nature.

In no dissimilar way the mental balance is saved from the dangers attending an attention concentrated on the laws of mechanical science by a just consideration of the constitution of the knowing faculty, and the conditions of knowledge. Whatever pursuit we are engaged in, we are acting consciously or unconsciously upon some theory, some view of things. And when the limits of daily routine are continually narrowed by the ever-increasing complication of our civilization, it becomes doubly important that not one only but every kind of thought should be shared in.

There are two ways of passing beyond the domain of practical certainty, and of looking into the vast range of possibility. One is by asking, "What is knowledge? What constitutes experience?" If we adopt this course we are plunged into a sea of speculation. Were it not

---

1 See further discussion in Rudolph V. Rucker's introduction to *Speculations on the Fourth Dimension: Selected Writings of Charles H. Hinton* (New York: Dover, 1980), vii.

that the highest faculties of the mind find therein so ample a range, we should return to the solid ground of facts, with simply a feeling of relief at escaping from so great a confusion and contradictoriness.

The other path which leads us beyond the horizon of actual experience is that of questioning whatever seems arbitrary and irrationally limited in the domain of knowledge. Such a questioning has often been successfully applied in the search for new facts. For a long time four gases were considered incapable of being reduced to the liquid state. It is but lately that a physicist has succeeded in showing that there is no such arbitrary distinction among gases. Recently again the question has been raised, "Is there not a fourth state of matter?" Solid, liquid, and gaseous states are known. Mr. Crookes[1] attempts to demonstrate the existence of a state differing from all of these. It is the object of these pages to show that, by supposing away certain limitation of the fundamental conditions of existence as we know it, a state of being can be conceived with powers far transcending our own, when this is made clear it will not be out of place to investigate what relations would subsist between our mode of existence and that which will be seen to be a possible one.

In the first place, what is the limitation that we must suppose away?

An observer standing in the corner of a room has three directions naturally marked out from him; one is upwards along the line of meeting of the two walls; another is forwards where the floor meets one of the walls; a third is sideways where the floor meets the other wall. He can proceed to any part of the floor of the room by moving first the right distance along one wall, and then by turning at right angles and walking parallel to the other wall. He walks in this case first of all in the direction of one of the straight lines that meet in the corner of the floor, afterwards in the direction of the other. By going more or less in one direction or the other, he can reach any point on the floor,

---

1 A reference to William Crookes (1832-1919), who invented the cathode ray in 1878. At this time, the universe was seen as being divided into two incompatible material: matter and ether. Electricity did not appear to fit into either of these categories. Crookes proposed that the "radiant matter" he found in cathode rays be identified as "a fourth state of matter," which was "neither solid nor liquid nor gaseous." Crookes was one of a group of scientist who believed in spiritualism. Describing the phenomena in mystical language, he believed that with the cathode ray he had "actually touched the borderland where Matter and Force seem to merge into one another, the shadowy realm between Known and Unknown" (qtd. in Leonid Ivanovich Ponomarev, *The Quantum Dice* (Bristol: Institute of Physics, 1993), 30. Cathode rays were identified as negatively charged atoms, i.e., electrons, by J.J. Thomson in 1897.

and any movement, however circuitous, can be resolved into simple movements in these two directions.

But by moving in these two directions he is unable to raise himself in the room. If he wished to touch a point in the ceiling, he would have to move in the direction of the line in which the two walls meet. There are three directions then, each at right angles to both the other, and entirely independent of one another. By moving in these three directions or combinations of them, it is possible to arrive at any point in a room. And if we suppose the straight lines which meet in the corner of the room to be prolonged indefinitely, it would be possible by moving in the direction those three lines, to arrive at any point in space. Thus in space there are three independent directions, and only three; every other direction is compounded of these three. The question that comes before us then is this. "Why should there be three and only three directions?" Space, as we know it, is subject to a limitation.

In order to obtain an adequate conception of what this limitation is, it is necessary to first imagine beings existing in a space more limited than that in which we move. Thus we may conceive a being who has been throughout all the range of his experience confined to a single straight line. Such a being would know what it was to move to and fro, but no more. The whole of space would be to him but the extension in both directions of the straight line to an infinite distance. It is evident that two such creatures could never pass one another. We can conceive their coming out of the straight line and entering it again, but they having moved always in one straight line, would have no conception of any other direction of motion by which such a result could be effected. The only shape which could exist in a one-dimensional existence of this kind would be a finite straight line. There would be no difference in the shapes of figures; all that could exist would simply be longer or shorter straight lines.

Again, to go a step higher in the domain of a conceivable existence. Suppose a being confined to a plane superficies, and throughout all the range of its experience never to have moved up or down, but simply to have kept to this one plane. Suppose, that is, some figure, such as a circle or rectangle, to be endowed with the power of perception; such a being if it moves in the plane superficies in which it is drawn, will move in a multitude of directions; but, however varied they may seem to be, these directions will all be compounded of two, at right angles to each other. By no movement so long as the plane superficies remains perfectly horizontal, will this being move in the direction we call up and down. And it is important to motive that the plane would be different to a creature confined to it, from what it is to us. We think of a plane habitually as having an upper and a lower side, because it is only by the contact of solids that we realize a plane. But a creature which had been confined to a plane during its whole existence would have no idea of there being two sides to the plane he lived in. In a plane there is simply length and breadth. If a creature in it be supposed to know of an up or down he must already have gone out of the plane.

Is it possible, then, that a creature so circumstanced would arrive at the notion of there being an up and down, a direction different from those to which he had been accustomed, and having nothing in common with them? Obviously nothing in the creature's circumstances would tell him of it. It could only be by a process of reasoning on his part that he could arrive at such a conception. If he were to imagine a being confined to a single straight line, he might realize that he himself could move in two directions, while the creature in a straight line could only move in one. Having made this reflection he might ask, "But why is the number of directions limited to two? Why should there not be three?"

A creature (if such existed), which moves in a plane would be much more fortunately circumstanced than one which can only move in a straight line. For, in a plane, there is a possibility of an infinite variety of shapes, and the being we have supposed could come into contact with an indefinite number of other beings. He would not be limited as in the case of the creature in a straight line, to one only on each side of him.

It is obvious that it would be possible to play curious tricks with a being confined to a plane. If, for instance, we suppose such a being to be inside a square, the only way out that he could conceive would be through one of the sides of the square. If the sides were impenetrable, he would be a fast prisoner, and would have no way out.

What his case would be we may understand, if we reflect what a similar case would be in our own existence. The creature is shut in in all the directions he knows of. If a man is shut in in all the directions he knows of, he must be surrounded by four walls, a roof and a floor. A two-dimensional being inside a square would be exactly in the same predicament that a man would be, if he were in a room with no opening on any side. Now it would be possible to us to take up such a being from the inside of the square, and to set him down outside it. A being to whom this had happened would find himself outside the place he had been confined in, and he would not have passed through any of the boundaries by which he was shut in. The astonishment of such a being can only be imagined by comparing it to that which a man would feel, if he were suddenly to find himself outside a room in which he had been, without having passed through the window, doors, chimney or any opening in the walls, ceiling or floor.

Another curious thing that could be effected with a two-dimensional being, is the following. Conceive two beings at a great distance from one another on a plane surface. If the plane surface is bent so that they are brought close to one another, they would have no conception of their proximity, because to each the only possible movements would seem to be movements in the surface. The two beings might be conceived as so placed, by a proper bending of the plane, that they should be absolutely in juxtaposition, and yet to all the reasoning faculties of either of them a great distance could be proved to intervene. The bending might be carried so far as to make one being suddenly appear in the plane by the side of the other. If these beings were ignorant of the existence of a third dimension, this result would be as marvelous to them, as it would be for a human being who was at a great distance—it might be at the other side of the world—to suddenly appear and really be by our side, and during the whole time he not to have left the place in which he was.

Appendix C: Other Works by Abbott

1. From *The Kernel and the Husk: Letters on Spiritual Christianity* (London: Macmillan, 1886)

[*The Kernel and the Husk* is a series of letters addressed "Dear —." The "husk" refers to religious miracles, while the "kernel" is faith. Abbott's discussion traces a path toward a rational and metaphoric explanation for biblical miracles. In Letter 2, Abbott gives autobiographical information along with a statement of his progress through religious questioning. In Letter 24, Abbott refers both to *Flatland* and Hinton's *A Romance of the Fourth Dimension*, but he rejects the idea that higher dimensions could provide rationalization for spiritual presence. This position is restated in the later *The Spirit on the Water* (1897), a selection of which is in Appendix C2, below.]

Letter 2, "Personal," pp. 7-19.

During my childhood I was very much left to myself in the matter of religion, and may be almost said to have picked it up in a library. I was never made to learn the Creed by heart, nor the Catechism, nor even the Ten Commandments; and to this day I can recollect being reproached by a class-master when I was nearly fourteen years old, for not knowing which was the Fifth Commandment. All that I could plead in answer was, that if he would tell me what it was about, I could give him the substance of the precept. Having read through nearly the whole of Adam Clarke's commentary as a boy of ten or eleven, and having subsequently imbued myself with books of Evangelical doctrine, I was perfectly "up," or thought I was, in the Pauline scheme of salvation, and felt a most lively interest—on Sundays, and in dull moments on week days, and especially in times of illness, of which I had plenty—in the salvation of my own soul. My religion served largely to intensify my natural selfishness. In better and healthier moments, my conscience revolted against it; and at times I felt that the morality of Plutarch's Lives was better than that of St. Paul's Epistles—as I interpreted them. Only to one point in the theology of my youthful days can I now look back with pleasure; and that is to my treatment of the doctrine of Predestinarianism and necessity. On this matter I argued as follows: "If God knows all things beforehand, God has them, or may have them, written down in a book; and if all things that are going to happen are already written down in a book, it's of no use our trying to alter them. So, if it's predestined that I shall have my dinner to-day, I shall certainly have it, even if I don't come home in time, or even though I lock myself up in my bedroom. But *practically, if I don't come home in time, I know I shall not have my dinner. Therefore it's no use talking about these things in this sort of way, because it doesn't answer; and I shall not bother myself any more about Predestination, but act as though it did not exist.*"[1] This argument, if it can be called an argument, I afterwards found sheltering itself under the high authority of Butler's *Analogy;*[2] and I still adhere to it, after an experience of more than five and thirty years. To some, this "Short Way with Predestinarians" may seem highly illogical; but it *works.*

Up to this time I had been little, if at all, impressed by preaching. Our old Rector was a good Greek scholar and a gentleman; but he had a difficulty in making his thoughts intelligible to any but a refined minority among the congregation; and even that select few was made fewer, partly by an awkwardness of gesture which reminded one of Dominie Sampson,[3] and partly by a grievous impediment in his speech. Consequently I had been permitted, and indeed encouraged, never to listen, nor even to appear to listen, to the weekly sermon; and as soon as the Rector gave out his text, I used to take up my Bible and read steadily away till the sermon was over. This sort of thing went on till I was about sixteen years old; when a new Rector came to preach his first sermon. That was a remarkable Sunday for me. To my surprise, when he read out his text, and I, in accordance with unbroken precedent, reached out my hand for the invariable Bible, my father, somewhat abruptly, took it out of my hand, bidding me "for once shut up that book and listen to a sermon." I can still remember the resentment I felt at this infringement on my theological and constitutional

---

1 [Abbott's note] That children, even at a much younger age than ten, do sometimes exercise their young minds to very ill purpose about these subtle metaphysical questions is probably within the experience of all who know anything about children, and it is amusingly illustrated by the following answer (which I have on the authority of an intimate friend) from a seven-years-old to his mother when blaming him for some misconduct: "Why did you born me then? I didn't want to be borned. You should have asked me before you borned me."

2 Joseph Butler's *Analogy of Religion, Natural and Revealed, to the Constitution and Course of Nature* (1736) provides a philosophical argument for morality. The work was required reading in universities, often serving as the text for oral exams, until the end of the nineteenth century.

3 A poor tutor in Sir Walter Scott's novel *Guy Mannering* (1815), "whose untuneable harshness [of voice] corresponded with the awkwardness of his figure." In the novel, he would pedantically draw out each syllable of a word when speaking, e.g.: "Pro-di-gi-ous!"

rights, and how I stiffened my neck and hardened my heart and determined "hearing to hear, but not to understand." But I was compelled to understand. For here, to my astonishment, was an entirely new religion. This man's Christianity was not a "scheme of salvation"; it was a faith in a great Leader, human yet divine, who was leading the armies of God against the armies of Evil; "Each for himself is the Devil's own watchword: but with us it must be each for Christ, and each for all." The scales fell from my eyes. After all, then, Christianity was not less noble than Plutarch's lives; it was more noble. There was to be a contest; yet not each man contending for his own soul, but for good against evil. A Christian was not a mercenary fighting for reward, nor a slave fighting for fear of stripes, but a free soldier fighting out of loyalty to Christ and to humanity.

But what about the doctrine of the Atonement, Justification by Faith, and the other Pauline doctrines? About these our new Rector did not say much that I could understand. He was a foremost pupil of Mr. Maurice, and in Mr. Maurice's books[1] (which now began to be read freely in my home) I began to search for light on these questions. But help I found none or very little, except in one book. Mr. Maurice seemed to me, and still seems, a very obscure writer. Partly owing to a habit of taking things for granted and "thinking underground," partly (and much more) owing to a confusing use of pronouns for nouns and other mere mechanical defects of style, he requires very careful reading. But his book on Sacrifice,[2] after I had three times read it through, gave me more intellectual help than perhaps any other book on Christian doctrine; for here first I learned to look below the surface of a rite at its inner meaning, and also to discern the possibility of illustrating that inner meaning by the phenomena of daily life. It was certainly a revelation to me to know that the sacrifice of a lamb by a human offerer was nothing, except so far as it meant the sacrifice of a human life, and that the sacrifice of a life meant no more (but also no less) than conforming one's life to God's will, doing (and not saying merely) "Thy will, not mine, be done." If one theological process could be illustrated in this way, why not another? If "sacrifice" was going on before my eyes every day, why might there not be also justification by faith, imputation of righteousness, remission of sins,

---

1   F.D. Maurice (1805-72), author of *The Kingdom of Christ* (1838) and *The Religions of the World* (1847), applied Christian principles to social reform and was a member of the Christian Socialist movement. He was dismissed from King's College, London, for his *Theological Essays* (1835), founded Queen's College for women and a Working Men's College (with Charles Kingsley) in 1854, and became professor of moral philosophy at Cambridge in 1866.

2   Maurice, *The Doctrine of Sacrifice Deduced from the Scriptures* (1854).

yes, even atonement itself? Thus there was sown in my mind the seed of the notion that all the Pauline doctrines might be natural, and that Redemption through Christ was only a colossal form of that kind of redemption which was going on around me, Redemption through Nature. This thought was greatly stimulated by the study of *In Memoriam*,[1] which was given to me by a college friend about the time when I lost a brother and a sister, both dying within a few weeks of one another. I read the poem again and again, and committed much of it to memory; and it exerted an "epoch-making" influence on my life. However, for a long time this notion of the naturalness of Redemption existed for me merely in the germ.

Meantime, as to the miracles I had no doubts at all, or only such transient doubts as were suggested by pictures of Holy Families and other sacred subjects, which exhibited Christ as essentially non-human, with a halo around his head, or as an infant with three outstretched fingers blessing his kneeling mother. As a youth, I took it for granted that God could not become man save by a miracle, and therefore that the God-man must work miracles. Further, I assumed that Moses and some of the prophets had worked miracles, and if so, how could it be that the Servants should work miracles and the Son should not? As I grew towards manhood, such rising qualms of doubt as I felt on this point were stilled by the suggestion (which I found in Trench's book on miracles[2]) that the miracles of Christ must be in accordance with some latent law of spiritual nature. It was a little strange certainly that these latent laws should be utilised only for the children of Abraham, and it was inconvenient that the miracles of Moses should be, materially speaking, so stupendously superior to those of Christ; but I took refuge in the greater beauty and emblematic meaning of the latter. Even at the time when I signed the Thirty-nine Articles[3] I had no suspicion that the miracles were not historical. Partly, I had never critically and systematically studied the Gospels as one studies Thucy-

---

1   Alfred Lord Tennyson's (1809-92) long poem *In Memoriam A.H.H.* expresses his grief for his friend A.H. Hallam. A series of poems, it expresses Tennyson's anxieties about social change, immortality, and evolution. It is known for hinting at natural selection in 1850 before Darwin published his theory in 1859.

2   Probably Richard Chenevix Trench's (1807-86) *Notes on Miracles* (1846). Trench held a theological chair at King's College, London, and additionally is known for his philological work, *The Study of Words* (1851). The origin of the *Oxford English Dictionary* is traced to a resolution he authored in 1858 that was passed by the Philological Society.

3   The defining statements of Anglican doctrine established in 1563. Adherence to them is required by all clergy of the Church of England.

dides or Aeschylus;[1] partly the miracles had always been kept in the background by my Rector and the books of the Broad Church School, and I had been accustomed to rest my faith on Christ Himself and not on the miracles; and so it came to pass that, for some time after I was ordained, I was quite content to accept all the miracles of the Old and New Testaments, and to be content with the explanation suggested by "latent laws."

But now that I was ordained, I set to work in earnest (the stress of working for a degree and the need of earning one's living had left no time for it before) at the study of the New Testament. Of course I had "got it up" before, often enough, for the purpose of passing examinations; but now I began to study it for its own sake and at leisure. While reading for the Theological Tripos[2] I had been struck by the inadequacy of many of the theological books that I had had to "get up." Especially on the first three Gospels—looking at them critically, as I had been accustomed to look at Greek and Latin books—I was amazed to find that little or nothing had been done by English scholars to compare the different styles and analyse the narratives into their component parts. For such a task I had myself received some little preparation. I had picked up my classics without very much assistance from the ordinary means, mainly by voluntarily committing to memory whole books or long continuous passages of the best authors, and so imbuing myself with them as to "get into the swing of the author." I had early begun to tabulate these differences of style; and in my final and most important University examination I remember sending up more than one piece of composition rendered in two styles. Though I was never a first-rate composer, owing to my want of practice at school, this method had succeeded in bringing me to the front in "my year"; and I now desired to apply my classical studies to the criticism of the first three Gospels. It seemed to me a monstrous thing that we should have three accounts of the same life, accounts closely agreeing in certain parts, but widely varying in others, and yet that, with all the aids of modern criticism, we should not be able to determine which accounts, or which parts of the three accounts, were the earliest. At the same time I began to apply the same method, though without the same attempt at exactness, to the study of the text of Shakespeare; in which I perceived some differences of style that

---

1   Classical authors commonly studied in university. Aeschylus was a Greek playwright and Thucydides a Greek historian.
2   The Tripos is the final honors examination in various subjects at Cambridge University. Abbott alludes to the very rigid reading list for the Tripos in his day.

implied difference of date, and some that appeared to imply difference of authorship.

About this time people began to talk in popular circles concerning Evolution, and alarm began to be felt in some quarters at the difficulty of harmonizing its theories with theology. With these fears I never could in the least degree sympathize. I welcomed Evolution as a luminous commentary on the divine scheme of the Redemption of mankind. That most stimulating of books, the *Advancement of Learning*,[1] had taught me to be prepared to find that in very many cases "while Nature or man intendeth one thing, God worketh another"; and it was a joy to me to find new light thrown by Evolution on the unfathomable problems of waste, death, and conflict. Death and conflict could never be thus explained—I knew that—but one was enabled to wait more patiently for that explanation which will never come to us till we are behind the veil, when one found that death and conflict had at least been subordinated to progress and development. So I thought; and so I said from the pulpit of one of the Universities in times when the clergy had not yet learned to call Darwin "a man of God." My doctrine was thought "advanced" in those days; but time has gone on and left me, in some respects, behind it. I should never have thought, and should not think now, of calling Darwin "a man of God," except so far as all patient seekers after truth are men of God: but I still adhere to the belief that Evolution has made it more easy to believe in a rational, that is to say a non-miraculous, though supernatural, Christianity.

In this direction, then, my thoughts went forward and, so far, found no stumbling-block. Guided by the poets and analytic novelists, I was also learning to find in the study of the phenomena of daily life fresh illustrations of the Pauline theology, confirming and developing my notion (now of some years' standing) that the Redemption of mankind was natural, nothing more than a colossal representation of the spiritual phenomena that may be seen in ordinary men and women every day of our lives; just as the lightning-flash is no more than (upon a large scale) the crackling of the hair beneath the comb. Good men and women, I perceived, are daily redeeming the bad, bearing their sins, imputing righteousness to them, giving up their lives for them, and imbuing them with a good spirit. This thought, as it gained force, was a great help towards a rational Christianity.

But now my feet began to be entangled in snares and pitfalls. I had begun the study of the Greek Testament, believing that it would bring forth *some* new truth, and assuming that *all* truth must end to the glory

---

1 By Francis Bacon.

of God and of Christ. "Christ," I said, "is the living Truth, so that I have but, as Plato says, to 'follow the Argument,' and that must lead me to the truth, and therefore to Him." But I was not prepared for the result. After some years of work I found myself gradually led to the conclusion that the miraculous element in the Gospels was not historical. A mere glance at the Old Testament shewed that, if there was not evidence enough for the miracles in the New Testament, much less was there for the miracles in the Old.

Before me rose up day by day fresh facts and inferences, not only demonstrating the insufficiency of the usual evidence to prove that the miracles were true, but also indicating a very strong probability that they were false. Often, as I studied the accounts of a miracle, I could see it as it were in the act of growing up, watch its first entrance into the Gospel narrative, note its modest beginning, its subsequent development: and then I was forced to give it up. Worst of all, that miracle of miracles which was most precious to me, the Resurrection of Christ, began to appear to be supported by the feeblest evidence of all. I had not at that time learned to distinguish between the Resurrection of Christ's material body and the Resurrection of His Spirit or spiritual body. Christ's Resurrection seemed to me therefore in those days to be either a Resurrection of the material and tangible body or no Resurrection at all. Now for the Resurrection of the material body I began to be forced to acknowledge that I could find no basis of satisfying testimony. I had heard an anecdote of the Head of some College of Oxford in old days, how he fell asleep after dinner in the Combination Room,[1] while the Fellows over their wine were discussing theology, and presently made them all start by exclaiming as he awoke, "After all[,] there is no evidence for the Resurrection of Christ!" I realized that now, not with a start, but gradually, and with a growing feeling of deep and wearing anxiety. If the Resurrection of Christ fell, what was to become of my faith in Christ?

Amid this impending ruin of my old belief I saw one tower standing firm. It was clear that *something* had happened after the death of Christ to make new men of His disciples. It was clear also that St. Paul had seen *something* that had induced him to believe that Christ had risen from the dead. That which had convinced St. Paul, an enemy, might very well convince the Apostles, the devoted followers of Christ. What was this *something*? It seemed to me that I ought to try to find out. Meantime, I determined to adopt the advice I gave you in my last letter—to stand upon the old ways and look around me and consider

---

1   In Oxford, the correct term would be a common room, but since Abbott is a graduate of Cambridge, he uses the term he is familiar with.

my path before taking another step. Circumstances had placed me in such a position that I was not called on to decide whether a clergyman could entertain such views as were looming on me, and remain a clergyman. I was not engaged in any work directly or indirectly requiring clerical qualifications; and as far as my affections and sentiments were concerned, I went heartily with the services of the Church of England.

So I resolved to put aside all theology for two or three years and to devote myself, during that time, to literary work of another kind. Meantime, I would retain, as far as possible, the old religious ways of thought, and, at all events, the old habits. None the less, I would not give up the intention of investigating the whole truth about the Resurrection. That there was some nucleus of truth I felt quite certain; and even if that truth had been embedded in some admixture of illusion, what then? Were there no illusions in the history of science? Were there no illusions in the history of God's Revelation of Himself through the Old and New Testaments? Might it not be God's method of Revelation that men should pass through error to the truth? This line of thought seemed promising, but I would not at once follow it. I would wait three years and then work out the question of the influence of illusion on religious truth.

An old college acquaintance, an agnostic, whom I met about this time, was not a little startled when I told him my thoughts. He frankly informed me that, though I was "placed in a painful position," I was "bound to speak out." I also thought that I was "bound to speak out"; but I did not feel bound to obtrude immature views upon the world, with the result perhaps of afterwards altering or recanting them. So I took time, plenty of time; I looked about me, on life as well as on books; I formed a habit of testing assumptions and asking the meaning of common words, especially such words as knowledge, faith, certainty, belief, proof, and the like. Believing that theology was made for man and not man for theology, I began to test theological as well as other propositions by the question "How do they *work*?" Meantime I tried my utmost to do the duties of my daily life without distraction and with the same energy as before, hoping that life itself, and the needs of life, would throw some light upon the question, "What knowledge about God is necessary for men who are to do their duty? And how can that knowledge be obtained?"

By these means I was led to see that a great part of what we call knowledge does not come to us, as we falsely suppose it does, through mere logic or Reason, nor through unaided experience, but through the emotions and the Imagination, tested by Reason and experience. Even in the world of science, I found that the so-called "laws and properties of matter," nay, the very existence of matter, were nothing more than suggestions of the scientific Imagination aided by experience. A great part of the environment and development of mankind appeared to have been directed towards the building up of the imaginative faculty, without which, it seemed that religion, as well as poetry, would have been non-existent. So by degrees, it occurred to me that perhaps I had been on the wrong track in my search after religious truth. I had been craving a purely historical and logical proof of Christ's divinity, and had felt miserable that I could not obtain it. But now I perceived that I was not intended to obtain it. Not thus was Christ to be embraced. There must indeed be a basis of fact: but after all it was to that imaginative faculty which we call "faith," that I must look, at least in part, for the right interpretation of fact. That Christ could be apprehended only by faith was a Pauline common-place; but that Christ's Resurrection could be grasped only by faith, and not by the acceptance of evidence, was, to me, a new proposition. But I gradually perceived that it was true. I might be doubtful whether Thomas touched the side of the risen Saviour, yet sure that Christ had risen from the dead in the Spirit, and had manifested Himself after death to His disciples. My standard of certainty being thus shifted, many things of which I had formerly felt certain became uncertain: but, by way of compensation, other things—and these the most necessary and vital— became more certain than ever. I felt less inclined to dogmatize about the existence of matter; but my soul was imbued with a fuller conviction of the existence of a God; and deeper still became the feeling that, so far as things are known to me there is nothing in heaven or earth more divine than Christ.

Thus at last light dawned upon my darkness; and when the sun rose once more upon me, it was the same sun as before, only more clearly seen above the mists of illusion which had before obscured it. The old beliefs of my youth and childhood remained or came back to me, exhibiting Jesus of Nazareth as the Incarnate Son of God, the Eternal Word triumphant over death, seated at the right hand of the Father in heaven, the source of life and light to all mankind. Like Christian in *Pilgrim's Progress*,[1] I found myself suddenly freed from a great burden—a burden of doubts, and provisos, and conditions which, in old days, had seemed to forbid me from accepting Jesus as the Lord and Saviour of mankind unless I could strain my conscience to accept as true a number of stories many of which I almost certainly knew to be false. In order to believe in Christ, it was now no longer needful to believe in suspensions of the laws of Nature: on the contrary, all Nature seemed to combine to prepare the way to conform humanity to that image of God which was set forth in the Incarnation. I did not,

---

1 Refers to the allegorical *Pilgrim's Progress* (1678, 1684) by John Bunyan. The main character is named Christian.

as some Christians do, ignore the existence of Satan (and almost of sin) which Christ Himself most clearly recognized; but I seemed to see that evil was being gradually subordinated to good, and falsehood made the stepping-stone to truth.

Through evil to good; through sin to a righteousness higher than could have been attained save through sin; through falsehood to the truth; through superstition to religion—this seemed to me the divine evolution discernible in the light that was shed from the cross of Christ. No longer now did it seem impossible or absurd that the Gospel of the Truth might have been temporarily obscured by illusions or superstitions even in the earliest times.

I think it must be now some ten years since I settled down to the belief that the history of Christianity had been the history of profound religious truth, contained in, and preserved by, illusions; an ascent of worship through illusion to the truth. A belief that has been fifteen years in making, and for ten years more has been reviewed, criticized, and finally retained as being historically true and spiritually healthful, you must not call, I think, "a transient phase." But I forgive you the expression. A dozen pages of autobiography are a sufficient penalty for three offending words.

Letter 24, "What is a Spirit?," pp. 258–66

MY DEAR —,

You take me to task for the abrupt termination of my last letter. I broke off, you say, just when you thought I was on the point of explaining what I meant by a spirit: "Surely you have some theory of your own and are not content with disbelieving other people's theories." Well, I thought I had said before that I am content to know merely this about a spirit, that it possesses capabilities for loving and serving God, or other nobler capabilities corresponding to these. But if you press me to set up some theory of my own that you may have the pleasure of pulling it to pieces, I will confess to you that my nearest conception of a spirit is a personified virtue. This cannot very well be quite right; any more than a carpenter can be like a door, or like anything else that he has constructed. But it is the nearest I can come to any conception that is not too repulsively material. And sometimes, when I try to conceive of the causes of terrestrial thoughts, and emotions, and spiritual movements, I find myself recurring to the antique notion, hinted at in one or two passages of the Bible, and I believe encouraged by some of the old Rabbis, that there are two worlds; one visible, terrestrial, and material, the other invisible, celestial, and spiritual; and that whatsoever takes place down here takes place first (or simultaneously but causatively) up there; here, the mere outsides of things; there, the causes and springs of action; the bodies down on earth, the spirits up in heaven.

This is but a harmless fancy. Let me give you another. You know—or might know if you would read a little book recently published called *Flatland*, and still better, if you would study a very able and original work by Mr. C.H. Hinton[1]—that a being of Four Dimensions, if such there were, could come into our closed rooms without opening door or window, nay, could even penetrate into, and inhabit, our bodies; that he could simultaneously see the insides of all things and the interior of the whole earth thrown open to his vision: he would also have the power of making himself visible and invisible at pleasure; and could address words to us from an invisible position outside us, or inside our own person. Why then might not spirits be beings of the Fourth Dimension? Well, I will tell you why. Although we cannot hope ever to comprehend what a spirit is—just as we can never comprehend what God is—yet St. Paul teaches us that the deep things of the spirit are in some degree made known to us by our own spirits. Now when does the spirit seem most active in us? or when do we seem nearest to the apprehension of "the deep things of God"? Is it not when we are exercising those virtues which, as St. Paul says, "abide"—I mean faith, hope and love? Now there is obviously no connection between these virtues and the Fourth Dimension. Even if we could conceive of space of Four Dimensions—which we cannot do, although we can perhaps describe what some of its phenomena would be if it existed—we should not be a whit the better morally or spiritually. It seems to me rather a moral than an intellectual process, to approximate to the conception of a spirit: and toward this no knowledge of Quadridimensional space can guide us.

What, for example, do we mean when we speak of the Holy Spirit, and describe Him as the Third Person in the Trinity? I hope you will not suppose—because I happen to be a rationalist as regards the historical interpretation of certain parts of the Bible, or because I have not disguised my dislike of the formal and quasi-arithmetical propositions in which the Athanasian creed sets forth the doctrine of the Trinity—that I reject the teaching of the New Testament on the nature and functions of the Holy Spirit. Literary criticism may oblige us to regard the long discourses on the functions of the Paraclete or Advocate in the Fourth Gospel as being in the style of the author and not the language of Christ; but it is difficult to suppose that the sublime thoughts in those passages are the mere inventions of a disciple of

---

1 [Abbott's note] *"A Romance of the Fourth Dimension,"* Swan Sonnenschein.

Jesus; and the characteristic sayings of Christ in the Synoptic Gospels bear cogent though terse witness to His acknowledgment of a Holy Spirit who should "speak" in His disciples, and "teach" His disciples what to say, when they were summoned before the bar of princes: "it is not ye that speak, but the Holy Spirit," Mark xiii. 11; "it is not ye that speak, but the Spirit of your Father which speaketh in you," Matth. x. 20; "the Holy Spirit shall teach you in that very hour what ye ought to say," Luke xii. 12. I need not remind you how large a space "the Spirit" claims in St. Paul's Epistles, and especially of the use which the Apostle makes of the triple combination of the Father, the Son, and the Holy Spirit. Even, therefore, if I could give no explanation of the whole of it, nor so much as put into words the faint glimpse I may have gained into the meaning of a part of this doctrine, I should be inclined to accept the existence of the Holy Spirit on the authority of Christ or St. Paul, as being a doctrine that does not enter into the domain of evidence, a conception of the divine nature from which I might hope to learn much, if I would reverently keep it before me and try to apprehend it. But I seem to have a glimpse of it. That influence or "idea" of the dead which, as Shakespeare says, "creeps into our study of imagination," and which reproduces all the best and essential characteristics of the departed—when this has once taken possession of us, do we not naturally say that we now realize "the spirit" of the dead, feeling that it guides us for the first time to the appreciation of his words and deeds? Now as God, the initial Thought, needed to be revealed to us by means of the Word of God, so the Word needed to be revealed to us by means of the Influence of the Word. Or, to put it more personally, as the Father needed to be revealed by the Son, so the Son needed to be revealed by the Spirit. Those who knew Christ merely in the flesh knew but little of Him, and had little understanding of His words. It was the Spirit of Christ that guided, and still guides, His disciples into the fuller knowledge of the meaning of His past life on earth and His present purposes in heaven.

I own, however, that I have sometimes felt at a loss when I have asked myself, "How is this Spirit a Person? And do I love Him or It? And if Jesus and the Spirit of Jesus are two Persons, then must I also infer two personalities for myself, one for my mortal terrestrial humanity, another for my immortal celestial spirit?" These questions are extremely difficult for me to answer with confidence: yet I feel instinctively that they have a profound and satisfying answer to which I have not yet attained; but I suggest some answer of this kind, "When we endeavour to form a conception of God we ought to put aside the limitations of human individuality. Now we cannot do this while we conceive of God simply as the Father, and still less while we conceive of Him simply as the Son; but we can do it when we conceive of Him as being an all-pervasive Power, the source of order and harmony and light, sometimes as a Breath breathing life into all things good and beautiful, sometimes as a Bono or Law, liking or attracting together all things material and spiritual so as to make up the Kosmos or Order of the Universe. The traditions of the Church have taught us that there has been such a Power, subsisting from the first with the Father and the Eternal Son, in whom the Father and the Son were, and are, united; and by whom the whole human race is bound together in brotherhood to one another and in sonship to the Eternal Father. What is this Being but the Personification of that Power which, in the material world, we call Attraction and in the immaterial, Love? Is it not conceivable that this Being which breathes good thoughts into every human breast should love those whom It inspires? And we—can we love our country, and love Goodness, Purity, Honour, Faith, Hope, and yet must we find it impossible to love this personified Love, this Holy Spirit? But if we love the Spirit of God, and the Spirit loves us, then we can understand how it may be called a Person."

I foresee the answer that might be given to these—I will not call them reasonings, say meditations. "All this is the mere play of fancy: you personify England, Virtue, Goodness, Hope, Faith, and the like; and such personifications are tolerable in poetry; but you do not surely maintain that such personifications have any real existence: in the same way, you may find a certain conception of the Supreme Being useful for the encouragement of devotion, but you have no right hence to infer that this conception represents an objective reality, much less God Himself." My reply is that in the region of theological contemplation where demonstration, and proof of the ordinary kind, are both impossible, I conceive I "have a right" to do this on the authority of Christ and St. Paul and the Fourth Gospel, and the general tradition of the Church. I would sooner believe that myself and my spirit have a dual personality; I would sooner recognize the presence of the Angels of England and France and the other great nations of the world about the heavenly throne, like the Angels of the seven churches of Asia or the Angel of the Chosen People; I would sooner acknowledge the actual personality of Hope, Faith, and I know not what other celestial ministers between God and man; I would sooner, in a word, believe that personality depends upon some subtle combination such as only poets have dimly guessed at, than I would give up the belief that there is beside the Eternal Father, and the Eternal Son, an Eternal Spirit, to the description of whom we can best approximate by calling Him personified Love.

Looking at the Spirit of God in this way I sometimes seem to discern a closer connection than is generally recognized between the Resurrection and the power of loving. You will remember that St. Paul constantly connects the Resurrection of Christ with the "Spirit"; Christ was "raised from the dead *in*, or *by*, *the Spirit*["]; and St. Peter says that Christ was "put to death in the flesh, but quickened *in the Spirit*." Now this Spirit is the Power of Love. Do we ask for an explanation of this connection? It is surely obvious that the Resurrection of Christ would not have directly availed men (so far as we can see) unless it had been manifested to them. But how was it manifested? We think it was by love: on the one hand by the unsatisfied and longing love of the sorrowing disciples, creating a blank in the heart which could only be filled by the image of the risen Saviour; on the other hand by the unsatisfied and longing love of the Lord Jesus Christ, dying with a purpose as yet unfulfilled. Thus—so far as concerns the influence of the Resurrection of Jesus upon humanity—it was the Spirit of Love that raised Jesus from the abyss of inert oblivion and exalted Him to the right hand of God in the souls of men. I dare not say that, if Jesus had failed to root Himself in the hearts of men He could never have been raised from the dead; just as I dare not say that, if St. Peter had not been inspired to say "Thou art the Christ," the Church could never have been founded on the rock of heaven-imparted faith. Let us avoid this way of looking at things, as being repulsive and preposterous, putting things terrestrial before things celestial. Let us rather say that, because the rock of faith was being set up by the hand of God in heaven, therefore at that same instant the Apostle received the strength to utter his confession of faith; and because Christ's Spirit had soared up after death to the heaven of heavens and thence was bending down lovingly to look upon His despairing followers, therefore they received power to see Him again, living for them on earth.

Yet as regards ordinary men, I cannot help occasionally reviving that same preposterous method which I would discard in the case of Christ. And starting from terrestrial phenomena first, I sometimes ask myself, Is it possible that the resurrection of each human soul may depend upon the degree to which it has rooted itself in the affection of others? The Roman Catholic Church teaches that the condition of the dead may be affected by the prayers of survivors; and many abuses have resulted from a perverted and mechanical misinterpretation of that doctrine; but how if the spirit of a dead man actually owes its spiritual resurrection, not indeed to formally uttered petitions, but to the silent prayers, the loving wishes, the irrepressible desires, of fellow-spirits on earth and in heaven? How if a man lives in heaven and in the second life so far as his spirit has imprinted itself on the loving memories of others above and below? "Has the dead man kindled in the heart of one single human being a spark of genuine unselfish affection?" To that extent, then, he receives a proportional germ of expansive and eternal life—might it not be so? And if it were so, then we could better understand how both the Lord Jesus Christ, and we mortal men, die in the flesh but are raised to a life eternal after death "in the Spirit" and "by the Spirit"—that great pervasive spiritual Power of Love which links all things in heaven and earth together.

I trust I have theorized enough to please you. I have done so because on the whole I think it best that you should see all the weakness, as well as all the strength, of my position—the credulous and fanciful side of it; as well as its breadth, its naturalness, its reasonableness, its spiritual comfort, its dependence on moral effort, its recognition of Law, its consistency with facts, and its absolute freedom from intellectual difficulties. Regarded in the ordinary way, as being the revivification of the material body, the Resurrection of Christ becomes an isolated portent in history; regarded naturally, it becomes the triumph of the Spirit over the fear of death, the central event of our earthly history. Central I say, but not isolated; because there are seen converging towards it, as it were predictively, all the phenomena of the evolution and training of the Imagination; all instances of true poetic and prophetic vision; the stars of heaven and all the creative provisions of night and darkness and sleep and dreams, nay even death itself. And what higher tribute (short of actual worship) can be paid to the personality of Christ than to say that "the phenomena of His resurrection are natural." I think if I were depressed and shaken in faith—as one is liable to be at times, not by intellectual but by moral considerations, when one feels that evil is stronger than it should be, both in oneself and outside oneself—it would be a great help to go and hear some agnostic saying with vehement conviction, "The resurrection of Christ was natural, purely natural." I should bid him say it again, and again; and I would go home and say it over and over again to myself by way of comfort, to strengthen my faith: "The manifestations of the Resurrection of Christ were purely natural. So they were. Things could not be otherwise. Being what He was, Christ could not but thus be manifested to His followers after death. It was the natural effect of Christ's personality upon the disciples; and through the disciples upon St. Paul. Then what a Person have we here! A Person consciously superior to death, and, after His death, fulfilling a promise which He made to His disciples that He would still be present with them! What wonder if He is even now present with us, influencing us with something of the power with which He moved the last of the Apostles! What wonder if He is destined yet for future ages to be a present Power among men until the establishment of that Kingdom which He proclaimed upon earth, the Fatherhood of God and brotherhood of man!"

2. From *The Spirit on the Water: The Evolution of the Divine From the Human* (London: Macmillan, 1897), chapter 2

[In this work, Abbott attempts to clarify and to distinguish the differences between understanding higher dimensions and his belief in Christianity, continuing to reaffirm the position he made in *The Kernel and the Husk* (Appendix C1, above). In doing so, Abbott is taking a very different philosophical position from that of Hinton.]

An Illustration from Four Dimensions[1]

We live in a world of three dimensions and find it hard to conceive of a world of four. But let us begin by imagining a world of (practically) two dimensions, in which all the inhabitants are thin Triangles, Squares, Pentagons, and other plane figures, so restricted in sight and motion that they cannot look out of, or rise or fall out of, their thin, flat universe. In such a Flatland nothing would be visible but lines.

Next, imagine a living Solid, looking down from a height on such a Flatland, and on the superficial figures—square, triangular, or otherwise—that constitute the homes of a city of Flatlanders and the bodies of the citizens.

He will see everything that is going on within every house and every Flatland body. The pulses, the throbbing of the heart, the changes in the brain that accompany the processes of thought—all will lie open to his view. He will be to them what some of them, perhaps, might be disposed to call the Eye of God. Yet he would not be a God. He would be simply a solid being looking at flat beings, a creature of three dimensions contemplating creatures of two.

Now suppose the surface of Flatland, though impenetrable to Flatlanders, to be of the nature of a watery superficies, penetrable by beings of three dimensions like ourselves; and imagine our Solid (which we will call a Globe) descending vertically into a Flatland chamber. It would be as when a ball slowly falls straight down on the surface of still water and sinks below it.

When the Globe touches the surface of Flatland he will break the surface with a small circle scarcely bigger than a point. When he sinks lower, he will break it with a larger circle. The circle will increase till

---

1 [Abbott's note] The author worked out the following conception in a little book called "Flatland," published in 1884.

the Globe is plunged up to his middle. Then it will diminish till he sinks below the surface. Then it will vanish.

Meantime what will the Flatlander see? A Solid he cannot see. But he can see the line of section made by the Solid as it cuts the plane of Flatland; and this line will represent to him a mysterious Being that has first entered his room (although doors and windows were closed), has then expanded, then diminished, then vanished.

Probably enough, he will call it Angel, Ghost, God, or Demon. But it will be simply a common solid creature manifesting itself to flat creatures, a being of three dimensions manifesting itself to beings of two.

Now try to conceive the existence of a world of one more dimension than ours, containing what we may call "four-dimensional" or "super-solid" inhabitants.

Speaking popularly, there would be a proportion, viz.:—As three dimensions are to two, so four would be to three. *What we are to Flatlanders, that the "Super-solids" would be to us.*

A "Super-solid," then, would see what is inside our homes and our bodies. Taking note of the workings of our brains, he might consequently anticipate our thoughts. He could manifest himself to us in our closed chambers, entering, increasing, diminishing, vanishing, at will. He could see and penetrate to the centre of our globe. Nowhere, in earth or heaven or beneath the earth, could we flee from his presence.

He, then, would be to us what some among us might be disposed to call the All-seeing and Omnipresent God.

But no Christian ought to be able—it is perhaps too much to say "*is* able"—to give the name of God to a Super-solid, who may perhaps be a wholly despicable creature, an escaped convict from the four-dimensional land.

The followers of Christ ought to feel that a good Flatlander is more like God than a Bad Super-solid, and that there is nothing essentially divine in being able to see the centres of all the stars in all the solar systems like dots on a sheet of paper.

This illustration from four dimensions, suggesting other illustrations derivable from mathematics, may serve a double purpose in our present investigation.

On the one hand it may lead us to vaster views of possible circumstances and existences; on the other hand it may teach us that the conception of such possibilities cannot, by any direct path, bring us closer to God. Mathematics may help us to measure and weigh the planets, to discover the materials of which they are composed, to extract light and warmth from the motion of water and to dominate the material universe; but even if by these means we could mount up to Mars or hold converse with the inhabitants of Jupiter or Saturn, we should be no nearer to the divine Throne, except so far as the new experiences might develop in us modesty, respect for facts, a deeper reverence for order and harmony, and a mind more open to new observations and to fresh inferences from old truths.

Appendix D: The Influence of Flatland

1. From A.T. Schofield, *Another World; or the Fourth Dimension*, 3rd ed. (London: Swan Sonnenschein, [1905]) by A.T. Schofield, M.D.

[Schofield, the author of several books on spiritualism, based his argument for spiritualism very heavily on Abbott's *Flatland*, giving large chunks of Abbott's writing in his publication and referencing Abbott's work by page number. His use of Abbott's work likely motivated Abbott to write *Spirit on the Water* (Appendix C2) in an attempt to distance himself and his work from mystical interpretations. However, Schofield's *Another World* was very popular and went into five editions: the first edition was in 1888 and the fifth edition was published in 1920.]

INTRODUCTORY

It is undoubtedly the cherished belief of the vast majority of mankind, whether they be Christian, Mohammedan, Hindoo, or Heathen, whether they be savage or civilized, in every quarter of the globe, that there is another world besides the material universe in which we live.

All unite in considering that world to be a higher sphere than ours, and its inhabitants to be more or less spiritual beings.

It is also generally believed that the beings of that spirit world can and do visit ours, manifesting themselves in a human or animal shape.

When we come, however, to further details of this higher world, we have every diversity of belief and superstition.

The only account and description of it to which we, as Christians, attach any credence, is found in the Bible, a book which we regard as a revelation of its rulers, inhabitants, and laws, given to man by the supreme Ruler, not only of the spiritual, but of our material world, God.

In our own persons we get confirmation of the existence of a higher sphere, in being able consciously to distinguish between our spiritual, intellectual, and moral selves and our bodies and brains, through which we act and by which we live.

Materialists will, we know, have none of this. To them, if true to their creed, there is, and can be, nothing beyond the material. Mind, morals, feelings, passions, are to them only protoplasmic changes of ganglion nerve cells, producing carbonic acid gas and water.

To them the almost universal consensus of opinion in favour of a spirit world goes for nothing, unless such a world can be demonstrated, handled, and weighed.

We therefore propose, in the following pages to discuss from a somewhat new point of view the question of the existence of such a world, what are its powers, its laws, and its relationship, with this universe, and in doing so, will observe how far these powers and laws, deduced by analogy from mathematics, correspond to the spiritual claims of the Christian religion.

I would here take the opportunity of acknowledging my deep indebtedness to the anonymous author of a small book, called "Flatland," which I have used extensively throughout, and without which I am quite sure the public would never have been troubled with these remarks; my object being to carry on the line of argument there brought forward, to what seems to me its true and necessary conclusion.

Finally, let me ask the indulgence of my more advanced mathematical readers for the many fallacies and "non-sequiturs" that doubtless abound, in spite of my true endeavours simply and impartially to draw none but legitimate and logical conclusions from the arguments and facts I have advanced.

PREFACE TO THIRD EDITION

Many speculations concerning the fourth dimension have been made since this book was first issued, notably that by Mr. Wells that it is "Time."[1] But no theory carries conviction, and indeed the whole is a speculation, the interest however of which remains untouched in the close parallel afforded between what would be true of a fourth dimension and all that is written or known concerning the spirit world. A few additions have been made in this edition.

A.T. SCHOFIELD.

CHAPTER I. THE LAND OF NO DIMENSION

We are all so habituated to take visible realities around us as a matter of course, and so accustomed to every variety of solid or material form, that why all the universe should be limited to solidity, or three dimensions, is only asked at rare intervals by a few of the more thoughtful among us.

---

1 H.G. Wells's *The Time Machine* (1895).

To make this plain. Even those unaccustomed to algebra will understand that if x represents three inches, or a line of this length, x^2 (x square) represents 3 x 3, or nine square inches on a flat surface, three inches each way; x^3 (x cube), again, represents 3 x 3 x 3, or twenty-seven cubic or solid inches, or a solid body measuring three inches every way. Hence we consider x as representing lines, x^2 squares, x^3 solids, and then comes the question, What does x^4 represent? For mathematics passes as easily from x^3 to x^4 as from x^2 to x^3, and yet while x, x^2, x^3, refer to objects known to all of us, the wisest can form no possible conception of what x^4, or a world of four dimensions, is like.

Perhaps, however, before disturbing our minds, and entering seriously upon the question as to whether there can be and is any object or world represented by x^4, and whether or no we can comprehend it, my reader will not be offended if, for the benefit of those less learned than himself, I labour in the simplest language further to explain these various dimensions.

To begin: *No dimension, or size in no direction*, is represented mathematically by a point, which is an object described as having no parts or magnitude....

One dimension (x), or *size in one direction*, is represented mathematically by a straight line, which is described as having length without breadth....

Two dimensions (x^2), or *size in two directions*, is represented mathematically by a superficies or surface, which is described as having length and breadth without thickness....

Three dimensions (x^3), or *size in three directions*, is represented mathematically by a *solid body*, which is described as having length, breadth, and thickness....

Four dimensions (x^4), or *size in four directions*, we cannot represent mathematically, nor can we describe in what direction its fourth dimension lies, nor can we draw, or even imagine it; the fact being that the whole material world which we can see, and of which we can speak, is a world of three dimensions (or x^3) and no more, nor is it possible for the mind of man to indicate or imagine any other direction than three—length, breadth, and height (or depth or thickness, etc.).

On this account it is that so many have denied the possibility of there being anything higher than a solid. To show the fallacy of this argument, then, we will consider the imaginary case of an inhabitant of a country where nothing but perfectly flat objects exist, when an endeavour is made to explain to him our own world of solids; and by putting ourselves in his place, and carefully observing the difficulty he, accustomed only to x^2 or flatness, would have in grasping x^3, or solidity, which nevertheless exists, we may understand better that the difficulty we in x^3, or solidity, have in our turn of grasping x^4, or the fourth dimension, is no argument whatever against the existence of such a world.

First of all, however, we will consider the still lower conditions of *no dimensions* and of *one dimension*.

Imagine, then, a world or universe consisting entirely and absolutely of a single POINT, a country which therefore possesses neither length, breadth, depth, nor height. Imagine (if you can) the sole being in such a world, and observe what his experience would be, as described in "Flatland."

"He is himself his own world, his own universe; of any other than himself he can form no conception; he knows not length, or breadth, or height, for he has no experience of them; he has no cognizance even of the number two; for he is himself one and all, being really nothing. Yet mark his perfect self-complacency, and hence learn this lesson, that to be self-contented is to be vile and ignorant, and that to aspire is better than to be blindly and impotently happy. Now listen! There arose from the little buzzing creature a tiny, low, monotonous tinkling, from which I caught these words. 'IT fills all space, and what IT fills IT is, what IT thinks that IT utters; and what IT utters, that IT hears, and IT itself is thinker, utterer, hearer. IT is the one, and yet the all in all.'"

This then gives us an idea of what a world would be that consisted only of one being, and that being having no parts or size.

Having duly performed this excruciating effort of imagination, and succeeded in realizing what nothing, or "Pointland," really is, the exhausted reader had better pause for five minutes before taking the next step higher into the more interesting world of one dimension, or "Lineland."

[Several passages from Abbott's *Flatland* follow.]

CHAPTER V. THE LAND OF FOUR DIMENSIONS MATHEMATICALLY CONSIDERED

In now summing up the result of all that has been said, and trying to carry the facts that have been observed in the relation of the first to the second, and the second to the third dimension into the relations of the third to the fourth, we will first of all consider this higher and unknown dimension as a mathematical figure, and secondly enumerate some of the probable laws of a world of such dimensions and its inhabitants, as deduced by analogy, and their possible relations with our world and its inhabitants.

Then we may further consider the actual facts around us bearing on the question, and compare these deduced laws of the fourth dimension with some of the claims of Christianity as stated in the Bible.

Let us then, first of all, consider the mathematical or geometrical side of the question, and inquire what would be the character of regular figures in the fourth dimension, arguing from analogy.

And in so doing, we must warn the reader that the subject is necessarily somewhat involved and intricate; but that nevertheless the conclusions arrived at are so fascinating and novel, that if he will only traverse the preliminary Sahara in patience, he will probably feel rewarded by the subsequent oasis he reaches in the summing up and application of the whole theory.

Let us therefore proceed to set forth the facts in order.

IN ONE DIMENSION we get—

(1) Straight lines,

(2) Varying only in one direction—length;

(3) Having two terminal points (or sides or outsides, the line between these being the inside); and

(4) Seen only (by a single eye in line with them) as points.

IN TWO DIMENSIONS we get—

(1) Surface or flat figures,

(2) Varying in two directions—length and breadth, also in number of sides and angles (we also get irregular figures of one dimension, but lying in two, as curved or crooked lines);

(3) Having not less than three[1] terminal points or angles, and not less than three borders or boundary lines, or sides or outsides (the surface of the figure being the inside); and

---

1 [Schofield's note] No flat figure can have less than three angles and three borders, viz., a triangle; for two straight lines cannot enclose a space. (Circles and curved lines are not considered, being really an infinite number of straight lines.)

(4) Seen only (by a single eye on a level with them) as lines.

IN THREE DIMENSIONS we get—

(1) Solids,

(2) Varying only in three directions—length, breadth, depth, also in number and regularity of sides and angles (we also get irregular figures of two dimensions, but lying in three, as curved or crooked surfaces);

(3) Having not less than four[1] terminal points or angles, and not less than four borders, surfaces, or sides or outsides (the contents being the insides); and

(4) Seen only (by a single eye[2]) as surfaces.

IN FOUR DIMENSIONS we get (by analogy)—

(1) Unnamed bodies,

(2) Varying only in four directions, length, breath, depth, and—, also in number and regularity of size and angles (we also get irregular bodies of three dimensions, but lying in four; as—);

(3) Having not less than five terminal points or angles, and not less than five borders, solids, or sides or outsides; and

(4) Seen only (by a double eye) as solids.

Turning now to consider some of the probable laws deducible by analogy from these data and the foregoing chapters, we may suggest the following, the general truth of which the reader will probably be now prepared to admit.

SOME OF THE RELATIONS OF A BEING IN ONE DIMEN-SION, WITH THE DIMENSION BELOW HIM AND THE BEINGS IN IT, *e.g.*, A BEING IN A FOURTH DIMENSION WITH THE THIRD (OUR WORLD) AND THOSE IN IT, ARE:—

---

1 [Schofield's note] A solid body cannot have fewer than four angles and sides, viz., a solid triangle. (Circular and curved bodies are not considered, being really an infinite number of straight lines.)

2 [Schofield's note] We see bodies as solids, not surfaces, simply because we have two eyes, and can see them from two points of view at once. The stereo-scope is founded on this fact.

1. He can enter or leave the world below him, that is, appear and disappear at will, and that without changing his form.
2. However near to the world below him, he remains invisible till actually in it.
3. He can be in closest proximity with the beings in the world below, and yet outside that world altogether, and therefore invisible.
4. From his dimension he can see and enter at will the inside of every living being and thing in the world below him.
5. When he enters the world below, he can never be wholly seen, and that part of him that is seen is always in the form of the world below him which he enters.
6. His voice, while still in his own dimension, would be heard (if hearing were possible) by a being of the world below as an internal voice, or a voice from his own inside.
7. His appearance and disappearance in the world below are not caused by any change of form or substance, but by his entering or leaving that world.
8. A world and beings of any dimension include all the shapes and characters of those below them, adding to them that further shape and character peculiar to the added dimension.

THE RELATIONS OF A BEING IN ONE DIMENSION WITH THAT ABOVE HIM AND ITS INHABITANTS, *e.g.*, ONE IN THE THIRD DIMENSION (OUR WORLD) WITH THE FOURTH.

1. All conception of a higher dimension is impossible, though capable of mathematical demonstration.
2. However vast and populous the dimension, to him it is absolutely and necessarily non-existent.
3. If he could hear such beings, the sound would appear to come from his inner consciousness, and not from his own world without.
4. If such beings enter his world, he can only see and comprehend that part of them that enters it. Such beings may directly enter his own inside.
5. And to him such part *always appears in the likeness of an inhabitant of his world* (the inhabitants of one world being always a partial likeness, or the likeness of a part, of those in the world above them).
6. He can never, by his own power, leave his own dimension or world.

7. While in his world, he can never see the true appearance or shape of any being in it, but only its exterior.
8. If raised into the dimension above, he at once perceives the true dimension and shape of every being in his own world.
9. The beings of the dimension into which he is raised, at first present the same appearance as the beings (now first truly seen) in his own dimension.
10. By close inspection and careful comparison the real difference can be discerned.
11. Even if the dimension above be visited and understood, it is impossible to describe it in the language, or to draw it in the figures, of his own dimension.
12. All such attempts are necessarily unintelligible, and sound foolish and irrational.
13. All attempts to understand or grasp the dimension above, without having entered it, are futile.
14. An eye in one's inside would, according to analogy, look in the direction of the dimension above.
15. Each dimension adds one new direction of size, space, capacity, and form to the one below.
16. The visibility of a being *does not depend on physical properties*, but on its position inside or outside of the world below him.

CHAPTER VI. THE LAND OF FOUR DIMENSIONS IN RELATION TO OURS OF THREE.

Turning now from analogies and theories to facts, we find in the first place an almost universal consensus of opinion amongst all nations, throughout all ages (with few and curious exceptions), that there does exist a higher[1] world than ours, invisible to mortal eyes.

Those among civilized nations who have doubted or denied its existence have done so in spite of their own feelings, and in virtue of a reasoning that denies anything that cannot be apprehended by the senses, in short, anything that is not "matter." The narrowness of such reasoning gives it all its exactness, and the materialist finds a satisfaction in denying all he cannot account for, or where the clear but limited light of his understanding fails to penetrate. Some minds, I suppose, prefer the well-trimmed order of a London square within its iron railing, or a well-stocked kitchen garden with its four high brick walls,

---

1 [Schofield's note] By higher is meant greater in qualities and powers. In speaking of this world, though the whole of it is included, it is mainly with that part of it that constitutes God's spiritual kingdom that we are concerned.

to the boundless prairie or the rolling moorland. The known can at any rate be made to yield a tribute to the complacent human wisdom which can classify, analyse, and otherwise ticket and name it; while the unknown is denied by our little philosophers, partly because the human mind cannot fully grasp it, and finds it easier to ignore it, and partly because the unknown refuses to be measured, weighed, and arranged, and thus furnish another trophy to the greatness of man's intellect.

It must not be supposed, however, that our patient reader has been asked to wade through all these pages merely to prove to our materialists that there is a world that finds no place in their philosophy; for the reader himself doubtless already accepts the fact of this world in a general way, and the number of absolute materialists is too small, and their convictions too strong, to be much shaken by the humble methods adopted here. We seek to do far more than this; we hope to show by analogy how the powers of this higher world, in many an unlooked-for particular, correspond with those that may justly be supposed to belong to x^4.

Let us now proceed to consider some of the phenomena of this unseen world, as current in tradition, as experienced by individuals, and as recorded in books—mainly in the Bible, this being the authoritative history accepted by all Christians of the spiritual kingdom.

All believe that this world is a higher one than ours; higher in the sense of being greater, wiser, more powerful; that it, like ours, contains inhabitants good and bad, and regions fair, and dark, and terrible. But we all feel that the goodness of some of its inhabitants on the one hand, and the evil of the rest on the other, alike transcend in every way all standards of good and evil here; and that, in the same way, both the fairness and the foulness and horror of its different regions transcend all ever seen by mortal eye, or that can be pictured by the human mind.

Most believe this unseen world to be densely peopled, and that in some way it rules over our own with a sway in every way greater, again stronger, and more comprehensive than that of any known earthly government.

Another curiously universal, instinctive belief and one by no means confined to Christianity, is, that when a man dies, part of him (his soul, or spirit) leaves this world altogether, to enter the higher one. And here we may turn aside to remark that the general belief that man has a spiritual nature—something beyond and above the highest ganglion cell in his brain, something that leaves the body at death, but abides in it through life— may be well illustrated by algebra.

Let, for example, the body, material and solid, be represented fairly enough by x^3, and the spirit, higher and possessing an unknown power, by x^4.[1] Then (x^3+x^4) represents the man in life, while $(x^3 + x^4)$ - x^4 represents the departure of the spirit (x^4) at death, which returns to its own dimension, while the body (x^3), which is left, returns to the earth to which it belongs.

If this, then, be true, as is surely believed amongst all Christians, that man *is* at any rate a complex being, having as definite a relation with the unseen world above him as with the visible world around him, a relation which is realized by all after death, then is explained the instinctive craving of all the human race, even apart from Bible revelation, after a higher world; hence, also, the capability to receive and understand its mysteries, and the possibility of communion with it even now.

[...]

In conclusion, we would briefly emphasize these following points.

If we have to any degree succeeded in showing the probability of that other world being of a higher dimension than our own, and that we have a link with it naturally in the spiritual part of our beings; we see most clearly established by analogy, that by no development of our mental faculties, by no advancement in science, by no cultivation of conduct or morals, in short, by no education or improvement of the human race, *per se*, can we understand, enter, or view this higher kingdom. Any comprehension, in short, of it, is not by cultivation, or strengthening even of that link we already have with it in our souls, but by a distinct revelation from that world to these powers within us, and a consequent elevation of these powers into this higher dimension. In relation therefore with Christianity (as we call this scheme of revelation), we see why the most highly cultured in the learning of the third dimension possess little if any advantage (nay, often the reverse) over the wayfaring man, though a fool, inasmuch as it is to both of them a distinct revelation, more easily received indeed in the latter case, since there is here no force of intellect to set aside, for the meaning of our

---

1   [Schofield's note] In taking x^4 here to represent spirits and hereafter the spirit world, it must be remembered that we are absolutely ignorant of what is really involved by this formula. As far as we know, the "material" is strictly limited to three dimensions, nothing in one or two being material, or having any substance whatever. It must therefore be distinctly understood that we firmly believe God is a spirit, and the other world a spiritual one, and that we have no wish or intention of materializing it in enforcing the truth of some of its laws by means of analogies drawn from a supposed fourth dimension.

Lord's saying is now clearly apparent, that except we become as little children, we shall *in no wise* enter the kingdom of heaven.

2. From C.H. Hinton, *The Fourth Dimension* (London: Swann Sonnenschein, 1904)

[In this work, which was very popular among theosophists and others interested in mysticism, Hinton discusses Plato's Cave and makes an analogy between the fourth dimension and a higher spiritual consciousness.]

Four-Dimensional Space

There is nothing more indefinite, and at the same time more real, than that which we indicate when we speak of the "higher." In our social life we see it evidenced in a greater complexity of relations. But this complexity is not all. There is, at the same time, a contact with, an apprehension of, something more fundamental, more real....

Now, this higher—how shall we apprehend it? It is generally embraced by our religious faculties, by our idealizing tendency. But the higher existence has two sides. It has a being as well as qualities. And in trying to realize it through our emotions we are always taking the subjective view. Our attention is always fixed on what we feel, what we think. Is there any way of apprehending the higher after the purely objective method of a natural science? I think that there is.

Plato uses this illustration to portray the relation between true being and the illusions of the sense world. He says that just as a man liberated from his chains could learn and discover that the world was solid and real, and could go back and tell his bound companions of this greater higher reality, so the philosopher who has been liberated, who has gone into the thought of the ideal world, into the world of ideas greater and more real than the things of sense, can come and tell his fellow men of that which is more true than the visible sun—more noble than Athens, the visible state.

Now, I take Plato's suggestion; but literally, not metaphorically. He imagines a world which is lower than this world, in that shadow figures and shadow motions are its constituents; and to it he contrasts the real world. As the real world is to this shadow world, so is the higher world to our world. I accept his analogy. As our world in three dimensions is to a shadow or plane world, so is the higher world to our three-dimensional world. That is, the higher world is four-dimensional; the higher being is, so far as its existence is concerned apart from its qualities, to be sought through the conception of an actual existence spatially higher than that which we realize with our senses.

3. From C.H. Hinton, *An Episode of Flatland: or How a Plane Folk Discovered the Third Dimension. With Which is Bound Up An Outline of the History of Unæa* (London: Swan Sonnenschein, 1907), 1-4, 6-9, 13-14

[C.H. Hinton published his own novel based on the concept of a two-dimensional world. However, Hinton aligned the geometry of his world along the edge of a disk, rather than the horizontal tabletop world of Abbott's. In this opening section, Hinton explains the geometry and physical nature of his world and its history. Aware of some of the criticism that had been raised about the physical possibility of Abbott's world, Hinton addresses such issues of how vision would work and the challenges his creatures would have in movement. In his discussion, Hinton also contemplates how the physical world would impact cultural and personal interactions, especially those between men and women.]

Preface

An objection is often made to the very word Flatland, and the term plane being—as if the existence of such a region and so circumstanced a people were impossible.

All such doubts find a ready solution in the Introduction to this narrative, in which is given a profound analysis of the structure of the people, the physical geography of the region, and a historical sketch of earlier events.

In dealing with the Episode [of Flatland] which forms the subject of the story however, a different plan has been taken, a different method pursued.

The attempt has been made to let the physical differences and the extreme limitations of the people fall into the background, so that with the kind of perception which recognises a nature akin to his own, the reader may pass to a comprehension of the situation through the feelings, acts, ideas and struggles of the actors themselves.

It is enough for the reader to remember, that at the time the narrative opens the inhabitants of Astria—these flatlanders, these Unæans—had arrived at a state of civilization which, though mechanically inferior to ours, yet in respect to the organization of the State, the conduct of business, the unequal distribution of wealth, and the charm of society, was not so very much unlike our own condition.

Introduction

Placing some coins on the table one day, I amused myself by pushing them about, and it struck me that one might represent a planetary system of a certain sort by their means. This large one in the centre represents the sun, and the others its planets journeying round it.

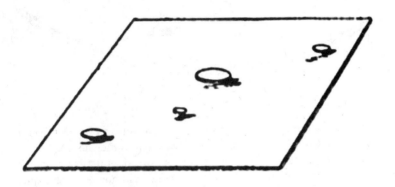

And in this case considering the planets as inhabited worlds, confined in all their movements round their sun, to a slipping over the surface of the table, I saw that we must think of the beings that inhabit these worlds as standing out from the rims of them, not walking over the flat surface of them.[1] Just as attraction in the case of our earth acts towards the centre, and the centre is inaccessible by reason of the solidity on which we stand, so the inhabitants of my coin worlds would have an attraction proceeding out in every direction along the surface of the table from the centre of the coin, and "up" would be to them out from the centre beyond the rim, while "down" would be towards the centre inwards from the rim. And beings thus situated would be rightly described as standing on the rim.

And I saw that if I supposed the surface of the table to be perfectly smooth, so that there was no impediment to motion along it, then these beings would have no notion at all that there was a surface on which they slipped. Since the surface is always in contact with every moving thing, the notion of it would be absent from their consciousness. There would be no difference in respect to it. And I saw that here

---

1 This is in response to Abbott's *Flatland* geometry.

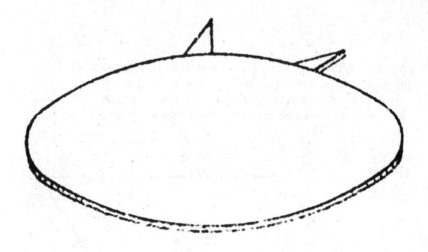

I had an image of a two dimensional world, a world in which the creatures of it would think that space itself was two dimensional.

We see that the discs which form these worlds must be supported somehow, but the beings of such a universe would not ask such a question—they would think that all the space there was lay in the extension of the movements they made, and would never think of any movement away from or into the table, being always in contact with it.

But it is very hard to realize how "out" from a disc, such as one of my coins, could be felt as "up" and inward towards the centre of it would be felt as "down." To ease my mind on this point I imagined myself standing on the equator of our earth, looking along it, then a great steel blade coming down and cutting the earth right through along the equator circle, and then coming down and cutting a slice parallel to the first. And then I imagined this slice of the earth and myself sticking against the steel blade, like the slice of a pea against a knife blade. In this way I gained the feeling of a being on a disc, with an "up and down," "away from and to" the centre of the disc.

But still I had a consciousness of another direction than those of "forward and backward"—along the rim of the disc—and "up and down" away from its centre and towards it. I could not help predicating myself with the sense of right and left—away from and into the steel blade. To lose this sense I must evidently change my notion of the constitution of my body. Without carrying the cutting so far as to imagine myself sliced, I imagined myself as made of very thin material, just of the width of the slice of the earth, and supposed that I myself and all the matter of the slice were of the same thickness, and stood out from the blade to exactly the same amount.

"If now," I said, "I was unconscious of this thickness, if the blade was perfectly smooth, and I and all the matter I knew slipped perfectly freely over it, I should have a two dimensional experience. My arm in moving, or my finger in pointing, could only move in contact with the blade, and I could never point in a third dimension. I should not think of it, for all motions of all things take place along the surface of the blade."

Thus it became apparent that without making the supposition that I was a mere line or triangle, or other geometrical figure, I could imagine myself as a two dimensional being.[1] If my thickness were very small and I was unconscious of it, if I could never move away from contact with a surface, my experience would be that of a two dimensional being. So, after all, it seemed possible that there could be real two dimensional beings. Now, if a thing is real, the only reason for not seeing it is either that it is small, or very far away—or some other reason. Hence I began to set about to try to discover these two dimensional beings, and learn all about them. I succeeded at last, and if I do not tell you how, I am afraid it is from no very worthy motive. For if I told how one could find out about them, I am afraid Mr. Wells or Mr. Gelett Burgess or some other brilliant author would begin to write about them, and to serve them up with all the resources of wit and humour.[2] In that case no one would listen to me. As it is I intend to have the pleasure of telling about them myself.

One thing always puzzled me from the beginning of the time when I began to think about these plane beings, and that is about their eyes.[3]

It is clear that they could not have two eyes beside one another as we have, for there is not the thickness in their bodies to place them so. Now, if they had two eyes, I wondered if one was above the other, or if they had one eye in front, another in the back of their heads. About this and other questions, I gained subsequently all the information one can desire. I have come to think of these creatures, from what I have

---

1   A reference to Abbott's *Flatland* characters.

2   H.G. Wells, well-known science-fiction writer and author of *The Time Machine*, used the fourth dimension as a plot device in "The Remarkable Case of Davidson's Eyes" (1895), "The Wonderful Visit" (1895), and "The Plattner Story" (1896). Gelett Burgess (1866-1951), known best today for his "Purple Cow" humorous poem, was a good friend of Hinton's and the author of his obituary. Burgess's writing on the visual arts helped introduce French Cubists to the United States.

3   Reviewers challenged Abbott about the physical possibility of vision in two dimensions.

found out, as very like ourselves, in different physical conditions it is true—but motives, aims and character, vary but little, however conditions differ. The only broad characteristic of difference I would draw is that they are not so massive as we. They are more easily moved to action, and political and other changes are brought to pass more easily than with us. They also take narrower views than we do, they do not look on things in the broad and tolerant way we do.[1]

[...]

The History of Astria

Astria is a plane world, along the rim of which its inhabitants walk. "Up" is away from the centre of the disc, "down" is towards the centre. To save myself the trouble of going into anatomical details, I will represent an Astrian, diagrammatically, by means of a triangle. And it will be conducive to the clearness of the reader's imagination if he will suppose the great sheet of matter against the surface of which Astria, its sun, and all the material bodies of that universe slip, to be disposed vertically. He will then gain a more real presentment of the feelings of motion and progression in this world.

The edge of the plane world of Astria is divided into two approximately equal portions by two oceans—the Black Sea and the White Sea. Since the daily motion of

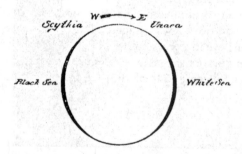

rotation of Astria takes place in the direction ... [west to east], the sun appears to rise over the White Sea, and the direction from the inhabited region to the White Sea is called "East."

In the earliest times the inhabited region was divided amongst two peoples, the Unæns and the Scythians. Of these the Unæans were by far the more civilized. In fact, all that gave Astria the promise of

---

1 Probably a sarcastic aside.

becoming the gem of her planetary system, was to be found amongst the Unæans, while the Scythians led a predatory nomadic existence. Yet, versed as they were in all the arts of life, the Unæans, from the dawn of history, were gradually forced back and conquered by the Scythians....

I will explain the cause of the Unæans' ill success. My rough and ready representation of the inhabitants of Astria, by means of a triangle, is sufficient to enable me to describe the main features of their bodily configuration.

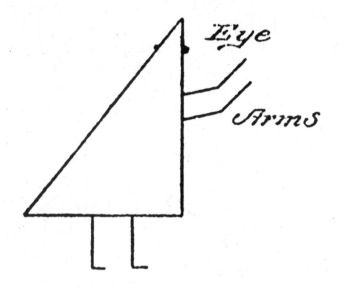

This figure of a triangle I use in a conventional way as a mark or symbol, which is simple and easy to draw, and which without any unnecessary complication enables me to make matters plain. It shows a thing I have often wondered at, namely, that there is a certain indication in the Astrian frame of being fashioned after the pattern of a higher existence rather than of complete adaptation to the exigencies of its narrow world.

Looking at the triangle which represents an Astrian, we see that on one edge are two arms and an eye, while on the other edge there exist no organs of sense or prehension. Thus, in going to the East, an Astrian could see his way clearly, and in working on anything, if it was placed to the East of him, he could operate on it conveniently; objects to the West, however, could only be seen by his bending over, and assuming a posture which, despite the suppleness of his frame, it was difficult to assume and painful to maintain for any length of time.

Objects to the West also could only be reached at in a very awkward and ineffective manner.

It seems to us as if it would be an easy thing for an Astrian to turn round so that he could face in the West direction. But to do this we would have to lift the thin body of the man away from the sheet against which it slips. Such an operation is, of course, inconceivable to the inhabitants of a plane world, and their bodies would not stand such an operation, for they are far too thin to be safely turned about and even temporarily deprived of the support of the sheet on which they slip. Every man in Astria was born facing the East, and facing the East he continued till he died.

Now I believe it is evident why the Scythians evidenced such a superiority over the Unæans in warfare. Scythian man had an advantage over a Unæan man of a kind that no skill or discipline could countervail.

The Scythian whom I represent as a shaded figure, could both see the Unæan plainly and deliver blows at him to good effect, while the Unæan whom I represent as an

unshaded figure, could only see the Scythian by a difficult exertion, and could only attack him or strike at him indirectly and backwards. [...]

In speaking of the Astrians, I have previously only drawn men's figures, which are ... all necessarily turned to the East. To represent a woman, however, it is necessary to draw a figure turned in the opposite direction, to the West.

Thus a Unæan woman, if her weakness and timidity were overcome by training, would be rightly framed to resist an attack from the West. The natural responsiveness of men to women and women to men,

Man · Woman

which we notice in our world, exists in Astria to a very highly accentuated degree. There a man cannot see his friend's face, because it is necessarily turned from him, but he can watch a woman's face and note the changes of expression his words call forth. The Unæans showed great chivalry in their treatment of women, and it was handed down as one of the most terrible horrors of that last period of their war, that actually a serious proposal had been entertained of women sacrificing womanhood, of hurling women into the contest against the Scythian oppressors.

Appendix E: Mathematical Background

1. Macmillan's Catalog of Geometry Textbooks (1884)

[A list of geometry textbooks available from Macmillan Publishers catalog in 1884 illustrating the range of approaches to the study of geometry. Charles Dodgson published a traditional Euclidean geometry textbook, while Francis Cuthbertson, who worked with Edwin Abbott at the City of London School, wrote a competing textbook that incorporated new approaches to teaching geometry.]

Euclid & Elementary Geometry

Constable.—GEOMETRICAL EXERCISES FOR BEGINNERS. By Samuel Constable. Crown 8vo. *3s. 6d.*

Cuthbertson—EUCLIDIAN GEOMETRY. By Francis Cuthbertson, M.A., LL.D., Head Mathematical Master of the City of London School. Extra fcap. 8vo. *4s. 6d.*

Dodgson.—EUCLID. BOOKS I AND II. Edited by Charles L. Dodgson, M.A., Student and late Mathematical Lecturer of Christ Church, Oxford.[1] Fourth Edition, with words substituted for the Algebraical Symbols used in the First Edition. Crown 8vo. *2s.*

***The text of this Edition has been ascertained, by counting the words, to be *less than five-sevenths* of that contained in the ordinary editions.

Kitchener.—A GEOMETRICAL NOTE-BOOK, containing Easy Problems in Geometrical Drawing preparatory to the Study of Geometry. For the Use of Schools. By F.E. Kitchener, M.A., Head-Master of the Grammar School, Newcastle, Staffordshire. New Edition. 4to. *2s.*

Mault.—NATURAL GEOMETRY: an Introduction to the Logical Study of Mathematics. For Schools and Technical Classes. With Explanatory Models, based upon the Tachymetrical works of Ed. Lagout. By A. Mault. 18mo. *1s.* Models to Illustrate the above, in Box, *12s. 6d.*

Smith.—AN ELEMENTARY TREATISE ON SOLID GEOME-

---

1 "Student" is what Christ Church called its faculty fellows. Those who attended classes were called "undergraduates," rather than students. A Fellowship was a college position, while Lectureships were funded by the university. The term "don" tended to be a generic term that was applied to all faculty, both Lecturers and Fellows.

TRY. By Charles Smith, M.A., Fellow and Tutor of Sidney Sussex College, Cambridge. Crown 8vo. *9s. 6d.*

Todhunter.—THE ELEMENTS OF EUCLID. For the Use of Colleges and Schools. By I. Todhunter, M.A., F.R.S., D.Sc., of St. John's College, Cambridge. New Edition. 18m. *3s. 6d.*

Wilson (J.M.).—ELEMENTARY GEOMETRY. BOOKS I.-V. Containing the Subjects of Euclid's first Six Books. Following the Syllabus of the Geometrical Association. By the Rev. J. M. Wilson, M.A., Head Master of Clifton College. New Edition. Extra fcap. 8vo. *4s. 6d.*

2. From Euclid's *Elements*

[The first extract is from John Casey's translation (Longmans, 1885). This edition, designed as a sequel to Euclid, was intended to serve as a school textbook and reflects the trend in Euclid editions after 1870. The postulates IV-V were called axioms XI and XII. The fifth postulate, here the 12th axiom, is commonly called the parallel postulate. In 1901, the Perry Movement called for a total divorce from Euclid in the teaching of geometry.]

Definitions
The Polygon
XXVI. A *rectilineal* figure bounded by more than three right lines is usually called a polygon.
XXVII. A polygon is said to be *convex* when it has no re-entrant angle.
XXVIII. A polygon of four sides is called a *quadrilateral.*
XXIX. A quadrilateral whose four sides are equal is called a *lozenge.*
XXX. A lozenge which has a right angle is called a *square.*

Postulates
I. A right line may be drawn from any one point to any other point.
When we consider a straight line contained between two fixed points which are its ends, such a portion is called a *finite straight line.*
II. A terminated right line may be produced to any length in a right line.
Every right line may extend without limit in either direction or in both. It is in these cases called an *indefinite* line. By this postulate a finite right line may be supposed to be produced, whenever we please, into an indefinite right line.
III. A circle may be described from any centre, and with any distance from that centre as radius.
[...]

Axioms
XI. All right angles are equal to one another.

XII. If two right lines (AB, CD) meet a third line (AC), so as to make the sum of the two interior angles (BAC, ACD) on the same side less than two right angles, these lines being produced shall meet at some *finite distance*.

[The second extract is from Sir Thomas L. Heath's translation (Cambridge: Cambridge UP, 1908). Here is the definition of a square and the five postulates in what would become the standard translation of Euclid. This translation was regarded as a return to the original form of Euclid. Heath would go on to translate all of the *Elements*, much of which had not been available in English in the nineteenth century.]

Definitions
Of quadrilateral figures, a *square* is that which is both equilateral and right-angled; an *oblong* that which is right-angled but not equilateral; a *rhombus* that which is equilateral but not right-angled; and a *rhomboid* that which has its opposite sides and angles equal to one another but is neither equilateral nor right-angled. And let quadrilaterals other than these be called *trapezia*.

Let the following be postulated:
1. To draw a straight line from any point to any point.
2. To produce a finite straight line continuously in a straight line.
3. To describe a circle with any centre and distance.
4. That all right angles are equal to one another.
5. That, if a straight line falling on two straight lines make the interior angles on the same side less than two right angles, the two straight lines, if produced indefinitely, meet on that side on which are the angles less than the two right angles.

3. The T.H. Huxley-J.J. Sylvester Debate (1869–77)

[From T.H. Huxley, "Scientific Education: Notes of an After-Dinner Speech," *Macmillan's Magazine* (June 1869): 177-84. Reprinted in *Collected Essays*, vol. III, 160-88. In these two essays from the textbook wars of the late nineteenth century, Huxley and J.J. Sylvester square off over the issue of whether the study of mathematics should be limited to that needed for the practical application or whether mathematics should be free of the limitations of the physical space and offer the opportunity for the imaginative play of the mind.]

If the great benefits of scientific training are sought, it is essential that such training should be real: that is to say, that the mind of the scholar should be brought into direct relation with fact, that he should not merely be told a thing, but made to see by the use of his own intellect an ability that the thing is so and not otherwise. The great peculiarity of scientific training, that in virtue of which it cannot be replaced by any other discipline whatsoever, is this bringing of the mind directly into contact with fact, and practicing the intellect in the completest form of induction; that is to say, in drawing conclusions from particular facts made known by immediate observation of Nature.

The other studies which enter into ordinary education do not discipline the mind in this way. Mathematical training is almost purely deductive. The mathematician starts with a few simple propositions, the proof of which is so obvious that they are called self-evident, and the rest of his work consists of subtle deductions from them. The teaching of languages, at any rate as ordinarily practiced, is of the same general nature—authority and tradition furnish the data, and the mental operations of the scholar are deductive....

[From J.J. Sylvester's 1869 Presidential Address to Section A (the Mathematical and Physical Section) of the British Association for the Advancement of Science. This speech was published in two parts, under the title "A Plea for the Mathematician," in *Nature* 1 (1869): 237-38, 261-63. After quoting Huxley's statement that "Mathematics is that study which knows nothing of observation, nothing of experiment, nothing of induction, nothing of causation," Sylvester adds his support to the call for a revision of how geometry is taught.]

I think no statement could have been made more opposite to the undoubted facts of the case, that mathematical analysis is constantly invoking the aid of new principles, new ideas, and new methods, not capable of being defined by any form of words, but spring direct from the inherent powers and activity of the human mind, and from continually renewed introspection of that inner world of thought of which the phenomena are as varied and require as close attention to discern as those of the outer physical world (to which the inner one in each individual man may, I think, be conceived to stand in somewhat the same general relation of correspondence as a shadow to the object from which it is projected, or as the hollow palm of one hand to the closed fist which it grasps of the other), that it is unceasingly calling forth the faculties of observation and comparison, that one of its principal weapons is induction, that it has frequent recourse to experimental trial and verification, and that it affords a boundless scope for the exercise of the highest efforts of imagination and invention.... the ever to be lamented Riemann[1] had written a thesis to show that the basis of our conception of space is purely empirical, and our knowledge of its laws the result of observation, that other kinds of space might be conceived to exist subject to laws different from those which govern the actual space in which we are immersed, and that there is no evidence of these laws extending to the ultimate infinitesimal elements of which space is composed. Like his master Gauss,[2] Riemann refuses to accept Kant's doctrine of space and time being forms of intuition, and regards them as possessed of physical and objective reality. I may mention that Baron Sartorius von Waltershausen[3] ... in his biography of Gauss ... relates that this great man used to say that he had laid aside several questions which he had treated analytically, and hoped to apply to them geometrical methods in a future state of existence, when his conceptions of space should have become amplified and extended; for as we can conceive beings (like infinitely attenuated bookworms in an infinitely thin sheet of paper) which possess only the notion of space of two dimensions, so we may imagine beings capable of realising space of four or a greater number of dimensions.

[...]

I should rejoice to see mathematics taught with ... life and animation [and] Euclid honourably shelved or buried "deeper than did ever plummet sound"[4] out of the schoolboy's reach, morphology introduced into the elements of Algebra ... the mind of the student quickened and elevated and his faith awakened by early initiation into the ruling ideas of polarity, continuity, infinity, and familiarisation with the doctrine of the imaginary and inconceivable.... The early study of Euclid made me a hater of Geometry, which I hope may plead my excuse if I have shocked the opinions of any in this room (and I know there are some who rank Euclid as second in sacredness to the Bible alone, and as one of the advanced outpost of the British Constitution)....

[From Sylvester's Commemoration Day address at Johns Hopkins University, 22 February 1877. In this address, Sylvester continues to define and explain his vision of mathematical study.]

Mathematics is not a book confined within a cover and bound between brazen clasps, whose contents it needs only patience to

---

1   See the Introduction, p. 12.
2   See the Introduction, p. 12.
3   Wolfgang Sartorius von Waltershausen wrote a biography of Gauss in 1856.
4   *The Tempest*, V.i.56.

ransack; it is not a mine, whose treasures may take long to reduce into possession, but which fill only a limited number of veins and lodes; it is not a soil, whose fertility can be exhausted by the yield of successive harvests; it is not a continent or an ocean, whose area can be mapped out and its contour defined: it is limitless as that space which it finds too narrow for its aspirations; its possibilities are as infinite as the worlds which are forever crowding in and multiplying upon the astronomer's gaze; it is as incapable of being restricted within assigned boundaries or being reduced to definitions of permanent validity, as the consciousness, the life, which seems to slumber in each monad, in every atom of matter, in each leaf and bud and cell, and is forever ready to burst forth into new forms of vegetable and animal existence.

Select Bibliography and Works Cited

A. Works of Edwin Abbott Abbott

[The following list is based on Martin Coonen's checklist, COBAC holdings in British libraries, and lists published by Thomas Banchoff and Ian Stewart.]

Selected Editions of Flatland

Flatland. A Romance of Many Dimensions. By A Square [i.e., E. A. Abbott]. London: Seeley, 1884.

Flatland: A Romance of Many Dimensions. New and rev. ed. London: Seeley, 1884.

Flatland: A Romance of Many Dimensions. 5th ed. Intro. William Garnett. Oxford: Basil Blackwell, 1926.

Flatland: A Romance of Many Dimensions. 6th ed. Intro. and rev. Banesh Hoffmann. New York: Dover, 1952.

Flatland. Intro. A.K. Dewdney. New York: New American Library, 1984.

Flatland: A Romance of Many Dimensions. Intro. Thomas Banchoff. Princeton: Princeton UP, 1991.

Stewart, Ian, ed. *The Annotated Flatland: A Romance of Many Dimensions.* Cambridge, MA: Perseus, 2002.

Film and Other Media Versions of Flatland

Flatland. Animated film. Adapt. by Carpenter Center for the Visual Arts, Harvard University. Narr. Dudley Moore. One reel 16 mm. Contemporary Films/McGraw-Hill, c. 1965.

Flatlandia. Animated film. Dir. Michael Emmer. VHS. Nicasio, CA: Great Media Co., 1994.

The Original Flatland Roleplaying Game. 1998. [Role-playing game]. By Marcus L. Rowland. Reissued 2006.

Flatland. Computer-animated film. Dir. Ladd Ehlinger, Jr. Screenwriter Tom Whalen. DVD. N.p.: Flatland Productions, 2007.

Flatland: The Movie. Videorecording. Dir. Jeffrey Travis and Dano Johnson. Screenwriters Seth Caplan, Dano Johnson, and Jeffrey Travis. Austin, TX: Flat World Productions, c. 2007.

The Anglican Career of Cardinal Newman. 2 vols. London: Macmillan, 1892.

Apologia: An Explanation and Defence. London: A. and C. Black, 1907.

Bacon and Essex : A Sketch of Bacon's Earlier Life. London: Seeley, Jackson, & Halliday, 1877.

Bacon's Essays. By Francis Bacon, Viscount St. Albans. With introduction, notes, and index by Edwin A. Abbott. 2 vols. London: Longmans, Green, 1876.

Bible Lessons. Part 1: Old Testament. Part 2: New Testament. London: Macmillan, 1870.

Cambridge Sermons: Preached before the University. London, Macmillan, 1875.

Christ's Miracles of Feeding. Cambridge: Cambridge UP, 1915.

"The Church and the Congregation." *Essays on Church Policy*. Ed. Walter L. Clay. London: Macmillan, 1868. 158-91.

Clue: A Guide through Greek to Hebrew Scripture. (*Diatessarica* Part I.) London: A. and C. Black, 1900.

The Common Tradition of the Synoptic Gospels in the Text of the Revised Version. With W.G. Rushbrooke. London: Macmillan, 1884.

A Concordance to the Works of Alexander Pope. By Edwin Abbott [Abbott's father], with an introduction by Edwin A. Abbott. London: Chapman and Hall, 1875.

Contrast; or, a Prophet and a Forger. [Being an investigation of the authorship of the 4th Gospel. Table of Contents, Introductions I. and II., Appendix V. and the titlepage of the author's forthcoming work: *From Letter to Spirit* issued with a special titlepage.] London: A. and C. Black, 1903.

Corrections of Mark Adopted by Matthew and Luke. (*Diatessarica* Part II.) London: A. and C. Black, 1901.

Diatessarica. A general title given to fifteen volumes published from 1900-17, separately titled *Clue: A Guide through Greek to Hebrew Scripture, The Corrections of Mark, From Letter to Spirit, Paradosis, Johannine Vocabulary, Johannine Grammar, Notes on New Testament Criticism, The Son of Man, Light on the Gospel*, and *The Fourfold Gospel*.

Dux Latinus: A First Latin Construing Book (adapted to "Via Latina"). London: Seeley, 1893.

"The Early Life of Cardinal Newman." *Contemporary Review* 59 (1891): 30-54.

"The Elders of Papias." *The Expositor 1* (1895): 333-46.

"Encyclopedia Biblica and the Gospels." *Contemporary Review* 83 (1903): 249-54.

English Lessons for English People. With J.R. Seeley. London: Seeley, 1871.

The Fourfold Gospel: The Founding of the New Kingdom or Life Reached through Death. 5 vols. (*Diatessarica* Part X.) Cambridge: Cambridge UP, 1913-17.

Francis Bacon: An Account of His Life and Works. London: Macmillan, 1885.

From Letter to Spirit: An Attempt to Reach through Varying Voices the Abiding Word. (*Diatessarica* Part III.) London: A. & C. Black, 1903.

"Genuineness of the Second Peter." *Southern Press Review,* April 1883.

The Good Voices: A Child's Guide to the Bible. London: Macmillan, 1872.

"Gospels." In *Encyclopaedia Britannica* (9th ed.), 1875.

Hints on Home Teaching. London: Seeley, 1883.

"Hours of Thought." Reprinted from *Modern Review* 1: 301ff. London: James Clarke, 1880.

How to Parse: An Attempt to Apply the Principles of Scholarship to English Grammar: With Appendixes [sic] on Analyses, Spelling, and Punctuation. London: Seeley, 1874.

How to Tell the Parts of Speech: An Introduction to English Grammar. London: Seeley, 1874.

How to Write Clearly. Rules and Exercises on English Composition. London: Seeley, 1872.

"Illusion in Religion." *Essays for the Time* 8. Reprinted from *Contemporary Review* 58 (1890): 721-42. London: F. Griffiths, 1909.

Indices to Diatessarica: With a Specimen of Research. [Compiled by Abbott's daughter Mary.] London: A. & C. Black, 1907.

Johannine Grammar. (*Diatessarica* Part VI.) London: A. & C. Black, 1906.

Johannine Vocabulary: A Comparison of the Words of the Fourth Gospel With Those of the Three. (*Diatessarica* Part V.) London: A. & C. Black, 1905.

"John as Correcting Luke." *The New World* 4 (1895): 459ff.

"Justin's Use of the Fourth Gospel." Reprinted from *The Modern Review,* July & October 1882. London: James Clarke, 1882.

"Justin's Use of John." *Modern Review* 3 (1882): 559, 716.

The Kernel and the Husk: Letters on Spiritual Christianity. London: Macmillan, 1886.

"The Latest Theory about Lord Francis Bacon." *Contemporary Review* 28 (1876): 141.

The Latin Gate: A First Latin Translation Book. London: Seeley, 1889.

Latin Prose Through English Idiom: Rules and Exercises on Latin Prose Composition. London: Seeley, 1875.

Light on the Gospel from an Ancient Poet. (*Diatessarica* Part IX.) Cambridge: Cambridge UP, 1912.

"The Logia of Behnesa, or the New Sayings of Jesus." *American Journal of Theology* 2 (1898): 1ff.

The Message of the Son of Man. London: A. & C. Black, 1909.

Miscellanea Evangelica. 2 vols. [Vol. 2 includes *Christ's Miracles of Feeding*.] Cambridge: Cambridge UP, 1913-15.

Newmanianism: A Preface to the Second Edition of Philomythus; Containing a Reply to the Editor of the "Spectator," a Few Words to Mr. Wilfrid Ward, and Some Remarks on Mr. R.H. Hutton's "Cardinal Newman." London: Macmillan, 1891.

"Notes from the Lecture-Room of Epictetus." *Expositor* 7th ser., vol. 1 (1906): 132ff.

Notes on New Testament Criticism. (*Diatessarica* Part VII.) London: A. & C. Black, 1907.

"On the Teaching of English Grammar." *Teaching and Organisation, With Special Reference to Secondary Schools; A Manual of Practice*. Ed. Percy Arthur Barnett. London: Longmans, 1897. 98-135.

"On the Teaching of Latin Verse Composition." *Three Lectures on Subjects Connected with the Practice of Education*. Ed. Oscar Browning. Cambridge: Cambridge UP, 1883.

"On Teaching the English Language." Vol. 1. *Lectures on Education*. London: College of Preceptors, 1872.

Onesimus: Memoirs of a Disciple of St. Paul. ["by the author of *Philochristus*"] London: Macmillan; Boston: Roberts Brothers, 1882.

Oxford Sermons, Preached before the University. London: Macmillan, 1879.

Parables for Children, With Illustrations. London: Macmillan, 1873.

Paradosis: or, "In the Night in Which He was (?) Betrayed." (*Diatessarica* Part IV.) London: A. & C. Black, 1904.

Philochristus: Memoirs of a Disciple of the Lord. London: Macmillan; Boston: Roberts Brothers, 1878.

Philomythus: An Antidote Against Credulity (A Discussion of Cardinal Newman's Essay on Ecclesiastical Miracles.) London: Macmillan, 1891.

The Promus of Formularies and Elegancies (Being Private Notes circ. 1594 Hitherto Unpublished) by Francis Bacon, Illustrated and Elucidated by Passages from Shakespeare. By Mrs. Henry Pott [Constance Mary Pott, née Fearon] with preface by Edwin A. Abbott. Boston: Houghton Mifflin, 1883.

The Proposed Examination of First-Grade Schools by the Universities. London: Macmillan, 1872.

A Protest Against Perturbed Criticism [of Bp. Joseph Barber Lightfoot by Prof. A.N. Jannaris]. By A.N. Jannaris. [Contains a letter, signed Edwin A. Abbott.] Suffolk: R. Clay and Sons, 1903.

"The Raising of the Dead in the Synoptic Gospels." *The New World* 5 (1896): 473-93.

"Realities of Christianity." *Contemporary Review* 59 (1891): 267-74.

Recent English Pedagogy. Hints on Home Training and Teaching. With lectures by Canon Farrar, Professors Huxley, Quick, Laurie, and Meiklejohn, and the contents of other recent pedagogical treatises. Hartford, CT: American Journal of Education, 1884.

Revelation by Visions and Voices. Essays for the Times 15. London: F. Griffiths, [190?].

Righteousness in the Gospels. London: Oxford UP, 1918.

"'Righteousness' in the Gospels." *Proceedings of the British Academy* 8 (1917-18), 351-63. Rpt. separately, London: Oxford UP, 1918.

A Shakespearean Grammar: An Attempt to Illustrate Some of the Differences between Elizabethan and Modern English. London: Macmillan, 1869. [A version is available in the Arden Shakespeare CD-ROM: Texts and Sources for Shakespeare Studies. Walton-on-Thames: Nelson, 1997.]

Silanus the Christian. London: A. & C. Black, 1906.

"The Son of Man"; or, Contributions to the Study of the Thoughts of Jesus. (*Diatessarica* Part VIII.) Cambridge: Cambridge UP, 1910.

The Spirit on the Water: The Evolution of the Divine from the Human. London: Macmillan, 1897.

St. Thomas of Canterbury: His Death and Miracles. 2 vols. London: A. & C. Black, 1898.

"Teaching of the English Language." *Every Saturday: A Journal of Choice Reading* 5 (1868): 655-58; *Macmillan's Magazine* 18: 33ff.; *Littell's Living Age* 97: 596.

Through Nature to Christ, or, The Ascent of Worship through Illusion to the Truth. London: Macmillan, 1877.

Via Latina: A First Latin Book, Including Accidence, Rules of Syntax, Exercises, Vocabularies, and Rules for Construing. [With key.] London: Seeley, 1886.

Secondary Sources on Edwin Abbott and His Works

Banchoff, Thomas F. "Flatland and The Man Who Wrote It." Brown University Library Center for Digital Initiatives. <http://dl.lib.brown.edu/flatweb/editions.php>.

Bell, Eric Temple. *Men of Mathematics*. New York: Simon and Schuster, 1937.

Borg, James M. "Abbott, Edwin (1808-1882)." *Oxford Dictionary of National Biography*, 2004.

Dewdney, A.K. *The Planiverse: Computer Contact with a Two-Dimensional World*. New York: Poseidon Press, 1984.

——, and I.R. Lapidus, eds. *The Second Symposium on Two-Dimensional Science and Technology*. London, ON: Turing Omnibus, 1986.

Douglas-Smith, A.E. *The City of London School*. 2nd ed. Oxford: Blackwell, 1965.

Farnell, Lewis Richard. "Abbott, Edwin Abbott." *Dictionary of National Biography (1922-1930)*. Ed. J.R.H. Weaver. London: Oxford UP, 1937. 1-3.

Farnell, L.R., and Rosemary Jann. "Abbott, Edwin Abbott." *Oxford Dictionary of National Biography*, 2004.

Gardner, Martin. "Mathematical Games." *Scientific American* (July 1980): 18-31.

Harper, Lila Marz. *A Century of Flatlands*. M.A. Thesis. St. Cloud State University, 1987.

——. "Mathematical Themes in Science Fiction." *Extrapolation* 27 (1986): 245-69.

Hipolito, Jane, and Roscoe Lee Browne. "Flatland: A Romance of Many Dimensions." *Survey of Science Fiction Literature*. Vol. 2. Englewood Cliffs, NJ: Salem Press, 1979. 792-96.

Jann, Rosemary. "Abbott's *Flatland*: Scientific Imagination and 'Natural Christianity.'" *Victorian Studies* 28 (1985): 473-90.

Johnson, Maria Poggi. "Critical Scholarship, Christian Antiquity, and the Victorian Crisis of Faith in the Historical Novels of Edwin Abbott." *Clio* 37.3 (2008): 395-412.

McGurl, Mark. "Social Geometries: Taking Place in Henry James." *Representations* 68 (1999): 59-83.

Rucker, Rudolf. [Rudy Rucker]. Introduction. *Speculations on the Fourth Dimension: Selected Writings of Charles H. Hinton*. New York: Dover, 1980. v-xix.

Smith, Jonathan. *Fact and Feeling: Baconian Science and Nineteenth-Century Literary Imagination*. Madison: U of Wisconsin P, 1994.

Sommerville, D.M.Y. *Bibliography of Non-Euclidean Geometry*. 2nd ed. New York: Chelsea, 1970.

Suvin, Darko. *Victorian Science Fiction in the UK: The Discourses of Knowledge and of Power*. Boston: Hall, 1983.

Valente, K.G. "Transgression and Transcendence: *Flatland* as a Response to 'A New Philosophy.'" *Nineteenth-Century Contexts* 26.1 (2004): 61-77.

——. "Who Will Explain the Explanation?": The Ambivalent Reception of Higher Dimensional Space in the British Spiritualist Press, 1875-1900. *Victorian Periodicals Review* 41.2 (2008): 124-49.

Other Works Cited

Ackroyd, Peter. *London: The Biography*. New York: Anchor, 2003.

Bacon, Francis. *The Essays of Francis Bacon*. 1908. Ed. Clark Sutherland Northup. Boston: Houghton Mifflin, 1936.

Banchoff, Thomas. *Beyond the Third Dimension*. New York: Scientific American Library, 1990.

Barrow-Green, June. "'Much Necessary for All Sortes of Men': 450 Years of Euclid's *Elements* in English." *BSHM Bulletin: Journal of the British Society for the History of Mathematics* 21.1 (2006): 2-25.

Basham, Diana. *The Trial of Woman: Feminism and the Occult Sciences in Victorian Literature and Society*. New York: New York UP, 1992.

Bentley, Nancy. "Literary Forms and Mass Culture, 1870-1920." *The Cambridge History of American Literature: Prose Writing 1860-1920*. Vol. 3. Ed. Sacvan Bercovitch. Cambridge: Cambridge UP, 2005. 65-286.

Bergamini, David. *Mathematics*. New York: Time-Life, 1963.

Blavatsky, Madame Helena Petrovna. *The Secret Doctrine: The Synthesis of Science, Religion and Philosophy*. London: Theosophical Publishing Ltd., 1888.

Blum, Deborah. *Ghost Hunters: William James and the Search for Scientific Proof of Life After Death*. New York: Penguin, 2006.

Booker, M. Keith. *Dystopian Literature: A Theory and Research Guide*. Westport, CT: Greenwood, 1994.

Brimblecombe, Peter. *The Big Smoke: A History of Air Pollution in London Since Medieval Times*. London: Methuen, 1987.

Brock, W.H. "Geometry and the Universities: Euclid and His Modern Rivals, 1860-1901." *History of Education* 4.2 (1975): 21-35.

Burger, Dionys. *Sphereland: A Fantasy About Curved Spaces and an Expanding Universe*. Trans. Cornelie J. Rheinboldt. New York: Crowell, 1965.

Cajori, Florian. "Attempts Made During the Eighteenth and Nineteenth Centuries to Reform the Teaching of Geometry." *The American Mathematical Monthly* 17 (1910): 181-201.

Carpenter, W.B. "Man the Interpreter of Nature." *Victorian Science: A Self-Portrait from the Presidential Addresses of the British Association for the Advancement of Science*. Ed. George Basalla, William Coleman, and Robert H. Kargon. New York: Doubleday, 1970. 411-35.

Chadwick, Owen. *The Victorian Church*. New York: Oxford UP, 1970.

Clarke, Bruce. *Energy Forms: Allegory and Science in the Era of Classical Thermodynamics*. Ann Arbor: U of Michigan P, 2001.

Cohen, Morton N. *Lewis Carroll: A Biography*. New York: Vintage, 1995.

Coonen, Martin. "Edwin Abbott Abbott: Primary and Secondary Checklists with Partial Annotations." *Bulletin of Bibliography* 56.4 (1999): 247-55.

Cox, H. "Study of Mechanics." *The Civil Engineer and Architect's Journal* (November 1846): 323-27.

Dodgson, Charles. "The Dynamics of a Parti-cle." *Diversions and Digressions of Lewis Carroll*. Originally titled *The Lewis Carroll Picture Book*. 1899. New York: Dover, 1961. 59-75.

——. *Euclid and His Modern Rivals*. 1885. New York: Dover, 1973.

Drake, Stillman. "The Assayer." *Controversy on Comets of 1618*. Trans. Stillman Drake and C.D. O'Malley. Philadelphia: U of Pennsylvania P, 1960. 183-84.

Fisher, John. Introduction. *The Magic of Lewis Carroll*. New York: Simon and Schuster, 1973. 7-18.

Gould, Stephen Jay. *The Mismeasure of Man*. New York: Norton, 1981.

Greenberg, Marvin Jay. *Euclidean and Non-Euclidean Geometries: Development and History*. 2nd ed. San Francisco: Freeman, 1980.

Hellman, Hal. *Great Feuds in Mathematics: Ten of the Liveliest Disputes Ever*. Hoboken, NJ: Wiley, 2006.

Helmholtz, Hermann von. "The Axioms of Geometry." *The Academy* 1 (1870): 128-31.

Henderson, Linda Dalrymple. *The Fourth Dimension and Non-Euclidean Geometry in Modern Art*. Princeton: Princeton UP, 1983.

Hinton, C[harles] H[oward]. *An Episode of Flatland: Or How a Plane Folk Discovered the Third Dimension, to Which is Added an Outline of the History of Unæa*. London: Swan Sonnenschein, 1907.

——. "What is the Fourth Dimension?" *Scientific Romances*. Vol. 1. London: Swan Sonnenschein, 1884. Rpt. in *Speculations on the Fourth Dimension: Selected Writings of Charles H. Hinton*. Ed. Rudolf v. Rucker. New York: Dover, 1980. 1-22.

Huxley, Aldous. *Letters of Aldous Huxley*. Ed. Grover Smith. New York: Harper, 1969.

Huxley, Thomas H. *Evolution and Ethics and Other Essays*. New York: Appleton, 1901.

Isaacson, Walter. *Einstein: His Life and Universe*. New York: Simon and Schuster, 2007.

Kant, Immanuel. *Critique of Pure Reason*. Trans. J.M.D. Meiklejohn, Ed. Vasilis Politis. London: Dent, 1993.

Lambridis, Helle. "Empedocles and T.S. Eliot." *Empedocles*. Studies in the Humanities No. 15. University: U of Alabama P, 1975.

Mill, John Stuart. *The Subjection of Women*. In *The Rights of Woman* by Mary Wollstonecraft and *The Subjection of Women* by John Stuart Mill. London: Dent, 1929. 219-317.

Mlodinow, Leonard. *Euclid's Window: The Story of Geometry from Parallel Lines to Hyperspace*. New York: Free Press, 2001.

Moktefi, Amirouche. "How to Supersede Euclid: Geometrical Teaching and the Mathematical Community in Nineteenth-Century Britain." *(Re)Creating Science in Nineteenth-Century Britain*. Ed. Amanda Mordavsky Caleb. Newcastle: Cambridge Scholars Publishing, 2007. 220-34.

Montesquieu, Charles de Secondat, baron de. *The Persian Letters*. Trans. J. Robert Loy. New York: Meridian, 1961.

Nicholls, Peter, et al. *The Science Fiction Encyclopedia*. New York: Doubleday, 1979.

Ouspensky, P.D. *Tertium Organum*. New York: Knopf, 1944.

Owen, Alex, *The Darkened Room: Women, Power, and Spiritualism in Late Victorian England*. Chicago: U of Chicago P, 2004.

Parry, Edward. *My Own Way: An Autobiography*. London: Cassell, 1932.

Pascoe, Charles Eyre. *Practical Handbook to the Principal Schools of England*. London: Sampson Low, 1877.

Peltonen, Markku. "Bacon, Francis, viscount St Alban (1561-1626)." *Oxford Dictionary of National Biography*, 2004.

Plato. *Republic*. Trans. Desmond Lee. London: Penguin, 2003.

Ponomarev, Leonid Ivanovich. *The Quantum Dice*. Bristol: Institute of Physics, 1993.

Richards, Joan L. *Mathematical Visions: The Pursuit of Geometry in Victorian England*. Boston: Academic Press, 1988.

Rodwell, G.F. "On Space of Four Dimensions." *Nature*. May 1873.

Rucker, Rudolf [Rudy Rucker]. *Spaceland*. New York: Tor, 2002.

——. *Gnarl!* New York: Four Walls, 2000.

——, ed. *Mathenauts*. New York: Arbor House, 1987.

——. *The Fourth Dimension: A Guided Tour of the Higher Universes*. Boston: Houghton Mifflin, 1984.

——. *The 57th Franz Kafka*. New York: Ace, 1983.

——. *Geometry, Relativity, and the Fourth Dimension*. New York: Dover, 1977.

Russell, Bertrand. "The Teaching of Euclid." *Mathematical Gazette* 2 (May 1902): 165-67; rptd. in *The Changing Shape of Geometry:*

Celebrating a Century of Geometry and Geometry Teaching. Ed. Chris Pritchard. Cambridge: Cambridge UP, 2003. 486-87.

Scholes, Robert, James Phelan, and Robert Kellogg. *The Nature of Narrative*. Rev. ed. Oxford: Oxford UP, 2006.

Scruton, Roger. *Kant: A Very Short Introduction*. Oxford: Oxford UP, 2001.

Sontag, Susan. *Under the Sign of Saturn*. New York: Random-Vintage, 1981.

Stewart, Ian. *Flatterland: Like Flatland, Only More So*. Cambridge, MA: Perseus, 2001.

Sylvester, J.J. "A Plea for the Mathematician." *Nature*. 30 December 1869.

Tatum, James. *Xenophon's Imperial Fiction: On* The Education of Cyrus. Princeton: Princeton UP, 1989.

Thompson, E.P. *The Making of the English Working Class*. New York: Vintage, 1966.

Weeks, Jeffrey R. *The Shape of Space*. New York: Dekker, 1985.

Zamir, Shamoon. *Dark Voices: W. E. B. Du Bois and American Thought*. Chicago: U of Chicago P, 1995.

Using 829 lb. of Rolland Enviro100 Print instead
of virgin fibres paper reduces your ecological footprint of:

Trees: 7 ; 0.1 American football field
Solid waste: 448lb
Water: 4,226gal ; a shower of 0.9 day
Air emissions: 983lb ; emissions of 0.1 car per year